Even Nectar is Poison

Mercer Addison

Mercer Addison
www.merceraddison.com

Publisher's Note: This is a work of fiction. Names, characters, places, and incidents are a product of the author's imagination. Locales and public names are sometimes used for atmospheric purposes. Any resemblance to actual people, living or dead, or to businesses, companies, events, institutions, or locales is completely coincidental.

Book Layout ©2013 BookDesignTemplates.com
Cover design by Gilded Heart Designs
Ordering Information: Amazon.com

Even Nectar is Poison/ Mercer Addison. -- 1st ed.
ISBN 978-0-9891947-1-6

Dedication

To my husband Ty, my rock and who keeps me on track. And to my sister Patsy who claims she is my #1 fan and who often says she is glad that Mom had me.

Acknowledgements

I'd like to give a sincere thank you to the following people. My family who has been there through the ups and downs deserves unique praise. Sending kisses to my daughter Whitney, my support beam and sounding board and who has been with me every step along this arduous path. Here's love for my husband who has spent many a lonesome evening in his recliner watching television while I spent lonesome hours writing on the computer. Special love goes out to my son, Michael, my stepson, Ryan, and my daughter-in-law, Sheryl. I certainly can't forget my sister, Patsy, and all of my dear family members who have given me encouragement to write.

Heartfelt thanks go to my devoted friends from work who I insisted read my manuscripts and tell me the truth, love you Mary R and Molly L. To Anna Brentwood, author, friend, critique partner of more years than I'd like to count, and for her wise wisdom throughout this process. There is no way I can forget my critique partners and fellow writers, C. Morgan Kennedy and Sarah Raplee who have amazing insight. And last but not least, this is for all the talented fellow writers at various writing organizations I belong to, and who have shown me how.

Irish Charm and Spell

For safety when going on a journey, pluck ten blades of yarrow, keep nine, and cast the tenth away for tithe to the spirits. Put the nine blades in your stocking, under the heel of the right foot and the Evil One will have no power over you.

Prologue

Dublin, Ireland, 1909

Donald McShane gathered the collar of his coat against the chilling rain and hurried across Parnell Street toward a darkened tobacco shop. Heading for a clandestine meeting in the back of the shop, he opened the door and slipped inside. A dim light from the back room beckoned and where male voices droned in anger and defiance.

Nods of welcome from men with thin faces and bright eyes met Donald.

"'Tis pissin' rain out there."

"Take to the heat, Lad. Warm yerself."

Donald nodded. Taking off his cap he knocked the water from the black cloth, and then replaced it.

Weaving his way through several bodies he went for the fireplace where hot coal burned. He put his hands close to the fire where the heat came off his sleeves in wispy threads of steam.

The air was sharp with the smell of wet wool and smoke.

A clock in the outer room chimed seven loud times.

As always, the area was packed with divided opinions. Half of the men present were members of the growing *Sinn Féin*, a peaceful organization, which Donald belonged to. The other half were part of the large established *Irish Republican Brotherhood,* made up of hot-headed firebrands who wanted to use force against the English. But no matter the means, both groups had a common goal, and that was for home rule. Tonight, they met to further their cause, by taking means to remove the hands of England from the throat and pockets of Ireland.

But not all Irishmen felt the same as these two groups, and some preferred being under England's thumb. Donald's employer was one of those men, and when he discovered Donald was a member of the *Sinn Féin,* he fired him on the spot. Still smarting from the injustice of it all, and with no way to feed his family, Donald had decided to leave the organization. Tonight would be his last meeting.

Spotting a friend, Donald made his way over to Aidan O'Connell, a proper Feinian man. Aidan, slim and with graying hair, made room next to him. Donald intended to ask his friend if he had work at his furniture store. When Aidan pulled out an already rolled cigarette, Donald accepted it and bent his head to the offered match.

"Did ye know yer brother Sam is here?" Aidan said, his gaze shrewd and locked onto the figure across the room.

Blowing smoke in the air and glancing to where Aidan pointed, Donald was surprised to see Sam leaning against the far wall. The last Donald knew of Sam, he was in Belfast working in the shipyards. The fact that he was here meant Sam was up to no good. Anything dark and against the law drew Sam McShane like flies to rotten meat. With a cigar clamped between his teeth, and his dark brows pulled into a perpetual frown, Sam's face seethed with defiance.

"Shite," Donald said under his breath. "'Tis the last man on earth I wanted to see here."

Smoke roiled thick from cigarettes, pipes, and cigars, creating a cloud of fog. Donald intently listened. Members of the *Irish Republican*

Brotherhood were urging violence against the English and defiantly brandishing hand guns. Others beseeched peaceful demonstrations. The meeting turned ugly.

"I say we fight the bloody English with bullets and not paper," Sam shouted, a wicked smile following his advice.

"Sure'n it's a battle ye be wantin', Sam McShane. Well I say go spill yer own feckin' blood and not mine," said Aidan, with spirit. His comment received ayes from the *Féin's*, and catcalls from the *IRB* members. "Rumor has it that ye've brought guns down from the north to give to the *IRB*."

"Aye, ol' man. Prove 'tis not rumor," Sam challenged.

Tom Clarke, the leader of the *Sinn Féin*, stood and with a cautioning tone dismissed the meeting and told them to go home. They put out their smokes, grumbled, but did as told.

As the men covertly spilled out into the wet, foggy air, Donald fell in step with Aidan. "Aidan, I was hoping to talk with ye about work. Would ye have an openin' in yer shop?"

"Sorry to say I don't. But I'm on me way to Collin's pub, let me buy ye an ale."

Before Donald could reply, Sam joined them. "If yer goin' to Collin's, I don't mind havin' a pint meself."

"I'm for home," Donald said. He wasn't inclined to share a drink with Sam, nor did he want his rebel of a brother in his house.

Donald often compared himself and Sam to the strong ends of magnets that no amount of force could push together. They clashed through life. Donald, at twenty-three and six years younger than Sam, was a family man who wanted to provide good things for his wife and two children. Sam, with no 'burden' of marriage to tie him down, did as he pleased. Although they differed as night and day in personalities, Donald suffered through the fact that in looks they were as similar as twins. The one distinguishing feature was Donald's hair coloring was brown, where Sam's was as black as his heart.

"How's Derry?" Sam asked with a tease, or was it a hint of *something else*?

Donald's eyes narrowed, and knowing damn well it was a hint of *something else*, said nothing.

Aidan, with his usual sprightly gait, was still fiery from the meeting. He continued arguing with Sam, trying to make him see the way peaceful demonstrations could make more progress with words than bullets.

"A gun pointed at the face of a disbeliever is more persuasive than words could ever be," Sam boasted.

Aidan scoffed. "Yer all a bunch of blatherin' eejits actin' like big men with your guns. Well, I'm here to tell ya, Sam McShane, that violence begets violence. Mark my words, yer flashy pistol will make trouble for us all." For emphasis, Aidan poked Sam's chest with his finger.

Sam slapped Aidan's hand away. "Leave off me, ya bloody blaggard. Ye have no right to touch me."

And in the light of the streetlamp and the misting rain, Donald saw his brother's jaw flex and the start of his vicious temper that the least insignificant thing could provoke.

"Ah, Lord above," Aidan said, and continued to goad. "It takes a puny man holdin' a gun to become mighty. Yer not a man, nor mighty in me eyes."

Sam snarled and pointed his gun directly at Aidan's face.

In the dim light, Aidan's face blanched white. He began shaking his head in disbelief, holding his hands up as if to ward off Sam's anger. "Shame on ye, McShane, scarin' me with yer evil gun. Put it away like a good lad. Let me buy ye a pint."

Sam cocked the trigger.

"Stop it, Sam!" Knowing what Sam was capable of, Donald launched his body at the gun and took Sam to the ground.

They scuffled. Sam gouged at Donald's face. Each tried to outdo the other, grunting, raw strength against raw strength, evenly matched. Rolling on the wet cobblestones, Sam's eyes glazed with hatred, his rage now directed at Donald. Without a doubt, Sam wanted to blow Donald's head off. Donald wanted to hurt Sam for all the savage heartache he'd strewn around over the years. But it was more than that with Donald. It was something deep and underlying, something that he wanted to forget about, but couldn't.

Aidan ran over, yelling at them to stop.

Donald's fingers inched up Sam's arm, stretching to reach the gun. His hand clasped Sam's and he wrest the gun away. Relieved that he now controlled the weapon, Donald got to his feet and started to move away. Sam tackled him, slamming Donald's body and face against the cobblestones.

The gun discharged. Its retort echoed loud like a church bell. A dog barked, and voices started up in the distance.

Aidan let out a cry. Donald rolled over to see his friend gripping his chest. Aidan staggered backwards against the stone building. As blood stained his jacket, Aidan slowly slumped to the ground. Stunned despair covered his face.

"Ah…no, Aidan," Donald railed, and scrambling over to his friend, tore Aidan's shirt open. "We'll get a doctor! Sam—get help!"

Aidan's bloody hand grabbed Donald's jacket lapel. "*Jaysus*…Donald…ye shot me…wasn't yer…" His head lolled to the side and his breath came out in a long sigh.

Horrified, Donald sobbed, "Nay, Aidan, I didn't mean for it to happen." Frantic, he wiped his bloody hands on his coat, his mind a muddled swirl.

Sam reached down and put his fingers at the base of Aidan's neck. He shook his head, and then jerked Donald away from the body. "Leave him, or it's the gallows for ya."

"Ah…no…no…I can't leave him lying here in the street. Not Aidan, not like a dead animal." Stunned at Sam's words, Donald's rushed out. "It was an accident, ya witnessed it—Jaysus, Sam, ye can tell what happened, aye?"

"Who'd believe me? Sam the liar and thief down from Belfast? They'll probably say I did it and yer takin' the blame. I've brought boxes of rifles with me for the IRB. I don't plan on gettin' caught with 'em." Sam picked up his gun and put it in his pocket. He began shoving Donald down the cobblestone street.

"I'm stayin' with Aidan." Donald shoved back, obligation overriding fear.

"Once the guarda find out what kind of meetin' ya came from you'll be jailed until they can sort this out. If they ever do. I'm off to Belfast, now, unless ye listen to me."

Giving in, Donald led the way running through the sleeping city toward home. His breath came out in heavy gulps. Water splashed high on his pants legs, chilling him to the bone.

"Ah…shite! I've lost me cap!" Donald said, and stopped. With no other choice, he turned and started back.

Sam was on him in a second, holding his arm in a tight grip. "'Tis too late. There'll be no going back now."

"They'll know it belongs to me. Why did ya pull yer feckin' gun in the first place? Damn ya to hell—Sam. Is there no middle ground with ya ever?" Donald's brutal words burst out as images of hanging blue-faced from the prison's scaffold flittered in his mind. That mere vision had him joining Sam in a fast run.

"I've got a plan, if yer willin' to abide by it, *boyo*. If not, then kiss me arse."

"What is it, Sam?" Donald glared at his brother. "Haven't ya done enough this night? What am I goin' to say to me family?" His world was crumbling and he wished it was Sam and not Aidan who'd caught the bullet. He wanted to destroy Sam's life like Sam was destroying his.

"We're goin' to get ya out of Dublin by ship. The same ship that brought me and the guns from Belfast. The captain's a member of the *IRB*."

Donald grabbed his brother's arm, stopping him from taking another step. "I can't run off and leave my family without food in the house, nor coin, I—"

"I'll see to 'em—make sure they get to Belfast and Mam's house." Sam shrugged off Donald's hold on him and hurried along. "Don't fret yourself."

'Don't fret?' Easy words coming from Sam when 'fret' was now wedged in Donald's mind, but having no other choice, he capitulated.

They approached the low rent district of drab row houses. Donald opened the door to his small home and entered the sparsely furnished room where a stone fireplace held a meager fire of coal. Sam was right behind him.

Derry stood from where she was sitting in the rocking chair close to the fire. Her face was pinched with worry as she reached out and stopped the chair's brisk rocking. She pushed at wisps of blonde hair that escaped from its tortoiseshell combs. Her ankle-length brown skirt and long-sleeved white blouse glowed yellow from the firelight.

"Donnie, what's wrong?" She plucked at the frayed neck of her blouse.

Donald swallowed hard. "Something terrible has happened." His eyes searched her blue ones. God above, how was he was going to tell her.

"Sam, sure'n it's a bad omen to see ya here. Donnie's trouble wouldn't have anythin' to do with you, aye?" She surprised Donald by being so bold.

"Hurry, get some clothes," Sam urged. He blew out the oil lamp and went to the window where he parted the lace curtains.

Donald pulled his bewildered wife upstairs into their bedroom. Striking a match, he quickly lit the oil lamp and replaced the glass chimney. The stench of sulfur mingled with the smell of roses, Derry's perfume. Beside him on the wall, his shadow loomed large as it mimicked his motions. He opened the dresser drawer and took out a shirt, and a union suit. Going to the peg on the wall, he snatched up his spare pants. His coat with Aidan's blood on it, he shed, and replaced it with his Sunday best.

"Get rid of me coat, Derry. Take it to the River Liffey. Weigh it down with rocks and throw it in."

"What are ya sayin', Donnie?" She stood close to him and wrung her hands together. "Tell me what's happened?" Her eyes glistened with unshed tears.

Donald stuffed his clothes into a battered satchel. "Ah…Jaysus, Derry. Aidan was accidentally shot and killed. I held the gun—Sam's gun. We—Sam and I were fighting over the gun and it went off. Accident—it was. And now I'm to take ship to God only knows where."

"Was it Sinn Féin business, or something more?" Her mouth quivered.

Snapping his satchel shut, he glanced at her. "Both. 'Tis always more with Sam."

"Please don't go. What will happen to us without ye?"

"Derry…I have no choice. They'll hang me or put me in prison for life. Sam won't stand up fer me. He's heartless, as ye well know. Get Colin to come move ya to Mam's house in Belfast." He silently thanked God for Colin, his patient younger brother that was without malice.

Helpless, as always, Derry slumped down on their bed's thick quilt. The vivid patches of color on the blanket were a stark contrast to their small, drab bedroom. A tiny wooden crucifix was in place over the head of the bed while on the headboard's spindly post, Derry's black-beaded rosary with a silver cross hung within easy reach.

He had always wanted to give her more, so much more. She was only twenty-two, and never a strong woman, depended on him for everything. Guilt washed over him in waves at the thought of leaving her—his family.

A cry sounded from the crib, and he quickly walked over to where Jilleen, his eleven-month-old, slept. She was awake and looked up at him with eyes the same color as his, a blend of brownish-amber that changed with their moods. She had his hair, unruly, wavy brown curls, especially the curl that mutinied down her forehead.

"Don't forget me, baby girl," he said in a ragged voice, a lump the size of coal now lodged in the back of his throat.

She whimpered and fisted her eyes, forcing Donald to scoop her up into his arms and hug her warm body close. He cupped the back of her head and nuzzled her, breathing her warm, familiar scent. He kissed her fat cheek.

"Da," she said and nestled her face against his shoulder. Her arm went around his neck where her finger and thumb latched onto his earlobe and tugged hard on it. She always did that, and he would tease that if she didn't stop it, she would stretch his earlobes down to his feet. He laid her back down and tucked her in.

He glanced over at Derry who sat on the bed working her rosary through her fingers. Their gazes locked as she said her rosary prayer.

"Jaysus," he cursed, and hastened to her side. He framed her face with his hands, and roughly pulled her up to meet his lips. She returned his kiss with equal fervor.

Loath to leave her, to end the kiss, he finally did. He whispered in a voice hoarse with emotion, "I love ya, Derry, and don't forget it." How could he tell her that her fears matched his, and that he was just as frightened to be leaving his family and hearth?

"Sure'n I love ye back, Donald. Don't forget us," her voice caught, forcing her into silence.

"Be assured, wherever I settle, I'll let ya know. Somehow, I'll write. Just think of our being apart like tomorrow, it always arrives," he said with sadness, his strength leaving him.

She nodded, and he knew his words were doing little to make her less frightened.

Donald slipped into the small storage room where his five-year-old son slept. He wanted a quick glance at Casey's sleeping face, a memory, anything to take with him.

A lamp already burned, and Casey his blond hair a curly riot around his head, stood next to his rumpled mattress. He was fighting with his suspenders, trying to hook one that kept flying loose. He finally got it attached. Donald could tell how fast he'd dressed. His shirt was buttoned one off all the way down and tucked into wrinkled knee pants. Below his knobby knees, his high-tops were unlaced. Next to Casey's feet was a stuffed knapsack made from a soiled pillowcase.

Surprised to see the knapsack, Donald asked, "Goin' somewhere?"

Casey nodded. "Aye, with you, Da. I heard ya tell Mam ya have to leave." He quickly pulled on his coat, and then grabbed up the knapsack.

The worried look on Casey's angelic face had Donald crossing to his son in two strides. He knelt and engulfed Casey in his arms. "I can't take ya with me, Casey. I don't know where I'm goin'. Ye have to be the man of the house and take care of yer mam and Jilleen. Can ya be strong and do that?" He placed the knapsack on the floor.

"I want to go with you, Da," Casey said, and started to cry. His small hands clutched the material of Donald's coat, unwilling to let go.

"Please, Son, I have no choice."

Desperate to pacify Casey, Donald unclipped his watch chain and removed his treasured pocket watch from his vest pocket. The gold case winked in the lamplight.

"My da gave me this watch the day I turned sixteen and became a man to him. Keep this watch until we're together again." He closed his son's stubby fingers around the prized possession.

Unable to remain any longer, to see the sadness in Casey's eyes, Donald whirled and clattered down the stairs. When he reached the bottom, the front door was open and a man from the Irish guards lay crumpled across the wet stoop.

Sam stood over the man's inert body. "He isn't dead. Let's go."

Without hesitating Donald snatched a recent photograph of his family off the sideboard and stepped out into the night.

Chapter One

New York City
April, 1912

It was Monday morning and out of habit, Donald arrived early at the clothing factory. The owner, Bruno Lapaglia, told him it wasn't necessary to start before the sun was up, and not to expect payment for the extra hours if he did. But in truth, Donald preferred it this way. The quiet allowed him to get his accounting work done before the factory floor became a scrambling mass of women and children and loud clacking sewing machines.

The morning air was frigid and with the furnaces not likely fired up at all, it would remain so. Lapaglia reasoned cold workers worked faster to get warm, while a warm room made a worker lethargic. Today, even the chilly room couldn't dampen Donald's happiness. From his suit coat pocket, he removed the object of his good mood, a letter from Derry that he'd carried for more than a month now. His thumb caressed across the blue ink of her spidery handwriting, the paper almost coming apart from being folded and unfolded so much.

'Dearest Donnie, I'm sailing on the Titanic out of Queenstown, April 12th, expect to arrive in New York on the eighteenth of April. Jilleen and Casey are well and excited to see their daddy. I will close now and hope to post this on time. Love, Derry.'

Smiling, he placed the letter on his desk. Soon, he would be able to hold her and his children. It was hard to believe that three long years had passed since he'd taken off in the middle of the night leaving his family behind, boarding a freighter heading for America. The captain of the freighter, a fellow Irishman, had allowed Donald to work off his passage by stoking boilers. Donald turned black with soot, and built muscles with each and every aching shovel of coal.

The freighter had discharged Donald at Ellis Island, where the federal immigration station with its tall domes and minarets waited. Grasping his satchel, he joined a long line of smelly, unwashed people carrying bundles. Mixtures of dialects from around the world bantered around him. Most wore somber black colored clothing while a few adventurous people wore their native dress of vivid bright colors. Men with families clustered around them made Donald envious and long for his.

Forced to endure a gauntlet of interrogations, Donald watched with trepidation as some people ahead of him were pulled from the lines and their coats were marked with large white chalk letters.

M for mentally ill.

C for criminal.

How could the inspectors tell with just a brief glance? Was the problem written on people's faces? Was it written on Donald's that he'd killed his friend? His fear of them labeling him a murderer made him uneasy.

When they took him from the line, Donald thought his journey was over with. Instead, they escorted him to the Registry Room where he answered more grueling questions. Did he have a job? No, he didn't. What was his occupation? When he said accountant, a kind-hearted inspector slipped him the name of Lapaglia's Garment Factory and told him the man was looking for help.

Donald stepped from the ferry onto lower Manhattan and got a crick in his neck from staring at the giant skyscrapers blocking the sun. The City was noisy and in constant motion with people, trolleys, horse-drawn wagons, and the new sputtering motor car. Already homesick, he could admit to himself he was also scared. He stiffened his backbone.

He soon discovered he'd left one poverty rat-infested country for another. He'd spent the better part of a year suffering grueling poverty and living in the Lower East Side in an old rat and cockroach infested building where even the wafting odors of cooking couldn't mask the stench of sewage and vermin.

Finally, able to afford an apartment across Manhattan in Greenwich Village, he moved to Bleecker Street. It was close to work, and far removed from the foulness he'd lived in. On the poverty scale, he was now several marks above the dirt-poor level he'd been in, and struggling to stay there.

When Donald first started at Lapaglia's, he was dismayed to learn the workers were forbidden to talk or hum on the job, if so they were docked pay. Ordered to deduct from their salary the use of a sewing machine, a fee for electricity, a fee for needles, thread and machine oil, he did as told. At first, he hated cheating people, but after three years on the job, he squelched his principles of honesty and wrote paychecks as ordered. He quickly came to the realization that Bruno Lapaglia's factory was among the worst for using child labor.

He was an accountant because God had blessed him with a special gift. From the time he was a little boy, he could add columns of numbers in his head in split seconds. His abilities had his father favoring him. He'd take him to the local smoke-filled pubs where he placed him on a bar and bet patrons money that Donald could add anything put before him and do it in his head. Performing like a trained monkey and spouting out added figures, Donald filled his father's pockets with spare change usually spent on an extra cut of meat for the family table. Growing up, Donald had taken beatings from Sam over this favoritism. And deep down inside he wondered if jealousy had forged Sam into the malcontent he'd become.

Fearing arrest, Donald had been in the country for half a year before he braved sending a letter to Derry by way of Colin, his younger brother. After letting Derry know of his whereabouts, Donald's big surprise came when he'd received a letter back telling him Aidan hadn't died. Aidan recovered from the gunshot and told the truth of it all. Derry begged him to come home. But his jubilation over being a free man and not a murderer was squelched as he wondered when Sam felt for Aidan's pulse just what in the hell his brother truly felt? Was it a thudding heartbeat or faint to the point of non-existence? One thing for certain, Sam had lied, because Aidan was alive.

Upon hearing the news, Donald had almost returned to Ireland, but didn't know what he'd do the day he came face-to-face with Sam. He knew what he'd like to do, but that would have put him in prison for life. With Ireland becoming more volatile against the British and with jobs getting sparse, Donald decided to stay put and sent Derry money to bring her and his children to his side. But Derry feared sailing and had refused to step foot on a ship.

And just when Donald thought she never would, she finally agreed…

…Trying to leave memories alone, Donald opened up a ledger book and attempted to concentrate on the columns of figures in front of him, but the only adding he was able to do was the longitude and latitude where he figured Derry's ship, the *Titanic*, had probably reached by now. Four days, in just four long days he would have his family with him.

Wanting so badly to surprise Derry, he'd purchased ready-made clothes for the whole family. Derry sent him the sizes the children now wore, but he'd ended up guessing at what they liked. He bought a fancy bottle of Payan's cologne from his friend Eldon's drugstore. The smell of roses reminded him of Derry and the lone bottle she always hoarded, allowing the tiniest of dabs from the glass stopper. His surprise for her waited on the dresser in their bedroom, and his intention was to dab it all over her body in an intimate moment.

The factory was starting to come alive. But with Lapaglia's policy about talking, he was surprised to hear constant chatter going on. A paperboy was hawking newspapers and doing so several hours earlier than the norm. Loud voices filtered up from the street. Curious, he started to get up and go look out the window when hollow footsteps echoed off the solid wood floor.

John Bartlett, a fellow accountant, approached. John was a big stocky man with red hair going to gray. The skin beneath his eyes drooped in baggy folds always making him look sad.

"Mornin', John. Yer early," Donald said.

John now stood in front of the desk. He carried a rolled up newspaper that he softly hit against the side of his leg.

Grinning, Donald pointed at the paper and raised a brow. "Sure'n ye've been reading about Taft and Roosevelt? I swear that's all this country thinks about is those two presidents. So, which one's got your goat this mornin'? Makin' ye all antsy like. Gotta be better news than…" Something in John's face made Donald's words die.

"Donald." John appeared miserable, his normal good humor squelched. "My…God, man, I don't know how to tell you this—"

"Tell me what? Ah…no, yer scarin' me." Something bad had happened and it was in the newspaper John held. Donald pushed off the chair, and hastened around the desk to tear the paper out of John's hand.

The headlines jumped from the page and took him by the throat. NEW LINER TITANIC HITS AN ICEBERG, SINKING BY

THE BOW AT MIDNIGHT, WOMEN PUT OFF IN LIFEBOATS…he read no more, couldn't.

"God no!" Donald ran out of the factory in a fast clip. He shoved through throngs of hysterical people that shouted and cried. They massed around paperboys calling out the story. With the *Times* still clasped in his hand, Donald headed toward the White Star Line office building three blocks away.

He joined a milling group of people on 9 Broadway outside the office of the White Star Line. Their eyes were wide, their faces masks of desolation. Donald forced himself to open the crushed paper and read. An early edition only, the paper told of an accident concerning the *Titanic* and an iceberg, that all were safe. By the time he finished the article, he had it in his mind that his wife and children were safely aboard the lifeboats.

"Are ya hearin' any news?" he asked the short, balding man next to him.

"I've heard the Titanic's been taken to Nova Scotia for repairs."

"The ship didn't sink, then?" Donald's hopes soared as high as the skyscrapers.

A woman beside Donald spoke up, "They just told us survivors are on the Carpathia and being brought to New York. They—"

"If the ship didn't sink, then what's with this survivor nonsense? They're passengers. They've been transferred to another ship so the Titanic can be repaired, that's all." He folded his arms. What the hell did anyone know, and concluded, they didn't know a bloody thing. Derry might still be in Ireland. He hadn't heard a word since she'd sent the letter telling him she was coming. Maybe she'd changed her mind. As that idea took root in his mind, he began pushing his way through the crowd and toward the office building.

Inside, it was pandemonium with people rushing everywhere. A troubled looking clerk glanced up from her desk. She quickly stood. "Sir," she said in a terse manner, "you shouldn't be in here. We've requested everyone remain outside, please go back out."

But Donald wasn't going to be put off so easily. "Wait a minute please." Removing his cap, he approached the desk. "My wife and two children were supposed to be on the Titanic. I'm thinkin' maybe they didn't board the ship after all. Do ya have a list of the passengers who boarded in Queenstown? That's all I want to know."

Her eyebrows, plucked to a thin line, slightly rose as she considered his request. "No, but I can bring you the Titanic's manifest and you can search for your family. Give me a few minutes." She disappeared into the back office.

After what felt like an eternity to Donald, she returned and placed a thick stack of papers on her desk and began sorting through it.

"Don't think you need to see the crew member's names and such." She continued to search. "You said they boarded in Queenstown?" She finally handed him several pieces of paper "This list is made up according to class of ticket purchased and in alphabetical order. These papers must remain here in our office, so just look and then you can leave." She settled in her chair.

The list was long. He searched for the M's. Ah…no.

McShane, Alana Darlene.

McShane, Creighton Donald.

McShane, Margaret Jilleen.

She was coming at his insistence, his badgering that he wanted her with him. And right now, he wished her fear of sailing had prevented her from making the voyage. But for the first time in her life, she'd apparently become brave enough to step on a ship with just the children.

He strode out of the office and pushed into the assembling crowd. Reporters reached for him begging to know what went on inside. Unable to talk, he brushed their grasping hands from his coat and started running, finally going down into the subway station.

He came out of the subway blocks away from his apartment and blindly walked home. Living on the fifth floor, he took the five flights of stairs in a blur. Finally reaching his door, he went inside where he collapsed against the living room wall and slowly slid down its side to land on his behind. To Donald, just thinking of the unknown, not knowing what happened out there on the freezing Atlantic made his blood chill. He hugged his knees to his chest, and burying his face wept deep agonizing sobs.

As shadows lengthened across the room he remained that way, numb in mind and body.

He didn't hear the knock on the door, didn't hear anyone enter.

"Donald."

He glanced up to see his friend Eldon Johnston who returned his stare with overwhelming sadness on his face. Lingering behind Eldon with uncertainty was young Joe Gillespie.

Donald stiffened and quickly dashed tears from his cheeks.

Eldon offered him a hand up and pulled Donald to his feet. Eldon's arm went around Donald, firmly patting his back. Donald wouldn't expect anything less from Eldon who had become a true friend since Donald first walked into the *Johnston and Son Drug Emporium* needing shaving soap. The young friendly druggist was quick to help him. When he realized that Donald was new from Ireland, he'd introduced him to his father Archibald. Donald had learned that there was no Mrs. Johnston for either man. Archibald's wife had passed away, and Eldon was a bachelor who hadn't found the right woman yet.

Now, as in the past, Eldon helped in his subtle way. After removing his fedora and brown suit coat, he smoothed his long dark sideburns and patted his hair down. He suggested they have coffee. When Donald agreed, Eldon rolled up his shirt sleeves while crossing the room and going into the kitchen.

Finally regaining his composure somewhat, Donald leaned against the kitchen doorjamb, watching Eldon work in the small area that consisted of a counter top, sink, cabinets, and a lone table pushed against the wall.

"How did ye find me?"

Eldon turned on the burner. "After I heard the news, I thought about what you'd do, where you would go." Reaching into the glass fronted cabinet Eldon rattled around and took out the tin coffee pot. Opening a jar of coffee grounds, he dumped several spoonfuls into the strainer. "So, I went to the White Star office and bullied my way inside. I asked about a belligerent Irishman. You left quite an impression with the woman working there. I'd no sooner left when Joe came running out of the crowd, shouting at me. He figured you might be here." Eldon screwed the lid back on the jar and replaced it in the cabinet.

"You've never bullied yer way into anything before," Donald said with a wry smile, glad that Eldon and Joe were here.

"Well, it was time to start. C'mon, Donald. Have a seat." Eldon nodded at him.

Donald pulled back the wooden chair and took a seat at the table.

Joe slipped his gangly body into the chair closest to Donald.

Nine-year-old Joe wore the same scared look he'd been wearing when Donald first met him. Donald, still living in the Lower East Side, saved the lad from having the hell beat out of him by Joe's employer old man Solberg. Donald would never forget that day, seeing the lad tossed out of Solberg's grocery store to land hard on the pavement. Solberg pummeled the boy, called him a liar, and accused him of giving grocery money away to that damn gang he lived with. Joe was no match for the store owner's meaty fists. Donald had run up to Solberg and pushed him away from the lad. When Donald found out that the little boy was just a year older than Casey, the mere thought of someone trying to harm Casey like the man was doing to Joe made Donald angry. Donald took the kid under his wing, and was glad to get him away from the gang he lived with and the rigors of street life. Joe stayed with Donald on and off. On the off days he slept in the back room of Ryerson's corner grocery store where he now worked delivering groceries.

Donald reached over to remove Joe's cap and hand it to him. Joe brushed his straight black hair out of his eyes. The kid was skinny as a rail and always a little disheveled. Joe's smile and his sparkling brown eyes could make a gruff person melt.

Joe piped up. "Maybe it's not as bad as it sounds, right, Eldon? Maybe everyone is safe. I want to meet your family, your boy Casey, and I just bet I do."

"I feel the same way as Joe," Eldon said from where he was pouring the coffee. "I mean, they keep bragging that the ship is unsinkable, right?"

Nothing on this earth was unsinkable but *Noah's Ark*, and that chilling knowledge bored into Donald's mind. "Aye, that's what I'm hearin'. It didn't sink, and everyone was put off into life boats." Now in denial Donald had to believe his family was safe. Donald watched as Eldon put three cups of steaming coffee down in front of them and pulled up a chair.

Donald stared at Eldon across the table. "Thank ya for comin' here." He sipped the hot coffee, not tasting it, not caring for anything but news of his family's rescue.

"You'd do the same for me," Eldon answered.

Again fate was sending Donald another disaster. It was like Aidan being shot all over again, the same numbing fear that crept up and clamped itself around his throat until he couldn't breathe. Unable to sit there any longer, he stood, and leaving Eldon and Joe where they sat, he went into his bedroom and shut the door behind him.

The cramped room reminded Donald of a wife who might never share it with him. Cots that Casey and Jilleen might never use were tucked under the bed. The sleeve of a white blouse he'd bought for Derry peeked out of the wardrobe. At the sight of it, he fell on the bed, cursing God, cursing the Titanic, but most of all cursing Sam.

Chapter Two

She gripped the sides of the lifeboat that shimmied and lurched while being lowered down the side of the doomed Titanic. Shrill screams from above forced her to look upward just as a small child was tossed over the ship's railing. The man who threw her was a blur in a long black coat with a thick, fur collar. As she fell, the little girl's face contorted with terror. She instinctively reached up to catch her, but the child's shoe painfully clipped her brow, knocking her off balance. She managed to clamp her arm around the child's waist, holding tight.

With the icy, churning abyss below, she fought hard to keep a firm grip on the struggling child. "Don't fight me—hold still!" she yelled, but unable to regain her balance, her free hand grasped at nothing but freezing air, she started to fall over the edge.

"Help me!" she screamed, "help—me!"

Olivia Marsh bolted upright in the bed. Her nightmare surrounded her like a dizzy fog and her heart beat against her chest in a flurry of rapid thumps. Realizing where she was, Olivia glanced around the dimly lit room to make sure she hadn't awaken her fellow survivors, especially the child sleeping next to her. But her cries must have been silent, for no one moved, and she heard deep breathing only.

Safe. She was safely aboard the rescue ship *Carpathia,* and in a stateroom given up by its original passengers. Shivering, Olivia felt the wool blanket covering her, wondering if she would ever be able to get the deep chill out of her bones. The ship with its constant pitch put her back in the lifeboat, the stark memories, the horror…

…Hours had passed since the Titanic had slipped underneath the Atlantic. The black sky was awash with millions of glittering stars that mantled the earth with dazzling glitz. How could it look so beautiful when death bobbed in white-faced silence and in such close proximity? The vicious cold stung her nostrils and invaded her lungs making it painful to breath.

The child in Olivia's arms screamed and pointed a mitten covered hand where the boat's meager lantern cast light upon the water. Olivia glanced alongside the boat just as warm urine from the girl soaked through both their coats.

"Oh—dear. Don't look, child—don't look." She quickly turned the little face away. Olivia couldn't help but stare into the lifeless eyes of the young woman who floated close by. Her shadowed face tipped skyward, her long blonde hair spread out over the white of her life jacket. The draft from the boat made her bob like a cork. Thankfully, one of the men reached out with his oar and gently pushed her body away.

"Mam—mammy," the child wailed in her Irish lilt, "please—I want me mam…"

Olivia's hand stroked the wilted, brownish curls. The child groaned and started shivering violently…

…Olivia shook her head trying to dispel the images chiseled into her mind. But she couldn't shake free of what she'd witnessed. Hundreds of people left in the freezing ocean because of their status in life. Especially their moans and screaming that sounded like a haunted choir, silenced only after freezing to death.

Olivia, trying to dispel the unforgettable from her mind, wiped tears from her cheeks.

She thought about the man who'd tossed the child—a father saving his family perhaps? He was a hero in her eyes, and one that deserved prayers and gratitude. She glanced at the child's closed eyes.

Without a doubt Olivia shouldn't have promised the little girl that she'd find her parents, for most certain the man who tossed her was the child's father and now dead.

Careful not to disturb the sleeping child and the other woman survivor in the next bed, Olivia lifted the heavy blankets and slowly got up. She looked at the time on her watch pendant. Half a day had passed since plucked from the glacial sea. She went to peer out of the porthole. Gone were the icebergs as tall as buildings and sheets of ice that the ship had to push through to get to the smattering of lifeboats. Rubbing her arms, she stared at the gray-green ocean. It looked angry and churned at the *Carpathia* as if intending to claim another liner. She shuddered.

Olivia didn't have to ask herself why she was here and not at the bottom of the Atlantic. She knew the answer. She'd been in first class and given priority to board the few available lifeboats. And that knowledge went against the very reason Olivia became a suffragette, *equality*. Well, she'd just gotten a good dose of what equality wasn't, hadn't she?

Born into money, the proverbial *golden spoon* in Olivia's mouth couldn't deter the tender spot she had for those less fortunate. While in college and taking a course in social studies, a field trip to a clothing factory where children labored had Olivia looking into small faces that were old before their time, some were missing limbs, and all were shy, grimy and barefoot. This despicable sight forced Olivia to seek out the nearest suffragette organization. A young twenty when she joined, and now just twenty-three, Olivia made her mark in the suffragette association by being outspoken and recognized as a woman who fought to establish child labor laws in the work force. Used to unruly crowds and shoved around by zealous factory owners, she had a reputation for cracking heads with a well-aimed picket sign.

Against her mother's wishes, Olivia had traveled from Manhattan to England to give a speech against child labor. If she'd thought the English were civilized gentlemen, she could think again because her speech turned into a riot of slamming fists. She'd taken a punch to the eye and told to go home. Her eye turned as black and blue as her ego, but she wouldn't let it deter her.

Had her parents heard about the sinking? Had Myron Prewitt? Thinking of Myron, she played with the ring he'd given her. He wanted to marry her, but she wasn't sure if she wanted to marry him. All she knew is right now she wished to be in his warm embrace, his dark handsome face next to hers, his moss-green eyes shining with attendance.

Movement behind Olivia had her turning away from the round porthole. Her fellow survivor, the woman in the other bed struggled to a sitting position. Her red hair was a tangle of long curls, and for a moment she appeared confused. Her confusion cleared and she pulled the pillow up behind her and leaned against the headboard.

"Me name's Noreen," she said in a thick Irish accent. "There's somethin' to be said about being one of the hundreds rescued, while thousands drowned. I dinna claim to know how God works, but last night he worked in mighty mysterious ways. I was in steerage, one of the lowest in the ship, well…not if ya count the stokers and the boiler room below us. When the water covered the floors, people panicked. I started up the stairs but the stewards had locked the gates, preventing us in third-class from comin' up."

"How did you get out?" Olivia asked, appalled.

"A man, a stranger to me, ordered me to stand on his shoulders. I did as told. He helped me squeeze my skinny body over the top of the gate. As I walked away, he called out to me from the other side of the gate, 'Good luck, miss, good luck.' I'll never forget the look in…his…eyes…" her voice trailed off.

"Oh…God," Olivia moaned. The vision so overwhelming she could hardly stand it. People, because of their status, were locked in like animals. She dropped her face into her hands and sobbed.

The little girl Olivia rescued thrashed around then bolted to a sitting position. "Casey!"

Olivia's head snapped up. She watched in curious silence.

The child yawned and rubbed her eyes with balled fists. She anxiously glanced around, and spotting Olivia the girl appeared to relax. She slipped from the bed and sat on the floor.

"Do you need help?" Olivia smiled at her.

The girl's brow puckered as she shook her head. She proceeded to put on her black cotton hose and ankle-high shoes of which she laced and tied. Clad in a flannel nightgown and plain muslin drawers, Olivia could tell she was an immigrant, undernourished and afraid of strangers.

The girl got to her feet and plowed through the blankets until she found the doll she'd kept in a tight grip even when falling. She held the doll in both hands, its porcelain lips painted in a permanent pink smile. The doll was dressed in a blue and white sailor suit with a matching sailor bonnet topping its blonde ringlets.

"Yer bad, Derry. I'm goin' to throw ya overboard," she said in her strong lilt, and violently shook the doll. As if realizing how harsh she was, she clutched the doll to her chest and patted its tiny back. "Good baby…be a good baby then," she crooned, her anger now gone. She nestled the doll under the covers and lovingly patted it.

Olivia stood and cautiously approached her. She knelt down and gently lifted the small chin, forcing those luminous hazel eyes to look at her. "I cannot help you until you tell me your name. Who are your parents? Please?"

She waited for a response, but just like on the lifeboat, none was forthcoming. Again she asked, "Why don't you let me help you? Your dolly is named Deary, but who's Casey, you called his name out—" A soft knock on the door interrupted her questions. "Who is it?" she called out, damning the timing.

"Steward Charman here," a male voice answered. "I have tea and biscuits. May I come in?"

"Please give us a moment," Olivia said, and glanced at Noreen who had pulled the blankets up to her chin. After Noreen nodded,

Olivia called out, "You can come in now." Olivia tried to smooth out the wrinkles in her blue skirt. Her hair was another matter, she'd long ago lost the pins holding her brown tresses up.

Steward Charman entered and set the tray on the table. He stuffed the metal tea ball with tea leaves and placed the tea ball inside the china teapot. "Would you like me to butter the biscuits?" he asked while clattering the lid back on the pot. His manner was like all the *Carpathia's* crew, sad yet helpful.

"No, thank you. We can manage now," Olivia said. "Oh, please wait. I was wondering if you have spare hairpins and toothbrushes."

The steward shook his head. "No. We ran out of both items." He shrugged and added with compassion. "I'm sorry…so sorry…" With nothing more to say, he took his leave.

"Noreen," Olivia said, "would you mind watching the child while I go topside and see if I can find any information?"

Nodding, Noreen yawned and rousted herself up. Her clothing was a mass of wrinkles. After taking several steps, she stiffly sat on the love seat. She leaned forward and began pouring the steaming liquid from the pot, creating a piquant orange aroma. She beckoned the child. "We'll have us a tea party. Would ya like to put sugar in the tea?"

The girl crept in front of Noreen who was smiling at her. She picked up the prongs and glanced at Olivia who nodded. Seeing this, the child began plopping square cubes of sugar into a cup.

Olivia, relieved, bent down to place a kiss on the child's pale cheek. "I'll be right back. Please stay with Noreen. Enjoy your tea and biscuits." But the girl wrapped her arms around Olivia's legs, clasping her as tight as a fashionable girdle. She looked up at Olivia with pleading eyes.

This wasn't going as expected. "I won't be long. You'll be fine here, I promise, little one. Why don't you give your doll some tea?"

Noreen piped up, "Here now, little miss, let's have a cup of cha together."

Finally the child released Olivia and went to stand next to Noreen.

Olivia pulled on her wool tweed coat and wrinkled her nose at the smile of dried urine. She left while Noreen kept the child busy.

The brisk wind topside swirled her dark hair about her face. She gripped the collar tight around her neck. Up ahead an officer was holding a clipboard of fluttering papers. Wanting to talk to him before he left, Olivia hurried to his side. Staring into the lined, unshaven face of the over-worked officer, she introduced herself and inquired if he had any information about the child. Was someone looking for her?

He scanned the clipboard, perusing the list of survivors. "Your description of her doesn't match any missing children reported to me so far." He fingered the paper. "Perhaps when we dock in New York there'll be a relative who'll recognize her. I'm praying that's the case. If it isn't too much of an inconvenience, would you mind taking care of her until we make port?"

"Of course not," Olivia said. "Do you have the Titanic's list of passengers?"

"No, we don't. But I have most of the survivors here. Our Marconi wireless operator will telegraph the names to the owners of the Titanic, the White Star Line in New York. They'll pass the information along to relatives and the newspapers. Are you listed, Miss Marsh?" He flipped the pages. "Ah…yes, there you are. Your family will be greatly relieved to hear you have survived."

"Thank you, sir. Your effort is truly appreciated."

The officer patted her arm with fatherly kindness. "Miss Marsh, let's pray by then the child will have told you her name and all about herself." He started to leave but stopped to turn back, a brief smile curving his mouth. "Will you need anything else? Do you have enough blankets, perhaps some hot tea?"

"I think we're fine for now, and tea was just brought to us."

Discouraged, Olivia went on deck where blanket-clad people were still milling everywhere. Some with haunted eyes passed by, some huddled on the deck in the brisk open air, and some sat in deck chairs staring out at the sea. At least the ship had sailed away from the freezing waters, but the cold was still biting. An overwhelming sadness curled around everything like a thick grey fog.

She began walking amongst the huddled survivors, talking to those who would listen. It wasn't easy. She asked if anyone knew or heard of someone named Casey, but all she got back were no's.

Disappointed and ready to give up and go back to the stateroom, Olivia glanced around the crowded deck. She saw a tall man moving through the milling people. Being a man amongst so many women, he stood out. His long black coat with a fur collar stood out even more. Olivia gasped, the man was the one who threw the child overboard. Maybe he's her father. Excited, and without any hesitation on her part, she started after him with lengthening strides.

Her skirt and coat hem hit against her ankles, wrapping around them, and she wished she could wear trousers like a man. "Damn this skirt," she cursed, and reached down to lift it up, exposing black cotton hose. She ran. Her heels clicked on the polished wood of the deck, attracting attention. "Sir—sir—please wait up," she yelled. But he disappeared around a corner. Fast behind him, she rounded the corner with such momentum her feet skidded out from under her. She grabbed the wooden railing to steady herself.

The man was now directly ahead. Olivia caught up with him. She grabbed his arm abruptly stopping him.

"What the?" he snapped out.

He stared at her, strikingly handsome with anger still evident in whiskey-colored eyes. His mouth relaxed into a deadly smile as his outrage appeared to fade. Short, dark black hair curled out beneath his bowler hat as he slightly nodded. "'Tis sorry I am to be rude to ye, lass. What can I help ya with?" he asked in a smooth Irish accent and studied her with the distinction of a jungle cat sizing up its prey.

"You threw a little girl into the lifeboat I was in. Actually, she landed in my arms. I thought maybe she's your child and you're looking for her." Olivia was disappointed to see him shake his head. "Do you know who she belongs to? She appears about four or five years old. It's hard to say since she's somewhat undernourished. Did you see her mother, her parents? Oh…and she calls her doll Deary. She yelled out the name Casey in her sleep." Olivia watched him, searching for any sign her words had meaning.

His face registered nothing. He shrugged. "Ah no, I don't know her. In truth, I don't remember throwin' her over the rail. Too much excitement, too many people, aye? I almost drowned before someone saved me. Now if there isn't anythin' else ya need, I'll be goin'."

He started to walk off, but again Olivia put her hand on his arm, restraining him.

"Please, are you sure? Was she standing next to anyone when you grabbed her up? Do you recognize anyone here that was with her? How about in Queenstown? Certainly there weren't that many people boarding in Ireland?"

His dark brow raised in amusement. "Ye think because I'm Irish that I boarded at Queenstown, aye? Sure'n it's none of yer business, but I got on the Titanic at Southampton, England with me wife Lillian. Albert Flynn's me name." His gaze roamed over her. "If by the saints, I hear anythin', ye'll be the first to know. But if her parents are on this ship, I'm thinkin' ya would have found them by now. Chances are they're one of those frozen souls left floatin' in the ocean. Mind if I ask yer name, lass, and yer stateroom number?"

She was reluctant to give her name to this man whose stare alone could make a store mannequin blush. "No, not at all. I'm Olivia—Olivia Marsh. The room is B121. You can contact me there or through a steward. Thank you for your time…er…Mister Flynn."

Looking amused, Albert Flynn doffed the curved brim of his bowler and left.

She was perplexed, what person wouldn't be happy to know they'd saved someone's life? Brag about it or even accept praise?

But even more confusing, while touching his sleeve she noticed his thick coat wasn't in the least bit damp, or mussed, and no salt brine dotted the fabric. Wouldn't he have lost his hat? Nothing substantiated his story that he'd been pulled from the freezing Atlantic.

With her finger pressed to her lips, Olivia narrowed her eyes in speculation. She watched Albert Flynn's long confident strides until he started down the stairs and disappeared.

Chapter Three

Albert Flynn went down the stairs leading to the bowels of the ship. As he closed in on the engine room, he could feel the steady vibration of the ship's giant engines on the metal walkway. Opening the riveted steel door to the boiler room, he paused to watch and listen to the stokers and firemen call out to each other as they worked. The noise coming from the giant boilers was deafening. The men glistened with sweat, their clothing and faces covered in black coal dust as they fed the yawning furnaces dousing the area in a red glow. Feeling the heat from where he stood, he decided against going in. He backtracked and headed in the opposite direction toward the third-class hold. A grim reminder that normally he would be in steerage, but with his good luck, he'd managed a second-class ticket on the Titanic. Things weren't so bad on this ship either.

As he walked, he took note of his surroundings. Large wooden crates stacked two high. Boxes shoved everywhere made the area a virtual nest of hiding places. Whenever he thought he'd found a place where someone small could hide, he stopped and searched. He went through boxes of food supplies, barrels, anything of interest. And just when he gripped the rough woven lid of a large wicker basket, a voice startled him.

"Hey, Mate, you're not supposed to be down here. What are ya doin'?" The steward approached. "You're not a Carpathia passenger. From the Titanic are ya? Don't tell me you're searching about for something to steal?"

"Nay, not stealin'. Not after all you've done fer us survivors." He rolled his eyes upwards and looked devastated, his theatrics excellent. "I just took a wrong hallway and ended up down here. Bless this ship, bless yer captain, and bless all of us who have lost so much in this tragedy." He hung his head in grief and sighed.

The steward's face grooved into lines of sorrow while he patted Albert's back. "Go on, be off with ya then."

Albert nodded at the steward and left. A quick glance over his shoulder showed the steward hadn't moved and still watched. Inwardly, Albert seethed, first the meddling bitch topside, and now the meddling bastard down here.

He hurried down the stairs into the third-class rooms. The stench of unwashed bodies in steerage was ripe. His mouth pulled into a grimace. He immediately knew that no information would be forthcoming from people jammed together, talking, some staring straight ahead seeing nothing, most still weeping. The smell had him lighting a cigar of which he puffed on and blew pungent gray smoke to filter into the area. It helped tremendously.

This ship was nowhere near as large as the *Titanic,* but big enough all the same. Finally knowing he couldn't check everywhere, he gave up for the day and moved on. He didn't like leaving unfinished business, but told himself he still had plenty of time before they would make port, at least three days. A lot could happen in three days. Hell, it only took a couple of hours for the mighty Titanic to sink.

As he made his way back up to second-class, he whistled, *No Irish Need Apply.*

She lay under the blankets and stared at nothing. In her hand was a rosary with jet black beads. Her thumb went over the round orbs as she mouthed, "Hail Mary, full of grace, the Lord is..." her words trailed off, her prayer to the rosary stilled.

No atonement from God would ever be forthcoming for such a monstrous sin.

Her sin.

Her eyes were swollen to reddened slits, and yet even now, tears continued to escape. *What have I done? Jesus, Mary and Joseph, what have I done…*

Heavy footfalls rang out in the corridor echoing louder as they came on. And then the key was in the lock and turned. The door abruptly opened creating a breeze that swayed the curtain around her bed. She could see through the opening in the curtain separating their bed from the other bed, and the rest of the shared second-class stateroom.

His mere presence filled the room. He looked menacing until he took off his long black overcoat and flicked a piece of lint off the fur collar. The coat was a grand thing to him. She hated it. He hung it on the wall peg, and then his bowler went beside it. He was a big man, tall, with a broad back, and large shoulders that pulled the seams of his suit taunt.

He moved out of her sight and she could hear the sounds of water from the faucet followed by the tinkling sound of a spoon hitting against glass.

The curtain parted and he stepped into their little alcove.

"Donald?" she said.

"Albert," he growled from beside the bed.

Yes…Albert. She must remember to call him Albert, but it was hard to do. Calling him Albert put her into the present when she'd rather be in the past. It was much easier, thinking of the past, staying there. She wished to God that Donald stood next to the bed, but it was Sam. She'd come to learn that he was nothing more than a common thief. And, to him, what was worth wanting was worth stealing. He showed no qualms about taking what wasn't his. He certainly showed no qualms about the biggest theft of all, his brother's family. And she'd allowed it.

"...Darlene?" he said, snapping his fingers close to her face.

She slowly focused on his looming form. "Did ye find Casey? Jilleen?" she asked with grieving hope that someone had put her babies in a lifeboat.

"I searched all over. He shouldn't have run off. Always running away, that boyo. And this time he took Jilleen with him."

"Casey's just a curious little boy, and Jilleen loves him so. They're inseparable. How can ye be so cruel and uncaring?" She began to cry and didn't have the strength to wipe her tears.

Spiteful, he spat out, "Don't forget, ya liked me well enough in Ireland before Donald came along, and ya liked me well enough after he left. Ya liked the money I gave ya, but I'd say ya liked me tool pumpin' in ya more. Say it, Darlene, ya liked being fecked best of all."

"Not at the expense of me children...never that." She groaned, stifled by the weight of guilt. "Yer a callous man, Sam—"

"Oh...so now yer goin' to play the grievin' mum, eh?" he ground out, mimicking her. "Lay it all on me shoulders. Ya knew what ya were doin' when ye boarded the ship in Queensland, knew ye were givin' them up. I told ya last I saw of them, Jilleen was runnin' after Casey, and me runnin' to catch them both. Bloody hell, Darlene, I was sloshin' in freezin' water up to me arse trying to get to yer brats. I yelled at them to stop, come to me. Too much confusion, people runnin' everywhere. Hell, I don't need to tell ya." He placed the glass on the floor and sat on the edge of the bed.

"Nooooo..." she cried, refusing to believe her golden-haired boy and sweet daughter were dead. Casey's enjoyment of life, his eyes bright with excitement forever closed. And Jilleen, her adorable little baby. One minute Jilleen was close by waiting to board the lifeboat, the next she was gone.

Derry railed at him, "What have ya done—what have we done? Jesus, Mary and Joseph, why did I listen to you? We're being punished, there's no escapin' this, never—never!" She started to come off the bed at him. Using her rosary, she slapped him across the cheek. The hard beads drew blood, creating a red welt.

His face darkened with anger. "Shuddup. Ye'll be bringin' the Captain in here." His large hands grabbed hers, stopping her barrage of slaps. He held her with a bruising grip.

"Oh…God…" she moaned, her anger turning to despair, her will beaten back. "What will Donald—"

"Donald nothing. Three years is a long time, aye? And it's not as if ya intended stayin' with him in New York. Now keep yer mouth shut and I'll get us off this ship and to the train as planned."

But she hadn't planned to go without her children safe in Donald's arms. "I hate ya, Sam McShane. Ye knew Aidan wasn't dead. Ye ripped me family apart. And for what? This? I've lost everything because of ya." She grabbed his suit lapels. He tore her hands from his coat and pinned them against the pillow. Pain shot up her arms, and seeing hatred coming from him, fear clamped her mouth shut.

"Get a hold of yourself—or by God—I'll…" His lips were on hers, moving against them, sealing her loud cries.

He released her arms, and she collapsed. He was too cruel, too mocking. He reached down to the floor and picked up the glass.

'What's that?" she asked.

"Laudanum. The ship's doctor claims it will help ya sleep." He slid his arm under her shoulders, lifting her off the pillow, holding her while she downed the liquid. "Ah…do be a good lass…be a good baby."

She drank the bitter draft, wishing it were strong enough to permanently close her mind to the thoughts of how the ocean kept reaching into her life, taking her babies, her mother.

Darlene had shadowy memories of her mother, Aisling, of flighty hands, a nervous laugh, and of a mother, who even though she tried, couldn't show affection. Days would go by when her mother was kept locked inside the bedroom. Constant visits from the doctor urged her father, Hoyt, to have her mother committed. He refused. Darlene remembered being young and asking what was wrong with Mam. Her father couldn't answer and acted as though it was something dark and terrible and she didn't need to know.

She'd learned the hard way concerning her mother, the mocking that cut her to her core. The cruelty of others.

"Darlene's mum's gone astray in the head," the children teased.

"Watch out, Darlene or ye'll do the same—astray…astray…" they mocked even more, making circles with their hands next to their ears and crossing their eyes like a loony.

She was six when the ridicule started and ten when it stopped. Her mother with a sly smile on her face had taken Darlene by the hand and slipped away to the seashore. While Darlene searched for shells, her mother put taunts and gossip to rest. She walked into the Irish Sea and disappeared under a monstrous wave of churning blue-green water…

"Mam," Darlene moaned out loud, and Sam casts a curious glance her way. He put the glass down and got in the bed with her. His hand clamped her chin as he turned her face toward his. "Do ya hate me?"

His face blurred behind her tears. She whispered, "Nay, how can I?"

Indeed, how could she?

Darlene fingered her rosary and thought how her life had been wedged between the two McShane brothers for so long she couldn't remember when it wasn't. *Sam—Donald—Donald—Sam.* She wanted to curse the day she'd met Sam, but if not for Sam, Donald would have never entered her life.

She had barely turned seventeen when Sam McShane came into their butcher shop. He already had a reputation of being a chancer, and a known thief. She stood behind the glass case and studied him as intently as he studied the meat on display. Tall, with black wavy hair and eyes the color of whiskey, he was most handsome.

He appeared not to like what was in the case and ordered a different cut of meat. Her father, Hoyt leaned close to her and whispered a strong warning to keep an eye on McShane. But the moment her father went into the back room, Sam leaned over the counter and opening the money drawer, deftly picked up some coins. Putting them in his pocket, he grinned and winked at her. His stare was bold, and signaling for her to come closer, he asked her to meet him on the beach in an hour.

After her father returned and placed the wrapped meat on the counter, she watched in wonder as Sam brazenly used the coins he'd just stolen to pay with.

Without a glance her way, Sam tipped his bowler and left.

Darlene, forced into shyness at an early age, preened from Sam's attention. After the shop closed, she told her father she was going for a walk. She went into her bedroom, plain in appearance with only a bed and a four-drawer dresser. An oval mirror hung on the wall. There was nothing frilly to indicate a young woman slept here. It was barren of life's souvenirs. No dreams of fancy happened here, only the fear that someday having gone crazy like her mother, she'd end up locked behind its solid brown door.

Opening the drawer she took out a red wool headscarf and tied it around her head. While her father bent over his ledger, she took her black coat off the peg and quickly left.

Nervous, Darlene left her small village of Portmarnock behind, and walked down the trail leading to the seashore. A place she'd never returned to after her mother died.

The wind carried the smell of salt and fish. She reached the beach where the surf came clawing in. The only other hearty souls about were two men who carried a rowboat over their heads, resembling a four-legged turtle, as they moved down the shore. She stepped into the dented sand made by someone's boots, perhaps Sam's. Each print, she noticed, were twice the size as hers.

Seagulls flew overhead, their shrill cries sounded like a warning to her. Go back! Go Back!

She now stood within a stone's throw from where she'd watched her mother go into the sea. Sam McShane stepped out from behind a large rugged boulder. Right now, Darlene wished wholeheartedly for a sane and well mother who was able to share all the firsts in her young life, like now, how to handle a first conversation with a man who made her words stick in her throat and give her the shivers.

As she approached him, Sam reached out and pulled her against his chest. "Yer a pretty little thing, Darlene O'Dea." His words blended with the howl of the wind.

He untied her scarf and took it off. The wind rushed along and whipped it down the beach. She started to go after it, but he wouldn't let her.

He kissed her. His tongue invaded her mouth, shocking her, and she started to pull away, but he held her tight. She didn't know if she liked the rough feel of his tongue, but responded by pressing hers against his. He finally broke off the kiss, his features now taking on a softer appearance, like he enjoyed what he was doing. He leaned down and kissed her neck, his hand going to her breast, squeezing. She gasped at his being so familiar with her body, he only laughed.

"Have ye never been kissed by a man?"

"Never," she managed to say. Other than her parents occasional pat, no other human had touched her. She found his exploring hands exciting.

"'Tis a virgin are ya now?"

She nodded, and his grin broadened. He removed his coat and put it down on the sand. When he gestured for her to lie down, she said no. But she soon learned the word no was not easily accepted by Sam McShane.

Before she knew it, he had unbuttoned her coat and parted it to fall off her shoulders and onto the boulder behind her. He began unbuttoning her blouse. She didn't stop him, her curiosity high. He pulled the straps of her chemise down over her shoulders, exposing her breasts, and used the straps to pin her arms beside her, he suckled her, changing breasts like he couldn't make up his mind. The pull on her nipples titillated her, and she felt an intense pleasure between her legs.

A light shower started, pattering against her bare skin, she ignored it. When he slowly helped her to lie down on his coat, she didn't complain, or try to stop him. He lay beside her, and for the first time ever, she touched another human in exploration. She removed his hat, allowing her hands to slowly trace his face, feeling coarse stubble, the formation of his skull, the multicolor in the depths of his eyes, and his hair tight with waves.

He deftly removed her long knickers. When he unbuttoned his fly, she watched in curiosity and saw a man's privates for the first time. He touched parts of her she'd only thought about touching. He rolled on top of her forcing her legs apart.

"What are ye doin'?" she asked in alarm, and struggled against him.

"I'm gonna show ya what a man and woman are put on this earth for," he said.

"Me da says never let a man touch me until I'm married to him." She tried to push him off of her, but he was too strong.

"No, lass," he said. "'Tis too late to act coy." He forced himself inside her, hurting her. She cried, he laughed and said it wouldn't hurt for long and to just wrap her legs around him and hang on.

For a month she slipped away to meet him and let him have his way with her. He destroyed her world by saying he'd had enough of Dublin and was going to Belfast to find work.

"I love ye, please take me with ya," she begged.

"Aye, I'll take ye with me," he assured. But he left without her.

Two weeks hadn't gone by after Sam's departure when a young man and an elderly woman came into the shop. Darlene glanced up from the counter, and thought Sam had returned for her. She cried out in joy. But a closer look showed he wasn't Sam at all.

Her father came out from the back, wiping his hands off on a towel. "Hello," he said. "What can I get for ye?"

The woman, with hazel eyes and graying hair beneath a small brimmed hat, smiled at him. "I'm Ina McShane, this is me son, Donald. I've heard my other son, Sam, does business with ye. I've come to make restitution if he owes ye money."

Hoyt O'Dea seemed puzzled, and said, "Nay, he was here but one time and paid me."

Donald McShane's sharp stare finally forced a smile from Darlene. She wondered if their visit had another reason, but she kept silent.

"Maybe we should buy some mutton?" Donald suggested to his Mam.

"Sure'n we could use the meat," the diminutive woman said.

Darlene couldn't help but compare Donald to Sam. Donald McShane thrilled Darlene as much as Sam did. She set about capturing his attention.

Her father liked him and was willing to let eighteen-year-old Donald court her. Donald never called her Darlene, preferring the snappy nickname of Derry.

"Derry O'Dea," he'd say.

She became his Derry, and tried to forget Sam who'd abandoned her almost two months ago. She told Donald about her mam killing herself and watched with a guarded expression if he was going to be put off. He wasn't and told her she was too young to realize how serious her mother's illness was.

They'd been seeing each other steadily for a month when Donald came to pick her up in a pony cart. A first for her as she'd walked everywhere she went. His face was eager with expectations as he shared future dreams and wanting a family of his own. After clattering along on the cobblestone streets, he lashed the whip in the air over the roan-colored horse and sent it down the grooved road to the beach. She held onto the bouncing cart with one hand and her straw boater with the other. The long black ribbons trailing over the back of the brim fluttered madly behind her.

They laughed as he sent the horse into a galloping race on the hard wet sand. Foam and pieces of shell flung up at them from the horse's giant hooves. The wind stole her hat and sent it sailing into the sea. She squealed that she'd lost her best hat. Donald pulled on the reins stopping the horse, and without hesitation went after the hat. He fought the playful, roiling surf as it crashed onto the shore. With a wide grin and his Sunday trousers drenched, he brought her hat back. She plopped the ruined boater on her head and laughed as water ran down the sides of her face.

As if the moment of giddiness was too much for him, he turned to her in sobering intensity and taking her face between his hands, thumbed the salt water coursing down her cheeks. She recognized his passion that now blended with specks of sand on his face.

"Will ye marry me?" he asked.

She longed to say yes, instead, she forced herself to say. "You're brother, Sam, he made promises to me…let me believe he loved…" She swallowed hard and wanted the earth to open up and devour her. "If ye no longer want to marry me, I understand," she said and hung her head in shame.

He tipped her face up with his finger. His gaze dug into hers, narrowed as her words revealed the truth. Donald said with forcefulness, "Forget Sam was ever in yer life. Be grateful it's me yer marryin' and not him."

...Be grateful it's me and not him...

The rosary fell next to her body. Sam picked it up, noticing the wear on the beads. The silver cross picked up the light. Jesus' body on the cross came into focus, the minute details of his agony made Sam smirk. He pressed his thumb against the image, blotting it out. He'd never been one for religion, didn't believe in God, and wasn't about to change. He made his own luck, and followed his own set of rules. *Sam's rules.*

He placed the rosary in her palm and folded her fingers over it. Her breathing became shallow. The laudanum had taken her away from life, away from hard truths. The ship's doctor cautioned him to use the laudanum a few times only. Too much laudanum with its tincture of opium could make her dependent on the drug, addictive was the doctor's warning. Sam wasn't concerned, a little drop here and there wouldn't harm her. He pulled the covers up over her shoulders, pausing to caress the silken strands of her hair. In due time he told himself, in due time she'll become the woman he liked fecking. In due time, she'll forget her brats, Donald, the past. Everything good always came to him in due time.

He reluctantly left her side, and parting the curtains went back into the small sitting area where he took in their quarters. "No bigger than a rat's arse," he grumbled.

It didn't matter that the Williams's, a generous elderly couple had given up their privacy to share their stateroom. The room was solid with nothing fancy about it. Several chairs framed a small wooden table between them. At least the room had a private washroom and a toilet, he'd give it that much. But it couldn't come close to the opulence of second-class on the *Titanic.* What a waste, all that beautiful wood, the fireplace mantels he'd carved and labored over, now at the bottom of the sea.

His face stung where Darlene raked the rosary across it, and he looked in the mirror to see the damage. Red welts and blood-flecked nicks started at his left cheekbone to end at his lower jaw. The sharp black beads did more damage than he'd thought. His face now matched his right hand with its red and swollen knuckles gotten from smashing in the nose of the steward who had tried to block him from bringing Darlene and Jilleen out of steerage. He was starting to resemble a prize fighter.

Traveling separate from Darlene, he'd set himself up nice and cozy in second-class on the Titanic. Darlene had purchased tickets in steerage with money sent to her by Donald. It was Sam's luck to be playing cards with some other gentlemen in the Titanic's card room when the ship shuddered to a stop. Working around ships, Sam knew something dire had happened, and a quick trip topside confirmed his worst fears. A giant iceberg loomed over the ship, and for the first time in his life Sam became afraid. No ship was unsinkable. He also knew that the affluent would be ushered to the lifeboats first and that there weren't enough boats for everyone. He ran to get Darlene and her brats.

He reached their room to find Darlene and Jilleen. Casey was gone. Sam ordered both of them dressed. From the nightstand next to the bed a white card fluttered to the floor. Picking it up he saw it was Darlene's health inspection card she used to board the Titanic in Queenstown. He stuffed it in his coat pocket.

Darlene begged Sam to find Casey and he promised to do so. Satisfied they were bundled in warm coats, he led them out.

People were everywhere, scared, jamming the corridors, talking, asking what had happened. Sam pushed past them, his grip on Darlene firm. At the top of the stairs a steward stepped in front of them barring their way. Sam smashed his fist into the steward's nose, crunching the bone. The man howled, his hand covering his nose, trying to stop the spurting blood.

Sam got them topside and maneuvered her and Jilleen into a group waiting for lifeboats. He warned her to get on a lifeboat and thrust a life jacket at her. Again she begged him to find Casey. He left her, but not to find Casey. He didn't give a feck about finding the lad.

…Sam straightened his suit collar and glanced out the Carpathia's small porthole, watching the horizon tilt first one way, then another.

A soft knock sounded on the door.

Ambrose and Bertha Williams slowly pushed open the door and entered. They paused to stare at him, their arms intertwined. Both short and overweight. Ambrose was clean-shaven, showing his thin slit of a mouth. Dressed for a vacation in the hot Mediterranean, the *Carpathia's* original destination, his suit was off-white, and the only blue on his white fedora was the hatband. Bertha's hair was hidden under a white, wide-brimmed hat. Her two-piece suit made her look like a white-breasted pigeon.

She shook her head causing the fold of fat under her chin to quiver. "Oh…my. Is your wife still unable to get out of bed?" She pulled the hatpins out of her hat, and taking it off, sighed while placing it on the table.

"Aye, she's still sick, delusional. Blames me for our children's death. Even hit me with her rosary," he said, and made a show of rubbing his cheek. "The doctor's given her some medication to help her sleep. I expect she'll be bedridden even after we arrive in New York. I can't see us continuing to our destination with her in such a bad way. Our children…"

"Mr. Flynn." Ambrose cleared his throat. "The Missus and I've been talking. We own a tenement building in Manhattan. It's in the East Village on Fourth Street. I'm afraid you're going to have to remain in the City until word comes down about…well…there's talk going around that ships are headed out to the site where the Titanic sank." He blew out a breath, his face sad. "Ah…recovering bodies.

If your wife is still unable to travel when we dock, you're welcome to one of my apartments. You can stay there free of charge until you get back on your feet."

Mr. William's put his arm around his wife and squeezed her shoulder. "Bertha has her mind set on seeing Greece, and…well…so do I. We're waiting to hear from Captain Rostron if our trip will be canceled, or if it will continue." With Bertha's help, he removed his coat and hung it on the peg next to Sam's. Next off was his fedora leaving a permanent dent around his gray hair.

Sam tried not to show his excitement. This was going so much better than planned it amazed him. "Sure'n it wouldn't be right fer me to impose—"

"Nonsense," Ambrose interrupted, taking a seat next to Sam. "We have a furnished apartment not rented out right now. Whether we go on our trip or not, we'd feel it's our duty to insist you stay there."

Bertha's mouth trembled as her hand nervously touched the brooch at her neck. "You need a place to grieve for your children. Those poor babies, all the little children, oh…my…I…" she stuttered.

Sam cocked his head at Ambrose. "Ye make it hard fer a man to refuse. By the saints, I thank ya." His shoulders slumped and his hand came up to cover his face. "Aye, to be separated from our children—wrenched out of our arms and put on a boat…we thought." His shoulders shook, he sobbed, and managed to shed a few false tears.

"My good man, my good man, do not grieve so. You'll make yourself sick." Ambrose looked as though he was the one who'd gone through the sinking. "How fortunate you were saved and put on a lifeboat."

"Sure'n I agree with ya." Oh…yeah, he'd managed to get himself off the sinking ship when most men remained behind. The righteous pricks. He'd hidden in one of Titanic's lifeboats. The remembered surprise of the ship's officer after he'd pulled the canvas tarp off exposing Sam cowering like a rat crouched down close to the ribs of the boat. The officer called him a rotten coward. The heated exchange with Sam telling the officer he didn't give a feck that women and children were first. No way was he going to die because of the captain's puking mistake.

Pulling a silver flask from his pocket, Sam quenched his thirst with one long swig of Irish whiskey. Shutting his eyes against the burn, he still bristled at being called a coward. At least he wasn't fish bait on the bottom of the Atlantic.

Sam offered Ambrose a drink. He accepted the flask and tipped back his head to take a nip.

Bertha Williams cleared her throat. "Mr. Flynn, when we get to New York we'll introduce you to Tom Meeks. Tom is our manager who takes care of the building while we're gone."

Bloody hell, but Sam's luck was changing, and the sinking of the *Titanic* just might be the best luck of all. He thought about the jewels and money left behind in the first-class staterooms. Money and jewels he'd managed to steal during the hysteria of the ship's sinking. But that wasn't all he was thinking about.

In his own panic he'd done something horrific in the one stateroom that filled his mind with images he'd like to forget. Or did he want to? A wry smile creased his mouth.

Chapter Four

April Eighteen

Donald, waiting for Eldon, mingled with the swelling crowd of anxious people. He glanced up at the giant archway of black metal curving high up over the entrance to *Pier 54*. The sign, noticeable for blocks around, was an imposing steel-girded structure with the words *White Star Line*, written in tall white letters. To Donald, the sign looked like a large black funeral shroud, the only thing missing was black bunting. Rainwater steadily poured off it to splash against the many black umbrellas passing beneath. Without Eldon, Donald couldn't get admittance into the pier, and with Eldon, getting admittance would be slim at best.

Pier 54, on Manhattan's Hudson River, was home to the *Cunard* shipping line, and the Cunard liner, the *Carpathia.* After a traumatic four days of waiting, everyone knew the ship was supposed to dock around nine tonight. The *Carpathia's* Marconi operators had telegraphed a complete list of survivors names to the *White Star Line.* The White Star office had in turn given the recorded names to the police, the newspapers, and to the relatives whose loved ones were on the ship.

Donald didn't have the coveted list of names to get him past the beefy policemen. But he wasn't going to let them deter him from getting inside the massive covered pier. He prayed Eldon's ruse would work. Donald looked down to see a discarded newspaper, the date three days ago. Big, black headlines screamed up at him, TITANIC SINKS FOUR HOURS AFTER HITTING ICEBERG, 866 RESCUED BY CARPATHIA, PROBABLY 1250 PERISH. He had a paper like it at home and knew the article word-for-word even down to the so-called partial listed names of the survivors.

Derry wasn't listed, nor was Jilleen and Casey.

Partial list.

Those two words fed his hopes.

Partial list.

He refused to believe they had perished, refused to believe his family was dead in the cold waters of the Atlantic. And yet, fear gnawed at him until he thought he'd lose his mind.

"God, let them be aboard the Carpathia," he blurted, his words riddled with hope.

The head of the port wanted to keep out the curious, the morbid thrill-seekers, eager reporters, and anyone else who didn't need to be here. Barriers of green lanterns strung on ropes girded the giant pier where the police kept the crowds back.

As dusk came on those seeking entry into the cavernous building had their credentials checked allowing them in. A long line of large wheeled automobiles rattled up to drop off people. A mounted policeman brushed by Donald. The horse's breath was hot against his face and its heavy hooves slammed down close to Donald's feet, forcing him back from the barrier.

"Donald!" Eldon elbowed his way through the thick crowd to get to him. "I've got what you asked for. I hope it works because these policemen mean business."

"We'll have to see, now won't we?" Donald replied with little enthusiasm.

"Well, don't blame me if it doesn't." Eldon opened his long coat and took out his pocket watch where it was snugged inside his vest pocket. "You said the ship's due around nine, right?"

"Aye." He turned to his friend whose face was shadowed beneath a wide-brimmed hat dripping rain. "I thank ye fer comin' here. But I'd expect no man to stand out in this pisser if he didn't have to. Give me what ye brought and go on home." Donald brushed dripping water off his nose.

"I'm not going anywhere. You shouldn't be alone at a time like this."

"I won't be alone for long, not after I bring me family off the ship."

"Donald, you better prepare yourself for the fact they may not be on the Carpathia—"

"Don't say anymore. They'll be there…they have to—" The blast of a ship's shrill whistle interrupted him.

Eldon held up a doctor's black bag and cautioned Donald to follow him. They hurried up to the blockade and the two policemen whose eyes narrowed at them in suspicion.

Eldon tipped his hat and lifted his bag. "The White Star Line asked me to bring medicine for the survivors who are ill or injured. They depleted their stores on the Carpathia." He pointed at Donald. "This is my assistant. I'm told frostbite is a big problem with a lot of people."

One of the policemen looked skeptical while the other didn't appear to know what to say. Inside the pier the crowd became loud. The ships on the river started blowing their whistles. People behind the officials strained at the ropes, threatening to break the restraints.

Distracted, the police motioned Eldon and Donald through.

They ran inside the large pier and barely made it in time.

Silence fell over the enormous crowd who hushed and peered toward the Hudson.

A large ship cut through the water.

It was the *Carpathia.*

Donald swallowed hard, his throat constricting into a balled-up ache. He braced his legs. Don't buckle on me now, he begged.

A flotilla of tugs, ferryboats, and ships flared their lights against the Cunard liner, welcoming her, lighting her way home. Out on the Hudson, the rain came down in torrents, and thunder cut loose to join the loud sirens and bells of the ships.

The *Carpathia* blasted her horn, the sound deep and riveting. The ship's black bow barely rippled the water as she slowly steamed toward home, her lone funnel reached into the night sky.

Donald glanced over his shoulder to see the press of faces, rich and poor alike awaiting loved ones. Most were sobbing, unable to pull their eyes away from the *Carpathia* being positioned against the north side of the pier.

Reporters lucky enough to get inside the covered pier tried to get the best pictures. Magnesium flashes kept going off like lightning.

As the ship's forward and aft blue-canopied gangways lowered into place, Donald, with Eldon following, began making his way toward the ship.

"Let me through, my family's waiting fer me." Donald pushed against the wall of bodies which gave way to let him pass. Seeing two gangways to keep an eye on, he positioned himself at the center where both merged behind a four-foot wooden fence put up to give the passengers a pathway to follow out of the pier.

He watched with anticipation as the ship's regular passengers disembarked and scurried past him as they followed the fenced off area. Some appeared surprised at the din surrounding them as they tried to get past the pushy reporters, seeking freedom from the limelight and the hubbub.

The raucous vibration of voices hushed as a young woman paused under the aft canopied cover. She wore a coat made from a blanket. There was something about her demeanor, as she gripped the railing, testing the solidness of it. Her gaze scanned the crowd. When someone behind Donald shouted out her name, her hand jerked up to cover her trembling smile. She ran down the walkway and into a man's embrace.

This scene continued and just as it looked like everyone had disembarked, Donald started toward the aft gangway but stopped. A lone woman appeared at the head of the forward walkway and paused to look out over the crowd. She held a little girl's hand. The child, wrapped in a blanket, clung to her mother, making him think of Jilleen, his wee lass, how frightened she must be.

"Olivia!" A man's deep voice shouted. The woman waved and started down the gangway. Her dark hair tumbled in disarray against her back as she walked inside the fence. Nearing Donald, her tired eyes trained beyond him, no doubt on the man who had shouted at her. She had a cut and nasty bruises on her forehead and eye.

"Olivia!" the deep voice impatiently called out again.

She waved and continued.

Donald watched her stiff-backed process. The child disappeared below the high fence barrier. With expectation, Donald turned back to the gangways, waiting for his family to disembark. But only a few stragglers came out.

And then nobody.

"God—no!" he screamed. Unable to contain himself any longer, he vaulted over the fence and sprinted up the nearest gangway. He no sooner stepped onto the deck when two thick-necked crewmen loomed in front of him, stopping him.

"Hey, mate, ya can't come on the ship. Get off!"

Donald pushed past them and took off running at a pumping clip, skirting a mountain of discarded life vests.

"Derry!" He ran toward where he thought the stairs down to third-class would be. "Casey—Jilleen—I'm here."

Feet pounded behind him. Someone shouted for him to stop.

He ignored them.

"Derry!"

Someone rushed up behind Donald and clamped their burly arms around his waist. The deck came up to meet him with a hard blow, scraping his knees and elbows, knocking the air out of him. Pain of not being able to breathe rendered him useless. He struggled for air. His cap was knocked off, and his head violently yanked backwards by the hair.

"Don't know what you're up to, mate," the crewman ground out. "You're not takin' another step on this ship."

Donald was jerked to his feet. His arms were pinned behind his back and leveraged upward. He grunted in pain. Several more men joined them. They formed a beefy guard in front of him.

He stared at a wall of blue uniforms. "I'm looking for me wife and children. My wife—Derry–ah–Darlene McShane. Jilleen me daughter. Casey my son." His words tumbled out as he tried to catch his breath. "I'm thinkin' they're still on the ship, aye?" Something in Donald's eyes, his voice, brought pity to the man for he released Donald's arms.

One of them patted Donald's shoulder. "See here, mate, all the passengers have left. Other than Mr. Flynn and his sick wife who's coming off by stretcher, all the survivors and passengers are gone. See for yourself, here are the names I checked off as they disembarked." He flashed the roster.

"I don't believe ya, they must be here and ye not know of them…please…." Donald wasn't used to pleading for anything, but now he did.

The crewman signaled for an officer who was approaching. "Sir, this man says his family must be aboard and—"

"Did you inquire at the White Star Line headquarters as to the complete list we wired ahead, Mister?"

"McShane—Donald McShane," Donald said hastily. "Aye, I have the list. But I believe my family's been left off."

"What makes you say that?" the officer asked.

"Because they were in steerage, and I'm thinkin' first and second class are listed, but not third class," he said with hope punctuating each word.

"You're wrong. Everyone removed from the lifeboats were recorded, and not by class. We took care to put them in alphabetical order." The officer cleared his throat. "I'm sorry…so sorry, but your family's not here."

Two men carrying a stretcher came up the gangway. They paused next to the first officer and inquired about the sick woman. The officer told them to go to stateroom 32B and ask for an Albert Flynn.

Donald stared into the gray eyes of the officer whose own face was slack with fatigue. Although reluctant to believe it, Donald knew he spoke the truth. "What do I do now?" he asked, defeated, unable to think. Inside, he was dying. The men before him blurred with his tears, and he hastily bent down to retrieve his cap. He wanted this nightmare to go away, to end, but somehow he knew it was just beginning. His little children—ah…no. His body shook with grief.

The officer put his hand on Donald's arm, his voice soft with sympathy. "I believe ships from Nova Scotia are recovering the dead and taking the bodies to Halifax. The White Star Line has set up a temporary office here inside the pier. They'll furnish you with a voucher for free train tickets to Halifax. You have my condolences…Mr. McShane. I'm sorry, so sorry for all the families who are living through this tragedy. I wish you luck in your journey." He signaled to a purser walking by. "Mr. Givens, escort Mr. McShane to the White Star office. Give him special treatment."

Overwhelmed, Donald reeled toward the aft gangway and Eldon who patiently waited.

Despite standing on solid ground, Olivia could still feel the airy roll of the ship beneath her. She stood next to Myron under the cover of the pier. Not knowing for sure who would be here to greet her, she had gladly gone into his welcoming embrace, loving the feel of his strong arms around her. He'd reassured Olivia that her father was waiting in his automobile for her.

Seeing Myron's curious glance at the child, Olivia didn't have time to tell him anything about her before a group of reporters rushed in. She inwardly groaned at the sight of them and darted a look down at the little girl standing close to her. Clutching Deary the doll against her chest, the child turned large eyes up at Olivia. Her small hand gripped Olivia's with amazing strength. Olivia could feel the little ones fear, and wanted nothing more than to get away from the circus now taking place around them.

Olivia, knelt down and brushing a curl from the child's face, talked in a soothing tone. "You'll be all right. These men only want to ask me some questions. We won't be long at all." The child remained silent, so Olivia stood and plastered a smile on her face.

"Miss Marsh—Olivia Marsh! Smile! Give us a picture won't you."

Camera's fired magnesium flares, and Olivia accommodated them all.

Paddy Riley from the New York Times always covered Olivia's suffragette rallies and speeches. The short, rotund reporter favored loud suits, and now wore one of yellow and brown plaid. His tongue darted out to wet the lead of his pencil and posed it over his notepad. "Tell me what it was like on the lifeboats. How'd ya get hurt?"

"Did you see John Jacob Astor—his wife?" shouted another.

"How about the Straus's? Guggenheim, did ya see Benjamin Guggenheim? Did you see the people on the ship when it went down? Tell us, Miss Marsh, and we'll put it to print." Holding paper and pencils in strong grips, they talked over one another as they jockeyed for position around her

Olivia opened her mouth to speak, to tell them of the horrors and the injustice committed, but for the first time in her life, she couldn't. There was no putting into words what had happened. There would be no relating about death and dying, not while this innocent little soul was clutching her coat for dear life, listening to every word. No, she'd keep mum to these reporters. No use telling them what she'd denied telling the little girl. That she was probably an orphan and only God knew her fate.

"Miss Marsh?"

Myron spoke up, "Miss Marsh just got off the ship, now is not the time for this." His arm went around Olivia's shoulder, protecting her. She smiled at him gratefully.

However, Paddy Riley wasn't one to be put off. "There's no better time than the present. We want the scoop and we want it from one of New York's finest suffragette's. C'mon Miss. Marsh, we're old friends, ain't we? I've covered all yer speeches for women and children labor rights. I bet you have a lot to say about an unsinkable ship sinkin'—ain't that right, Miss Marsh? I bet you have a lot to say about the world's finest liner now at the bottom of the Atlantic…huh."

"Paddy Riley," she said, almost scolding, "You always show up at the most opportune time don't you? And after reading some of the articles you've written about me, I'm not sure if you're friend or foe." She waited for a response from the lively reporter in the gaudy suit. Even though Olivia didn't always agree with what he wrote, albeit sensationalized, it was truthful.

"For sure this is bigger than suffragettes whacking men with picket signs." Again, he posed his pencil over his paper and quirked a sandy brow at her.

"Well, Mr. Riley, if you'll come by my home tomorrow, I'll give you an exclusive." She took his pencil and wrote her address on his notepad. "I believe I have a story to tell you, and certainly one I want printed. But right now, I'm exhausted, and freezing." She pulled her coat collar tight and shivered.

Myron scowled at the bunch surrounding them, and said, "You heard her, that's the end of it for now."

As the reporters drifted away, Myron's eyes, the color of a new leaf, swept over her and then glanced at the child. "I'd like to hear your story before the rest of the world does. You took quite a knock on your forehead."

"Yes I did. Hit in the eye by an Englishman while giving my speech. And then clipped by this little girl's shoe during the sinking has left me with a rather colorful face. It no longer hurts though."

"That's good to know. Let's go, your father's waiting." He put his fedora back on.

Her father wasn't a demonstrative man, and she wondered how he was going to react upon seeing her. "How is father?"

"Fine, just fine."

"Well, I'm sure he is. He's too ornery to be otherwise," she said, affection coloring her tone. She noticed stubble on Myron's usually impeccable face and voiced her concern. "You're tired. It must have been a long day."

"Make that a long four days. The waiting has put us all through the ringer. I can't tell you how happy your family and I were to see your name on the survivors list."

At long last he bent and kissed her cheek, chaste, droll, and keeping with good manners. Myron would never break his rigid code of morals and make a display in public by really kissing her. She frowned, come to think of it, he'd never really kissed her in private either. Just once, right here and now, she wanted him to make her toes curl, say to heck with propriety and bend her backwards and kiss her until she begged for mercy.

"...Olivia, did you hear what I said?"

"Yes, Myron, I heard. But before leaving here, I want to get a list of the Titanic's passengers. Let's go to that office over there."

People were assembling outside a makeshift office where a large sign read, *White Star Inquiries.*

At first Myron appeared not to understand, and then comprehension dawned as he tilted his head at the child. He bent down and softly addressed the child. "Here now, I don't think you need the blanket anymore." He removed the blanket to leave the child snug in her woolen coat. Myron then picked the child up. Pure horror covered the girl's face, and she opened her mouth to cry out. Olivia was quick to reassure her Myron wouldn't hurt her.

They started toward the office. A lot of others had the same needs and she fought against the rush, moving with the expertise of someone who snaked through large mobs on a daily basis.

"Olivia," Myron said striding beside her. "Why not wait until tomorrow to do this? There will be less people around." His height and size helped cut a path for them.

"I can't wait until tomorrow. Maybe her parents or someone else is here looking for her. If I were to miss them, I'd never forgive myself. I need to try, Myron."

Against sharp protest from the crowd, she pushed her way to the front of the line. "Excuse me…excuse me, I was on the Titanic. Please—I must get past. Excuse me!"

Myron moved in front of her, and with the child's arms locked around his neck, he opened up a path for Olivia.

Inside, the office was uproarious with people shouting and seeking answers. The air in the room was sharp with the strong smell of wet woolen clothing making it reek like a stockyard.

Olivia, spotting a clerk, moved forward. "Sir, I have a little girl from the Titanic. She won't speak, so I don't know her name. I need a list of the passengers on the Titanic, especially third-class."

"Steerage only?" The clerk, a man with thinning hair and stubble asked while reaching under the counter. He pulled out sheets of paper.

"One would think so, but give me everything but first class," Olivia said. "I also need to leave her description with this office. Maybe someone's inquired about her."

"We have several lists started on clipboards over there," he said while pointing to Olivia's right. "Go fill it out with her description and your name and address. The newspapers are also getting information from them." He handed her the list of passengers, and wished her luck.

Myron, taking the child with him, left Olivia's side and was already writing information down on a clipboard. Olivia silently blessed the man for his help.

She started to join them when the outer office door burst open. A purser from the *Carpathia* escorted a man into the room. The stranger's face was a mask of wild apprehension, as he glanced around, seeing but not seeing. Several men paced behind them. As he drew near, his gaze locked with Olivia's. His eyes held unbelievable sadness, grief.

He paused next to her, and manners had him grabbing his drenched cap from his head. Short brown curls plastered against his forehead and she watched a droplet of water trickle down his cheek then drip onto his soaked coat.

"C'mon, McShane, let's get your ticket for Halifax." The purser urged.

"You mean tickets," another man behind him spoke up.

McShane's head snapped around in disbelief. "Ah, no, Eldon, ya needn't be thinkin' to go up there with me. What about the drugstore?"

The man, Eldon, shrugged. "I'm not letting you go up there alone, Donald. Not with me knowing what you're going to be facing trying to identify your family. So, don't even think it. Dad will be okay. There are a number of people who can help him."

Olivia listened to the rapid exchange between them, thinking what a good friend this Eldon person was. And then a sad smile broke across McShane's face as he shook his head and humbly said, "Then 'tis thanks I be givin' ya."

As though she was an afterthought, he glanced at her and nodded. His face closed up, and the haunted look reappeared as he followed the purser.

Olivia couldn't get over how much Donald McShane resembled Albert Flynn. However, she did have to admit Donald McShane only gave off grieving emergency, certainly none of the menacing discomfort she'd felt with Albert Flynn.

"Sir," she said, stopping an office worker as he made his way back toward the inner office. "Why are you sending people to Halifax?"

"It's where the dead from the Titanic are being taken." He started to push by her, but she grabbed his arm.

"The dead?"

"Why, yes. The dead. Fifteen hundred of them, ya know. Gotta take them somewhere. Ships are sailing out of Halifax, pullin' them out of the water, still wearing life vests they say. A special train is taking agents from our line up to Halifax. They're taking others who have a need to be there, family members and the like."

Olivia's mouth fell open, but he left before she could say another word. He was right, the bodies had to go somewhere. It was something she hadn't thought about. But now she did. Donald McShane was going to Nova Scotia to try to find his family. *Precious Lord, please wrap your arms around this man…and everyone who has lost so much.*

"Olivia, it's getting late. Let's go meet your father. I'm sure he's wondering what's happened to us." The little girl in Myron's arms had nodded off, her head on his shoulder.

Olivia glanced at the list in her hand. Curiosity concerning Donald McShane made her turn to the M's. Skimming down the list, she spotted the names. Alana Darlene McShane, Creighton Donald McShane, and Margaret Jilleen McShane. His whole family, my God. Compassion for this stranger overwhelmed her. She couldn't begin to absorb what he was going through, and his heartache became her heartache.

"Olivia." Myron started to leave.

"Myron—wait," she called out, and folding the list, shoved it into her pocket.

She hurried after him and leaving the covered pier behind, stepped through the large arched doorway and out into the downpour.

As they approached the Studebaker Limousine parked on a side street away from the crowd, Hugh, the family's uniformed chauffeur, quickly vacated the open-sided driver's seat and hurried to open the back passenger door. Rain doused his black oilcloth slicker making him resemble a sleek seal. He promptly opened an oversized umbrella and held it aloft.

Walter Marsh emerged from the black hardtop. Well over six feet and with an authoritative presence, he greatly resembled former president Teddy Roosevelt, even down to the rimless glasses he removed from his nose and placed in his breast pocket. His mouth, firm and narrow, pulled into a tight smile under a steel-gray mustache. He was a dynamic fifty-nine.

"Olivia, my girl," he said in his deep baritone, and pulled her into a bear-like embrace.

Cocooned against her father's giant body, Olivia felt like a child. His familiar scent of cigar smoke, mustache wax, and Violet Witch Hazel aftershave wafted about, comforting her.

"By God, I told them naysayers my girl wouldn't go down with any damn ship, that you'd find a way out of it. And damn it to hell, I was right." Again he hugged her close, finally parting to give her a generous grin, his eyes moist.

She rejoiced at his tears, her father here and now, showing his love in front of others. "Yes, Dad, the ship didn't take me down, only my heart along with hundreds of poor souls who didn't make it." She glanced at the automobile's rain streaked windows. "I take it mother didn't come with you?"

"Your mother's waiting for you at home. She swooned after hearing news of the ship and took to her bed. She'll be all right once she sees you so fit."

Olivia sighed and nodded. She expected nothing less from her mother, but right now having her mother here would have meant the world to Olivia.

A dog barked from inside the car. His moist black nose pressed against the window breathing cloudy circles on the glass, and she couldn't help but smile. "I see you brought Sparks."

"Yes, I did." Walter raised a speculative brow while turning his attention to the little girl held by Myron.

Sensing his curiosity, Olivia said, "Dad, I have quite a story to tell you about this little one. She's a survivor from the ship."

"Then it's a good thing I brought Sparks along. He'll be good company for her. I know you have a lot to tell me, especially about the child. But right now let's get out of this blasted rain."

Olivia nodded at the chauffeur who held the umbrella over their heads. "Hugh, it's good to see you."

A wide grin creased his skinny face. "And the same to you, Miss Marsh. As Mr. Marsh said, it was a relief to know you've survived." Quickly opening the door, he shooed the small black and white Boston terrier away.

After climbing into the car next to her father, Olivia immediately took the child onto her lap, trying to comfort her. A painful ache filled Olivia as she kissed the small cheek. Tomorrow, she'd be telling her story to Paddy Riley, and insist he take the little girl's picture and plaster it all over the papers. Paddy better deliver.

Her jaw tightened. If the child's parents or family aren't found, this little one isn't going to an orphanage. She vowed no harm was going to come to this child.

Sparks jumped on Myron's lap and stared at the strange little newcomer. They smiled at the dog who wore a nervous look made even more so by his large bulbous eyes and darting tongue. His muzzle was white and he had a mask of black surrounding his eyes, ears, and most of his body, the only other exception was the white on his chest and front legs. He squirmed and sniffed the doll, his pink slobbery tongue licked the girl's hand. She began to timidly pet the dog's sleek black and white head. Sparks appeared to love her caress's and kept licking her hand as though she was a piece of prized meat he'd found in his bowl.

"Sweetheart, this is Sparks, our dog," Olivia said, "and from the way he's licking you, I'd say he's excited to meet you."

The silent girl kept her attention on Sparks, stroking him.

"Darn it, if only she'd talk, tell me her name. I've tried for the last four days to get her to say something—anything. All I heard her say was Deary and Casey. I've never felt so helpless. She should know by now that I only intend to help her, not hurt her."

"Same way you acted when you were little," her father said.

"What do you mean? You've always told me I started talking sentences before I was a year old, and I've never stopped. When was I ever silent?"

Walter chuckled. "Of course you rattled on like some scolding bird. But when you got mad, you'd sulk and not say a thing for hours."

"I guess you're right, but I don't remember being a sulky child." She couldn't help but smile and leaned back against the leather seat.

"Well, you wouldn't." He raised a bushy brow at Myron. "Sometime you and I will talk about this girl of mine."

"Dad!" She scowled as Myron grinned at her father. She quickly changed the subject. "I've invited a reporter to stop by tomorrow for my story. And my story's about this child. I also want to tell how third-class passengers were deliberately locked up and couldn't get out."

"Whatever do you mean, daughter?" Walter leaned forward.

Myron shifted to make better eye contact with her. Both men wore narrowed yet unbelieving stares.

Olivia, mindful of the child's feelings, indicated such to both men and tactfully said, "I was told certain gates, were locked…keeping hundreds of people below…the crew…so many stayed behind…" her voice faltered, the white faces, the screams…

"Terrible—terrible tragic events. I'm sorry you had to see such." Her father patted her hand. He hesitated, as if weighing his words. "I understand Senator Smith has already started an investigation into the sinking. You should tell the Senator your story."

Olivia nodded. "Perhaps you're right, Dad. I'll leave all of the gruesome details for the Senator if I'm summoned."

His whole persona glowed with pride. "That's my girl."

Jilleen gingerly stroked Sparks's furry head, the adults conversation faded as her fingers scratched the inside of his ears. She'd never had a dog, but did have a little orange kitten at Grandmum Ina's. She missed Grandmum. But mostly she missed Mam and Casey. Where were they? Frightened and confused, she wanted to tell Olivia, about Casey and Mam. But she didn't think Casey would want her to, so she clamped her mouth shut and obeyed her missing brother.

She held her dolly a little tighter. Her arm hurt where Uncle Sam had grabbed it and threw her overboard. She should tell about mean Uncle Sam. Sparks stared at her with his large, round eyes. Without a tail or a long nose, Sparks was funny looking, but she liked him. She stopped petting him. He pushed his nose against her hand, forcing her to continue. She smiled.

Casey always told her Da was gentle. Casey loved Da something fierce and made sure she knew all about him as soon as she was old enough to understand. He would occasionally let her touch the shiny watch Da left in his care. Casey had brought it with him. She wanted her da. She thought he'd be at the ship for her tonight, but he wasn't. He'd sent her Derry doll all the way from America.

The dog lurched and swiped a wet drippy tongue across her nose. Giggles erupted from her. "Sparks, stop that," she said, and wiped his wet slobbers off her nose. She patted the top of his head. His mouth widened in a tongue-hanging grin.

"See there—you can speak when you want to." Excited, Olivia continued, "Will you please tell me your name? I can't help you if you don't."

Jilleen wondered if she dare tell. She finally whispered, "Jelee."

A puzzled look crossed Olivia's face. "Her lilt's so strong, can you understand her?"

"Somewhat. Did you say, *Jelly*?" Myron asked.

"Ah, no, Jelee," she repeated shyly. She didn't know if she liked Myron. He was tall and dark like Uncle Sam and she was frightened to death of her uncle. Olivia's father glanced at her and she wanted to shrink into the seat. He reminded her of the big, woolly bears she'd read about in picture books. She couldn't help but watch him reach into his pocket and remove a small slim package with pictures of fruit on it. Picking at the end of the package to open it, he took out something wrapped in thin foil paper, of which he unwrapped.

"Here, have a stick of fruit gum. It's not food, so don't swallow it. You just keep chewing it." He handed the fruity smelling gum to her, and she gingerly accepted it. "Since you're talking maybe you can tell us how old you are?"

Jilleen watched him take another piece of gum from the package and rolling it up, pop it into his mouth. He offered the package to

Olivia and Myron who shook their heads. Jilleen rolled up the gum, then closed her mouth over it and chewed. She'd never had chewing gum. As the juice slipped down her throat, she decided she liked the sweet taste. After chewing the gum for a while, she figured it was all right to tell them her age. She scrunched her brow, folded her thumb, and held up four fingers. "I'm this many," she said, and smiled. She quickly patted Sparks.

The grownups squinted at her in the dim light inside the car.

"And now that we know you're a big girl of four, how about telling us your last name and all about yourself?" Olivia asked.

She liked Olivia. She was pretty and nice. Olivia wouldn't hurt her. But Casey had told her not to tell anyone. Mam always said she must obey Casey, he knew best. No, she wouldn't tell her last name.

"Were you with your mother and father?"

Jilleen slowly shook her head. "Casey." Her lips began to quiver. She didn't want to cry, but couldn't help it. The gum almost fell out of her mouth and she pushed it back with her finger. "Where's me Casey?"

"Casey? Was that your father's name?" Olivia's eyes shone with excitement.

"Ah, no, Casey's me brudder. He's this many," Jilleen said and held up eight fingers.

"And your mommy, do you know what her name was?"

"Mammy."

"What did other people call her, your father, what did he call her?"

"Derry. Daddy's gone away." She held up her doll, trying to keep Sparks's curious nose away from it. "Daddy gave me Derry." She snuggled against Olivia's bosom and sighed with the small amount of security she now felt.

Myron shifted Sparks's body on his thigh, the dog so intent on the little girl in Olivia's lap he didn't notice. The car headed up Eleventh Street, parallel with the Hudson River towards the Marsh's mansion on the Upper West Side. As the large-wheeled tires splashed into water-filled ruts, jostling them, Myron enjoyed being thrown against Olivia's arm. He'd never seen her so rumpled, disheveled, and wantonly gorgeous. And if this was what she looked like first thing in the morning, then he couldn't wait to marry her. Right now, he wanted to run his hand through her hair. But with her father sitting on the other side of her, he didn't dare, nor would society's stiff upper lip allow it. Despite the curly tendrils of hair tickling her face, her profile was strong, her aquiline nose straight, and her chin jutted just the right amount to remain feminine. Olivia's brown eyes held a certain softness for the child while reassuring her everything was all right. He'd never seen Olivia holding a child so close, and her maternal reactions startled him somewhat. Yet, he was glad to see it, thinking once he married her and she had their child she would give up her demonstrative work with the suffragettes.

He thought back on his own childhood, and of his parents Grace and Emil Prewitt. According to his parents, he'd had two brothers and a sister who died in infancy from childhood diseases. He'd been the only child to make it to adulthood. Even the rich couldn't keep lethal illnesses from crossing their doorstep.

His family wasn't from stuffy old money, his family's fortune was new, and made on the backs of textile workers. But wasn't it all like that? Didn't someone need the brains to put a business together, and wasn't someone always down in the trenches doing the grunt work? His father had been a young entrepreneur with a knack for business. He'd started with one dollar and turned it into millions. Perhaps the location had something to do with it. While others had set up shop in Manhattan, Emil Prewitt started small in South Brooklyn while most of the land was still farmland. He'd built a red-bricked medium sized factory, hired laborers from around the poor area, and started producing cloth. Years ago, a larger one with Prewitt and Son Textiles written on the front replaced the original factory. Myron could thank his father for all he'd achieved.

Living in a tall stately mansion in Brooklyn Heights, and with his mother lavishing her only child with anything he could possibly want, Myron had turned out spoiled and was the first to admit it. He'd grown tall and solid built and didn't need a mirror to know he was more than handsome. The prostitutes he often visited to relieve his sexual agony told him of his prowess, calling him a great lover, and with no false sense of modesty, he agreed with them.

His mother, thinking it was time he married and give her a grandchild, had started taking him to her charity functions. The Prewitt's had money to burn and his money had taken him to a charity luncheon hosted by the *Women's Charity League.* He'd been seated beside Merilee Marsh, Olivia's mother. Upon meeting and conversing with Mrs. Marsh, he couldn't help but glance past Mrs. Marsh and stare at her daughter Olivia Marsh, the dark-haired beauty who appeared thoroughly bored with the ongoing proceedings. The only time she appeared interested was when the speaker announced the amount of money being donated to the *New York Foundling Hospital*, and to local orphanages, and that brought a mere flick of her elegant eyebrow. He was in love with Olivia Marsh and would do anything to have her.

He knew Olivia wasn't just another pretty woman. She was a firebrand, a famous suffragette with values as high and lofty as hot-air balloons. She'd taken her fight for women's rights to the capitol and the oval office. He'd accepted her values, one of which was relatively close to his. What could it hurt to let women vote? Nothing at all. But the moment she turned to child labor and started unknowingly stepping on his factory's toes, it became a different matter. She was taking a different path, one he didn't want her to go down, and one that would take her away from him. Their values or lack of values now collided. His failing virtue was being a factory owner who kept it a secret from Olivia that he had children working in it. Olivia's virtue was being a suffragette and fighting against this very thing. He knew he should tell her goodbye and go his separate way, but he was in love with her. And love, dear sweet fickle love, could get inside a man's head and mess him up for the rest of his life.

He deluded himself in thinking her near brush with death would change her and force her to leave the movement. Seeing the determined lift of her chin and with the child now in her charge, he knew it wouldn't happen. If he wanted Olivia for his wife, he was going to have to get her away from the suffragette organization.

Chapter Five

Jilleen grasped Olivia's hand while craning her neck upward at the tall house. She stared open mouth at a lone figure in one of the upper windows looking down at them. She didn't want to go into the big scary house. She wished to be back in Ireland at Grandmum Ina's cozy little cottage with Mam and Casey. Olivia started toward the stairs leading onto the wide porch, but Jilleen dug her heels in, refusing to take another step.

Walter quickly walked up the steps and opening the door politely held it. "Olivia?"

Sparks scooted inside and then poked his head back out. He woofed once and then disappeared.

"Give me a minute, Dad. You and Myron go on in."

Jilleen found herself being picked up by Olivia, then carried up the steps and set down on the wide porch. Olivia knelt down, and took Jilleen's hands within hers.

"What is it, Jelee?"

"Scarit, me's scarit of the big house." Her lips quivered as she met Olivia's kind eyes and smile. She clutched her dolly tightly against her chest.

"Everything seems scary at night. But inside there are warm fires, food, and my family who you shouldn't be afraid of. I was raised here. The old nursery still has toys in it that I played with when I was a little girl your age. There's a rocking horse and a big dollhouse that I'm sure you'll like. Besides, I'll be with you."

Jilleen felt lost, forlorn, and strange. Her secure little world had changed from familiar faces to strangers. She wanted Mam and Casey. She was shy about meeting more people, even if it was Olivia's mam. She sucked in her bottom lip and frowned. "I don't like this house."

"It'll be all right, you'll see. Now do be a brave girl and let's go inside where it's warm. I'll not leave you alone, I promise."

She ducked her head and whispered, "Promise, 'Livia?" Exacting from Olivia what she would ask of her brother, expecting nothing more or less from her.

"Yes, I promise. Cross my heart." And Olivia then made a cross over her bosom.

Relieved to see such a pledge, Jilleen allowed Olivia to take her inside.

Olivia was greeted by the familiar smell of Rosewood furniture polish, flowers, and her father's cigar smoke wafting in a thin gray cloud from the study. The entry floor gleamed with gray marble. Right in the center of the foyer was a large, round, ornate mahogany table with a large ceramic vase overflowing with colorful, fragrant flowers. Her mother, no matter the season always made sure that particular vase held flowers, imported or otherwise to greet her many guests. Despite its opulence, the house felt light and airy. A sweeping staircase backed the entry, and in the study to the right of where they stood, she knew her father and Myron waited for her. Yes, she was home, elated to be here, and yet she couldn't relax.

She watched Stella Lippencott, matriarch of their house servants, move across the shiny floor with her determined stride. Despite the late hour, Mrs. Lippencott was crisply starched. Her body was slim as a Whippet, and her gray hair slicked back into a severe tight bun nary a strand dared to escape from.

"Oh…Miss Olivia," she cried out, "What an ordeal you've been through. How well you look, and we can praise the Lord for that." She stepped behind Olivia and helped her out of her coat. Pausing to sniff the thick tweed, she wrinkled up her nose and blurted out, "My goodness—this will have to be cleaned."

"Have it cleaned then donate it to charity. I'll never wear it again. It brings back horrible memories that I want to put from my mind."

Mrs. Lippencott nodded and put the coat on the table. She smiled at the child. "Well…and who do we have here?"

Olivia took Jilleen's hand and leaned toward her. She pointed at Mrs. Lippencott and said, "Jelee, this is Stella Lippencott. She keeps our house tidy and running in good order. There is no need to be afraid of her. Mrs. Lippencott, this is Jelee. We met in the lifeboat."

"Nice to meet you, Miss." She fussed about, helping the child out of her coat. "Should I have this cleaned, Miss Olivia or thrown away?" Her lips compressed into a crinkled slit.

Even from where Olivia stood, she could smell the dry urine emanating from the wool material. "Please throw the coat away, but not before tomorrow, she will have need of it." Olivia smiled at Mrs. Lippencott.

Jilleen gasped loudly, and quick as a rabbit, she grabbed her coat back, protecting it against her body. "Not me coat. Don't throw me coat away—me da bought it."

Startled, the housekeeper reached for it, but Jilleen shied away. Mrs. Lippencott's quizzical blue eyes looked at Olivia, and then swept over Jilleen. She smiled down at the child and Jilleen offered a meek one in return while edging closer to Olivia. Jilleen clutched her coat and dolly even tighter.

"Jelee, please give Mrs. Lippencott your coat. It will not be thrown away. We'll need it tomorrow for pictures, and then it'll have to be cleaned."

Jilleen's face set in an uncertain scowl. "D'ye promise?"

Olivia's eyebrow arched high as she tried to keep from laughing. "My list of promises to you is getting quite long, isn't it? And I'm sure you'll be able to remind me of each one if I should forget them, right?" She grinned at the girl's innocent face. "Now give Miss Lippencott a proper greeting." After Jelee offered a soft hello and handed her coat back, Olivia took a deep breath and let it out. For now, another step in the right direction had been taken. She made a mental note to inquire more about the father who bought the coat, but now was not the time to do so.

"Mrs. Lippencott, is mother upstairs and awake?"

"She is, Miss Olivia, and waiting for you."

"Have you heard from Nathan?"

"Yes. Your brother was telegrammed the news, and we received word back from him. Upsetting as it all is, I don't expect he'll be able to leave Oregon and come home." With her arms full of coats, Mrs. Lippencott used her head to point towards the open doorway. "There's a warm fire in the study. Would you like something to drink? How about the youngster, something hot for her?"

The only thing Olivia wanted to do was go to bed, but that wouldn't be possible yet, so she simply said no, they didn't need anything. Taking Jelee's hand, Olivia entered the study where Myron turned from the fireplace to smile at her.

Sparks had claimed his spot dangerously close to the fire screen where he stretched out. He snored loud wheezy whistling grunts through his short snout.

Jelee made a beeline for the dog and squatted next to him.

Olivia's father sat in his comfortable brown leather chair and puffed on his favorite Romon Allones Cuban cigar. Smoke roiled in a gray clouded aura around him. He picked up a telegram from the table next to him and handed it to her. "From, Nathan."

Olivia took the small square of paper with its short message. While reading, she pictured her brother's handsome face and heard his caring voice. Finished and taking a deep sigh, Olivia folded the paper and handed it back. "I wish Nathan was here. I do miss his teasing outlook on life, and could use his good humor right now. I'll have to write him a long letter and tell him all that's transpired." She smothered a yawn with her hand.

"Go to bed." Her father urged.

She met his forceful stare with a tired smile. "Yes, Dad, I'm going."

"Your mother's waiting, so take Jelee and pop up to see her before she thinks no one cares about her. I've asked Myron to spend the night with us, no sense in him trying to get home this time of night. Hell, it's closing in on midnight."

Olivia could swear her father had more gray in his hair than she remembered. Acting on impulse, she kissed his cheek.

He gripped her arm and met her stare straight on. "Daughter…you will never know how worried I've been. Actually broken hearted at the mere thought you might have died. But the thought that I'd lost you without telling you how damn proud I am of you almost did me in." He politely stood.

For the first time in her life, Olivia peered into her father's spirited gray eyes and saw love, real love. He wasn't blustering or putting on airs. His fear at almost losing her had surfaced for her to see. And those poignant feelings pulled from her emotions she always carried for him but had squelched over the years with his seemingly indifference of her.

"Thank you, Dad. What you just said means more to me than surviving, it means the world." She went into his open embrace of which he held her tight.

"I've always been in your corner, Olivia, always." He stepped back and nodded, his gruff exterior returning. "Your mother's waiting." He directed a bearish grin at Jelee. "Still got your gum? Don't swallow it, it'll mess your insides up." He chuckled at her surprise, and grinned when she pushed the gum between her lips at him. "Good girl."

Olivia laughed at the teasing. "Father, you're incorrigible! Myron, I'll see you at breakfast."

Myron approached her and whispered, "It won't be long before we're married and we won't have to say goodnight in a study."

Surprised to hear him speaking with such conviction, Olivia changed the subject. "Thank you for being at the pier tonight. I couldn't have made it without you."

"Yes, you would have, but I'm glad I was there," he said. "Go see your mother, you look exhausted."

Smiling, Olivia could only nod. Taking Jelee by the hand, she left them to their talk, smokes, and drinks.

Walter smiled as his daughter led the child from the room, and he wondered what kind of reception they would both get upstairs. He flicked ashes from his cigar into the ashtray. Outward he appeared gruff and acted tough, a façade he used for his banking and the business world in general. Inside he was still shaking. Never in his life had he come so close to losing one of his cherished loved ones. His world had almost collapsed when he thought Olivia had died. And that got him thinking he hadn't shown her enough love, or his son, or his wife Merilee. He realized he'd fallen into the nasty habit of taking his loved ones for granted. He vowed to change.

Always driven, it was up to him to care for his family, to provide the best, and keep churning out money. He'd started in his early twenties and set his sights high. Realizing money could be had in real estate, he bought up buildings and parlayed them into big profits. In ever expanding, rapidly changing Manhattan, he tore down a rickety wooden building and built his bank. No wood for him, status was made in brick. His fortune could be categorized as recent, not brought over centuries ago from England like his wife's ancestors had done.

Merilee was a rightful Bostonian from old money made from shipbuilding, and she married him against her family's wishes. He was an upstart in the financial world, a young man of twenty-seven, but only worth several million. According to Merilee's family, he should have at least nine or ten million more before he proposed. He'd gone to Boston on business and met Merilee during a dinner party held at her parent's mansion overlooking the harbor. Five years younger than him—she was beautiful with dark intelligent eyes, black glossy hair, and a penchant for subtle flirting of which she did across the table at him. Captivated, he made up his mind that he wasn't leaving Boston without her, and didn't…

…The clinking sound of crystal brought Walter back to the present and Myron who was pouring drinks. Myron turned, and after handing Walter his glass, settled into a chair.

While sipping his brandy, Walter studied Myron. He didn't know how he felt about this young man who appeared in love with his daughter, but was more than willing to see what would transpire from the relationship. "Tell me, Myron, if you'd gone to London with Olivia, and returned on the Titanic, what would you have done? Remained behind? Or got in a lifeboat with her?"

Myron shrugged. "That question has gone through my mind more than once. I'm just glad it wasn't a choice I had to face."

Having watched Olivia's arrival from the window, Merilee Marsh knew her daughter had a little stranger in tow. Just like Olivia when she was a child, stray dogs, cats, wounded squirrels, it didn't matter, she would drag them home to care for. Olivia, to Merilee's despair had too much of Walter in her. She bore his zest for life, had his tenacity to turn things to her advantage, and his soft spots for the unfortunate. Right now, Merilee assumed the *unfortunate* was in the guise of the child keeping Olivia from her side.

Merilee, born and bred in high society, cut her teeth on the book of social structure, manners and correct behavior. She butted heads with Olivia at every turn. She disliked the suffragette organization, didn't want women's right to vote and thought women should leave politics to the men. She wore blinders as far as children working in factories went, and yet gave generously to hospitals, orphanages, and church charities. Right now, her goal in life was to get Olivia away from the suffragette movement. She wanted her daughter married to Myron, had ensconced herself in his corner, and would do whatever necessary to see it happen.

In a prideful snit, and feeling neglected, she downed the last of her sherry and roused herself off of her settee to go place the glass next to the crystal decanter. Eyeing the liquor and deciding to have another, she pulled the glass stopper from the bottle when the soft tread of feet coming down the hallway made her pause. Quickly replacing the lid, she hurried to pose gracefully upon the settee and wait for her daughter who should have immediately come up here to be with her.

Olivia led Jelee through the sitting room and into her mother's bedroom. She paused in the doorway. Her mother, elegantly reposed on a silk covered settee awash with colorful pillows and cushions, returned her stare. Her billowy blue dressing gown fanned around her like the ripples of an aqua sea. She didn't look fifty-four, and in the dim light of the bedroom and the fires glow, Olivia thought they could pass for sisters. The smell of Jasmine, her mother's expensive French perfume, permanently filled the room along with large bouquets of flowers. In the background, a rumpled bed was testimony she'd been in and out of it.

The dark flash of her mother's brown eyes more than confirmed she was angry with Olivia for failing to rush to her side.

"Olivia, there you are, at long last," she said in her clipped Bostonian accent, her tone biting.

"Mother, I'm just pleased to be *alive* so I can stand here and tell you hello." Olivia pasted a smile on her face but stood her ground and kept holding Jelee's hand. Olivia longed for her mother to rush over and take her in her arms, cry, and tell her how happy she was that she'd survived, but her mother remained planted on the settee. "I was delayed at the White Star office and came as soon as I could. Father and Myron are downstairs."

Merilee moved to a sitting position and deftly arranged the flowing chiffon of her sleeve.

Olivia watched her mother's head tilt and her sharp gaze sweep Jelee with interest.

"What's that sticking to your hip like a barnacle and looking like a wide-eyed hoot owl as it peers at me?"

Olivia tampered the biting retort on the end of her tongue and tried to treat her mother respectfully. "*That* is a person, Mother. Her name is Jelee, and she's from the Titanic. Jelee will be staying with us until we find her family."

"She's from third-class, an immigrant, correct?" Merilee studied Jelee like she was a specimen under glass. "What if you can't find anyone who claims her? Then what?"

"I don't know the answer to that question. The other answer is yes, she was probably with a family immigrating." Olivia, swallowed back tears and the ache in her throat. Why in the heck did she allow her mother to evoke such reactions from her. "Mother, I know you're tired, we're all tired, but can you please show a little compassion for Jelee who was wrenched from her mother's arms and literally tossed into mine?"

Releasing Olivia's hand, Jelee hid behind her.

Merilee's thin dark eyebrow flicked upward. "I'd rather you didn't use that tone with me. Leave it for the factory workers and fat politicians you attack over child labor and the right to vote." She sighed, acting put out. "You need to marry Myron and settle down. Give your father and me grandchildren. Instead, you bring an immigrant under our roof. What country is she from? Do you even know that?"

"Ireland," Olivia snapped and withheld the words she wished to say. "Fight fair, Mother. We have a child here I'll not see traumatized more."

She watched her mother rise and move elegantly to the dressing table, the silk of her nightgown swished with every step. Opening a tiny jeweled pillbox, she popped a little round tablet into her mouth and downed it with water.

"You're right we always spar with each other. I'm tired, and believe it or not, I've been extremely worried about you. Whether you realize it or not, I do love you, Olivia."

She surprised Olivia by approaching and embracing her. Olivia tried to relax against her. But her mother's body felt unyielding. She wished her mother had a large bosom, flabby arms, and a person who could give a hug and know how to mean it, anything besides the svelte beauty she was.

They broke apart and Merilee beckoned Jelee. "Come here, child, let's have a look at you."

Jelee remained plastered against Olivia's skirt forcing Merilee to take her by the hand and bring her forward. She tilted the child's chin upwards studying her. "My word, she's a pretty little thing, isn't she."

Surprised at her mother's comment, Olivia could now see Jelee's large upturned hazel eyes, her rosy mouth, and the brown curls that framed her face in a long, curly halo. Yes, Jelee's pretty, and she was relieved her mother recognized it. But, the last thing she wanted was for her mother to think of Jelee as one of her charity projects and exploit her.

"You must get rid of that nightgown she's wearing—it reeks of who-knows-what. Get her something nice and clean from the linen trunk. What are your plans for finding her relatives?" Merilee pushed a button that would ring in the servant's part of the house.

Olivia, surprised by her mother's concerns, thought perhaps her mother felt it better to capitulate than argue over someone that would probably be gone in a few days. Why make a fuss and upset her perfect world, she practically read her mother's mind.

When her mother asked about the Titanic, Olivia told about her experiences, how Jelee was tossed into her arms, the lifeboat, the Carpathia. She informed her mother about Paddy Riley's planned visit. She was still telling all when Mrs. Lippencott came into the room and announced their beds were ready and a hot bath drawn.

It was almost one. Everyone was drooping, especially Olivia and Jelee.

Olivia delicately held her hand over her mouth and yawned. "I'm drained, totally exhausted. Goodnight, mother. Oh, and please let me sleep late."

She led Jelee from the room.

"'Livia?" Jilleen whispered and tugged on Olivia's skirt.

"Yes, little one?" Olivia smiled down at her as they moved through the long hallway towards her bedroom.

"What's an immergent? Is it bad?"

Chapter Six

It was closing in on one in the morning, and Sam had just settled Darlene into bed. He stood in the cramped living room and puffed on his cigar. Good old Ambrose Williams had stood by his word and generously brought them to his tenement building here in the East Village. He'd bragged to Sam how he'd converted an abandoned department store into three stories of apartments. Sam thought the building at one time stood glorious, probably before the Civil War, but with its metal fire escape zigzagging down the outside front, stopping shy above the front entrance, it looked junky and unkempt. Williams had also bragged his building here on East Fourth Street was away from the Lower East Side which was so stacked with immigrants that one couldn't move or breathe the foul air.

The inside didn't look much better to Sam. Given a small set of rooms at the front of the building, the furniture was a hodge-podge mixture of second-hand Victorian. A stark overhead bulb burned bright. The room had a maroon, camel backed sofa, plus a sideboard with plenty of drawers. A radiator popped and hissed as it heated up.

The Williams's who lived down the main hallway were leaving early the next morning for their delayed trip. Sam would be glad to see the last of them. He'd grown tired of their constant fawning and worrying over Darlene. They'd introduced him as *Albert Flynn* to the manager, Tom Meeks, a bookish man with a friendly smile on his homely face. Sam concluded the unassuming man wouldn't get in his way.

The *Carpathia,* or what Sam hoped was still inside the ship, was on his mind. He needed to return to the ship—soon. He headed toward the bedroom and Darlene.

The bedroom, he smirked, was barely able to fit a wrought iron bed and wardrobe. The walls faded, garish, cabbage rose wallpaper made him wonder how one could sleep with such a display. This wasn't what he had in mind for Darlene, but it was free and for now it would have to do. He felt the scabs on his face where the rosary had raked it. Almost healed.

Darlene was still sleeping and he thought it just as well. Perhaps she'd quit crying over her brats soon. Try as he might, he couldn't conjure up guilt or sadness over his deception about Casey and Jilleen. It was to his advantage for Darlene to think they had perished. Damn it—he should be enough for her. He didn't want to share her with Donald's kids.

He approached the bed and sat on the side of it. Darlene's face was relaxed, her eyelids thin and delicate enough he could see tiny pale blue veins under the skin. He started to kiss her cheek, but stopped himself. He didn't want to wake her, didn't want to see the anguish in her eyes, or the tears that would fall from them.

Darlene.

He refused to think of, or call her by *Derry,* the nickname Donald had given her. Her fingers twitched, causing her gold wedding band to flash in the lamplight, reminding him as long as Donald was alive he couldn't marry her. The day Donald had put that ring on her finger everything had changed for Sam…

…He'd returned to Dublin, where he'd gone to his mam's house to find nobody at home. Catching a ride on a horse driven cart with a sidecar, he was bounced on the hard seat all the way to Portmarnock. To his surprise, a hearse with its team of horses was behind the butcher shop. Worried something had happened to Darlene, he hurried up the back stairs and into the living quarters where a wake was in process.

Hoyt O'Dea, Darlene's father, was laid out all peaceful like in his wooden coffin.

Darlene stood next to Donald. Her belly, round and big with child, stretched against the black material of her long dress. Her bright hair was pulled back in a bun. She dabbed at her tears, appearing not to see him, but Donald did. With a quick comment to Darlene, Donald came over to him and acknowledged Sam with a curt nod. Sam's mother, Ina along with Colin slipped next to Sam as well. They whispered hello. Speaking in muted tones, his mother told Sam that Darlene's father had died from a heart attack. The shop was sold to pay off Hoyt's debts. Donald, having worked for Hoyt, and living here with Darlene, would be moving his lovely wife to Dublin. Wasn't it grand they were giving Ina her first grandchild?

Sam's gaze darted to where Darlene still stood, their eyes locked for a moment. Her brow knotted and she glanced away, but not before her face flushed pink, a blush he could create with a mere kiss. Well, he wouldn't be kissing her now, would he?

The priest started his eulogy. Everyone went silent and listened about a man's life that some did, and some didn't, know a thing about. The priest didn't utter a word that Hoyt's wife had gone mad and killed herself. But he did talk about Darlene, and how sad that hard working Hoyt O'Dea would never know his grandchild.

After the priest finished speaking, he nodded at several men who reverently stepped forward. They closed the wooden lid over Hoyt's stark face then nailed it shut. Donald, along with his brother Colin and several others, picked up the coffin, carried it down the stairs, and out to the black draped hearse waiting to take it to the cemetery.

Darlene started down the stairs and Sam made a grand display of taking her hand to help her. "I was coming back fer ya, Darlene, why didn't ya wait?" he growled under his breath.

She paused and glared at him. "You, Sam McShane, are the biggest liar in all of Ireland. I want nothin' to do with the likes of you."

But he wasn't giving in. He badgered her down the stairs while she was being careful not to fall. He became cruel. "Did ya tell Donald I shoved me tool in ya first? That ya laid down and spread yer legs for me and begged me not to stop?" He wanted to add to her sorrow, wanted to stomp on it, grind it in that he was first with her. How dare she marry his brother and try to make like she was happy having done so?

They reached the bottom of the stairs where Darlene reminded him that he'd left her with promises to take her with him. She was now Donald's. Her back stiffened. She awkwardly sped up, but he was right behind her.

"I need to talk with ya," he urged. "How many months with child are ya? When did ya marry Donald?"

She scoffed. Her scent of fragrant roses washed over him, and despite her burgeoning pregnancy his desire for her heightened. He held himself back and seethed inside.

Donald hurried over to lock his arm within hers. He stared at Sam. "Go away, Sam. Leave us be." They took their place behind the horse-drawn hearse and the priest.

The procession began, leaving Sam to stare after them. Why did he leave Darlene in the first place? Did he love her at the time? He didn't think so. He was out for himself only. He had no time to yoke a woman around his neck, or take the 'burden' as it was called when a man got married. Women were the least of his concerns, making the coin and lots of it was. But seeing Darlene with Donald made him pause. And like always, he began to silently reason with himself, arguing she should be his, and sulking that she wasn't. He wanted to knock that smug, gloating look from Donald's face.

The darkness was starting to unfold in his mind. It changed his mood from one of tolerance to an uncontrollable rage. He wanted to run after Donald, slam his fists in his face, stomp him to the ground. He slowly uncurled his hands where his fingernails had cut deep grooves into his palms.

He left the village and returned to Belfast where he found work close to the Belfast shipyards doing fine carpentry work that would go into the liners. During this time, he enhanced his talent as a thief. He always tried to be at the docks when incoming ships berthed, melding with the workers as a dockhand unloading the large steamer trunks and cargo. It was easy to open the trunks and remove the jewelry and other items of monetary value. As his accumulation of money grew, he thought about going to California where riches abound, perhaps San Francisco where there would always be a need for a carpenter of his caliber.

Sam often thought he was close to finding the proverbial pot of gold, could swear he was born to do so. Certainly luck had a hand in what happened to him as he moved through life. Even the time he spent in jail had served to teach him, harden him, and cement his thoughts that those who put him in there were wrong. He'd been right to steal. Even the night of the *Sinn Féin* meeting had turned golden. What luck, what stupidity on Donald's part to trust that he'd felt no pulse coming from Aidan. Even as Aidan's pulse beat steadily under his fingers, something dark and indescribable made him say Aidan was dead.

The strong wake from behind Donald's ship hadn't settled into smooth water before his brother Colin had moved Darlene and her brats right into his mam's house in Belfast, and right into Sam's life. But Darlene had changed since her younger days as an eye-catching lass. She often spent time by herself in the bedroom she shared with Casey and Jilleen. Soft mutterings would come from the room.

Wondering who in the hell she was talking to, he'd hurried to fling the door open. No one was there, only Darlene sitting on the bed with her rosary in her hands.

His mam asked both him and Colin if they noticed Darlene was different, like she was physically in the room with them, but wasn't with them in her mind? She also reminded him Darlene's mother was crazy and killed herself. Sure he'd noticed her strange behavior and knew the story about Aisling O'Dea, but what the feck. To him, Darlene was just a shy soft-spoken woman. He'd lived for years with the want of Darlene tucked inside and he wasn't about to let anything shatter his image of her.

He'd fantasized about having her again, and just when he thought he never would, he could. One small step at a time, he put his plan into action. Whenever he went to visit Mam or his brother Colin, he made sure to be around Darlene when she was alone. He'd constantly remind her that she was the wrong Mrs. McShane and watched with delighted malice as doubt veiled her face.

He was careful not to let his mam suspect anything. But the kids did. Every time he got anywhere near Darlene, Casey was quick to follow, staring up at him with eyes narrowed in suspicion. He tried buying their friendship with toys and food, but that didn't work, they rejected him, their dislike evident. Casey would talk about his da, showing off the pocket watch Donald had given him, bragging that he was taking the watch to America. Jilleen, not remembering her da would parrot Casey about loving her da so much. Sam couldn't stand them, especially Casey. Somehow, he was going to get rid of the lad, put him in boarding school.

He'd planned to seduce Darlene again, bring back old memories of how virile a lover he was. But he was the one ending up seduced because he fell in love with her, and by the Saints, she with him.

She'd come to him in a panic one morning bearing a letter and money from Donald, telling her it was time to come to him. Sam was not about to lose her. He made plans, and she'd bought it. He would go to England, board the *Titanic* under a different name. After they arrived in New York he'd told her they'd leave the children on Donald's doorstep, and then disappear.

Meeting Lillian Denbury was a different matter. She'd slipped into his scheme like a wild growing weed. He'd met her in a smoke-filled pub in Southampton, England where he waited for the *Titanic.* Lillian was seated alone. Not many women frequented a pub without a male escort, but she had. While she sat in demure silence he'd boldly approached her, a glass of ale in each hand. Her blonde hair and blue eyes reminded him of Darlene. Lillian, having just lost her father to a sudden fever, was going to America to join her aunt who lived in New York City.

He was more than willing to spend time with her. He even flashed a wad of money at her, promising to give her some if she would pretend to be his wife while boarding and also on the ship, be Mrs. Albert Flynn. He took Lillian to the theatre. They had dinner together, but not one to settle for a simple good night kiss at the door, Sam talked his way into Lillian's bed, a good feck in exchange for gifts was his way of thinking.

Derry could feel Sam's presence. Knew he was next to the bed, probably watching her sleep. Sam's indifference about Casey and Jilleen's death puzzled her. She didn't like it.

She thought how their plan had turned into a sick travesty. Take the ship to America, make Donald think you're coming to him, Sam had urged. You'll leave Donald and then it's away to San Francisco for us. *Think of it Darlene, the sand glitters like gold. They have oranges growing on trees.* His words excited her and she believed him, even when he stuck her down in steerage while he played the fancy man up in second-class. He'd told her not to let the kids see that he was aboard. But he didn't need to worry as both she and Jilleen were seasick the first couple of days and took to their beds. While Casey roamed the *Titanic* playing, she and her precious daughter were up to their chins in covers with a puke pot next to the bed.

Not long after sailing, Casey came running down to their cabin breathlessly blurting out he'd seen Uncle Sam walking on the second-class deck with his arm around a woman. This startled Derry, why would Sam be with a woman? She'd lashed out at Casey, calling him a liar. He'd never lied to her a day in his short life, there was no need. His blue eyes had filled with dismay knowing she was siding with Sam over him. Seeing the hurt she'd caused her wee lad had her thinking she couldn't go through with Sam's plan. But how could she get out of it? Perhaps tell him when they reached Manhattan. Her mind muddled at the thought. There was no way out.

Next to the bed, Sam cleared this throat.

She began reciting the rosary, her fingers sliding over the round black orbs trying to find strength and courage from the Lord, but other voices joined in sounding like slithering hissing snakes, all talking at once. Her fingers slowed as she whispered in a faltering voice, "I believe in God, the Father Almighty. Creator of heaven and earth…Jesus Christ…only Son…"

The voices mocked her, "You have no son…God is Satan…you killed your son…"

…She moaned. Her golden boy…her angel. Jilleen…sweet baby. A tear coursed from beneath her lashes. Derry opened her eyes to stare at the faded pink roses on the wallpaper. The roses had human eyes staring back at her. Her heart beat with a sickening swish, her fingers clutched the blanket and she quickly pulled it over her face shutting out the grotesque images. She slowly inched the sheet off her face. The eyes were still there glaring at her.

The wall whispered, a hundred voices at once. "You failed your children—children—children—children," the voices echoed. "Whore, slut! Kill yourself—kill yourself."

She put her hands over her ears and screamed, "Go away—leave me alone!" She bolted upright. Throwing her hands up to protect her from the wall's terrible wrath, she tried to scramble from the bed.

Startled to his feet, Sam grabbed her upper arms in a bruising grip. "Darlene? Who are ya talkin' to?" The strong look he always wore now wary.

She put her hands over her face and slowly spread her fingers to peer at him. "Can't ya hear them? Voices. Their talkin' right now, telling me awful things," she said. Horror-struck, she grasped at his shirt front, practically popping the buttons, trying to convince him.

Sam drew near and cocked his head, listening. "I don't hear anything except yer squawking. Ya must have been dreamin'." He started to help her back down.

"No—don't!" She fought. "Don't—don't! I hate the wall! Move the bed!"

"I'm not moving the bed. There's nothing on the feckin' wall but wallpaper. Stop it—Darlene!" This time he strong-armed her back down and covered her. She turned away from the wall, casting a fearful glance over her shoulder at it.

Nothing was there, only faded roses, and whispers that sounded all around her.

"Here's the medicine the doc said to give ya. Maybe it'll take away yer nightmare." He leaned over and lifted her up.

She gladly accepted the drink and let the bitter liquid flow down her throat. He dabbed at her mouth and placed her head on the pillow. She pulled the blanket around her chin and watched as he started to turn off the lamp next to the bed.

"Please, leave it on."

He shrugged and did as she asked. Watching him grab his suit coat from the peg, she tried to rise up on her side but her arm was too weak to hold her. "Ah…no…are ya going out?" she cried.

"Aye, but only for a while. 'Tis a little walking and thinking I need to do. Just around the block, darlin'. I won't be gone long." He pulled on his coat.

"Don't go…don't leave me alone, not, here, strange…place," she pleaded, her tongue feeling thick, her mind starting to shut down.

.

Chapter Seven

"Nooo! Don't—Uncle Sam—don't!" Casey screamed, his legs a blur of kicking, hitting, grabbing for a post, a side rail, his Uncle's arm, anything to keep from being tossed over the side of the Titanic. But his fingers were pried from the rail he held with a death grip.

"Nooo!" Tossed into space, he fell alongside the Titanic, his arms windmilling. Down—down—he fell to splash into the mind-numbing cold water. He thrashed around, trying to surface, but unable to swim, couldn't, and was grabbed by the tentacles of freezing water and darkness. He gave in to the chilling grip, and slowly spiraled downward into the dark abyss, a slight trail of air bubbles leaked from his mouth doing a crazy dance towards the surface.

"Nooo!"

Casey's eyes popped open. Realizing he'd been holding his breath, he gasped for air. Covered in a sheen of sweat, he groped to feel the sides of the wicker basket, his safe haven for the past four days. Relief had him sagging. He grabbed the wool blanket and pulled it over his shivering body. He should be safe with Da, not hiding in the hold of a ship, waiting until he thought it was safe to leave.

He thought how happy he'd been about coming to his da in America. Even down in steerage, his family still had a cabin. The beds were soft and had hardwood bedposts. He thought the cabin was nicer than his room back at Grandmum Ina's. With Mam and Jilly seasick, he'd been left to his own devices. The ship became a giant toy for him to play on. He became a pirate, the captain of all thieves and cutthroats. The crew allowed him to be adventurous on the decks, but told him to stay away from first class. He didn't obey. He went where he could, and shouldn't go, starboard and aft, first, second, and third promenades, the dining rooms, he'd explored it all.

Having fashioned an eye patch out of one of Mam's handkerchiefs, he was running and hiding from imaginary foes when he'd almost collided with Uncle Sam strolling on the second-class promenade. His uncle had a pretty lady on his arm as they paused to look out over the ocean.

Casey's breath caught in his throat. He quickly ducked inside the sliding doors of the palm court. His excitement was dashed, his trip ruined. This meant his uncle was going to America the same as him. From that day on, Casey kept a sharp eye on him.

He'd tried telling Mam about his uncle, but it upset her and she'd lashed out at him, calling him a liar. Those words cut him something fierce. He stopped being a pirate. Instead, he slunk around, watching, and learning enough to know his uncle had the blonde lady with him in a second class cabin.

He could well remember snapping awake when the Titanic stopped. The steady vibration stilled. Curious to know why it did so, he'd quickly dressed and leaving Mam and Jilleen sleeping went topside. Not many were about at this late hour, and when he'd stepped outside he'd almost walked into his uncle.

Careful to stay behind him and out of sight, Casey followed him out on deck and saw the iceberg. It towered over the ship, and was too close. Some of the ship's crew investigated the iceberg, peering over the railing, gesturing and talking to one another. Casey shrank back to hide when his uncle turned around and took off in a fast run, going in the direction of third class.

Frightened, now sensing something bad had happened, Casey had followed his uncle as he rousted his Mam and Jilleen out of bed. He'd even watched as Uncle Sam saved his mam and sister by knocking out the steward who wasn't going to let them pass.

Following at a safe distance, he heard Mam screaming that *He* wasn't with them, begging Sam to go back to steerage to find him. Casey started to run up to his uncle and tell him not to go, that he was safe. But when his uncle headed toward the first-class suites instead of steerage, Casey followed. He wasn't the only one. The woman he'd seen his uncle with earlier followed his uncle right into an elegant stateroom.

Casey peered around the doorjamb where his uncle was busy stuffing his pockets with sparkling jewelry and money left right out in the open. Casey listened.

"I see you're concerned enough about me to make sure I'm safe on a lifeboat." The woman accused Sam in a surly voice while adjusting the straps on her life jacket.

"Get out of me way, Lillian. I have no use for ya now. Go up to the boats." Sam turned back to his stealing, leaving the suite and going into the next.

The woman kept dogging him. Again, he told her to go topside, wait to get into a boat. But she wouldn't leave him alone and started to pick up a pearl necklace. He swatted her hand away, and shoved her out of the room.

She immediately huffed back in and stood with her finger wagging at him. "I want the loot your stealin', luv," she said. "I think that pearl necklace dangling from your hand will look smashing around my neck." Her chin stuck out and her blue eyes dared him.

He shook his head.

"Then I'll be going straight to the ship's warden and tell him about you. He might take a grand interest in a passenger stealing during a time like this."

She held out her hand for the jewelry. But Sam, his jaw flexing in anger, picked her up by the neck and propelled her backwards to slam her body against the dark paneled wall.

When the woman opened her mouth and started screaming, Sam crammed the pearl necklace inside it, silencing her. She snapped her head back and forth making a gagging sound. She beat at him with closed fists, her bulky life jacket a hindrance. Sam's face turned purple with rage as he held her up, her feet kicking against the wall.

"How do you like me hands around yer neck—not as pretty as a necklace, aye?" he said, savagely pressing his thumbs against her windpipe.

Her eyes bulged.

Casey's throat closed up as he watched the woman trying to pry Sam's hands from her neck. A loud explosion shook the ship, throwing him to the stateroom's floor. Screams came from the deck.

The woman became limp. Sam released her.

As her body slid down the wall, he pulled the necklace from her mouth. The beads clicked against her teeth one-by-one as the necklace roped from her mouth.

She sat, her legs spread like a collapsed puppet.

Sam bent over her body, and removing a small card from his pocket, quickly shoved it inside the woman's coat pocket.

Casey gasped.

Uncle Sam stared right at him with eyes glowing like a night animal. "Ya feckin' little snoop. I'm goin' to break yer Goddamn neck!"

"Nooo, Uncle Sam!" he screamed. Jumping to his feet, he began backing away. His uncle came toward him. Casey rushed down the hallway, heading back to where his mam and sister were.

"Casey—Casey!" Jilleen's little voice called, as she ran toward him. "We're over here, goin' on the boat, hurry!"

"Jilly, Uncle Sam just killed a woman…we've got to tell Mam! Hurry—now—let's go! Ah…no! Run—Jilly!" he screamed in terror. His uncle ran past him and grabbing up Jilleen threw her overboard.

Hearing his sister's screams, Casey, wild with fear bolted. He pushed through the frightened crowds. Someone grabbed him up by the coat collar. He turned around to see his uncle had him. Casey fought, practically pulling his body out of his coat, but his uncle held fast. Casey, no match against his strength, was tiring. He feared following Jilleen, and knew his little sister was dead. She couldn't swim, nor could he.

While carried toward the ship's railing, he yelled, "Help me—help me!"

By now, a wild furor had broken out, and no one was paying attention to a boy throwing a fit. Casey fought hard, reaching for a handhold, anything solid. He locked his toes on the rail of the ship and held onto his uncle's coat sleeve. It was a useless struggle. His uncle pried him loose and wearing a sneer of triumph, hurled him overboard.

He hit the water like a rock and started sinking. The freezing water was thick with thrashing bodies. Casey felt a hand grabbing his.

A man pulled him out of the churning waters and deposited him in a lifeboat. "Here ya go, laddie," he said in an Irish accent, and quickly turned to help someone else.

Casey sucked in air. He coughed and vomited up salt water.

The woman next to him immediately pulled him to her bosom and gently stroked his wavy, curly hair. "Ellie my girl," she said. The smile she had for him belied the frightened, wild look on her face. She wrapped a woolen headscarf around his blonde curls and comforted him by pulling a blanket over the both of them. "There now, me luv, isn't it grand we're safe." She crooned in a sing-song voice, sharing her warmth with him.

Casey understood the woman wasn't in her true mind, at least not right now. In a way she reminded him of his mam. He played along and was happy to rest his head against her bosom and become her daughter. He was wet, miserable, and thought for sure he'd lost his little sister. Mam, he figured, got on a lifeboat. And he was certain his Uncle Sam had gotten on one too. The woman next to him pulled him against her cork life jacket, practically abrading the skin off his cheeks. But he didn't care, and thought her constant hugging had probably saved his life.

His lifeboat had floated several miles from the others and was next to the last to be loaded onto the *Carpathia*. As he stood shivering beside the woman with the wild cast in her eyes, they were signed aboard by the *Carpathia's* officer as Mrs. Bessie Graham and daughter Ellie Graham. Assigned cots in the public smoking room on B-deck they sank onto the hard canvas and fell into an exhausted sleep.

Early that evening, Casey woke up to see the woman sitting on her cot and staring at him like he was a spook. She pulled on her round glasses, her gray eyes again staring him down.

"You're not Ellie. You're not my daughter," she shrieked, and seized him by the ears, pulling him off the cot.

"Ouch," he yelled. "Stop it! Yer hurtin' me ears!" By now he was panicking.

"You little liar," she said and tugged harder forcing him to his knees.

Casey could see people starting to approach. He wanted to get away before one of those people was Uncle Sam. Hating to do so, he started hitting her arms. She yelped and let go.

He grabbed up his blanket, and shoes, and plowed through the loitering bystanders. With his ears still burning, he flew down the stairs. Seeking safety, he stumbled into the large storage area not far from the galley. A large wicker basket with a lid on it was just what he needed. He tossed in his stuff and tumbled inside.

While in hiding, he carefully snuck around and tried to find out if his mam or Jilleen were on the boat. The captain had posted names of the survivors. No one by the name of McShane was listed. He wondered what happened to his mam and Uncle Sam. His uncle would throw an old woman in the water to save his rotten life. The murdered woman's bulging eyes and the sound of those beads being pulled from her mouth were captured in Casey's mind forever.

A day later and usually stealing food from the nearby food galley, Casey, feeling lonely and cut off from everyone, decided to eat a meal in the third-class dining room. He also wanted to snoop around. He was sitting at the long table, swinging his legs and slurping hot clam chowder. He liked the crackers and crushed them into his soup.

The lady next to him took a bite of her sandwich and then sipped her tea. "Yer a lovely lad," she said. "I do believe we will be in New York day after tomorrow. Do you have relatives waiting for you there?"

"Aye, me da," he answered, and hoped it was so. But if he and his family weren't listed as survivors, why would Da go there? He had to tell him about Uncle Sam.

He put a spoonful of soup in his mouth and almost choked on it when he glanced up to see Uncle Sam entering the room.

Sam stopped and looked around with that dead-on stare of his.

Casey's hair stood on end.

With no other way out of the room, he slipped from the chair, and crawled underneath the long table. He created gasps from startled people, and ducked kicking shoes. He quickly made his way to the door.

Uncle Sam spotted him and gave chase. Casey raced down the stairs. Knowing the *Carpathia* as well as the crew did, he managed to elude his uncle. He'd gotten his answer about Uncle being alive. But now, to Casey's dismay, Uncle Sam knew for sure that he wasn't dead…

…Tonight, he'd anxiously waited for the *Carpathia* to dock. The deep horns blasting from the other ships excited him, letting him know he was getting closer to being with Da. When he started to leave the ship along with everyone else from steerage, his uncle was standing at the top of the stairs waiting to pounce. Casey turned around and ran back here to his basket.

Reluctant to do so, he now felt it was safe enough to leave. He just wasn't sure where to go or what to do. His eight-year-old mind had only one goal right now and that was to find his da.

He eased the basket lid up just enough to peer out. One lone light burned in the nearby corridor. There was no one about. Feeling safe to do so, he flipped the lid off and got to his feet. He pulled on his coat and felt inside the pocket for his father's watch. Somehow the solidness of it made him feel better.

Casey reached inside his other pocket for his da's address that Grandmum Ina had stuffed in there before he'd left Ireland.

It was gone.

He panicked and started searching around, he picked up the blanket and gave it a good shake. The paper was nowhere to be found. He tried to recall the address, but couldn't. How was he going to find his da?

Now shaken to have lost his only security, he took up the meager items he'd managed to steal. Some matches, bread, a cooking pot to use as a weapon. He wasn't sure he'd need them, especially the pot. Just in case, the blanket and everything else was tucked inside the converted pillowcase. The name *Carpathia* was embroidered on the case in navy blue lettering. Tossing the knapsack out, he crawled out of the basket and peered around.

He started topside.

His chest pounded. No one passed him, no one challenged him, and no Uncle Sam stepped out of the shadows to grab him.

The gangway did a slow up and down rise as he eased down it, and on to the covered pier. The chilly night air hit him and he took a deep breath. He stared up at the big ship and wished he were back inside the basket. Piles of water-soaked debris, discarded food wrappers, newspapers and an occasional hair ribbon littered the area making him feel even lonelier. Sad that he'd missed out on the reunions.

The light from some kind of a guardhouse reflected off the puddles, and he could see a lone figure sitting inside. Relieved to see another person, he started toward it. As he got closer to the shed, a man dressed in a blue uniform stepped out.

He immediately held up a lantern and began shouting, "Hey! What are you doing here? This is off-limits. I'll bet you're part of that gang. C'mere." He started running toward Casey. "What's in the sack? Why it's a pillowcase from the Carpathia. Ya little thief….c'mere to me."

"Nay, I'm not a thief, I'm lookin' fer me da."

The intense look on the stranger's face frightened Casey who dallied no more. He ran down the pier's staircase, his footfalls the only sound echoing in the giant building. He ran outside and past a rope barricade. His feet splashed in deep puddles, the cold water drenched his knee-pants and shoes as he ran. He ducked around the corner of a building and breathlessly peered around it.

No one was there. The guard must have gone back to his guardhouse.

Trying to catch his breath, he sank down on the sidewalk. A stack of boxes across the alley shifted, one fell over, startling him. Afraid of what he couldn't see, he started to get up. An animal, its eyes glowing in the dark, meowed.

"Here, cat—kitty—kitty," he called softly. The cat meowed, and with its tail pointing to the sky, it padded over to Casey. He stroked the cat's head, noticing it was missing half an ear. The cat, skinny with matted orange colored fur, looked as haggard as Casey felt. It lay down beside him and Casey continued to pet it, feeling the cat's contented vibrations through its boney side.

Sam approached the ship's gangway. It looked different without the pandemonium that had surrounded it earlier. He figured Casey was still inside the ship somewhere, probably down with the stores and too frightened to come out. He no sooner started up the ramp when a guard, holding a lantern approached him.

The man appeared suspicious. "What are ya doing? No one's allowed on the ship."

Sam took off his hat and held it contritely against his chest. "I'm lookin' fer me boy. He was on the Carpathia. I couldn't get here sooner, came down from the North. He's about so high and has curly blond hair." Sam held his hand up past his waist.

The guard scratched his chin whiskers. "I just chased a young kid away matching that description. Not more than ten minutes ago. I yelled at him and he shot down the street like the devil himself was after him." The guard pointed. "Went that way."

Casey reluctantly left the cat behind. As he walked along, the tall, dark buildings looked foreboding and sinister. Some of the electric streetlamps dimly burned, others were completely out. He didn't know what to do, or where to go, and hoped to find a police station.

He had to pee, so he stopped and pulling out his wanger, pissed into a puddle. Grandmum Ina would have clattered him a good one for that. An empty can with a peaches label on it lay in his path and a good kick sent it loudly rolling in front of him. When he reached it again, he gave it another kick, the sound echoed off the tall buildings. Steam was coming up from vents in the sidewalk and he stood on one of them, feeling the warm rush.

Attracted by lights in the windows of a building a short distance away, he started toward them, reasoning that lights meant people. He reached the building with the lights burning, and shifted the heavy knapsack to his left shoulder. It didn't take him long to realize no one was around. A lone bulb was burning on a window display of women's hats. He heard a noise behind him and glanced up to see Uncle Sam's ghostly reflection looming behind him. Casey's body turned to mush. He froze.

"Hello, *boyo*." His mouth curved in a wide grin as he reached for Casey.

Casey found his mettle and screamed at the top of his lungs, the sound echoing down the empty street. He turned and swung his knapsack. The cooking pot thudded hard against Sam's head, clobbering him a good one.

Stunned, Sam staggered backwards.

Seeing his chance, Casey dropped the knapsack and ran for his life. His footfalls echoed loudly around him.

So did his uncle's.

He could feel his presence closing in on him.

"Stop—Casey! I'm here to take ya to yer mam. She cries fer ye, won't give me a minutes peace," Sam shouted.

"I don't believe ya! Yer lying!" He stumbled and righted himself. He darted down another street, trying to miss the bricks lying in jumbled piles.

"Stop running, boyo."

"Noooo. Ye want to hurt me 'cause I saw ya kill that lady." His side developed a stitch. It hurt to breathe.

"C'mere ya little shite."

Sam's cold hand slipped inside Casey's coat collar, jerking him to a stop.

A brick came hurtling out of nowhere and slammed against Sam's leg.

He cussed, releasing his hold on Casey.

Casey took off running.

His uncle was right behind him.

Another brick slammed against the ground. Sam cursed again.

Realizing his uncle had stopped his pursuit, Casey turned to watch but kept walking backwards. Uncle Sam was rubbing his arm and cautiously peering around.

Laughter eerily echoed off the buildings under construction. Snickers and whistling appeared to be coming from both sides of the street.

Another brick forced Sam to duck, and then a deadly barrage came at him. One connected against his shoulder making him yelp.

Sam started backing up. Pointing at Casey, he edged out, "Ye've not seen the last of me, lad."

The next brick knocked his bowler hat off. Not bothering with it, Sam turned and ran. Heavy bricks dogged his heels, splattering and breaking against the street's cobblestones.

Alone and standing in the middle of the street, Casey peered at the dark and sinister shadows. He tried to swallow, but his dry tongue filled his mouth. Soft laughter echoed all around scaring the bejapers out of him.

"Hey, sissy boy, where did you get such pretty curls?" The voice, young, yet menacing sounded behind him.

Casey whirled around. No one was there, only laughter hung in the air. He heard scuffling sounds all around him. His scalp prickled. The shadows began to move as dark figures crept towards him. Now was the time to run.

Feet pounded right behind him.

Someone tackled him, bringing him down in a brutal skin-scraping bounce against the cobblestones.

He fought, throwing punches, landing a good one against his attacker's jaw. Casey's arms were pinned. His assailant sat on his chest, and grabbed his face. Not knowing what to expect, Casey slit an eye open and peeked. A teenager, not a bogeyman had him. The kid was now grinning back at him. His dirty brown cap was turned backwards over shaggy blonde hair, his nose long, and his face in shadow from the street light burning on the sidewalk next to them.

His eyes glimmered. The kid was getting heavy and acted like he had all the time in the world.

"What's yer name, and who was the bloke trying to get ya?" He grinned, showing two overlapping front teeth.

Two other boys just as ratty looking joined him and stared down at Casey.

"Bite me shite, ya blaggard!" Words boiled out of Casey's mouth as he tried to buck the kid off his chest.

But he wasn't budging. He laughed and tweaked Casey under the chin.

"Whoa! Listen to the little Mick would ya! I take it a blaggard is something bad in Ireland?"

"Hoodlum, that's what ye are. Now get off me, I can't breathe," Casey rasped out, drawing in a ragged breath.

"What's yer name? And who was after ya?"

"Creighton, me—name's Creighton. Get off!"

The boy laughed. "Creighton is it? Now that's a name to match yer pretty curls." He leaned close, and smacking his lips together made mock kisses.

Casey threw a surprise punch that landed hard against the kid's lip, cutting it. But instead of getting mad and popping Casey back, the kid simply chuckled and wiped blood from his lip.

"I like ya, Creighton. Ya got moxy. My name's Frankie Doyle." He searched Casey's pockets, and pulled out a pocket watch. "Hey, where did ya get this? Steal it from the bloke chasing ya?"

Casey bucked hard, dislodging Frankie. He lunged for the watch. "Give it back. That's me da's watch!"

Frankie shook his head and held the watch at bay. "Whew…scrappy aren't ya! You'll have to earn it back, Creigh…ton. That's a mouthful, gotta nickname?"

"Casey."

Frankie stood and slipped the watch into his pocket. "Meet the rest of my gang. We're the Wharf Rats. This little guy is Benny Hart.

He thinks he's nine, but livin' in an orphanage since he was real young, he's not sure."

"I am nine," Benny said with emphasis. Smaller than Casey, Benny was tough looking with thick cheeks and a pug nose. His bottom lip stuck out past his upper giving him a permanent pout. He pushed his brown cap toward the back of his head revealing a shorn scalp. "Hi," he said, and adjusted his empty newspaper bag.

Frankie continued. "This here's James Kelly, best pickpocket around. But you'd best call him Jimmy."

Jimmy, tall and lanky, had a gaunt face splotched brown with freckles. "Got me a new hat thanks to the man chasing ya." Jimmy, wearing Uncle Sam's bowler, winked at Casey. He reached up and tilted the hat to a jaunty angle showing off his thick red hair. "And since we're telling ages, I'm claiming to be about fourteen. Frankie, the watch thief, says he's sixteen, but I'd say he's more like fifteen."

"I'd say more like seventeen if we're stretchin' the truth," Frankie said with a smirk.

"Why don't ya know how old ya are?" Casey asked.

Jimmy shrugged. "Some of us were left at orphanages when we were young. And that's all you need to—"

The sound of a car chugging in the distance alerted the boys to move on.

"C'mon, Casey, I think the coppers might be coming."

"Coppers?" Casey asked.

"Aye, coppers—police. The minute they see ya, they'll throw ya in the hoosegow and forget ya. C'mon."

"What's a hoosegow?" Casey joined the boys hurried gaits.

"It's jail, and someplace ya never want to go. If ya do, you'll never get out. They do terrible things to boys in the hoosegow. Buggering is one of them," Frankie said.

"What's buggering?" Casey did his best to keep up with Frankie.

Jimmy laughed. "Buggering? Ya don't know what buggering is?" He hooted. "It's when someone, usually a man, gets into your pants and ya don't want them there."

"Oh…aye, now I know." Casey was ashamed to admit he really didn't. Jimmy had given him a good idea of what it was, and he wanted no part of it. His grandmum had always told him to let no one touch ye that ye didn't want touching ya, and if ya think ya do, then ya better think again. Her meaning was as curvy as a country road, but now he had it straight.

They went down into a subway station, a first for Casey. When they came to the turnstiles and coin meters, the boys put in slugs and pulled them back out with attached strings. They got on an arriving train and took a seat. The train was almost empty this time of morning. Casey was fighting sleep, and it seemed he wasn't on the train long at all before it stopped and they got off.

The boys ran down dark smelly streets close to the waterfront, continually checking behind them. They even sent Jimmy back to make sure no one followed. Finally, they stopped in front of a boarded up building. Jimmy stood guard while Frankie lifted up several squeaky boards hiding a door. One at a time the boys ducked under the boards and hurried inside.

Frankie secured the boards behind him and locked the door. He lit a lantern and handed it to Jimmy. They were in a musty smelling foyer piled high with trash.

They made their way up dark dilapidated stairs, the lantern lighting their way. And just as Casey thought he couldn't take another step, they reached the third-floor landing and hurried inside a good-sized flat.

The smell hit him first, of pee and filth. He crinkled his nose hardly able to stand the stench that now mingled with the lads unwashed bodies. He peered at his surroundings. Several fancy parlor lamps were now lit, the sulfur from the match still acrid and strong, the wicks slightly smoking. The chimneys on the lamps were cracked, but the bases holding the oil were intact.

Casey was dismayed but tried not to let on. Cockroaches scurried for the walls. An old brown-velvet sofa was pushed against one wall, and lining the others were mattresses loaded with holey, woolen blankets. A kitchen cabinet stood on three legs, the fourth corner of the cabinet was propped with stacked books. It was missing drawers and had plates and cups stacked about. A red metal matchbox along with a salt and pepper shaker was on top. The counter held a hot plate fueled by kerosene.

This was home to the boys and one they were willing to bring him to. He gladly accepted their hospitality. It sure wasn't Grandmum Ina's cozy nest, no nighttime story was going to be read here, and no goodnight kiss was going to follow the story.

"Don't ya have a mam or da?" Casey asked.

"Nope," Jimmy said. "We told ya we're orphans. Benny and I were in orphanages, but ran away. Not at the same time, or the same orphanage. Those places are tough to live in. Here we answer to no one."

Frankie held up his left hand that was missing his little finger and half of the one next to it. "Got 'em caught in a machine while working in a box making factory. No more of that work for me." Frankie took off his jacket. He yawned while pulling down his suspenders to reveal a dirty union suit. He scratched his armpits and rump, and then plopped down on one of the mattresses and started unlacing his boots. "This place ain't much, but its home to us."

Jimmy pulled a can of soup from each of his jacket pockets. "I hit old man Solberg's earlier tonight and got these. Serve the old fart right after firing Joe." He turned to Casey. "You're lucky we were out so late tonight. With all the excitement over at the Pier we went there to watch the ship come in. Man the crowds were huge. You would have thought the president was in town. But we didn't do any stealing, leastways not there, not with people so upset about the Titanic sinkin'."

Benny dropped his newspaper bag on the floor and pulled a handful of coins out of his pocket. He handed them to Frankie.

"Speakin' of that ship. I got a lot of money today. The Titanic's sinkin' had paper's flying out of my hand—"

"Ya shuddup about the Titanic!" Casey stormed. "I was on that ship."

"Liar!" Benny shot back. His face wrinkled into a scowl making him look like he could go a few rounds and easily win.

"I'm not lyin'. I was with me mam and sister. We sailed from Ireland." Casey stood his ground and glared.

Their mouths were agape, and they looked at him with something between admiration and disbelief.

"Why ain't ya drowned then?" Benny wasn't going to let this go.

Casey's jaw clenched. And thinking Benny was stupid, he blurted out. "I almost did. Somebody pulled me out of the water and into a lifeboat. I was on that ship tonight, the Carpathia."

Jimmy walked over to the kitchen cabinet and emptied his pockets of penny candy, fruit gum, and other edibles. At last he turned to Casey. "Did yer mother and sister die?"

"I don't know."

"What do ya mean ya don't know?" Benny pushed.

Casey shrugged. He wasn't telling anything to these kids, especially Benny. "Just that. I don't know." He tried not to cry even when his little sister's screams and his mam's face was the only thing he could think of.

Grabbing a spot next to Frankie on the mattress, Casey unlaced his shoes and toed them off. He covered himself with the musty smelling blanket. "And, ye, Frankie Doyle, will be givin' me da's watch back, or I'll be takin' it."

Feeling secure for the first time in days, Casey wilted against the mattress. Wanting to stay awake with the rest, and fighting sleep as long as he could, his eyes kept closing and he finally drifted off.

"D'ya believe him, Frankie?" Jimmy asked.

"Yeah, I do. He'll tell us in good time."

Jimmy blew out all the lamps but one, and that one he turned down to a low, soft glow. When Frankie glanced at him questioningly, he shrugged and said, "For the little Mick, just in case he wakes up and is scared."

"Blow it out, Jimmy. That man might have followed us, and if he's snoopin' around back he can see the light."

Jimmy did as told.

Used to moving around in the dark, the two boys found their beds.

"Anyone see Joe lately?" Benny asked.

"Nope." Jimmy said while settling under his blanket. "I haven't seen him for about a month or more. Expect he's staying in the Ryerson's backroom. Can't blame him. It's warmer than this dump."

Frankie pulled the musty smelling blanket up to his chin. Anyplace was warmer than this rat infested hole, but it was home. And home was here in the Lower East Side and the waterfront where most of society didn't dare to tread. He absentmindedly fingered his maimed hand, thinking…always thinking.

He was born a loser, and born to a whore of a mother who couldn't tell him who his father was. One of the many *uncles* who frequented her bed was a sure shooter. She'd take those uncles, over five or more a day, behind her closed bedroom door until Frankie became wise enough to know what she was.

"Frankie, can ya go to the store and steal us something to eat?" She would constantly ask.

"Yeah, Ma."

"Frankie can ya go to work in the factory and bring home some money?" She pulled her dirty blond hair back into a bun.

"Yeah, Ma." He was eleven.

His mother became quite good at dodging the truant officer who would knock on the door and yell that Frankie was supposed to be in school and did his mother want him to grow up stupid?

What good would it do him to read and write? He never learned.

Bitter about the life he led, his mother's constant whining for him to bring in some money, forced him into a factory making paper boxes. He was happy to get away from the grunts and moans coming from his mother's close door. For over twelve hours a day he stood next to a cutting machine, its knife sharp, and him always on guard. But the day came when he was exhausted, let his guard down, and watched in horror as his little finger and half of the one next to it lay on the box in front of him. As blood ran down his arm that he clutched against his chest, he screamed, and screamed.

A ruined hand for two dollars and fifty cents a week.

He lost his job, his drive, and was already an old man before he turned thirteen.

His mother always thin, was now gaunt. Constantly coughing, she started bringing up red phlegm. Men stopped coming to her.

"What's gonna happen to us, Frankie?" she would always ask.

"I don't know, Ma. Don't rightly care," he'd say. Knowing his answer was cruel, he'd retract it and sooth her anxiety with a nicer one. "I can steal stuff and sell it to the second-hand shops. They'll pay me."

"What if ya get caught, what will happen to me?" she asked, not caring that he stole, only that he might get caught, then what?

Frankie looked around the cockroach infested flat he and his mother called home and thought, indeed, then what?

...Behind him in on the mattress, Casey moaned and began thrashing about. Frankie gently nudged him and he settled down.

Outside, Sam took in the dark empty depilated buildings around him. One of these abandoned structures held his nephew and he was going to find out which one. He flexed his shoulder that throbbed from being hit. Good thing they didn't hit his head or he'd be dead in the street.

By staying far behind the boys, he'd managed to follow them onto the subway and discovered they were several miles from the Williams's tenement. Knowing Casey's whereabouts here on the lower east side, Sam could relax for the first time in days.

Puffing on his cigar, he blew a thick funnel of gray into the air, and knew without a doubt that his nephew wouldn't be going anywhere soon. He pushed away from the building and headed north towards the apartment and Darlene.

Chapter Eight

The church bells in Halifax began to toll. The deafening clamor resounded throughout the city and reached Donald on Citadel Hill. From his vantage point next to the watchtower, Donald could see Halifax Harbor and for miles beyond. The normally busy harbor was subdued. Closed to all shipping traffic, one lone ship steamed into port with her flags flying at half-mast.

The ship, the *Mackay-Bennett* was arriving with the first load of bodies.

It was the thirtieth of April and the giant clock on the tower read nine-thirty in the morning. Donald used his hands to shade his eyes, cutting the glare from the water that sparkled like silver in the sunlight. If Donald thought waiting for the *Carpathia* was hard, this was by far worse. At least while on the pier in Manhattan he had hope. Here, none existed.

He'd accepted his family had perished. All that had happened before he met Derry and what happened afterward, he could blame on Sam. The man was a blemish on the beauty of life, a canker. And Donald's tolerance of his brother had turned into hatred so deep that if he had Sam standing right here, he'd kill him and feel justified in doing so.

He'd missed three years of seeing his children grow, and in his mind, they were just as he'd left them. His children would never grow up, he'd never be able to kiss them, hold them, and give comfort. He'd never look into Casey's blue eyes again and see them shine with excitement and curiosity. He'd never be able to feel Jilleen pull on his earlobe, and sigh against his chest. All he had left was an outdated photograph, and five short years of memories before leaving Ireland.

The *MacKay-Bennett* blew its horn, forlorn and echoing.

Through tears that blurred his vision, he watched the death ship until it was out of sight, its wake a mere ripple.

Due to The White Star Line's courtesy, he was able to be here. The Line took care of his and everyone's expenses. They were also going to stand for the costs of burials. Donald figured this was the Titanic's owner's way of purging their guilt over the sinking.

Without a doubt, Donald planned to bury his family in Dublin. He was leaving the harsh reality of New York behind and returning home. He longed to see his mam.

Halifax reminded him of Ireland. It had a lazy way about it, just like Dublin. Perhaps it was the old soul look about Halifax, the cragginess of its people, which brought about comparisons.

He began walking to the Halifax Hotel where Eldon waited for him. An information bureau was set up inside the hotel where employees of the White Star Line received telegraphs sent from the ships on recovery duty. Donald understood the ships captains were burying bodies at sea especially the ones in too bad of shape to be embalmed, or damaged beyond recognition. Would it be too much to ask of God to bring his cherished loved ones back to him intact? He didn't dare ask, for none of his prayers were answered so far. He felt compelled to turn his back on a God who would let this tragedy happen in the first place.

The bells kept up their funeral knell that ricocheted around the city. Their insistent tolling split his head in two, and he wanted to scream to stop the madness! But his was a small voice in a City bereaved. As he headed down the sidewalk toward the hotel, store owners in their way of paying homage, had put pictures of the *Titanic* in their windows and draped black bunting around them. Another constant reminder.

Tomorrow would come, and everyone would go their separate ways and continue on with their lives. He hated tomorrow, hated to see the sun rise on another day, hated to see it set, and for him the world became dark.

"Donald, don't you think it's time to go down to the curling rink?" Eldon asked, and using a napkin wiped his mustache.

Donald pushed his coffee cup away. His lunch of fried fish and scalloped potatoes went uneaten. He took out his watch from where it was tucked inside his black vest pocket. It was after one. Eldon was right, he couldn't put it off any longer. By now, the officials had more than ample time to get the bodies organized for viewing.

Thankful to have Eldon along, Donald figured he'd strained their friendship beyond the breaking point, especially the times his temper flared, and he took his anger out on Eldon. But good-natured Eldon just took it in stride, appearing to ignore his outbursts about the owners of a ship so ill-equipped to handle such a disaster that it made him want to puke at the injustice.

Donald, along with Eldon, approached the Mayflower Curling Rink on Agricola Street. The rink, normally a place of gathering to pit ones skill against another in the game of curling, was now a giant morgue.

A simple picket fence surrounded the two-storied, red brick building where an official with a badge stood by the front gate.

Donald showed his letter of identification to the official and watched the man's face fold with sadness.

"Go on in," he said and pointed at the front steps.

The air inside the room was foul with the smell of sweat, tobacco smoke, and the heavy pall of fear. A nurse with a white cap and soft features was stationed behind a desk that held smelling salts and restoratives.

No way was Donald going to faint. The nurse bit her lower lip and accepted his list that she checked against hers.

"Mr. McShane," she said with a low whisper. "We have your wife's body."

Pole axed, Donald cemented his legs. No fainting, not here, not ever.

"Steady, Donald," Eldon cautioned, and put his hand on Donald's shoulder.

The nurse stood and asked if he needed help.

"No," Eldon replied. "Thank you."

Donald faintly heard the nurse tell Eldon where they should wait. He allowed Eldon to guide him to a chair against the wall.

He collapsed onto the hard wooden seat. Again, Donald's hatred for Sam twisted his guts. His brother's mocking face wavered in front of him.

Eldon leaned forward to rest his arms on his thighs, his movements catching Donald's attention, dragging him back from the hell his mind had a tendency to go to more often than not.

"Do you want me to go in with you?" Eldon asked, his dark eyes full of concern.

Donald's first inclination was to say yes. But not knowing what horrors he would be viewing, he thought it best Eldon waited for him here.

"Nay, Eldon, one doesn't ask a friend to walk into hell with him. But I'm thanking ya just the same for the offer." No words could express how much he appreciated Eldon being here with him.

He waited.

The door leading into the giant curling rink opened, and a man and woman, weeping, propped each other up as they stumbled out. So deep into their grief, they appeared not to notice when another couple helped them from the building.

"Mr. McShane…Donald McShane?" A tall, thin man with wisps of hair sticking straight up from his balding pate glanced around the room. "Mr. McShane?"

Donald reluctantly stood, and started toward the man waiting by the doorway.

"Mr. McShane, please come with me, sir," the man said. "We'll try to make this as easy for you as we possibly can. All you have to do is view her face. Her health inspection card to board the Titanic was inside her coat pocket."

He led Donald into the cavernous curling rink. Some of the windows on each side of the room were shuttered while a few were left open to accept daylight. The overhead lights, spaced sporadically, didn't help much. All Donald could see was rows upon rows of canvas-enclosed cubicles where grieving relatives were escorted to view their loved ones.

The man Donald followed led them past the cubicles and upstairs to the second floor. Here, canvas shrouded bodies with stenciled numbered canvas bags were stacked on ice and lined foot to head with barely enough room to step among them. Men were scurrying around, trying to keep some kind of decorum in a scene so grisly it was almost impossible to do.

The smell hit Donald full in the face. He muttered under his breath, trying not to breathe too deeply, but it didn't help. Nothing helped.

Expecting to be shown one of the bodies on the floor, he was surprised to be ushered into yet another room dissected by a canvas curtain. A lone body shrouded in a white sheet lay on a table.

"Mr. McShane, this is Doctor Jacob Tory, our local coroner and examiner." His escort was quick to turn Donald over to the distinguished looking man wearing a white frock coat and standing next to the body.

"Not a mortician?" Donald said while making the man's acquaintance by nodding.

The doctor stared at Donald. "Actually, at times I'm both. But I'm a coroner by trade."

Donald knew what a coroner did.

Appearing to study Donald, the doctor cleared his throat. "You appear a strong man, Mr. McShane, and you will need your strength. We have your wife. She fits your description of her and the inspection card inside her pocket leaves no doubt of her identity. I just want you to be aware she may look somewhat different to you, even though she was one of the first bodies to be removed from the water—"

"I understand what yer tellin' me. I'll do this for Derry."

Coroner Tory walked around the table, and putting his hands on the sheet, slowly began to lift it.

Donald reached out and gripping the man's wrist, gently stopped him.

"Ah…don't. Please let me do this." He couldn't stand the thought of a stranger displaying his wife's body. As minutes ticked by, he stood with his one hand clenched into a fist, his gaze on the shrouded figure, unable to move

The examiner nudged him. "Mr. McShane…maybe… I should—"

"Nay, I can do it." And he slowly began lifting the material away.

Her blonde hair came into view first. Then her face with closed eyes, mottled alabaster skin and a blue tinged mouth.

Donald sucked in air, the sound loud and sharp. He gripped the table for support as his chest squeezed and his breath stopped. After a few seconds he found his voice. "That's not me wife—that's not

Derry," he blurted, highly agitated. He was relieved and angry at the same time, and damned God for putting him through this again.

Coroner Tory's face went slack with surprise. "But her health inspection card identifies her as such. She had to be inspected and this card had to be filled out and stamped before she could even board the Titanic." He reached across the table and put his hand on Donald's shoulder. "Remember, she's been in the water, albeit freezing cold, perhaps she just looks different to you?"

Before the examiner could stop him, Donald pulled the sheet off her and stared at the stranger. She was dressed in her undergarments, long lacy drawers, a chemise with pink ribbon threaded through the lace of it, and black cotton tights. Her arms, stiff at her sides, were ravaged by long wide gouges.

Donald opened her chemise to bare her chest and paused at the sight of the thick autopsy stitches crisscrossing her chest and abdomen. He steeled himself against the defilement of her body. His knuckles brushed against skin that was no longer the warm pliable flesh of a living woman. The cold rubbery feel of death made it easier to touch her, detach his mind from what he was doing. He told himself to think of her as a doll, a toy, anything but a human being.

"Mr. McShane," the coroner blustered, "What are you doing?

"Me wife had a dark mole on her back, close to her left shoulder." He lifted the body by the shoulder, slightly turning it, inspecting it. "Do ya see one here? I don't." He gently laid her back down and lifted her left hand. "She also had a long scar right here on her thumb caused by cutting herself peelin' potatoes. This woman has neither a scar nor a mole. I don't believe saltwater would make them disappear, aye?"

"No, you're right, they would still be there."

Donald noticed something strange. In haste, he pushed her golden hair away from her neck. Tilting her head back revealed dark mottled bruises around her neck in the shape of long thick fingers.

"What in bloody hell is this?" Surprised to see the bruising, Donald glanced over at the doctor.

At that moment the curtains parted, and a man stepped inside and stood next to Doctor Tory.

The examiner pointed to the middle-aged man next to him. "Mr. McShane, this is Inspector Mulhall from the police."

Donald nodded at the man whose inquisitive eyes scanned his face in return, searching for truths, catching a lie, doing his job. Donald knew without a doubt from the marks on the woman's throat she'd been strangled.

Examiner Tory cleared his throat and let out a deep sigh, his hand going into his pocket. "I must say I'm relieved to know she isn't your wife. That's the last thing I want to tell a grieving husband, is that his wife was murdered. This woman was already dead when she went into the water. Strangled. Her larynx crushed."

"Mr. McShane," Inspector Mulhall said, "do you have any idea who she is? Was she traveling with your wife?"

Worked up, he pushed his cap off his forehead. "How do ya expect me to know what happened on the ship? Sure'n I don't know who this woman is. Part of me wishes she is me wife, so I could at last know…have solid proof my wife is dead. Now I have none," his voice cracked.

He was angry that he was still living this hell. Here was a woman no one knew, a woman his wife had probably befriended. And even more sorrowful to him was that he didn't have Derry's body to take home and bury, knowing somehow that mounded dirt over a grave helped to make it final, eternity taking over, withering his grief, helping him to go on living. But it wasn't happening.

Mulhall said, "I didn't mean to imply you know who this woman is. It's just the scene for this murder is resting on the bottom of the Atlantic. Possible witnesses are lost as well. Our only clue is your wife's inspection card in her pocket. I find all this both strange and interesting. Since I know she isn't your wife, I'll try to find out who our mystery woman is. If I can."

A man came in and began setting up his camera on a tripod.

"What's happenin'?" Donald asked.

Doctor Tory answered. "We're taking pictures of all the dead ones we can't identify. We're sending the photographs to newspapers around the world. Trying to find who belongs to whom. It's not good to put people in unmarked graves and not know anything about them. I'm afraid we already have too many we'll never know who they are." He pulled the sheet up to the woman's neck and arranged her hair somewhat.

The photographer began taking pictures. His flash fired. The smell of magnesium blended with the smell of decay and embalming fluid.

Mulhall put his black fedora back on and nodded at Donald. "I'll be taking my leave. Before you go, McShane, leave your address and how to reach you with the examiner here." He left. The photographer was right behind him.

The coroner handed Donald the inspection card. It was warped from being wet but now dry it was legible. There it was, Derry's name, the date and time she left Queensland. It even listed her cabin number on the Titanic. Donald read the card more than once. He imagined Derry accepting it, her blonde hair blowing as she stood on the wharf, and her trying to quell Casey and Jilleen who he knew would be running around excited for the adventure ahead. He finally put the card into his pocket.

The woman's dress and shoes were beside her folded coat. Doctor Tory picked up the coat, and as he did so, tiny grains of salt fluttered to the floor. He unfolded the coat that gave off an odor of decay. Both of the sleeves had long jagged cuts in them.

"What made the tears?" Donald asked.

"She was probably sucked through a broken window, or a porthole," Coroner Tory said. "The force from the sinking blew out the porthole glass. Survivors also told the newspapers that the forward funnel fell. When it toppled it ripped an opening inside the ship clear down to the hull. Everything that could float came out of the ship. Most of the bodies wearing life vests floated to the surface, as did hers." He gently covered the woman, leaving only a tuft of hair sticking out.

Donald knew he would never forget this moment, or the woman's pale waxen face. He wondered what she must have looked like when she smiled. Did her eyes dance with glee? Could a man make her blush? He could do all those and more to Derry.

The examiner cleared his throat and said, "Mr. McShane, the MacKay-Bennett only brought in one child's body. A little blonde boy that's around two years. Certainly not even close to the age of your son. Captain Lardner of the MacKay-Bennett made the decision to bury over a hundred at sea. Their bodies were too far gone for embalming. The morticians on board the ship kept detailed descriptions of every body, numbered them, and placed their personal items in a canvas bag." He paused as if weighing his next words. "You'll need to go over the entries and check the descriptions. And we still have three ships out there looking for bodies, hoping to find those carried away from the site by the currents—"

"So, yer tellin' me I need to wait in Halifax until the ships have picked up all the dead? That I have to wait here for more bodies to be brought in and try to identify me wife and children?"

"Yes. I wish to God I wasn't. The whole of Halifax grieves. I'm so sorry."

Chapter Nine

Olivia sat in the den at her mother's writing desk which held stamps, pens, and fancy engraved stationary. The den, decorated for the women in the house, held dainty furniture with intricate carved legs, and brocaded cushions.

Olivia dipped her fountain pen into the ink bottle and pulled the tiny lever on the pen that sucked the black ink into her Parker pen. In the upper right hand corner of the fancy stationary she wrote *May Fourteen* in a flourish, and then stopped.

The date was poignant.

Tomorrow it would be exactly a month since the *Titanic* sank. A month ago that Jelee was thrown into her life, and in that short time Olivia had become more than attached, she loved the child dearly. Olivia fingered the black bow tie of her white blouse with her left hand, and began to write with her right.

Dear Nathan, the nib scratched across the paper as she started to tell her brother everything that happened, but couldn't. Instead, she tried to be light and airy and tell him about her life including Jelee.

Jelee's bubbly laughter floated in from outside, distracting her. Olivia stood, and after smoothing the wrinkles in her pink and black striped skirt, she went to the French doors and looked out.

Jelee, wearing a green dress and white pinafore, was trying her best to get a red hoop to roll, but Sparks was constantly leaping at it or through it, causing the toy to crash onto its side. Olivia couldn't help but smile as Jelee wagged a finger at Sparks, scolding him. Sparks instantly rolled onto his back, his front paws dangling, his body practically coming off the ground as he squirmed. The little girl squatted down and rubbed the dog's belly.

Jelee would sometimes talk to the adults, but mainly answered what was asked of her. The newspaper story that appeared weeks back about Jelee had brought out many who hoped to be a relative. One couple even insisted she was their poor sister's child, and were so convincing Olivia started to let them take her. Luckily, Jelee had put up a fight, screaming and kicking, saying, *"No-no-no, 'Livia, no!"* So much so, that when Olivia said she needed to have their story about their sister investigated, they took off and never returned. And they were just one of many. Some wanted a child to exploit, while others just wanted a child. It became so bad, whenever there was a knock on the door, Jelee immediately ran upstairs to hide in her room.

Paddy Riley, the reporter who had written the article and taken such lovely pictures of Jelee, had dropped by to see if anyone claimed her. He suggested a follow-up story, but Olivia refused, they had tried once, and that was enough. Olivia would have tried on her own to find more information, but with only two names to go on, and neither one of those matching the *Titanic's* manifest, it had become nigh on impossible.

Olivia could smell the delicate Jasmine scent preceding her mother's soft steps. Turning around, she watched her mother pulling on white gloves as she breezed toward her. Her hat, wide-brimmed and midnight blue canted at a jaunty angle. She was tall and graceful in her blue, lightweight duster for traveling.

"Mother, you're lovely. Going out?" Olivia pasted on a smile. She turned back to check on Jelee, and peered through the glass squares of the doors.

"You've forgotten this is my Women's Charity meeting day." Merilee dipped her head to look outside. "Well, it was another night of the entire household being startled awake by the girl's screaming for somebody named Casey."

Olivia turned to her mother. The past month hadn't been easy for Olivia either. Jelee's plaintive cries woke her up more often than not.

"Yes, Mother, I know, and I'm sorry. But think of poor little Jelee, so frightened, still living the nightmare of it all. I have my family, she doesn't. She's lost everything but her doll. Put yourself in her place. Please, Mother, can't you find some compassion for her?"

Merilee clucked her tongue. "There is none to be found when one loses sleep. You need to discourage the child from crawling into bed with you. She should stay in her own room."

Olivia thought about Jelee standing next to her bed, hiccupping from crying, and knew there was nothing else she could do but pull the child's trembling body into her arms and kiss away her tears.

"How could I possibly send her back to sleep alone when she's so disturbed?"

"Don't get too attached to her. It's time you let her go."

Smarting at her words, Olivia turned back to the window. Jelee was still playing with Sparks. "Go? Where am I supposed to let her go to? An orphanage? You know how I feel about that."

"It's out of the question for you to adopt her. I'll ask around at my charity meeting. Maybe someone will know of couples wanting children. The longer she stays here, the more attached you're becoming to her. It isn't a good thing, Olivia, not good at all." She turned to leave and Olivia fell in step beside her.

"Mother, think about it. What harm could it do to have her become part of our family? We could give her a good education. Father's fond of her. And...well...I love her dearly."

Merilee stopped shy of the front door that Hugh held open for her. "She's an immigrant. We can't understand half of what she's saying. I doubt she'll ever lose her undesirable accent. This is nothing I want for our family, to raise someone else's child. I doubt she'd ever be accepted into our circles. Why, I'd rather give her to Mrs. Lippencott—"

"You make her sound like a piece of furniture to be given away," Olivia said in anger. Why did her mother have to live by societies rigid rules? Olivia hated them, hated the thought of giving Jelee away, and knew she couldn't do it. She'd thought a lot about getting her own house so she could raise Jelee. She didn't care one bit if adopting Jelee would put her mother in a dead faint.

"The answer's no, Olivia. Not under my roof." Merilee smiled at Hugh and started past him. "Let's go, Hugh. I'm going to be late for my meeting."

Olivia stood on the porch and watched them leave. The car slowly traversed the long driveway, but stopped at the gate and stayed there longer than necessary. Trying to see what was happening, she thought she saw a man walking away from the car. Probably someone lost and asking directions. After the car turned onto the street, Olivia closed the door.

Distraught about their conversation, Olivia went back inside the study and watched the unsuspecting child romping with Sparks. Suddenly, Jelee came to an abrupt stop. Her head cocked to one side as she stared toward the tall, dense, clipped yew hedge surrounding the back yard. Sparks started barking and tore out in the direction Jelee was staring at. For a brief moment, Olivia thought she saw a man in a bowler hat, right where the tall, wooden gate separated the hedge, and right where Sparks was now raising a ruckus.

Olivia jerked open the French doors and quickly stepped outside. "Jelee!" she called out, and lifting her skirt, took off running. She rushed past a white-faced Jelee and hurried to the gate.

"Who's out here?" Olivia quickly opened the heavy latch and stepped out onto the sidewalk. "Sparks, stay!" she commanded, but the fearless little terrier streaked past her.

He took off down the sidewalk where trees formed a canopy of dark shadows and glittering sunlight.

"Oh—you darn dog. Sparks—come back here!" She had no choice but to go after him. She scanned the area, noticing several men briskly walking along. Another across the street was climbing into a car that the driver was cranking. None of them wore black bowlers.

Sparks started yelping. Worried that he'd been injured, Olivia rushed around the corner to see Sparks scampering toward her. The black fur of his side wore what looked to Olivia like a muddy boot print.

She pointed inside the gate. "Sparks, get your behind home—right now!" Sparks cut his bulbous eyes up at her then back down the sidewalk from where he'd come from. He barked, his hackles standing stiff.

"Inside, Sparks," she ordered and stomped her foot for good measure. Olivia started to follow Sparks but stopped when she stepped on a rolled up newspaper. Curiosity had her picking the paper up and unrolling it. On the front page was the picture of Jelee and the article Paddy Riley had written. Olivia's name as a contact person and her address circled in pencil. This was no fluke. The person who was trying to get past the gate was after Jelee.

Unsettled, Olivia stared at the long green hedge surrounding the property and edging the sidewalk. A squirrel scolded from a nearby tree branch, and birds flitted around. Her skin prickled as if someone was watching her and she couldn't get behind the gate fast enough.

While forcing the rusty bolt back in place, she reminded herself to have the lock replaced with a better one.

Sparks's short nose plastered against the ground as he sniffed along the thick bush. He lifted his leg to pee, and then continued to follow the hedge until he disappeared around the front of the house.

Jelee was nowhere around. Olivia paused next to the tall fountain with a statue resembling Aphrodite. Water cascaded out of the statue's urn to splash into a large circular basin. Wind blew through the trees, rustling the leaves, raising the flesh on her arms. The call of birds, the noise beyond the yard, the dark shadows in the garden now felt menacing. Even the sun's bright warmth couldn't dispel her apprehension.

Olivia picked up Jelee's doll. The doll, treasured, and given by a father who had no doubt drowned, was never far from Jelee's sight. To leave her behind showed the depths of Jelee's fright. Olivia, knowing exactly where to find Jelee, headed inside.

Jilleen squirmed under her bed until she reached the wall. Her mouth opened trying to gulp in air. Ah…no…she started crying, Uncle Sam had found her, called her name, and waved at her to come to the gate. When she refused, he'd reached over and tried to unlock the bolt.

She remembered the big ship, her brother Casey screaming at her to run from Uncle Sam—he'd killed someone. For sure, she'd run away before she'd let Uncle Sam get her. But what if he hurt Olivia? She wouldn't be able to stand it if anyone hurt Olivia.

Should she tell what Casey told her Uncle Sam did on the big ship? She hadn't promised Casey not to. For now, she thought it best to keep silent. She wondered about her brother, did he make it off the ship? She thought maybe so. Casey could take care of himself, he certainly took care of her. Even at Grandmum Ina's he was always there for her. Casey was smarter than anyone she knew. She wondered where her mam was. Why didn't she come for her after her picture was in the newspaper? Maybe Mam didn't get on a lifeboat after all.

Jilleen's stomach hurt. She didn't understand why any of this happened.

The door opened and she could see Olivia's shoes flicking the hem of her black and pink striped skirt. The next thing she knew, Olivia was on her knees and peering under the bed at her. As always, seeing Olivia's kind eyes and nice smile calmed Jilleen.

"There you are. Are you all right?" Olivia said with relief.

The girl nodded making Olivia grin. She urged her to come out from hiding. "Would you like to have lunch with me? I think cook has made an apple pie just for you."

Jelee squirmed out from under the bed. Olivia, still on her knees put her hands on Jelee's arms. She found the child's transformation remarkable. Her cheeks were starting to plump out and turn rosy. She scowled less, and if Olivia could keep Jelee from being frightened to death, her nerves would settle, allowing her to live like a normal child.

"Jelee, listen to me." She tucked a brown curl behind Jelee's ear. "I will never let anyone hurt you, do you understand?" Getting a slow nod, Olivia continued, "But someday, and I hope it's soon, you're going to have to tell me your last name, your parents' names, and all about your life in Ireland. As I have told you before, if you don't, neither I, nor anyone else can find out who you are. Did you see who was at the gate just now?"

Jelee shook her head, her brow pushed down in a frown. "Nay."

Disappointed and wondering if Jelee was telling the truth, Olivia let out a mock groan. "Well, I've got to get off my knees, this floor hurts." She got to her feet and walked Jelee over to the rocking chair next to the tall window.

Olivia situated the child on her lap and watched as she leaned forward to stare out the window, searching the backyard. Appearing to be satisfied no bogyman was out there, Jelee settled back against Olivia's bosom. Olivia's feet sent the chair rocking and the antique rungs squeaking a soothing tempo. Inside, Olivia was strung taunt.

"Jelee, did you know the man who threw you off the big ship?" To her disappointment, Jelee's little face closed up and a glimmer of fear filled her eyes.

Give her time, Olivia told herself, *don't be so anxious.* But after what just happened at the gate, she wondered if Jelee's being tossed over the side of the ship was to save her, or to kill her.

And that wasn't all she was thinking about. Albert Flynn wore a bowler, a black bowler.

Sam McShane, attired in a new store-bought suit of brown linen, loudly whistled while strolling down the sidewalk. He'd just come from the elevated train that ran from the Upper West Side to Greenwich. He'd give Manhattan some credit for its transportation system, and having traveled the City, he knew it well enough to know the Williams's tenement building was just a notch above the slums of the Lower East Side.

He acted like a man of leisure, but his mind whirled. Things were going great. He'd just been to the fancy house where his niece lived, and close enough he'd almost had her if it wasn't for that stupid looking dog. Finding Casey was a different matter. He kept going back to the old abandoned area where he thought the boys lived. He watched and waited, but the opportunity to grab Casey hadn't happened, not yet anyway. At least he now had his thumb on both kids.

He'd also met by pure happenstance, the grand dame herself, the Missus Marsh, all hoity-toity and chauffeured in a Studebaker limousine. He'd purposely stepped out in front of the car as it started to exit from the driveway. The wide-eyed driver brought the car to a jolting halt to keep from hitting him. Sam had minded his manners and doffed his new hat at the lady in the backseat, before walking away. Her resemblance to her daughter was uncanny, older but with a dignified presence the rich had about them.

He pulled out his solid-gold pocket watch, also stolen from the Titanic, glad it wasn't on the bottom of the ocean along with its owner. Plenty of time to drop by a drugstore and get more laudanum for Darlene, and then just enough time to go past Donald's apartment to see if he'd returned home yet. Not that he wanted to see him. His brother had been gone over three weeks, and he just wanted to keep tabs on the bloke's whereabouts.

Sam laughed out loud at thoughts of Donald up in Halifax trying to find the bodies of his family, and at all the corpses he probably had to wade through. Let Donald be heartsick for a change, just like he'd been for so long, wanting, and desiring Darlene. Now, he, Sam, had it all, or would just as soon as he finished up here. How convenient Donald thought his family dead, and would no longer be looking for them. Oh…aye, sunken ships silenced lips.

He paused in front of a drugstore with a large wooden mortar and pestle sign outside. The store was not too far from Donald's place. Maybe it was time for a change. Go to a different druggist with a new prescription for Lillian Flynn. The bell peeled as he opened the door and sidestepped to allow several customers out.

With a purpose, he made his way down an aisle toward the back of the store and the druggist who was busy working. He paused next to the counter and waited patiently finally clearing his throat, getting the man's attention.

"Sorry, didn't see you there." The elderly druggist approached.

The druggist smile faded to one of surprise. He stared at Sam, making Sam wonder if he needed to wipe his nose. "Ah…that's fine, aye. You'll be findin' me in no hurry. 'Tis a grand day. I need this filled." Sam handed over the forged prescription. He was proud of his abilities to sign the doctor's name to the little slips of paper. When the man kept staring at him, he finally asked, "Is me face manky…em dirty?"

"No…ah…no, sorry. I didn't mean to stare," he said, and read the prescription. "For Lillian Flynn, right?"

"'Tis true, for Mrs. Flynn. Me poor wife's ill, hearin' and seein' things that aren't there. We were on the Titanic. I expect the ordeal made her go a little mad. I'm puttin' me hopes into the medicine. Maybe it will calm her down, make her well."

"On the Titanic? Then I must congratulate you on being saved." The druggist met Sam's gaze.

"Aye, one of the lucky few from second class, and with memories I'd rather be forgetting," Sam said. He pointed at the prescription still in the druggist hand.

The druggist cocked a white bushy brow at him. "Laudanum will not cure a sick mind. It will keep her drugged, sleepy, unable to function, and unable to overcome whatever is making her ill. But I'm sure this…ah…doctor…Shilling told you so, right?"

Inside, Sam seethed that the druggist had the gall to lecture him. However, instead of losing his temper, Sam made his face appear sad and drooped his shoulders. "Aye, he did. Me poor wife. I'm not sure what to do next. But if you'll fill that prescription, 'tis for certain I'll be doin' what the doctor says is best for her."

The conversation was finished for Sam. Wanting to look around the store, he started down the aisle, picking up merchandise and putting it back. Finally, he stopped at the perfume display, where he picked up a bottle of Payan's perfume. He lifted the delicate glass lid on each one, smelling, until he found the one similar to what Darlene wore. The scent when he kissed the soft flesh at the base of her throat that made his wanger stiff. Roses, that's it, roses. He took the perfume to the counter where the druggist had placed a brown bottle of laudanum.

"This as well," Sam said, and pulled out his billfold. He picked up his wrapped purchases. "What's the name of your store?"

"Johnston and Son. I'm Archibald Johnston." He held out his hand. "My son and I run it together. And your name, sir, I never asked. I apologize for being so rude…but you loo—"

"Nice to meet ya." Sam pumped the man's liver spotted hand. "My name's Flynn, Albert Flynn."

Young Joe Gillespie came ripping into the drug store. He'd found a nickel and intended to use it for an ice-cream soda and nothing was going to stand in his way. Hurrying toward the soda fountain with his usual zest, he plopped down on the nearest stool. He glanced at the mirror behind the counter and caught a side view of a tall man leaving. Not paying much attention to the customer, Joe's mind was on the treat he was about to have.

"Hello, Joe." The druggist approached with a smile that stretched his white mustache.

"Howdy, Mister Johnston." Joe looked up at the wall poster showing a frothy soda with ice cream dripping down its sides. He wanted one just like the picture.

"So, Joe, how's the job at Ryerson's?"

"Fair…fair. How about a chocolate soda with three scoops of ice cream?" He slapped his nickel on the counter and watched Mr. Johnston look at the coin and his raise his eyebrows in question.

The druggist shrugged and tossed the coin in the cash register drawer. "I think you're expecting a nickel to buy you a good ten cents worth of ice cream. But that's all right. For you, Joe, I'll make it work." He got busy making the treat Joe was salivating for. "Tell me, did you by any chance notice the man who just left here?"

Mr. Johnston placed the soda on the counter in front of Joe. Not only did it have *four* scoops of ice cream, he'd gone heavy on the chocolate.

"Sorta. Why, did he do something wrong?" Joe couldn't lick the sides of the glass fast enough to keep up with the spilling liquid. Giving up, he picked up the glass and downed a big portion of it, the soda dripped onto his shirt, the chocolate tasted sweet and delicious.

"No," Mr. Johnston answered. "But he looked enough like Donald that for a moment I thought Donald and Eldon had made it back from Halifax. He's even Irish. Didn't see him, huh?"

Joe swallowed a big bite of ice cream and shook his head. "Nope. Boy, this is good, Mister Johnston, tastes great."

"Why don't you call me Archibald? Save yourself some words?"

Joe grinned at the elderly druggist. He liked the old man who was as friendly as his son, Eldon. And Joe liked Eldon as much as he did Donald, well maybe not as much, but close. Besides a friend of Donald's was a friend of Joe's. "Not being disrespectful, how about I call ya Archie? Shorten it even more."

"That I could let you do." He chuckled. "I'm expecting Eldon and Donald back anytime. Eldon telegraphed yesterday to say they would be home today."

Joe could see sorrow on Archie's face, and his curiosity got the better of him. "Did Donald find his family?"

"No."

"Not a one of them?"

"None of them, Joe. And I expect we will need to handle Donald with extra kindness. I know when I lost my wife Myrtle Rose, my world stopped spinning. But for Donald to lose all three of his loved ones, I can't even imagine his grief."

Joe knew what it was like to be without a family. He wanted Donald to be happy. He owed Donald a lot, loved him like a father, and admired him even more. He drained his soda, and no longer able to enjoy the day, stood. "Expect I'll go now and wait for Donald at his flat. He asked me stay there. Maybe it's a good thing I am."

"I thought you were sleeping in the back room at Ryerson's."

Joe smiled and nodded, liking his good fortune of warm rooms instead of the cold abandoned building the gang had. "Both places. Some nights I crash at the store, others I stay with Donald. He asked me to stay at his place while he went to Halifax. Ya know, in case someone might drop by with news about his family."

"I see. Are you done delivering groceries for the day?"

"Yeah."

"Hold on, then. I have a newspaper article for you to give Donald." Archie left to get the paper.

While he was gone, Joe waited on the stool and began spinning the seat, his long skinny leg whipping it around. When it was going fast enough, he pulled his feet off the floor, the counter shot by in a dizzying whirl.

"Joe! Stop it before you drill that stool through the floor," Archie scolded.

Joe used his foot as a brake. Coming to a stop, he grinned at Archie.

"Here's the article. Make sure Donald gets it. Off with you now."

He accepted the paper, and unable to read very well, briefly glanced at the article which had a picture of a little girl and something about the *Titanic*. "Who's the girl?" Joe asked.

"She was on the Titanic. They put her picture in the paper hoping to find her parents. I don't want to leave no stone unturned. Donald should see this child's picture just in case she might be his daughter. I think she looks like him, and I couldn't live with myself if I tossed the paper before Donald had a chance to see it."

Joe folded the paper and stuck it under his armpit. He just wished things were different for Donald and remembered how happy he'd been about his family coming to America. He quickly went towards the door, smiling back at Archie who waved.

Sam smirked at the five-story brick building Donald lived in. Skinny alleyways ran on each side of it and clotheslines with flapping clothes drying in the wind crisscrossed from building to building looking like the flags on ships. A woman on the third floor wearing a brown headscarf hung out her window and reeled in her clean wash.

Once inside the building, he read the list of tenants' names. Donald lived on the top floor in 501. Easing up the stairs, he reached the door to Donald's. It was unlocked so he slowly let the door swing open.

He entered with caution and called out softly, "Donald?"

The place was small and clean, with a few articles of clothing scattered about. He picked up a kid's blue sweater and, wondering whom it belonged to, tossed it back on the floor. The worn, wine-colored sofa had a blanket on it, wadded up like it had been hastily tossed aside. A large wooden rocker was positioned next to a small end table.

He went into the bedroom. The bed with its simple head and footboard, made him gloat. Darlene would never share this bed with Donald—never. A new rosary for Darlene draped from the headboard, blue in color with a silver cross made him burst out laughing. In his humor, he accidentally knocked over a bottle on the dresser. He picked the bottle up and saw it was the same kind of perfume he'd just purchased for Darlene. As he held the delicate bottle, the rage started inside of him like white heat. He threw the bottle hard across the room shattering it against the wall. Glass tinkled onto the floor. Perfume streaked in floral trails down the blue paint.

"Donald! Donald—are ya home?" a young male voice called.

The smell of roses flooded the room.

Sam hid behind the bedroom door.

"Who's in there? Donald?"

Hearing glass break, Joe put the newspaper down on the sideboard. The bedroom door was open but he couldn't see if Donald was in there. He edged close to the door. The floorboards squeaked beneath him. He peered inside and saw perfume oozing down the wall. The smell of roses was overpowering.

"Donald?" he said in a quivering voice.

His mouth went dry as he stepped inside the room, his eyes still on the wall. He felt movement behind him and reacted by putting his hands up in self-defense. A heavy blow against the back of his head drove him to the floor.

Chapter Ten

Donald's mouth dropped open at the sight of Joe sprawled out on his bedroom floor. He rushed to the kid's side and dropped to his knees. "Joe!" he exclaimed and turned him over with care. Donald's gut restricted at the sight of the kid's chalky white face, he prayed the lad would be all right.

He gently shook him. "Joe?"

The lad's eyelids fluttered open. "Donald?" He appeared disoriented. Joe started to rise but Donald stopped him.

"Don't move. What happened to ya? Are ya hurt?"

Joe pointed to the back of his head. "Yeah, I was hit right here."

Donald ran his fingers through the kid's dark hair, feeling his scalp, finding a good sized lump.

"Ah…good, at least yer not bleedin'. Whatever it was hit ya hard, lad. Here, let me help ya up." He put an arm around Joe's boney shoulders and helped him to sit on the side of the bed. "Better?"

Joe nodded.

Donald offered to get a wet cloth. "Stretch out if ya get dizzy," he ordered. He went out to the kitchen and put a washcloth under the spigot.

Upon his return he placed the cold cloth against Joe's bump, and then had Joe hold the rag in place. "Keep that against your scalp for a while, it should take the swelling' down. Feelin' any better?"

"Yeah, sure."

"Can ya tell me what happened here?" Donald sat next to him.

Joe made a feeble attempt to grin. "Well, I had a soda at Johnston's. Archie told me you'd be home today. Anyway, I came here to wait for ya. When I stepped inside the place, I heard a loud sound in your bedroom, so I came in here. Perfume was leakin' down the wall. The next thing I know—bam—I'm whacked." He snapped his fingers.

"Someone was in me home? I don't have anythin' to steal. Strange, aye?"

Unsettled that a stranger had come into his home, Donald walked around the bed. The bottle of perfume he'd bought for Derry was lying in splinters on the floor. All that was left was a piece of the stopper and the label, a profile of a pretty woman. The smell was strong, overpowering, and he fought for control, fought to keep his grief at bay, fought against the scent that was Derry's favorite, and fought to keep Joe from seeing his grief.

"I best be cleanin' this up." And not waiting for Joe's reply, he got out the broom and dustpan and took a wet soapy rag with him back into the bedroom. He swept up the shards of glass. He scrubbed the wall and the floor trying to wipe away the scent and memories he no longer could abide. At least the perfume wouldn't be around as a reminder.

Joe got to his feet and held onto the footboard. "Maybe he was looking for food and I surprised him."

"Yer makin' sense, Joe. What else could anyone want in here? I don't understand about the perfume thrown. Ya probably kept them from stealin'."

With Joe following him, he went into the kitchen and lifting the checkered curtain covering the pipes under the sink, emptied the dustpan into the garbage can.

They both went into the living room where Donald took off his suit coat and hung it on the hat rack next to the door. Unbuttoning his black vest, he plopped down on the sofa where he loosened his tie and pulled the black shiny material from around his neck.

"How'd it go for ya while I was gone?" he asked, rolling his neck to make it pop.

Neither one wanted to bring up the inevitable, that Donald's family was lost to him.

Joe shrugged and took the chair facing him. "Fine. Nothing went on." His brow furrowed as he viewed Donald with question-filled eyes.

Donald felt compelled to say, "'Tis all right, Joe. I think Archie must have told ya I didn't find me wife and children's bodies. So, it's there to gnaw at me forever. But I'll get by, somehow."

Joe pushed his hair out of his eyes.

The both of them sat there not saying a thing. And Donald wondered if this was how it was always going to be. Were people going to shy away from saying anything, knowing if they did they were opening up his grief, forcing him to live it, think it again?

"Oh, I forgot!" Joe exclaimed. "Archie sent ya this, said to make sure ya got it." He went over to the sideboard and began searching for something. "I put it right here," he said slapping the wooden top, "right next to the picture of yer family. Ah…gosh, Donald, Archie sure wanted ya to have it. Funny it's gone." He leaned down and looked on the floor and all around, his face wearing a puzzled frown.

"What was it, Joe?"

Joe scratched his head. "A newspaper article. Archie showed it to me. It had a picture of a little girl from the Titanic. Archie said they were trying to find her parents or anyone that knew her. He really wanted ya to see it. I'm sorry it's lost."

"Ah…don't give it another thought, aye? I'll find out about it from Archie. Right now, I'm going to try to rest."

A soft knock on his door had Donald going to answer it. He opened the door to see a tall middle-aged woman. She was dressed in black from head to toe, but her hat, a wide brimmed fluff of black and purple feathers belied her need to wrap herself totally in mourning. A mixture of brown and gray strands of hair escaped beneath her hat. Her eyes, direct and the color of storm clouds, scrutinized him.

"Mr. Donald McShane?" she asked in a British accent.

"Aye," Donald answered, wondering what she wanted.

Joe came to stand next to him.

"I'm Vivian Denbury." She hesitated. "If you don't mind, I would rather not have a conversation standing in the hallway."

Donald felt his face grow warm, and said with haste, "Of course ye don't, but I don't know you."

"And you never will if you're going to leave me out here." Uninvited, she brushed by him and came to a stop in the middle of his living room. She took a moment to look around. "My, but it does smell pretty in here. I expect a rose bush to be growing right here in the living room." Not waiting to be asked, she made herself comfortable on the sofa where she removed her gloves and then situated her purse on her lap. She left her hat in place.

"Mrs. Denbury, this is Joe Gillespie." Donald pointed at Joe who simply acknowledged the stranger with a brisk nod.

"I'm Miss. Denbury. It's nice to meet you, young man."

"Ah…Miss. Denbury, can I offer you some tea?" Donald asked.

And seeing her nod and smile, Donald sent Joe to start the kettle. Still wondering why she was here, Donald sat beside her.

"Mr. McShane." She opened her purse, took out a clipped newspaper article, and handed it to him. "I cut this out of the Brooklyn newspaper listing the dead from the Titanic and showing pictures of those who were not claimed in Halifax. Not a very pleasant sight I might add, but totally necessary."

She tapped a long slender finger against the lone picture. Donald's eyes immediately went to the dead woman found with Derry's health card. Somehow the photographer had managed to make her appear asleep and take away the ravages of death.

Vivian Denbury continued. "After reading this and getting over my shock, I contacted the authorities in Halifax to let them know this was my niece Lillian. A…Inspector Mulhall up there…suggested I contact you."

"Aye, I was there when this picture was taken. 'Tis sorry I am for your loss." He peered at her, seeing sorrow and unanswered questions.

"That's what the Inspector told me." Her composure faltered and she pulled a lacy handkerchief from her purse and wiped at her tears.

Donald, perplexed and uncomfortable, managed to put his hand on her shoulder and tried to give her comfort.

After a few minutes, she took a deep breath. "I'm sorry about that. I vowed not to break down while I was here. But, Lillian, her name is…was Lillian Denbury, and she's my brother's only child. After my brother passed away, I asked Lillian to come live with me in Brooklyn. Lillian was excited about coming to New York, and even more about sailing on the Titanic."

The teakettle let out a shrill whistle. Joe, who sat listening, was quick to run into the kitchen and snatch it off the burner. He poked his head around the doorway. "Miss. Denbury do you take sugar?"

"Please, two lumps."

"Hope ya don't take milk 'cause Donald don't have none."

"That's quite all right," she said in a soft voice.

Joe came from the kitchen, holding a steaming cup, watching where he walked, careful not to spill it. He handed it to Miss Denbury. She accepted the plain, white china cup and saucer. After blowing on the hot liquid for a few seconds, she gingerly took a sip and placed the tea on the small end table.

"Thank you, Joe," she said.

"Yer welcome." Joe tossed a well-mannered smile at Donald and went back into the kitchen.

"Ah…Mr. McShane, I suppose you're wondering why I've come here to talk with you about Lillian."

"Aye, my thoughts exactly. I'm wondering where I fit into all of this?" Donald said, and then watched with interest as once again she pilfered inside her purse and took out a letter.

"Inspector Mulhall suggested I talk to you before I send this letter to him. He wanted you to read it. Lillian sent me this letter from England about three weeks or so before she sailed." She removed the letter from the envelope and handed it to Donald.

A floral smell of some kind wafted up from the paper.

Dear Aunt Viv,

How excited I am to be coming to live with you. I thought this month would never pass, and now it's April and I will be sailing soon. I have traveled to Southampton to await the ship. At the alleged speed the Titanic is supposed to travel, perhaps the ship will bring me to your doorstep long before this letter reaches you. The hotel here is a bore, and I can't wait to see Manhattan, Brooklyn, and all the exciting places you have told me about New York.

I miss father terribly. His death has left me quite bereaved. I am bringing you the family photographs he wanted you to have.

But that's not all my news, Auntie. I have met a dashing handsome man and although I pray more comes of it, I'm afraid it is not to be. He is sailing on the Titanic, but doesn't plan to tarry in New York. Alas, he plans to continue across the continent to California. He has treated me to the theater and dinners.

As the Titanic docks, look for my grin and hearty wave, and of course I'll be wearing the wonderful hat with bright red feathers you sent me.

Your loving niece,

Lillian

Donald rubbed his mouth with his fingers, thinking. Did Derry lose her health card on the ship? Was that the answer? Maybe Lillian Denbury found it? There were a lot of unanswered questions popping to the surface, and he wanted answers.

"Sure'n yer niece never said the man's name?" he asked, and was disappointed when she shook her head. He had another question to ask, one he didn't want to ask, but had to. "Ah…did the inspector tell you that yer niece was…er…strangled?"

Her mouth quivered. "Yes, he did. And that's so puzzling. Why would anyone want to harm her? I've always thought of my niece as a sweet girl. Of course Lillian was a mere child when I left England. But we corresponded regularly." She dabbed at her moist eyes and wiped her nose. "Do you think she suffered much?"

He tried to ease her grief. "She looked quite peaceful when I saw her. Please, Miss Denbury, try puttin' it from yer mind."

"That's impossible to do." Rifling through her purse, she took out a small business card and gave it to him. "You can reach me here at my millinery shop. Lillian was supposed to learn the trade and help me out."

Donald read her card. "Yer shop is called, *The Vexing Veil*?"

"Yes, it is. You see, a veil not only sticks to a woman's mouth, it sticks to ones eyelashes, and in general most women find the veil most vexing. But, fashion always rules over comfort." She stowed her letter in her purse and snapped the clasp shut. "I must go now. Please come for a visit sometime, luv."

Donald saw Vivian Denbury to the door. Her niece's letter was engrained in his mind, more for what it didn't say than for what it did.

After what had happened in her backyard today, Olivia called Paddy Riley at the Times newspaper and insisted he come over immediately. Myron had dropped by for an impromptu visit and she was glad he had.

They were in the drawing room where Paddy's drink went untouched, and Olivia's tea had turned cold. Myron slowly drank his bourbon, listening.

Olivia, agitated and unnerved, stood next to Paddy Riley, and thumped the newspaper she'd found at the gate. "I'm telling you, Mr. Riley, the person at the gate was after Jelee. This newspaper article you wrote proves it. I thought maybe I was jumping to conclusions, but this changed my mind." She handed the newspaper to the reporter. "Also, Jelee took off running as if she was frightened to death. She hid under the bed and I had to coax her out."

"Did you see the man?" Paddy asked.

Olivia shook her head. "Only his hat—a black bowler. I think I spotted his arm reaching over the gate."

"Thinking you saw something is not actually seeing it." Paddy squinted at Olivia. "But this would make one concerned." He tapped her address that had been circled. "Maybe it was a delivery man, or a well meanin' stranger coming to answer your ad?"

"Fiddle-faddle. That was not a delivery man. And if he was a well-meaning stranger like you say, why didn't he come to the front door like all the others asking for Jelee?"

"Hmmm…it does sound like he was going to bypass the household and take her right out of the yard," Paddy said.

"My sentiments exactly," Olivia said, happy Paddy agreed with her for a change. "Albert Flynn wore a bowler." She stopped pacing long enough to cast a heated glare at both Paddy and Myron. "I know—I know hundreds of men wear bowlers, including you, Mr. Riley. But there's only one Albert Flynn, and I strongly believe he's the man I saw toss Jelee off the Titanic."

"Perhaps you're imagining it all?" Myron finished off his bourbon.

Olivia bristled and said, "I can't believe you just said that. I'm not one to ever imagine anything as dire as this. And…you weren't on the ship when I confronted Albert Flynn. You didn't see the malicious grin on Flynn's face, or the look in his eyes as if I was daring to uncover things about him." She put her balled fist on her hip and stared him down.

"You've been on edge ever since you got off the ship. Try thinking it through. No sense getting all worked up." Myron tried to placate her and made the situation worse.

"Myron, I'm not on edge!" she retorted. "And I—"

Merilee breezed into the drawing room interrupting Olivia, and forcing Myron to pop to his feet.

"Goodness me, I didn't think my charity meeting was ever going to end. Mrs. Lippencott told me you were in here." She smiled at Myron, and raised her brow in a questioning arch at Paddy. "Olivia? What's happened? Why is Mr. Riley here? Certainly you're not going to have another article printed about Jelee, bringing more riffraff to our doorstep?"

"Of course not, Mother. I've asked Paddy Riley here as a friend, not as reporter. Mr. Riley has offered his services to help me find Jelee's family. He has great connections. And after what happened today, I need his help even more."

Merilee elegantly held out her hand for the reporter. "Welcome to my home again. I hope you can find Jelee's loved ones."

Paddy, dressed in a bright green and orange plaid suit, accepted Merilee's offered hand. "Sure'n I'm pleased to be seein' ya again. And if ya don't mind me sayin' so, I can see where yer daughter gets her beauty," he said, and grinned.

Merilee returned Paddy's smile as Myron approached. "Myron, how good to find you here."

Myron took her hands and kissed both cheeks. "Yes, I had business at Walter's bank so thought I'd drop by to see Olivia. We were listening to Olivia's concerns."

Merilee went over to the serving tray and poured herself a miniscule amount of sherry. "Olivia, you were saying something happened here today that made you need Mr. Riley's help? Would you mind telling me what's going on? And please, sit down, Olivia. Your pacing gets on my nerves." Merilee settled onto the sofa next to Myron, and placed her sherry on the decorative table in front of her.

Paddy moved to another empty chair.

Olivia, unable to sit, remained standing and told her mother what had happened and her suspicions about Albert Flynn.

"When was the man here?" Merilee asked.

Noticing the puzzled frown her mother wore, Olivia replied, "Today, not long after you left. Why?"

"No reason, really," Merilee answered. What does this Albert Flynn look like?"

Olivia's mind went back to the Carpathia, of staring Albert Flynn in the face. "He's tall with black wavy hair, Irish accent. I would imagine most women think he's handsome. Too me, he's dark and sinister," she said and continued, "not to mention those eyes of his. They were the color of whiskey, feral like. He has a way of staring right through a person." Her skin goose bumped and she shuddered.

"And you think the man here today is the same man who tossed Jelee off the ship? That he was possibly here to take her?" Merilee reached for her crystal glass and took a dainty sip of her sherry.

"Yes, I do, Mother. And if the man here today is Albert Flynn, I want Mr. Riley to help find him before he returns." She almost told them about Donald McShane and his resemblance to Albert Flynn, but didn't. One man at a time to investigate was enough.

Chapter Eleven

Under Frankie Doyle's watchful eye, Casey emptied his pockets of stolen goods. His stash was pathetic. A battered pocket watch, and some coins he'd actually found on the street. Not much for a day's work, but he was still learning how to steal and keep his ears from being ripped off his head by a potential victim. Today, he'd been caught with his hand on a man's watch. The man had boxed his ears a good one while threatening to throw him into the dreaded *hoosegow.*

Jimmy Kelly dumped several billfolds and a leather pouch on the table. He picked up the pouch and gasped in surprise. "Well, fuck the money!" he blurted while dumping the contents on the table.

The boys watched as four silver dollars rained out and began rolling.

"Jeepers! We're rich!" Jimmy scooped up some of the silver dollars while Frankie reached out to catch the coins before they rolled off the table.

Frankie showed off one of the coins. "Looks like we're going to eat good for awhile…eh…guys."

"I was hopin' to buy shoes. We can all buy shoes, and still have plenty for food. Whaddya say? Ya guys want new shoes?" Jimmy urged while flipping a coin in the air.

"Yeah!" They all chorused.

Benny grabbed up a floral tablecloth from off the floor and wrapping it around his waist, started prissing around, acting goofy. "I'd like some new pants before I have to start wearing tablecloths and look like a girl. My ass is hangin' out the back of these." He dropped the cloth and turned around to wag his behind revealing a good-size hole in his knee pants where his grimy union suit showed through.

"Yeah, we all need new pants," Frankie said.

Jimmy agreed. "I say we get long legged pants. Think of it, Frankie, no more of these little boy knee-pants for you and I?"

Frankie grinned at Jimmy whose eyes were shiny with anticipation. "Yeah, Jimmy, grown-up duds for us." Frankie started coughing, a deep hacking sound, that took him awhile to control. He used his sleeve to wipe his tears.

They continued going through the other billfolds Jimmy had pilfered but there was little in them, a few bills, nothing much.

Benny took out his meager earnings paid to him by the newspaper for selling papers and placed it on the growing stack.

Casey felt bad. He was uncomfortable about stealing, hated doing it, but Frankie told him he'd either steal or get out. Being alone frightened him more than stealing. He liked the boys and needed what protection they offered. He hadn't seen Uncle Sam since the night the boys pelted him with bricks. But Uncle Sam could still be watching him. Uncle Sam was evil.

He'd learned by accident that Jilleen was alive and where she was. He was using the makeshift toilet, a smelly tin bucket they'd put in one of the other dilapidated apartment rooms. He was literally going to wipe his behind with a piece of newspaper when he spotted Jilleen's picture on the front page.

Just to know she'd survived being tossed from the ship made him giddy with happiness. He wanted to go and see Jilleen, let her know he was alive. Maybe Da read the article and went there to claim her. If so, then maybe he'd left his address with the people. Being a good reader, Casey read the month-old article and wrote down the address. Jilleen had given her first name, but seeing it written as Jelee, he'd chuckled and thought, *Ah, Jilleen, they can't even say yer name right.* Since the article was seeking information about his sister, he knew without a doubt that Jilleen had kept their pact of keeping promises, and not sharing secrets. Casey also figured if he'd seen the paper about her, so had his uncle.

Frankie shook his head at their good fortune. "Shoes and clothes it is."

"I think we'd better stop stealin' for a while," Jimmy said. "The fella I took this leather pouch from chased me. I thought he was going to catch me, but I ran in front of a trolley. He had to stop for it to pass." Jimmy picked up the paper checks he'd taken out of the money pouch and, without giving them a second glance, went to toss them in their slop bucket. Flies took to the air then settled on the bucket again.

"Could be. Where did ya steal this from?" Frankie asked.

Jimmy raised a ginger brow and said, "I've been goin' down to the financial district. Ya know, Wall Street, where the people think they're high and mighty. That's where I ran into this guy. I think he owns a cigar shop."

Frankie nodded. "Ya need to show Casey how to steal a watch without gettin' his ears boxed." Sniffing, he used the back of his hand for a handkerchief.

They all hooted at Frankie's suggestion.

Benny opened a can of peaches, and using his fingers, scooped one out before putting the can on the table. "I'm hungry, let's eat."

Casey wondered if Frankie would give him money for a new pair of shoes. He peeked down at his shoes where the toes turned up from their dunking in the ocean. His pants were in worse shape than Benny's. Casey didn't know if he should ask Frankie or not. Maybe he hadn't picked enough pockets to share in the goods.

As soon as he got his pocket watch back from Frankie, he had planned to go to the hoosegow as they called it and find his da. But now that he was a thief, he wouldn't be able to ask for their help. The boys had put fear in him about ever stepping foot inside the hoosegow. Frankie told him they'd arrest him the minute he did. How would the police know he was a thief if he didn't tell them, Casey had asked Frankie. Well if he wasn't recognized as a thief, just one look at him the coppers would know he was an orphan. For sure, they'd take him to an orphanage which was even worse than jail, or so Frankie said. Casey believed everything Frankie said.

Frankie had told Casey all about the gang. Frankie and Jimmy had started the gang years ago. It was funny because they started to pick the same pocket at the same time. That's how they met and formed a friendship becoming close as brothers. Benny wasn't part of the gang then. Other boys were. At one time the gang had about twenty boys in it, but they were long gone, having split for other boroughs, died, or been arrested.

Casey listened to his friends chatter on. For now they were happy, but he couldn't help but wonder what would happen to them. "Frankie, where did yer mam and da go?" Casey asked.

"I never knew my dad, only my mother. She put on a great show of cryin' and tellin' me she loved me. I asked if she *loved me* so much why she didn't feed me. Men came and went from my mother's bed. I thought I had a ton of uncles, but as I got older I realized she was a whore. No wonder I never knew my old man. Hell, he could have been anyone. She started coughin' a lot, getting real skinny, sick like. The men stopped comin' around.

"One day she didn't get out of bed. When I tried to wake her up, she was stone cold dead. I went to get the landlord. All he did was mutter about not gettin' his rent. Then he became nasty and said he wasn't paying for her burial and for me to get the hell out. Next thing I know I'm standin' in a graveyard for people who can't pay, lookin' down at a cheap pine box. Men with shovels told me to get lost, that I didn't need to see them toss the dirt in. I left and never went back. Don't think I could find her grave now anyways."

Jimmy's face took on a harsh look. "I was in an orphanage but ran away. I left behind a younger brother and two sisters cryin' so hard they couldn't talk. Don't know what happened to any of 'em. Never went back. Maybe they were adopted by someone nice."

"What about yer parents?" Casey asked Jimmy.

Jimmy pushed his hands into his pockets and rocked on his heels. "Don't know—don't care. We were dumped on our aunt's doorstep when I was nine. Wasn't there a month before she rounded us up and hauled us off to the orphanage." His theatrics about not caring didn't fool anyone.

Little Benny spoke up. "I was seven when my daddy left me and my little sister in an apartment we shared with the rats. I tried stealin' food to feed us. One day these tall men came bustin' in, sayin' we had to go to an orphanage. My sister was cryin' and askin' how will our daddy find us? I bolted out the door. They chased me, but couldn't catch me. I ran right into Jimmy. He brought me here to the gang.

"I knew my little sister was at the orphan asylum on seventy-third. Once in awhile I'd go stand by the fence to watch her playin' outside. Finally, no matter how long I waited, she no longer appeared. Don't know what happened to her." His gaze sought out each kid as his mouth settled into a sad slit.

Casey felt the boys sorrow. It was how he felt. But his sorrow couldn't begin to match theirs. They'd never known love like he had. His Da, Mam, and Grandmum. Jilleen. They'd all loved him and he loved them back.

Jimmy picked up one of the silver dollars and flipped it. "Enough of that shit. What say we go and have a hot meal tonight? I'm tired of eating canned this and canned that. I say steak and potatoes sound real good. Whaddya say, fellas, or what is it Casey calls us? *Boyos?* What do you say, boyos?"

Relieved, Casey knew he was going to be included in getting new clothing and eating good food. Casey liked Jimmy best of all. Jimmy was a good friend.

Chapter Twelve

The two o'clock sun beat down on the restive crowd forming around Olivia and her group of suffragettes. Chatting amongst themselves, the women, two dozen in number, went to pick up their picket signs and flyers.

Olivia, waiting to start her speech, tugged at her high-necked white linen blouse. Uncomfortable, she discreetly unbuttoned the top two buttons, but found no relief. She stood next to her dark green Model T Runabout that had the top removed. The Ford was last year's birthday gift from her father.

The sun winked off the chrome in blinding intensity as Olivia climbed inside to stand on her car's back seat. She glanced around at the mob of women, children, men, and certainly recognized the riff-raff paid to heckle her.

Directly behind Olivia was her target, Lapaglia's Clothing Factory and Bruno Lapaglia. Her speech was aimed at the man's factory and his nefarious work practices.

A fellow suffragette with bright red hair blew loudly on her whistle to quiet everyone down. "Ladies and gentlemen, please accept the flyers being passed out to you. Come hear us speak tonight at the Union Hall."

The suffragettes quickly circulated flyers advertising the speech set for that evening. On the flyers, *Men especially invited*, was printed in bold black lettering. Some people read the announcements word for word, while some, mostly the men, immediately balled the paper up and tossed it to the ground. Others were folded and put into purses.

Olivia held up a large wooden sign with a magazine article affixed to it. The page taken from the *April twenty-seventh Woman's Journal* was a cartoon of the *Titanic* with a sea creature's tentacles reaching for the *Titanic*. Each tentacle was labeled, *Child Labor*, *White Slavery*, *Sweatshops*, *Firetraps*, and a variety of other names. Another ship coming to the rescue had its smoke stack belching the words, *Votes for Women*.

Olivia spoke in a loud carrying voice. "The caption under this cartoon reads, *'When women cannot vote, the ship of state is like the steamship Titanic with only half enough lifeboats.'*" She paused for affect, her gaze scanning the crowd. "I was on the Titanic. And since this cartoon came out just fifteen days after it sank, at first I was offended and appalled. But the more I thought about it, the more I could see the correlation between the two. Yes, it is cruel to use such a horrendous disaster to point out a cause, but is the Titanic's disaster any worse than what we are doing to our children?

"Death and maiming of children in factories each year far exceeds the death tally of the Titanic. I can guarantee you Senator Smith is making sure all *ships* in the future will be equipped with enough life vests and life boats to save each and every person aboard. Why don't we do the same for our children? Save them, give them a life vest by keeping them out of the factories."

The line of suffragettes held up bold signs printed with, *Save Our Children, Factory Inspections Needed, Abolish White Slave Traffic, Pass Child Labor Laws.* They shook them furiously at the crowd.

Paddy Riley, doing his job, moved around the crowd. His photographer was taking pictures.

Olivia put her sign down on the seat. Wisps of hair stuck to the back of her neck, tickling, and she reached up to remove her hat and drop it on the seat. Despite the round, dark glasses hiding her eyes, she still squinted against the glaring sun.

She spread her arms wide as if to embrace the crowd. "People, the reason I am here today is to bring to your attention the exploitation of children being worked to death in factories such as the one right behind me." For emphasis she turned and pointed to Lapaglia's Clothing Factory where children as young as nine were forced to work thirteen hours a day. "Children don't belong in factories, they belong in schools getting educated. They belong at home under a parent's supervision."

"Yeah, well who is going to put food on a poor mother's table, when a child is all she's got to send out and bring in a dime," one woman shouted at her.

"And what good is your child if he or she ends up dead? How will you spend your dime? If you are able bodied, then you need to go to work, the child would be better off staying home alone then sent to the likes of this place." Olivia could tell she hadn't pulled the women over to her side. This was a tough crowd, apparently depending on the factory.

Olivia watched with great interest as the owner, Bruno Lapaglia, came outside and listened to her protest. Short and balding, a no-neck ape of a man, he wore a gray vest, and had his shirtsleeves rolled up past his elbows. He picked his teeth with a toothpick, and appeared to be bored with all the commotion.

While wishing to sic her suffragettes on the man, Olivia smothered her dislike for him, and instead met Lapaglia's narrowed gaze.

She spoke directly to him. "Your factory has children under the age of ten working in it. The children are running dangerous cutting equipment that can chop off fingers. These are jobs grown men should be doing, and getting paid much more than the forty-eight cents a day being paid. Why can't you understand this? By giving the job to a man instead of a child, it will make for better output."

She pointed directly at Lapaglia. "You! I'm talking to you."

All heads turned to where she pointed.

"You're the owner of this factory, right?"

He nodded, stepping a little closer, his dark eyebrows pulled down over even darker eyes. "I am and proud of it. Who do ya think made the blouse you're wearing?"

"Not anyone working in a factory like yours. I personally know who sewed this blouse, a woman who does her own work, and pays her staff of grown women fair wages."

"Do I hear ya sayin' you're rich enough to afford to have your clothes sewn in a private shop? Well not everyone can afford such luxuries. I suggest you take your expensive clothes, your loud mouth, your spinster friends with their signs, and get the hell away from my business."

"You cannot order me around." She fumed and turned to the crowd. "People, take a good look at Bruno Lapaglia and take a good look at your clothes. If they have a Lapaglia label you are wearing clothing made by a child. Think of those small fingers sewing and laboring for hours."

The vision Olivia painted was vivid, and from the shocked look on some of the women, she felt they were coming over to her side, starting to see her views.

A tall man walked out of the factory and, pushing through the throng, came to stand next to Lapaglia. The newcomer took off his dark suit coat and flung it over his right shoulder. He removed his cap to wipe his forehead on his white shirtsleeve. At first Olivia thought he was Albert Flynn, but he wasn't. Olivia recognized him from the night the Carpathia docked. She remembered his name, Donald McShane. He put his cap back on and bent his head to say something to Lapaglia. She couldn't believe he worked here for this…this…unscrupulous, insidious piece of scum. Her kind thoughts about Mr. McShane were replaced with instant dislike. He stood there chatting with Lapaglia like they were brothers or something. For a brief moment he made eye contact with her. His gaze was one of indifference.

Catcalls and cursing by the restless men in the crowd pulled her back to the job at hand and she quickly turned her attention back to her listeners.

"Read your flyers. We're having a rally tonight at the Union Hall. We need women to join our cause. Won't you please join us? Help us to put these deplorable factories out of business. You parents out there. What do you want for your child? A better life—or no life?"

A young woman, thin yet bosomy, poorly dressed and holding a baby, stepped up next to the car. "It's easy for you to say. Ya were probably born rich. I need my Jamie to work in the factory. I need him to bring home the money I can't."

"You seem able-bodied, why can't you work instead of Jamie?"

"Because I'm breast feeding his little sister."

Olivia started to retort, but something slammed against the right side of her head sending her glasses flying. Pain deep and cutting was the last thing she felt.

Donald was stunned to see a brick hit the woman's head and her crumple in the seat like a limp doll. Hearing gasps and screams from the crowd, he started for the fallen speaker.

Lapaglia grabbed his arm restraining him. "What are ya doing? Ya help that bitch you're out of a job."

In an instant Donald saw his income, food in the cupboard, and a roof over his head go with the way of Lapaglia's words. But Donald would stop to help an injured bird, certainly this woman was like that, delicate and wounded.

Having his fill of the man, Donald pushed his boss away. He spat out, "I'd help anyone hurt. She's bad off."

With Lapaglia shouting after him that he was fired, Donald ran toward the injured woman. A reporter along with a photographer was converging on the car at the same time. Donald jerked the back door open and tossed his jacket on the front seat. The woman was unconscious. She lay in disarray, half on and half off the seat, blood coursed down the right side of her face and neck, spreading bright red onto her blouse. Pictures were snapped, and Donald pulled her skirt down to modestly cover her knee-length drawers.

"Get off me back!" Donald ordered the photographer away.

He knelt close to the suffragette and placed his hand at the base of her throat. Satisfied to feel a strong pulse, he quickly grabbed a handkerchief from his hip pocket and parted her hair above her ear where blood was seeping out. The piece of brick lying next to her was a good size. She needed a doctor, quick. He pressed his handkerchief against the wound.

A redheaded suffragette, screeching like a wild bird, jumped onto the car's running board. "Olivia—Olivia, are you all right?" She leaned over to grab up the woman's limp hand, and rapidly patted it. "Oh my—the blood. Please help her—we have to get Olivia to a doctor." Her eyes widened. "Look out," she warned.

Too late, Donald was grabbed from behind and roughly shoved away. One of Lapaglia's men, a hired goon Donald disliked, started dragging the injured woman out of the car.

The suffragette on the car's running board descended on the man like an avenging angel and whacked his head with her sign. "Get away from her—you pig!" The wooden sign was lethal. "Leave her alone!" She pounded his head, forcing the thug to drop Olivia who now hung halfway out of the car. "Help me—they're trying to hurt Olivia," the woman yelled.

Bleeding from the side of his head, the man ducked away.

Donald fought his way back toward the injured woman's side. He'd almost reached her when Lapaglia rushed in front of him and pulled the woman to the ground with a hard thud. Donald grabbed Lapaglia by the shoulders, preventing him from doing her further damage.

"Bloody hell—Lapaglia! Stop this—it's wrong," Donald shouted.

Holding Lapaglia was like stopping a wild bull. He jerked his boss around to face him, trying to put a stop to the brawl. But Lapaglia stared through him and Donald recognized someone so intent on doing damage they're beyond reason. Donald drew his fist back to land a blow but someone grabbed his arm, stopping his punch.

All the suffragettes had joined in the fray.

A robust looking woman swung her sign at anything that moved. When she eyed Donald, he yelled out, "Darlin', I'm not the enemy." He pointed at Lapaglia's man. "Hit him."

Her chins bounced, as she took aim and busted her sign over the man's head.

Fists and signs were flying. Suffragettes were riding on men's backs, brutally beating them with their signs. Innocent bystanders got nailed. Male bystanders got a good look at lacy drawers and shapely legs. The cursing would have made a preacher blush, and shockingly, the women were doing most of it.

Someone landed a haymaker against Donald's eye and mouth, busting his lip. As pain exploded through his face, Donald hit the ground hard, skidding on his butt. Tasting the tang of blood, he swore the man used brass knuckles. He tried shaking it off, and popping to his feet, threw a knuckle-buster that sent the man sprawling. Donald clutched his hand, his bleeding knuckles stung. He headed straight for Lapaglia. Dropping the man with one hard blow, Donald stopped the fight and permanently ended his employment in Manhattan with one bone-crunching punch.

Shrill police whistles sounded in the distance.

A bystander yelled, "The coppers are coming."

Everyone scattered, all but the suffragettes standing around Olivia's car. They bled from cuts, their hats were askew, and blouses torn to reveal a peek at frilly chemises.

A heavy-set woman winked at Donald from where she sat on Lapaglia's chest. "Thank you for your help," she said, and blew a lock of hair out of her eye.

Donald drew in a deep breath. "Be sure ya tell the police this man…er…Lapaglia attacked…er…the woman giving the speech."

She nodded. Lapaglia groaned and raised his head but she popped him with her sign, knocking him out again.

Another suffragette, still breathing heavily from the fight, approached. "We don't have a lot of time to stand around talking. Can you take Olivia away from here?"

Surprised at the question, Donald shrugged. "Aye, I can take her to me place, 'tis close. Can ye drive this thing?"

"No," the suffragette said in a hurry. "I have to stay here and direct everything. Tell me where you live and I'll send a doctor over."

Donald gave her the needed information. He started to lift the wounded woman when the reporter ran over and helped place her on the back seat.

"I'll drive ya," the reporter offered.

Donald glared at the man. "Ya took the lass's picture while she was knocked out. Why should I let ya drive us anywhere?"

"Aye, I did, and Miss Marsh will no doubt give me what for when she sees it. But, it also will show how she was injured. I'm a friend of hers. Let's go." And not waiting for an answer, the reporter told his photographer to keep on taking pictures.

After cranking the car until it sputtered to life, Donald ran around and jumped in the back with the injured woman.

The reporter squeezed the bulbous horn, forcing people to scatter. They turned the corner just as a paddy wagon full of police arrived on the scene.

Still trying to catch his breath, Donald managed to rest the wounded suffragette's head on his lap. They'd called her Olivia. It suited her, he thought. He parted her hair above her right ear to check for damage. The cut was still bleeding, so he ripped the sleeve from his shirt and applied pressure.

"Is she all right?" Paddy tossed a quick glance over his shoulder.

"She's still bleeding," he said. "Ya need to hurry." He tongued his lip tasting the coppery tang of blood. His eye wasn't feeling too great either.

With Donald shouting the way from where he sat, the reporter sped down the street, honking his horn, gesturing at people to get out of the way.

"I'm Paddy Riley from the New York Times. I always cover Miss Marsh's speeches." He glanced over his shoulder and had the gall to grin. "This, I admit, is the best I've ever attended. What a brawl. Can't wait to get the story written up."

"I'm Donald McShane. Do I hear ya say you're going to be exposing Lapaglia's factory?"

"That I am, but it won't be easy. I'd bet on me poor mother's grave Lapaglia ordered the brick thrown at Miss Marsh."

"Well there's no denying that. Provin' it is a different matter. I live right there." Donald pointed at his apartment building.

Paddy brought the car to a rattling stop in front of the brick building. "What floor do you live on?"

"The fifth," Donald said.

Between the both of them, they were able to carry Olivia up the stairs and into Donald's home.

The cab pulled into a parking slot in front of a café with a dark green awning over the door. Merilee Marsh, dressed all in black, peered out the cab's window. She was in foreign territory, in an area called Little Italy. Men, women, and children moved along the sidewalk like a human river. Unwilling to risk finding another cab, she leaned forward. "Please wait here. I shouldn't be long at all."

The driver nodded but didn't bother to get out and open the door. Merilee, used to Hugh waiting on her, realized this driver was ill bred and lacked in social graces. Glaring at him, she opened the door and gathering her long skirt, stepped out. She was careful to pull the veil on her hat across her face.

She pushed through the crowd toward the restaurant. She paused in front of the large plate glass window with *Café* written in large, sweeping white letters. Peering through the letters, she could see a lot of activity going on inside. The establishment looked like one of those *Bohemian* places she'd heard about. She took a deep breath and opened the door to step inside the small, unpretentious room.

A myriad smell of cooking food and brewing coffee came on strong. The café itself was loud with voices, and thick with smoke from cigars and pipes. The men outnumbered the women. Most of the men afforded her a glance of curiosity then went back to tipping their glasses or consuming their food. The sound of utensils scraping against plates was almost louder than the conversations going on.

She resented being here.

"Excuse me, madam." A waiter, with a long white apron tied around his waist, nudged past her holding high a tray of sizzling steaks. She moved out of the way.

To her relief, in the far back, the person she'd come to meet stood, allowing her to see him. He remained standing while she approached and slid into the booth. He took his seat across from her. As she removed her black gloves, one hand at a time, she couldn't ignore that he was ill-at-ease and extremely agitated.

Stiff-backed and getting to the point, she said, "Well?"

"Something's gone terribly wrong," Myron said.

With Olivia stretched out on his bed, Donald set about making her comfortable. While unlacing her shoes, he paused to wipe sweat from his upper lip. His bedroom was stifling, warmer inside than out. The heat caused his split lip to throb and sting. Paddy was in the kitchen filling a basin of water.

Donald's ripped shirt-sleeve fluttered as he worked the high top shoes from Olivia's feet. He fumbled with the tiny pearl buttons on her blouse, the delicate white lace of the collar dyed red with her blood. Finally having success with the buttons, he parted her blouse to reveal a soft cotton chemise, threaded with a green ribbon. He quickly removed the ruined blouse. Covering her with the sheet, he put his hands modestly under the cover and slipped her skirt off.

Paddy brought in a basin of water that he placed on the seat of the wooden chair next to the bed. Pulling on his collar, muttered, "Damn, it's hot and stuffy in here." Sweat beads formed on his face and receding hairline. Taking out a handkerchief he wiped his face while going over to the window and forcing it open.

"Aye, and it'll only get worse." Donald wrung out the washcloth in the ceramic basin and dabbed at the blood. Olivia let out a soft moan, her brows furrowing. He stopped to see if she was waking up. She remained unconscious.

A knock on the door had Paddy hurrying to answer it. Donald watched from the bedroom as the doctor carrying his black bag stepped inside. After the doctor removed his fedora and suit coat, Paddy led him the short distance to the bedroom.

The doctor, a short man with a swelling paunch, approached the bed and set his bag down. "Young man." He nodded while fitting his glasses atop his nose. "Name's Brown, Doc Brown." He glanced over his spectacles at the patient.

"I'm Donald McShane."

The doctor listened to Olivia's heart, moving his stethoscope from one area of her chest to another, his eyes narrowed in concentration. He lifted her eyelids to check her pupils. When he finally looked up and nodded, Donald took it as a good sign. The doctor began examining her head.

"Is she going to be all right?" Paddy asked from the foot of the bed, his normally tough attitude melted with concern.

"I believe so. She has a nasty cut, and I suspect a concussion. She'll be unconscious for several more hours or so. I'm going to stitch her scalp. What about you?" he asked, giving Donald the once over. "Want me to fix your lip?" He poked around inside his bag, pulling out needles, catgut, and other supplies he needed.

Donald smiled and winced. "Nay, I'll be all right. Sure'n I've taken worse hits than this."

"Is that so? What's this young woman's name? How did she get hurt?"

Paddy was quick to say, "Olivia…her name's Olivia Marsh. Miss Marsh is a suffragette, and was givin' a speech. I guess the factory owner didn't like what she was sayin'. Some lout threw a brick at her."

"A speech you say?" The doctor set about pulling Olivia's hairpins out and then cut her hair to the scalp right over the wound. Ushering the two men out, Doctor Brown went into the kitchen to wash his hands and while there he sterilized his needle and scissors.

Waiting in the living room, Donald and Paddy tossed small talk at each other. Finally unable to stay away, Donald went back into his bedroom. The doctor had sewn the wound shut, and said he'd put in over fifteen stitches. He was now busy cleaning up and putting his instruments away.

"She'll need to remain here. I don't want Miss Marsh moved or disturbed. With that kind of wound, I expect her to sleep through the evening. When she wakes up, make sure she's lucid and knows her name." He told Donald what kind of symptoms to watch for. If needed, he offered to return and check on her in the morning.

Donald picked up the basin and followed the doctor out. He dumped the bloody water in the sink and walked with Doctor Brown into the living room where the physician shrugged into his suit coat and snatched his hat from the rack. When he didn't leave, Donald realized he was waiting for his fee.

"Oh." he said. "How much?"

He pursed his lips for a moment. "Let's make it fifteen dollars."

Donald didn't let the doctor see him gulp. It was a lot of money to Donald who no longer had a job. He pulled out his wallet and paid the doctor. "Ya think she'll be better by mornin' aye?"

Doctor Brown situated his fedora on his head. "She took a nasty hit. Trying to reform men that don't see anything but the almighty dollar is a dangerous line of work. They will remove anything or anyone who gets in their way. Apparently, Miss Marsh is well known for her reform fight. But one day if she's not careful, it might get her killed."

Finding that thought unsettling, and not wanting to have another dead body on his conscience, Donald nodded, and saw the doctor out.

After shutting the door, he turned to face Paddy Riley.

Paddy grinned at him and said, "You have quite a left hook."

"It felt good to throw a few punches, especially at rodent shite like Lapaglia." He smiled at the reporter, thinking Miss Marsh was lucky to have a friend like him.

"Ya don't seem like the type to turn up at a rally just for the sport of it."

Donald had a wry grin. "Yer right. I hate to admit it, but I work…eh…worked at Lapaglia's. I was done for the day and left during Miss Marsh's speech. I could see things were goin' to get nasty. I tried tellin' Lapaglia to go back inside, ignore the woman, that the suffragettes would soon be gone. But he wasn't having any of my advice. Told me where to put it. Actually fired me arse right on the spot."

"Well, I'm thinkin' Miss Marsh will be glad ya were there to help her," he said while glancing around. "I don't see a telephone in here. Is there one in the hallway?"

"Ah…no, the closest one is down at Ryerson's grocery store. D'ye need me to make a call?"

"No, I'm goin' to call the Marsh's and let them know what's happened, and where to find Olivia. I'll go make the call then be right back."

Donald gave the energetic reporter directions to Ryerson's. As Paddy turned to leave, he paused next to the picture of Donald's family and picked it up.

"Your family?"

"Aye. They were comin' to me on the Titanic." Donald stood next to the flamboyant reporter and took the picture from him. After looking at it with intense emotion, he placed it back where it belonged. "Ya know, I went to Halifax and tried to identify their bodies. But I came up empty handed." Donald paused, horrible visions of the battered corpses he'd viewed still fresh in his mind. "I'm sure you reported on the Titanic and aftermath, aye?"

"I did."

"Something puzzling happened while I was lookin' at bodies up there," Donald said and continued, "A woman who'd been murdered on the ship had my wife's inspection card in her coat pocket. The murdered woman's aunt came to see me awhile back. She'd recognized her niece's picture in the paper. The woman told me her niece's name was Lillian Denbury."

Paddy quickly took out his notebook and began writing. "Aye, I knew a woman was murdered on the Titanic. Our newspaper ran the story and pictures from Halifax. There was an Inspector Mulhall asking for information."

Donald nodded. "Inspector Mulhall talked to me when I was up there. Lillian Denbury wrote to her aunt about a man she was interested in. Another strange happening is the day I arrived home from Halifax someone had been here in me home, actually surprised young Joe who stays with me, hit him on the back of the head."

Paddy's sandy brows pulled together and his blue eyes filled with questions. "Was anything stolen?"

"Nothin' here to steal. But a bottle of perfume was smashed against the bedroom wall."

Paddy kept writing. "I'd like to help ya with this, McShane. Nothin' about this makes sense, and I don't like things that don't make sense." He slid his pencil over his ear and stuffed the notebook back into his pocket.

"Have ya lived in New York long?" Donald asked.

Paddy nodded, his eyes taking on a shine. "Since I was nine. My father unable to make a go of it in the old country loaded us up and brought us here. I had three brothers and two sisters. All dead but two of us. My dad dug ditches and my mother worked her fingers raw sewin' clothing in our apartment. All I remember is stacks of cloth and clothes and shoving them out of the way to get around.

"I was still wearin' knee pants when I started at the Times as a runner. Then I began writin', going out and gettin' the good stories. 'Tis said I'm the best reporter the Times has. Maybe someday I'll be editor-in-chief." He laughed and started for the door. "I'll go make that call."

Donald moseyed back into the bedroom and paused next to the stranger in his bed. Pulling up the chair, he leaned back until the wall stopped him. He'd seen her before, somewhere, maybe a poster with her picture on it. She was quite the forceful woman, like a hurricane brewing over the ocean to come ashore with a punch. He'd never known a woman who had so much zest and nerve. She had nerve to stand up to men who wanted to hurt children, and a certain zest for life about her, like she enjoyed being alive, even living dangerously.

At least he'd helped this woman by not turning his back on her and that gave him some comfort.

He continued to study her. She had an elegant profile, a straight nose, and full pink lips. Despite the gauze strip holding her bandage in place, her hair fanned out dark against the white of the pillowcase.

Used to blonde tresses covering the pillow next to him, he swallowed back the pain. He'd bought the bed for Derry. He thought she'd be the only woman to ever sleep in it, curl up next to him, snake her arm over his side to rub his chest, and that their next child would be conceived here. Now he had no wife, no children. He splayed his hand across his chest, feeling the hurt start to creep back in.

Olivia wore earbobs, small, black shiny things hooked through holes in her ears, and the jet beads reminded him of Derry's old rosary that hung from the bedpost for as long as he was married to her. He glanced at the new rosary he'd bought her and thought he should put it away, put away all the reminders.

His gaze trailed down Olivia's long smooth neck where his search stopped at the base of her creamy skin. He let his chair fall forward with a thud and inched just a little closer.

Longing to feel her pulse, he placed two fingers against the base of her throat. She felt incredibly soft, softer than he was used to feeling, but just as soft as Derry. He hadn't touched a woman in years, not since he'd held Derry in his arms before running away from Ireland.

He squinted, and thought back to better times before Sam had tricked him, sent him to run like a dog in the night, leaving his family and everything familiar to slip aboard a freighter like the common criminal Sam had him thinking he was.

Donald continued to rest his hand, drawing strength from her steady swishing pulse, allowing himself the feel of another human being, realizing how grievingly sad, lonely, and depressed he'd become. In a strange way, he drew comfort by just having her close. Wounded and unconscious, not knowing she was in his care. His gaze strayed to where her frilly chemise rose and fell with each breath. He tried to place the delicate scent coming from her, some kind of flower.

A slight gasp had him looking into her eyes now wide open and staring at him. She shrank back as if he was *Jack the Ripper* or someone equally sinister. He jumped as though caught with his hand in her drawers.

"Ah…shite!" he yelped, windmilling his arms as his chair went over backwards and hit the floor. Still sitting in it, his feet in the air, he'd lost all dignity as he looked up at Olivia Marsh who peered over the edge of the bed at him. She'd pulled the sheet up to her neck and squinted at him with pain filled eyes. Embarrassed, he scrambled to his feet and quickly righted the chair.

"Ya weren't supposed to wake up for a while yet, sure'n that's what the doctor said." He felt like a kid caught stealing penny candy, and sheepishly grinned at her.

"Mr. McShane, it is you, isn't it?" She appeared puzzled while settling back on the pillow, making the bed springs slightly squeak.

"Aye 'tis me…er…McShane…Donald."

She started to touch her head. "Oh…my…I hurt. What happened?"

He quickly stopped her from touching her bandage. "You've been stitched up. Expect yer going to have one blastin' headache." He peered at her. "How do ya feel? Drowsy? How many of me do you see? The doctor said to ask."

"Well, I see *one* of you. A banged up *one* of you with a cut lip and a black eye." She turned his hand over fingering the cut and swollen knuckles.

Her eyes were full of questions, so he told her about the suffragettes and the violent free-for-all. He told her Paddy Riley had driven them here in her car. Donald embellished on how they'd both carried her up five flights of stairs.

When he had her wincing and laughing, he relaxed in the chair again. "Mind if I ask how ya know my name?"

"You really don't remember do you? I guess I wouldn't expect you to, not under the circumstances. I noticed you at Pier fifty-four, the night the Carpathia docked. You came into the White Star office."

That night blasted back into his mind like a surging wave, and though he never wanted to think about it again, here it was.

"I thought ya looked familiar, but I couldn't place ya. I remember now, walking down the barrier, ya had a little girl with ya. How is yer daughter?"

A trace of a smile flicked the corners of her mouth. "The little girl isn't mine. I was in a lifeboat and she landed in my arms when someone threw her off the Titanic. I've been trying to find her parents, but can't. I think they were lost with the ship."

He tried to recollect what the child looked like, but couldn't. It was all a frantic blur to him, and he preferred it remained so. She asked if he'd found his family, her voice hesitant. He said no and nothing more, the pain still too raw.

She squeezed his hand. "I've never had a man fight for me. Despite the fact that you work for Lapaglia, I need to thank you, Mr. McShane."

"I'm like all immigrants, I needed a job when I came to America. If it makes ye feel better, I no longer work at Lapaglia's. When I went to yer aid, he fired me. And yer friends would make ya proud of 'em. Their picket signs are wicked, used them to hit good and hard."

Her eyelids began to droop. She nestled into the down of his pillow, and giving him a ghost of a smile fell back asleep, leaving him once again in silence.

He had enjoyed talking with her and realized he was missing a great deal of things in life. Companionship being one of them.

His stomach growled. He thought about eating something while she slept. Going into his small kitchen, he'd no sooner opened the cabinet and began moving cans around, trying to decide, when there was a loud knock on the door. Before he could open it though, Paddy barged in. He was like a storm entering one's home. He moved with hurried intent, but paused to glance toward the bedroom.

Closing the door behind Paddy, Donald spoke in a low tone. "She woke up and talked to me for a bit. Then she dozed off again. She was lucid, so I think she's going to be fine."

"Good—that's good news. Olivia's father, Mr. Marsh, will be stoppin' by." He pulled on his watch chain and removed his watch from his plaid vest pocket. Opening the gold lid, he squinted at the face before snapping it shut. "Half past five, I've got to get goin' to the office. Don't want to miss my deadline. Does the subway run close by?"

"The elevated train is several blocks over. Can ya not drive her auto?"

Paddy relaxed into a laugh. "I'd rather not. I'll leave it."

A loud knock sounded on his door again. Just as he started for it, the door swung open and a tall, older gentleman walked in and glanced around.

"Mr. Riley—where's Olivia?" The man whipped off his hat and tossed it to land on the hat tree.

Donald watched Paddy lead the way into his bedroom. Feeling like a stranger in his own home, he followed and stood at the foot of his bed while Mr. Marsh leaned over his daughter. His face was etched with concern. The second he saw her bandaged head his mouth went dangerously narrow. He gently ran a hand over her forehead, careful not to wake her. Olivia moaned, her eyelids tightened, but she remained asleep. He fussed with the sheet that really didn't need fussing with, but Donald figured it made him feel better.

A worried frown creased Mr. Marsh's craggy features. He pointed to the door, and then followed them out. They'd no sooner reached the living room when Olivia's father turned and said, "I intend to find the bastard who hurt my daughter, and then I'm going to snap him like kindling."

"Mr. Marsh, I'm Donald McShane. I brought yer daughter here to me place after she was hurt. The doctor said she has a concussion, but she'll be all right." His jaw tightened as he stepped forward and held his hand out to Olivia's father.

Walter Marsh pumped Donald's offered hand. "No malice intended toward you, McShane. Mr. Riley told me about your heroic efforts on Olivia's behalf. It's seeing her so damaged, and not knowing the extent of her injury makes me want to kill the men who did this." He searched Donald's face but he didn't ask what happened. "McShane, forgive my bursting into your home like I did. I have nothing but my daughter's welfare on my mind. I—"

"Mr. Marsh," Paddy interrupted. "I've gotta leave now and get my work done at the paper. I was there to cover the story at Miss Marsh's request. Normally I'm sittin' on the fence concerning the suffragette movement and factory owners. After today ya can read yer morning paper and not choke on yer coffee when ya read what I'm goin' to write." He picked up his brown bowler and placed it on his head.

"Mr. Riley, how are you getting to your office?" Walter asked.

"By the 'el' train. I drove your daughter's car here."

Shaking his head, Walter rocked on his heels. "To show my appreciation for what you've done, I'll have my chauffeur drive you to your office."

"How will you get back home tonight?"

Walter chuckled. "I can drive Olivia's car. But, if McShane doesn't mind, I'm staying here tonight. Would you tell my chauffeur I need him to get in touch with Merilee and tell her I'm here? I tried earlier but she wasn't home." Upon Paddy's nod, Walter glanced at Donald and was gracious enough to enlighten him. "Merilee is my wife, Olivia's mother. No need to worry her about us."

Donald had to agree, and admired the way the man walked through life with complete confidence. His orders would be carried out without question, and Donald wondered what it would be like to have money mold him into a man of power like Mr. Marsh.

"Oh…and Mr. Riley, tell my chauffeur I want him to stop by Lüchow's and bring McShane and myself some dinner. Tell him to order off the menu, he knows what I like. How about you McShane, what do you like to eat?"

"Anything, I'll eat anything," Donald said, thinking anything would be better than soup.

"How about a good T-bone steak?" Walter raised a thick eyebrow, and not waiting for an answer, patted Mr. Riley on the shoulder.

And Paddy, ever the reporter, said to Donald, "McShane, it's been grand makin' yer acquaintance. I'll be lookin' into what ya told me." He nodded at the two men and closed the door behind him.

"Make yourself comfortable," Donald said.

Walter Marsh appeared to relax for the first time since arriving. He took off his double-breasted suit coat and loosened his tie. He then went for his suit pocket and the three cigars nested there.

He offered one to Donald. "Care for a smoke?"

"Not right now, thank you."

While Walter lit up, Donald went into his kitchen searching for some sort of an ashtray. Finally grabbing up a jar lid, he took it back to where Walter had made himself comfortable.

Donald sat on the sofa, his hands on his knees, and thought he must look stupid. It was hard to relax in the presence of such a man. Walter Marsh puffed his cigar as though he thoroughly enjoyed every gray wisp of smoke he blew into the air. The man was solid, big, bold, and Donald realized he resembled old roughrider Teddy Roosevelt, even down to the pince-nez glasses now perched on his nose. One thing for sure, Walter Marsh looked totally out of place in his small apartment, and made Donald more than aware of its shabbiness.

"Would you like something to drink?" Donald asked.

"Depends on what you're offering."

Donald stood and going into his small kitchen where he opened the glass fronted cabinet. He searched around, picking up bottles. "Whiskey, or brandy?"

Walter nodded at him. "Irish whiskey?"

"None other," Donald said and grinned. He poured them both two shots. Taking the glasses back into the living room, he handed the liquor to Walter who was quick to clink his glass against Donald's.

Both men knocked back their drinks, and exhaled as the liquor lit a fire in the back of their throats, finding camaraderie in a shared drink.

"Damn that's fine whiskey," Walter said. "Listen, McShane, what Mr. Riley said before he left echoes my sentiments. I understand you stepped right in and helped my girl. I'm grateful. This happened in front of Lapaglia's factory?"

Donald went to bring the bottle back and poured them another shot. "Aye. Lapaglia was standing out front when it happened. I tried to get him to come back into the factory, ignore the suffragettes, but he refused. Felt he was going to hurt yer daughter. We…well we exchanged blows. I knocked him out. Ah…Mr. Marsh, until I hit Lapaglia, I was employed by him."

Walter flicked his ashes in the jar lid, and sipped his drink. "Was? So you were fired?"

"Aye. Fired right on the spot."

"My bank does business with Lapaglia. Why in the hell would he hurt my daughter?"

"Maybe he doesn't know Miss Marsh is your daughter?" Donald wondered about a man who would hurt an acquaintance's daughter. He also wondered about Walter Marsh doing business with Lapaglia and thought he must know the kind of man Lapaglia was.

Walter tamped out his cigar and let the last of the smoke trail out of his mouth. "I agree. I'd like to think he doesn't know the connection. One doesn't bite the hand that feeds them, or in this case, the bank that loans them money. What do you know about Lapaglia?"

"I know his business practices are lower than a snake. He docks people's wages for the smallest infraction, like talkin' and humming. Charges them to use his sewing machines, charges them for machine oil, thread. Even workers bringing their own machines are charged for using his electricity. He was always askin' me if I could find something to dock them for." Donald leaned back and crossed his ankles. The whiskey and good company helped him relax, a feeling he hadn't had in a month.

"I like hearing you're familiar with the factory," Walter said and raised his eyebrows. "May I ask you to do something for me?"

Donald perked up. "I probably should say it depends on the askin', but I'm inclined to say, aye. What are you needin', Mr. Marsh?"

"Do you think you could go back to Lapaglia's? I'd like you to nose around Lapaglia's office and see if you can find out if this attack against Olivia was intentional. Most important, I want to know if Lapaglia knows who Olivia is. Can you do this?"

"Aye." Donald reached into his pants pocket and taking out a key flashed it along with a grin. Perhaps a bit of intrigue would help take the melancholy out of his miserable life.

"Is that what I think it is?" Walter asked, and he too was grinning.

"Aye, the key to Lapaglia's back door."

"Come see me at the bank when you have something to tell me. I keep my personal life separate from my livelihood. My son Nathan runs my bank out in Oregon State. But neither my wife nor my daughter knows about my banking practices. I fully intend to keep it that way." He leaned forward and rested his forearms on his thighs. "You mentioned you no longer have a job. What do you do besides fight for my daughter and get yourself hurt?" Walter laughed, and leaning back he interlaced his hands across his stomach.

Donald couldn't help but chuckle. "I worked in the accounting department."

Walter's eyes narrowed as they settled on Donald. "Accounting, huh? Nice profession. Are you good at it?"

"I think so. Here, I'll show ya."

Donald went to the sideboard and opening a drawer foraged for a pencil and paper. Finding what he was looking for, he took them back to Walter.

"Put down a row of figures, make it as many as you want."

Walter did as told and made up five columns, ten deep with various numbers, and handed it back to Donald. Donald glanced at it then wrote the sum in the corner. He handed the paper back. Walter flicked the pencil up each row, adding, and when done, his answer matched Donald's to the number.

"Well, I'll be damned," he said, and scribbled down a longer and wider string of digits and gave it to Donald. "Add and divide these."

Once again, within seconds, Donald took the pencil from Walter and wrote the answer below the first one.

This one turned out correct, and by now, Walter was grinning from ear to ear. "Don't know how you do it, McShane, but I'd like to offer you a job in my bank. I could use a good man like you."

The thought of returning to Ireland was heavy on his mind and he replied, "Just because I can add numbers doesn't mean I know about banking."

"I'm sure you'd be a fast learner. And your helping my daughter didn't get past me either. Most men threatened with their livelihood would have ignored what happened. You didn't. I like bravery and loyalty in a man. With that in mind, I'm making you an offer of accounting manager. You appear smart enough to learn the banking business." He took the paper, scribbled down a figure, and handed it to Donald. "That's what I'll start you out with. You don't have to answer right now. Take your time, think it over, and then get back to me."

Donald stared at the figure and tried to act nonchalant, like he was offered this kind of money everyday. He cleared his throat and asked, "Is this yearly, sir?"

"Monthly." And before Donald's mouth could hit the floor, Walter's face crinkled into a wide grin. "I bet you've already added what it'll come to per year, right?"

"Aye, Mr. Marsh, I have." Donald nodded. Maybe things weren't so bleak after all "Since losing my family on the Titanic, I haven't had much to stay here in America for, and was set to return to Ireland. Being fired, I was more than ready to go. But you've given me hope. And if ye don't mind, I'm acceptin' yer offer right here and now."

"Good. Be at my bank first thing Monday morning." Walter leaned forward and patted Donald's arm. "I'm sorry to hear about your family—so sorry. Perhaps you could come to my home and talk with our little miss who Olivia rescued from the Titanic. It might help to have a fellow Irishman talk with her. But then again, I don't want to cause you further pain. She won't give her last name and she pronounces—"

Donald's front door flung open, and Joe came striding in, interrupting Walter. "Whooee! That's some auto out there," Joe said, and taking off his cap twirled it around his finger then sent it to land on the sideboard. "Hope I own a rig like that someday."

"Ah…Joe, hello," Donald said. "And I bet ya will own a rig like that. Eh…ya didn't get inside it…did ya?"

"Nope. But I squeezed that big old horn by the driver's door. Didn't ya hear it up here?" Wearing a big grin Joe sauntered over. He glanced at Walter, curious like.

"Joe, shake hands with Mr. Walter Marsh. Mr. Marsh, this is Joe Gillespie. He's been staying with me ever since his old boss made the mistake of punching him in front of me. Joe works for Ryerson's delivering groceries."

Walter offered Joe his hand. "Glad to meet you, young man."

After shaking Mr. Marsh's hand, Joe leaned forward and squinted at Donald's face. "Wow! What happened to your kisser? Were ya in that brawl at Lapaglia's? Last I saw the coppers were hauling women and men off to the hoosegow."

Holding his bruised jaw Donald nodded. "Sure'n I was. Not proud of it. But I helped Mr. Marsh's daughter who is in me bed right now, and who owns that shiny automobile out front ya like so much. She's injured worse than I am."

Joe took a chair and after plopping down, he picked up the small sack he'd carried in. Pilfering through the sack, he pulled out a package of Oreo Biscuit Wafers and held up the chocolate treat. "Ever have these?" he asked the grownups. "Mrs. Ryerson gave them to me. They're new, supposed to be better than Hydrox cookies. It's what the big ol' sign on her wall says."

"Not right now, Joe. Mr. Marsh has ordered steak dinner. You can join us. Why not save them for later?" Donald could have saved his breath, as Joe bit into the chocolate treat sending crumbs tumbling down his shirt front. The kid could eat the whole box of cookies and a steak.

A knock on the door sent Joe scrambling to answer it. The smell of a delivered dinner filled the room with the delicious odor of cooked meat and potatoes. Joe grabbed the food boxes from the startled chauffeur, and stepped aside.

Walter put money in his chauffeur's hand and gave him further orders about going home and telling Mrs. Marsh where he was.

Donald took the food from Joe and after placing it on his table he put down mismatched plates and eating utensils. They set about cutting into the juicy steaks. Halfway through the meal Donald told Walter this was the first time he'd ever had cooked food delivered.

Later, after the meat, peas and carrots were long gone, Walter sat enjoying his cigar. Donald poured them another whiskey to celebrate his new job.

It wasn't long before Joe became fidgety, drumming his fingers against his knees, until he finally blurted out, "Do ya know how to play Flinch, Mr. Marsh?"

Donald stifled a groan. Joe was good at Flinch, too good. If one played for more than toothpicks, he cleaned you out.

"Now, Joe, maybe we shouldn't," Donald said.

"Maybe we should," Walter quipped, reaching into his pocket for change. "I like a good game of cards."

Joe flashed Donald a look of impish anticipation and hurried to get the deck of cards.

The oil lamp on the sideboard was turned down, its rose-colored globe casting a pink glow. Donald was sleeping in the chair, Walter snored on the couch, and Joe with his pockets bulging with change and having eaten all the Oreo wafers, had left to sleep in the back room at Ryerson's.

"Help me…"

The voice was low enough it almost didn't wake Donald, but it did. His eyes shot open to see Olivia leaning against the frame of the open bedroom door. The white of her chemise and drawers glowed in the dim lamplight.

"Help me…" she whispered a moan, her arms out in front of her reaching.

Donald was out of the chair in a flash, his long stride propelling him across the room. He caught her just as her knees buckled.

"The water…the water's so cold…I don't want to die…not now…."

"Shhh…" Donald soothed, and picking her up, carried her back into his bedroom. He pulled the chain to switch on the overhead light. The lone bulb, dim, and hidden beneath a frosted cover gave off some light. As he laid her down, she refused to let go of his shirt, the material balled tight within her fist.

"No…no…they'll drown me," she whimpered. "The dead, they're pulling my legs."

Now unsure of what to do, he thought to lie next to her, just until she settled down. She shivered as though she was cold instead of being in the hot, stifling apartment. Wanting to help her, he encased her within his arms and nestled her head against his shoulder. He gently rubbed his hand up and down her arm. She was shaking, her skin moist with perspiration.

"I'm cold…so cold…oh…God, we're going to die." Her breath tickled against his skin. She began to cry soft little sobs that reminded Donald of a tiny kitten so scared it could barely get a good meow out.

"Olivia," he said, his mouth next to her ear, trying to wake her. "Yer safe in me home, not the ocean." He continued to stroke her arm, patting it, slowly bringing her out of her nightmare. Her eyes were large and tear-filled. Sad eyes, he thought. At last she relaxed and released her hold on his shirt.

"Do ya know who I am?" he said.

"Yes, I know who you are, and where I am," she spoke in a gentle whisper. "You saved me today and again just now."

"Just now?"

"You drove away the demons of guilt that surround me when I sleep."

"What guilt?" he said.

"The guilt of being one that survived while so many didn't. I keep wondering why."

Donald released her and shifted off the bed to sit on the chair. He reached across the covers and took her hand within his patting it softly like a child's. "Ya saved a little girl, that's why yer still alive. And yer still trying to save children. Today was a darn good example."

"Thank you. You're very kind." She squirmed into a more comfortable position. Her movements caused the bedsprings to squeak and the beads on the rosary to rattle against the headboard. She turned her head toward it and reached out to finger the silver cross. "Yours?"

"No. God abandoned me the night the Titanic went down. I no longer pray. This was for me wife, Derry."

Her hands fell to the sheet. "Derry? Is that your wife's name?" Her mouth parted with surprise. "How do you spell it?"

He didn't know what to make of her agitated state, but he complied. "D-e-r-r-y. It's a nickname for Darlene. Her name was Alana Darlene, but she never went by Alana, only Darlene, and I was quick to shorten it even more. She was a proper lass, me wife, me sweet Derry."

"Mr. McShane, if it wouldn't be too painful could you tell me your children's names?"

She lay looking at him, and he thought she'd forgotten to breathe.

"My son was named Creighton after my father, but since that's a mouthful, we called him Casey. He would have been nine his next birthday. And my little daughter, not even a year old when I left Ireland, is…was four."

"And her name?" Olivia asked.

"Margaret Jilleen." His little earlobe pulling Jilly…his baby daughter.

"Margaret?" She gripped the sheet in clenched fists.

Donald wondered where all this was going. "After me wife's grandmother, but we called her Jilleen. She took after me, had me hair. Miss, Marsh, if ya don't mind…I'd—"

"Oh…my God," she said and started to get up.

Alarmed, Donald gently put his hands on her shoulders. "Ya can't get up—"

"Olivia, are you all right?" Walter said from where he stood in the doorway.

"Dad, I didn't know you were here." Olivia stretched her arms out to him. "Oh, Dad, there's so much to tell you…and I…and I…" She started to sob. He sat on the bed and she held onto him, her face buried against his chest.

Walter patted her shoulder with a strong hand.

"I'll get the headache powder the doctor wanted ya to have," Donald offered, and left them alone.

"Daughter, what is it? You're trembling. McShane didn't—"

"No, he was only helping me."

She thought about telling her father about Jilleen, but decided not to. She was still reeling from the news herself. Before she told Mr. McShane, or her father, or anyone for that matter, she wanted to hear the truth from Jilleen. She wanted Jilleen to admit to being a McShane. For if by the slightest chance Jilleen wasn't McShane's daughter, Olivia didn't want to be the one to open up a chasm of hope for him and have it close back up.

Her head felt like it was being hit by a sledgehammer. She didn't know if the pain was from her injury, or from what Donald had told her.

She changed the subject. "Dad, I'm scared. There was something about the crowd today, like I was being targeted."

"Don't worry, Olivia. I'm sure it was just a mischief maker trying to scare you off."

"You'll never know how glad I am to see you here tonight. Is mother here?"

"I've been here all evening. And in all fairness to your mother, I came here straight from the bank. Your reporter friend, Paddy Riley was supposed to call her from his office."

Olivia could only nod, accepting and not accepting. If mother wanted to be here, she would be here no matter what. And her absence injured Olivia more than a thrown brick ever could. Why? Just once, why?

Walter cleared his throat. "I've gotten to know McShane somewhat. He seems an upright fellow. I've asked him to come to our house and talk with Jelee. Maybe he can help her. I understand he lost his family in the disaster."

"Yes, yes he did."

And she thought he might just be getting one of his children back. She was relieved to see Donald approaching with the promised powder and glass of water.

She smiled at him through her pain.

Chapter Thirteen

Donald, having left Olivia and Walter sleeping in his apartment, now stood across the street from Lapaglia's factory where busted signs and paper littered the street. At four in the morning the quiet was a stark contrast to yesterday's brawl. Since Lapaglia was too cheap to hire a night watchman, Donald figured now was a good time to get inside the place.

He crossed the street and hurried down the alley behind Lapaglia's factory where large barrels overflowed with foul smelling garbage. Donald's approach frightened several crows feasting on rancid scraps. The birds cawed and fluttered away.

He heard someone whistling. Trying to make out who the person was, Donald stopped and waited. He was surprised to see a lone man jiggling the doorknob to Lapaglia's checking the lock. At first the long-legged stranger eyed Donald with suspicion and paused. Donald purposely approached, and standing under the light over the door, allowed the man to see the bruises on his face.

The man broke into a grin. "Were ya in that brawl yesterday? Did ya let one of those ladies…those suffergits…hit ya?" He slapped his knee and busted out laughing. His teeth were decayed and a wad of chew swelled his cheek. He spit a brown stream next to Donald's boot.

"Don't make me laugh, aye. It'll make me lip bleed again," Donald said, and gingerly felt the scab on his lip. "Next time, I won't be so quick to get involved. Not if I know there's going to be wooden signs and lethal women involved." He paused. "Who are you—what are you doing here?"

The man's humor dried up. He answered Donald's question with one of his own. "What about you? It's early enough, ain't it? Why are ya here in this alley?" he asked, his sharp scrutiny never wavering.

"I work for Lapaglia. Hired to put the scare in those suffergets ya mentioned. It's getting so bad an honest man can't make a livin' without gettin' picketed. And you?"

The man spread his coat open and hooked his thumbs under his belt. "Same as you. Hired yesterday by Lapaglia as a night watchman. He seems to think those ladies might try to damage his factory." He spat on the ground again.

"I agree with Lapaglia. Those women are like cockroaches, everywhere, all the time. I like to get an early start, so if ya don't mind," Donald said and held up his key. And wishing for the luck of the Irish the key still fit, he put it in the lock and turned. He let out a sigh as the door swung open.

The watchman shrugged and followed Donald inside. "Ya won't mind if I come inside with ya? Thinking to take the early mornin' chill off."

Donald wanted to tell him this would be the last place to get warm in, but didn't. Instead, he gave the man a friendly slap on the back and after turning on several lights, went about his business. The man he noticed was quick to head into another part of the factory where the toilet was located.

Donald took the stairs two at a time and then went inside Lapaglia's office. He pulled the chain on the overhead light. The place smelled like Lapaglia's sweaty body. Bolts of cloth leaned against the wall. Donald approached Lapaglia's desk cluttered with pattern books, sewing notions, and a plate of unrecognizable dried food. He started his search with the desk by dropping the plate in the garbage can, and then pushed a stack of patterns out of the way.

He found his accounting ledger on Lapaglia's desk. Knowing full well that Lapaglia had brought it in here to see if he followed orders, curiosity had Donald going over it. New additions docked those that left their machines during the brawl. Lapaglia was squeezing blood out of his workers where there wasn't any left to squeeze. Donald knew Lapaglia's foremen enjoyed snitching, fondling the female workers, anything to make an employee's life miserable. And Donald was ashamed to have welded the ink pen that made the deductions and wrote the puny paychecks. No wonder Olivia's suffragettes picketed this place. He put the ledger down, and continued searching.

Just when he thought it was hopeless, that he'd never find anything here linking Lapaglia to Olivia, he noticed an open order book peeking out underneath the pattern books he'd shoved aside. Picking it up, he fanned through it. A notation was hastily scrawled on a page which had nothing to do with orders. Two names were written there, one meaningless, the other practically jumped off the page at him. He tore the page out and shoved it in his pocket.

He glanced around, making sure he wasn't overlooking anything. A wall calendar drew his attention. The calendar was made for Lapaglia's factory, and had his name on each page, the month was June. Thursday the sixteenth was circled, and Olivia Marsh, suffragette rally, written in pencil. And that wasn't all. Blazoned across the squares for next week was, *Eliminate The Bitch.* The words written with such hatred that the pencil had gouged through the paper. Donald's stomach knotted, he had all the proof he needed. He ripped the page from the calendar, folded it, and then shoved it in his back pocket. He went to the mezzanine window where he scanned the work floor for the watchman. All was clear, so he quickly opened the door and pounded down the stairs.

Feeling bold, Donald left by the front door. He no sooner stepped outside into the morning air and plowed right into Lapaglia's stocky body. Donald watched as a stunned looking Lapaglia stepped backward. Lapaglia's fedora helped shadow eyes that were purple and swollen. Donald knew he'd personally given his former boss one of those black eyes.

Lapaglia became furious. "What the hell are you doing here? I fired your sorry ass."

Donald stood his ground. "I need me job so I came back to grovel, plead fer ya to take me back." He took off his cap and dramatically clutched it to his chest.

"You hit me in the face." His former boss pointed to his shiner. "Do you think for one second I'd let you back inside here? I'm blacklisting you. Already put the word out you're not to be hired by any factory around here. Go to hell, McShane." He held out his hand flexing his fingers.

Donald dropped his key into the man's meaty palm. "Sure'n there is no changin' yer mind?"

"Get the fuck off my property!"

Not wanting to press the issue or his luck, Donald walked off, glancing over his shoulder to make sure none of Lapaglia's goons followed him. None did.

A paperboy stacked his papers on the corner. Ahead, cars and trucks were grinding down the street. All of a sudden Donald's life didn't appear so bad. As he approached home, he noticed Olivia's Model T was gone. Fearing it was stolen, he hurried up the stairs and eased inside his apartment. But he could have saved himself the trouble of being quiet. Walter and Olivia were gone, and only a note with two twenty dollar bills from Walter remained on the table.

'McShane. I expect your not being here has something to do with what I asked you to do for me. Have taken Olivia home where our doctor is meeting us. Will see you Sunday at my home.' It was signed *WM* in a fast flourish.

Donald took out the pages from the order book and the calendar. He read them again. The page from the order book he didn't plan to share with anyone, not even Walter Marsh. However, the calendar page with its damning scrawl he would give to Walter on Sunday.

He opened his dresser drawer and put the evidence inside it. Derry's inspection card was there so he took it out and sat on the bed with it. Lillian Denbury had this card in her coat pocket. With her blonde hair and blue eyes, she could easily pass for his wife. He read the card again. *Contract ticket number 35868. Immigrants and Steerage passenger. Port of Departure: Queenstown. Date of departure: 11th April 1912. Name of Ship: SS Titanic. Name of passenger: Alana Darlene McShane.*

With a puzzled frown, he abruptly stood. And going into the living room he opened the sideboard's top drawer. He pushed aside letters from his mam. At last, finding what he sought, he took out the thick, crinkled list of the *Titanic's* passengers given to him in Halifax. Flipping to steerage, he started reading, searching.

Lillian Denbury wasn't listed.

He flicked the pages to second class, no Denbury. First class didn't have her listed either. In fact, Lillian Denbury wasn't listed anywhere on the ship's manifest. He hurriedly grabbed up his jacket, and locking the door behind him, took off for the nearest telephone at Ryerson's groceries.

He held the receiver in one hand and waited for the switch board operator to put his call through to Vivian Denbury.

She answered on the fourth ring. "Hello, you've reached the Vexing Veil hat shop."

"Miss Denbury? It's me, Donald McShane. You came to visit awhile back?"

"Yes, Luv, I remember you quite well. Do you have news to tell me?"

He moved out of the way of a customer and said in a rush, "Did you know yer niece's name isn't listed on the Titanic's manifest?"

"Yes, I did. Inspector Mulhall told me. That's why he was interested in the man Lillian referred to in her letter. With her not naming him, I don't know how he'll ever find the man. We don't even know if he survived the sinking."

"I don't understand how the inspector can investigate your niece's murder from Halifax."

"Neither do I, and in truth, I don't think he's doing it with much expectation of ever finding the killer."

Donald couldn't agree more. After promising to keep in touch, he hung up.

How could Lillian Denbury travel on the ship and her name not be on the manifest? With disjointed thoughts spinning around in his mind, he left Ryerson's and headed for Eldon's drugstore.

Chapter Fourteen

A whisper of a breeze stirred through the large trees surrounding the Marsh's backyard. Honeysuckle vines arched up over the gazebo sweetening the June air with pale yellow flowers.

Olivia took a deep breath, enjoying the heady fragrance. Two days had passed since her injury and she was still having slicing headaches. Dressed in a white linen sack of a dress, she reclined on a white wicker lounge with a thick cushion underneath her and plenty of pillows for her back.

Both Myron and her mother fussed over her like she was a delicate piece of china. They'd made sure a warm throw covered her legs. A book of poetry by Keats was on her lap, and a glass of lemonade sat within easy reach.

Olivia let out a sigh, and fingered the stitches above her ear that felt like brush bristles. She'd swept her hair up in the back and anchored it with a butterfly-shaped comb. Try as she might, she couldn't concentrate on the lovely stanza on the page in front of her, so she pulled the ribbon page-marker in place and closed the book. She glanced over at Myron who was engrossed in the New York

Times. His handsome dark head tilted downward and he fingered his silk tie as he read. Earlier, he'd asked her permission to remove his suit coat. It now lay over the nearby chair.

Her mother, resplendent in a skirt and blouse of cool white linen, was sitting in a wicker chair not far from her. In the latticed shadows, gray hairs were daring to thread throughout her mother's black glossy hair. She watched her mother work on a complicated embroidery pattern of purple iris's. Normally without stress, today her mother appeared on edge and kept knotting the purple thread. Tsking under her breath with exasperation, she took up her scissors and clipping the threads, pulled them all out and started over.

Jelee, along with her doll and Sparks, was sitting on a blanket spread on the lawn. Olivia watched the child as she played with a miniature porcelain tea set. Jelee urged Sparks to drink. The dog was trying to lap up lemonade from the tiny rose covered cup but his tongue kept getting stuck. Normally, Olivia would have laughed at the funny sight, but since the other night when Donald McShane had told her about his family, she had no humor at all.

She couldn't help but think about him. A man extremely different from anyone she'd ever met. He had a tantalizing hard-edge about him. His busted lip and black eye, all endured while trying to protect her. Imagine, a total stranger had chosen her over his job. Yes, something about him definitely pulled at her. But, she feared Jelee was going to be the biggest pull of all.

A headache hit, the pain sharp and blinding. Her book dropped with a loud splat against the wood floor. "Oh," she exclaimed.

Her mother paused, her needle in the air, purple embroidery thread dangling. "Perhaps this wasn't such a good idea after all. Do you want to go back inside?" she said, worried.

"Maybe you should be in bed." Myron leaned over and picked up her book. "Want me to help you to the house?"

Olivia managed to shake her head as the pain webbed across her skull. "I'm fine. I get such a stabbing pain at times it almost makes me stop breathing. Thankfully, it fades fast. The doctor said the headaches will stop after a while and I'll be good as new."

"I'm sure the doctor knows best, don't you agree, Myron?" Merilee said.

Myron nodded and hid himself behind the paper again. Turning the page, he let out a low whistle. "Well, just look at you, Olivia," he said. "On second thought…maybe you shouldn't. I never—"

"What do you mean?" she said suspiciously.

"Nothing, it's a picture of you in your automobile after you were hurt. Never mind, it's really not important."

"Give me that." Olivia reached over to take the paper from his hands. The picture was of her spilling out of her car. Her legs were up in the air and her knee-length white drawers were showing. Mr. McShane was leaning over her coming to her aid. The caption under the picture told about suffragette Olivia Marsh instigating a riot and attacked in front of Lapaglia's Garment Factory. The article emphasized that Miss. Marsh was viciously wounded and almost killed. *Who was dangerous enough to order the brick thrown the reporter asked?*

"Thank goodness Paddy Riley was there. I think this is the first time the truth about my suffragettes has been written. At least the article tells about Lapaglia's devious practices. I'm told he locks them in during working hours. One would think the fire at the Triangle factory and the workers that died from being locked in would be a deterrent to Lapaglia, but I guess not."

Myron leaned forward and said, "The article's well written, interesting to say the least. I just never thought Paddy Riley would publish such a compromising picture of you."

"Let me see it, please," Merilee said, and took the paper from Olivia. "This is terrible. I don't need to say I told you so, but I will. You must stop doing this insane suffragette activity. You could have been killed." Merilee kept staring at the page. "I suppose this man leaning over you is the one who helped you out, and who your father hasn't stopped praising ever since?"

"Yes, it's Mr. McShane. If it wasn't for him, I might be dead. The suffragettes told me Lapaglia's men were trying to drag me out of the car, and that Mr. McShane jumped right in and helped me."

Myron took the paper back. "I guess we owe a good deal of gratitude to this…er…McShane fellow. Hear he landed a few good punches. Says here that the riot ended with several suffragettes along with Lapaglia and his men put in jail. Here's another picture of them being loaded in the paddy wagon."

"Yes, I was informed about their jail experiences by my suffragettes who were delighted with all the publicity. They think it helps our cause. I wonder if Mr. McShane gave Paddy Riley the information written here about Lapaglia's factory practices. I don't think Lapaglia has a defense against that kind of behavior." Olivia watched her mother place her sewing beside her, and then take a dainty sip of her lemonade.

"Listen to this," Myron said, "Murder victim on the Titanic named. This is certainly a day for shocking news isn't it?" He leaned forward and handed the paper to Olivia.

The article, on the second page of the front section, was a byline from Halifax. It had a picture of a pretty, young smiling woman who was the murder victim. The article rehashed the story about the mystery woman mentioned in prior papers and now proven murdered on the *Titanic.* Her aunt had come forward to identify her. The murdered woman's name was Lillian Denbury. The authorities asked if anyone knew of her or had seen her with a male companion on the *Titanic* would they contact an Inspector Mulhall at the Halifax Investigation Department, or the New York City Police Department.

Olivia studied the woman's picture, trying to remember if she'd passed her on the Titanic's promenades, but she didn't think so. The article piqued Olivia's interest. This was the second time the name Lillian came up involving the Titanic. Mr. Flynn had said his wife's name was Lillian.

"A woman murdered?" Merilee scolded Olivia. "Perhaps all these happenings will be an insight for you to give up this dangerous line of work."

"Mother, I'm sure there is a logical explanation concerning this woman. And her death really has nothing to do with the riot." Olivia shifted into a more comfortable position. "I'm only sorry I was unconscious when the brawl really got going. I'd like to have seen Mr. McShane fighting with Lapaglia. The person who the law should be arresting for good is that awful factory owner. Why should I let him scare me away from doing what's right? If I can make a difference in just one child's circumstances, it will be worth it."

But her mother wanted the last word. "Don't you agree with me, Myron? She should give it up. I'm sure you will not want her to continue with this line of work after you're married, by then you will be—"

Jelee came running up to Merilee, and holding out her glass, said, "Can I have more ade?"

"It's *may* I have some more please." Merilee corrected Jelee then filled her glass with the sweet tangy liquid.

Jelee gulped the lemonade followed by a soft burp. Both of those actions had Merilee admonishing Jelee that it was unladylike to gulp and burp.

Olivia swung her legs off the lounge and sat up. Trying to steady herself, she beckoned the child closer. Jelee was wearing the green and plaid dress Olivia recently bought her. Upon closer inspection, Olivia could see grass stains on her white pinafore.

Olivia's heart swelled with pride as she put her hand on Jelee's back. How could she not love the darting little smiles Jelee always offered her, and the giggles that would sometimes burst forth? But now and almost with dread, she had to prove to herself and everyone involved if Jelee was or wasn't Donald McShane's daughter. She knew he hadn't answered the newspaper article about Jelee because he was in Halifax at the time.

She leaned close to Jelee's ear and whispered, "Sweetheart, I need you to go to my desk. In the top drawer you'll find sheets of paper folded together. Please bring me those papers."

Jelee took off running. Sparks, rousted out of his sleep, playfully chased behind her nipping at her heels.

Jelee had no sooner left when Olivia's father appeared. He stepped inside the gazebo, taking them in with one fast sweep. "Is there any lemonade left?" His big body made the room shrink, and the wicker snap as he settled into a chair.

"Yes, dear, we have plenty," Merilee said, and poured a glass for him. "Did you see our daughter in the newspaper?" She handed the drink to him.

"Yes, I did. Thought it was enlightening. I liked Paddy Riley's take overall. Myron, how are you today?"

"Fine, sir, just concerned about Olivia."

"As we all are." Walter downed the pale liquid, his throat working, emptying the glass in one long drink. Finished, he set the glass back on the table and stifled a belch. "Myron, if you don't mind, I'd like to talk with Olivia in private."

"I suppose that goes for me too?" Merilee said. When Walter agreed, she stood. "I'm getting sleepy just sitting here anyway. I have plenty to do inside. Myron, would you mind helping me with my embroidery basket?"

Myron stood and stretching his long arms outward, tried to work the kinks out of his back. "I don't mind at all." He leaned down and Olivia accepted his kiss on her cheek.

Jelee dashed in and handed the papers to her. "Did I get the right ones, 'Livia?" she asked in her soft voice.

Olivia smiled at her. "Yes, these are what I want. The bees are buzzing around your teacups. You should go pick up your dishes and dump the lemonade out of them. Be careful not to get stung."

Waiting until everyone left the gazebo, Olivia turned to her father who had moved into Myron's vacated chair. "Dad, I need to talk with you, but you've aroused my curiosity by sending Myron and mother away. What is it you wanted to tell me?"

"I shouldn't be telling you this, but in light of your injury, you should know for your own safety."

"What is it? You make it sound dire." Feeling something akin to fear, she shifted to see him better.

"A reliable source told me you were targeted to be hurt. There was a payoff involved. That's all I know about it. I'd like to talk with your friend Paddy Riley. Perhaps he can find more information. You need to be careful, Olivia. No more speeches until we find out who is behind this."

Her skin prickled. Hearing someone had paid to have her hurt was frightening. She racked her brain, trying to think who hated her enough to silence her. It was daunting. Every factory owner she'd picketed over the last several years would make the list. And she could add a few New York politicians as well.

"Perhaps you're right. I'll stop picketing for a while. With these bad headaches, I wouldn't be able to do much anyway."

"What did you want to tell me?" he asked.

She pulled in a deep breath and slowly let it out. "Well…I think we can stop searching for *Jilleen's* parents." She expected the look of surprise on her father's face, and he didn't disappoint.

"You called her Jilleen, not Jelee?"

"Dad, I know Donald McShane told you he lost his family on the Titanic." Olivia handed the list to her father. The paper crackled as he opened the list she'd read numerous times since Thursday's rally and her encounter with Mr. McShane.

"I take it I'm supposed to be reading McShane's family listing?"

She nodded and took a deep breath. "Would you read it out loud?"

"Alana Darlene, Creighton Donald, and Margaret Jilleen." He repeated, "Margaret Jilleen. Jilleen?"

"I keep wondering how I missed it before. Margaret Jilleen. Jilleen…Jelee. She told us her rightful name in the car. Only Jilleen's Irish accent had changed the sound of it, at least to us, but not to her. She accepted our inability to pronounce her name with the aplomb of youth." Olivia glanced at her dad and continued. "The day I was hurt, Mr. McShane told me his wife was called Derry. It's a nickname for Darlene. Her full name was Alana Darlene. He had a son named Creighton, but called Casey for short. His daughter was Margaret Jilleen."

Walter was startled to the edge of his chair. "Hellfire—Olivia! This means we have McShane's—"

"Daughter," she finished for him. "Yes, I believe we do. That first night in the car, Jilleen had told me her mother's name was Derry, but I'd mistakenly thought the doll's name was Deary. By now, Jilleen has probably found comfort in calling the doll by her mother's name."

"Well, it's a good thing he's coming here. The sooner the better don't you think?" He handed the list back to Olivia. She folded it and placed it on the wicker table.

"First we have to make certain she is Jilleen McShane. If she is his daughter, Mr. McShane must be the one to tell her." Olivia's mind was awhirl with all the complications, and she damned herself for always wanting to do the right thing. Who was going to help her through this, make it right for her? Who was going to mend her heart now breaking with the mere thought of losing Jilleen? Her insides were as tangled as her mother's embroidery thread.

"Olivia, I know how hard this is for you," her father said as if reading her mind. "But it's the best thing for our little miss. Donald McShane is a fine man and the happiness he will gain is beyond comprehension. What joy it'll be for us to give his daughter back to him."

Olivia could only nod at her father's wise words. And forcing herself to do it, she called Jilleen over.

Jilleen, now wearing an old, gray golf hat Walter had given her, was dumping her toys inside the stroller. She took her doll and carefully laid it on top of the dishes. She came running, her curls bouncing below the hat cocked sideways on her head.

"Aye, 'Livia?" she said.

Olivia took Jilleen by the shoulders and gently pulled her close. She removed Jilleen's hat and brushed a curl off her forehead. Without further delay she asked, "Are you Margaret Jilleen McShane?"

Jilleen gasped.

"That's your name isn't it? Jill..leen? Only we all thought you were saying Jelee. And…McShane is your last name? A fine Irish name, McShane." And she couldn't help but think of the fine young Irishman who would soon be claiming his daughter. She had caught this little one for a reason. Now the reason was here. But where was the joy in it? She couldn't think past the pain of giving up Jilleen.

"How d'ye know me last name?" Jilleen squirmed, staring at them both.

And Olivia could see her young mind trying to figure out if it was all right to admit the truth. "By the list you just brought me. Was your mother's name, Alana Darlene?"

Again Jilleen nodded. "Aye...Derry. Me mam…Derry."

"And Creighton is Casey, your bother?" After another nod of affirmation, Olivia hugged Jilleen to her bosom and kissed the top of Jilleen's head. Olivia glanced at her father who nodded encouragement.

"I love you, Jilleen. Like a daughter, I love you," her voice shook.

"I luv ya too, 'Livia. Don't cry."

Oh…God, how could she not? Where was the strength she was so noted for? Where was her strong demeanor? But this was so different. Her strong demeanor, her heart was in a million aching pieces. Yet somehow, she managed to put on her best smile. She tweaked Jilleen's nose and replaced her hat.

Jilleen turned the hat to the side. "Then yer not mad at me fer not sayin' me last name?"

"Of course not. Everything is going to be just fine. I'm going inside now. Go get your doll and come in as well." Her headache had webbed to a throbbing crescendo and she groped for her father's arm.

He stood and helping her up, linked her arm within his, guiding her out from the gazebo. "It's going to be all right, daughter, you'll see."

Jilleen started to push her stroller and follow Olivia and Walter. She glanced over at the pretty flowers growing tall and thick on the edge of the yard. Maybe flowers would make Olivia happy again. Running over to the flowers, she began picking the daisies and some tall purple things she didn't know the name of. The purple ones had thick stems she struggled to break, but they were too strong. She put her bouquet on the ground and used both hands. Finally, the flower stem broke and she put it with the daisies. She wrestled with another one of the purple flowers.

"Psst," said a voice from the other side of hedge.

Pausing to make sure she heard right, she fingered the flower and glanced around for the gardener, wondering if she was in trouble for picking the flowers.

"Psst," again the voice beckoned.

"Who's there?" she asked timidly.

"Jilleen," the young voice said again.

Recognizing the voice, but not believing it, she stepped past the flowerbeds. Dropping to her knees she wormed her way into the thick hedge, parting it. A blond head popped into the hedge's opening, scaring her. She squeaked and fell backwards on her behind.

He grinned at her.

His blue eyes twinkled.

Forgetting where she was, she cried out, "Casey! Casey! Casey! Ye didn't drown—ye didn't get drownded! Ye didn't drownded!" All of a sudden, she didn't feel so lonely.

Casey laughed at her. And she laughed at him looking so funny with his head sticking through the hedge with little green leaves stuck to his curly hair.

"Jilleen, I gotta hurry. I've been waitin' a long time fer them people to leave. Me friend Jimmy's here. He helped me find ya."

Her brother forced his arm through the thick, stiff hedge and took her hand. The feeling of her brother's warm hand squeezing hers felt so familiar. His hands had patted her when she'd fallen, had fed her when mam had been too busy to do so. He'd taken care of her since she was born, and holding his hand meant she still had family.

"Where ye be livin'?" She had to know. "Can I go with ya then?"

He slowly shook his head, "'Tis best I don't tell ye. Someday we'll be together. But ya have to stay here for now."

She scrunched up her face, close to tears. "Casey, could ya not find our daddy?"

"Nay, but I will. I'll find him, Jilly, and he'll help us. I found you, didn't I?" he blurted. "Are ya being treated fair then?"

"Aye, 'Livia is so nice. And Sparks her dog, he likes me too." She couldn't help but notice he was wearing different clothes, newer, yet rumpled and smudged. "Where's yer hat?"

"I lost it in the ocean." And he didn't have to say anything else. They both knew how he lost it.

She took off Walter's old cap and handed it to him. "Here, take this. Ye need a cap, aye."

After settling the cap on his head, cocked just a little sideways to take up the loose fit, his face became fierce looking and he whispered, "I've something to tell ya, Jilly, but ya have to promise not to tell anyone, 'specially the people yer with. Promise?"

Only after she crossed her heart and pledged never to tell did he continue.

"Ya have to be careful. Remember what I told ya just before being tossed off the big ship?"

"About the lady Uncle Sam killed?" Yes, she remembered, and sucking in her breath couldn't help but nod. Her happy mood was ruined. "Casey, Uncle Sam's been here by the gate, tryin' to get me."

"Ah…no—Jilleen! He's after me too. He's mean. He'll harm those around us—maybe kill them. I'll find Da. Stay inside, don't play outside—"

"Jelee?" Myron was walking across the lawn towards her. She glanced back at Casey, but he had already squirmed back from the hedge as though he'd never been.

"Casey?" she whispered, "Are you there?"

"Aye, but I have to go. Don't tell anyone about me, or about Uncle Sam. Promise?"

"I promise. Bye, Casey." But he was gone, and all she could hear was the fading sound of his shoes against the sidewalk. She picked up the flowers and put them in the stroller. The news about her uncle squelched any happiness she felt.

"Were you talking to someone?" Myron asked. Using his hand to shade the sun from his face, he stared directly at the spot where Casey had been.

"Nay, to meself. I was trying to pick those flowers for 'Livia." She pointed at the thick-stemmed purple ones.

Myron dug into his pants pocket and pulled out his pocketknife. "Here, let me get them, they're called irises and the stems are too thick for you to break." After a few swift cuts with the sharp blade, he had a handful of colorful flowers that he handed to her. "Olivia will like these."

Jilleen could see Olivia waiting at the back door for them. Sparks shot from the house and went right to the spot where she'd talked to Casey. He sniffed all around the area, his moist nose close to the ground. He then went directly to the hedge and lifting a leg, peed.

"Sparks, come." Myron whistled for the dog.

Jilleen fell in behind him and pushed the stroller that bumped up and down on the lawn. She hoped her brother could stay away from Uncle Sam. Casey's warning for her to be careful and forced promises left her confused about what to tell and what to keep to herself.

The boys ran down the sidewalk, their shoes thudding against the cobblestones. They passed tall imposing houses peeking over hedges like the one surrounding the big house Jilleen was in. Casey ran to keep up with Jimmy's longer strides. Casey was the happiest boy around. Jilleen knew he was alive and that she still had family. Finding her safe and happy was all he cared about right now. In order for Jimmy to bring him here, he'd told Jimmy about his Uncle Sam. He told his complete story from the time his da was forced to leave Ireland, his mother and uncle's odd behavior back in Belfast, the *Titanic*, the murdered woman, all of it.

"Stop, Jimmy, I've a stitch in me side," he said and stopped running. While Jimmy waited for him to catch up, Casey dug around inside his pants pocket. Taking out a dime, he flipped it high, and then caught the coin as it fell. "I'll buy us a soda, want one?"

"Sure."

Casey had come to rely on Jimmy for a lot of things. He'd even cautioned Casey they needed to be more careful. His uncle might not care who'd get hurt if he came after Casey. They were going to find where Uncle Sam was staying. Jimmy said if they knew where his uncle was living, they could watch out for him better and find out what he was up to. Casey figured his mam was with Uncle Sam, and that hurt most of all. It was as though she'd stopped loving him and Jilleen. He couldn't understand how she could not want to be with Da.

They boarded a packed elevated train.

Casey glanced around making sure his uncle wasn't following them. Nowadays, he looked over his shoulder a lot. The train tracks, high off the ground, ran down streets parallel with tall buildings. Only upper floors were visible. Casey noticed the buildings were shabby, with awnings over the windows, the wash stringing across alleys. The train let out a jarring whistle.

"That's some house yer little sis is livin' in."

"Well 'tis only until I find me da. Then we'll be together and he don't live in no big fancy house. His letters to mam said he had a nice apartment for us."

Jimmy's body swayed with the rocking of the train. The sun's glare through the window made his red hair blaze. "Yer old man must live in the tenements somewhere. Can't ya remember anything about the address?"

"Village something."

"East Village…ah Greenwich Village?"

Casey shrugged. "I never paid attention. Thought Da would be meetin' us."

Chapter Fifteen

Derry stood next to the front window of their apartment. For the first time in weeks she was up and not lying in bed drugged. Her mind was permanently fogged with whispery voices.

On the table beside her were supplies for a bath. Sam had told her to go down the hall to the bathroom and wash up. She didn't like to leave their room, and would do anything to remain behind the locked door. Delaying her bath, she parted the lacy curtains and peered out. The day was clear with people strolling along. Children's excited chatter forced her to shrink back and let the gauzy curtain fall back into place.

Her hand darted nervously to her throat as the sounds of children brought memories of her own babies. Casey's eyes so blue they rivaled the sky. He had her eye color. She reached up and wrapped a strand of blonde hair about her finger. Casey, her golden boy. He had her hair. She closed her eyes as memories of her wee lass Jilleen aroused an ache so intense that sometimes she thought to join her daughter in death. Jilleen's bubbly giggle, her trusting face so like Donald's, it was all becoming too much to bare. Their deaths were her fault. Guilt chipped away at her hardly leaving anything to live for, and the dark tunnel enveloping her, cinched a little tighter.

Sam scowled over his paper at her. "Go take your bath. You're startin' to stink."

Something in the paper had put him in a sour disposition, like he'd eaten bad food, but she wasn't about to ask. Besides, he wouldn't tell her anyway. Sam was a man of many secrets. Unable to put her bath off any longer, she picked up her things and started for the door.

"Take your dress off and get in the tub—ya hear me," he ordered as if reading her mind. "Fill the bathtub, and soak. Be sure to wash your hair."

She opened their apartment door and fearfully peeked out into the hall toward the bathroom. Relieved no one was about, she hurried down the dimly lit hallway. She reached for the doorknob and the safety of the bathroom, when the toilet flushed, and the door swung open.

A man stepped out.

She gasped and stepped backward. Her supplies clattered to the floor.

"Sorry, didn't mean to frighten you," the stranger said, holding his hat.

Like a captured rabbit, she watched in paralyzed silence, looking at the back of his thinning brown hair as he knelt down and hastily picked up her items.

"Here," he said, and standing stuffed them back in her arms. "I'm Tom Meeks from upstairs. I was on my way out and decided to use the downstairs…er…well, never mind. You're Missus Flynn, aren't you?" he asked.

Derry hugged her bath items to her chest and nodded. She stared at the bathroom door, her intent to get away from this man as fast as she could. "Let me by," she whispered, and pushed past him to slam the door on any reply he might have.

Quickly turning the key, she raggedly drew in a breath and listened to his fading footfalls.

She went to the pedestal sink where she pushed the rubber plug into the drain hole. She glanced at the large claw-footed bathtub. With no intentions of obeying Sam, she dropped the lavender scented soap into the sink's hot water. She unbuttoned her dress to the waist and pried her arms out of the narrow floral-printed sleeves. The top flopped around her hips.

Derry leaned forward to scrutinize herself in the mirror. The face peering back wasn't hers. Fine lines had embedded below both eyes, and a line had gouged itself vertically between her eyebrows. She frowned at the face, making the line groove deeper.

Something in the mirror caught her eye. She turned to stare at the dark wooden bookshelf against the wall close to the toilet. A stack of periodicals and newspapers were piling up on the shelves. The newspapers weren't here before, were they? Maybe they were and she didn't notice, or more like she didn't care.

Curious, she knelt down on the small black and white tiles of the floor and shuffled through the papers. Usually, the voices stopped her ability to concentrate, so she'd almost given up reading. The papers in her hand were about the *Titanic*, the headlines large and bold. Not wanting to read about what she'd lived through, she halfheartedly continued to sort and stack the papers. Thinking they were all about the ship's sinking, she picked up the last paper in the stack.

She gasped.

Jilleen! Her little girl was on the front page. She moaned, her hand covering her mouth to stifle the screams of joy wanting to escape. Jilleen was alive! Mother of God—Mary Mother of God, her baby was alive. Her legs collapsed and she sat down hard on the floor.

Read it Derry, read what it says, she told herself.

WHO IS THIS LITTLE GIRL? The banner glared in bold headlines.

Oh…God, Jilleen, her baby alone in a strange city. She absentmindedly scratched the bare skin at her throat. Jilleen looked sad, like she'd been crying, her little lips in a familiar pout. No one knew who she was. Apparently, she'd only given her first name, and they'd spelled it wrong, making it sound like jelly one puts on bread. The article gave the address where Jilleen was staying. She was somewhere here in the City. Oh…God…Derry moaned, she wanted her daughter.

She hadn't caused her daughter's death after all.

Please let me have my baby.

The paper was dated several days after they had docked. She didn't know today's date. Maybe Sam would take her to get Jilleen. Nay, she didn't think so.

Maybe Donald had read this and now had Jilleen. Nay—aye?

Derry feasted on her daughter's face like a starving person given food and couldn't get enough. She ran her hand across Jilleen's image, remembering the soft feel of her daughter's skin, her luminous eyes that always held trust. Those eyes in this article were large and frightened. She tried memorizing the address, but gave up and tearing the article out of the paper held it pressed against her bosom.

Voices began whispering in a loud frenzy, *"Go to Donald, he'll forgive you. No, he thinks you're dead…all dead."*

Where had she lost Donald? Why? Sam had been before Donald. Sam—Donald. Donald—Sam.

…The voices converged on her, all shouting at the same time, *"Fill the tub—lie down in the water, go to sleep Derry, go sleep in the water."*

She put her hands over her ears trying to quell the urging whispers, warning them away. She fought against the voices, refusing to accept them as part of her being.

She'd kept asking Sam if he could hear them talking, but he'd scoffed at her, and told her what she needed was a good feck, and he was certain she'd hear even louder voices singing in her head before he was finished with her.

The water turned cold in the sink, the soap gone soft, and still she sat, thinking. It dawned on her Jilleen was on the *Carpathia.* Sam said she wasn't.

She didn't hear the heavy tread on the floor. A knock on the door and a voice softly calling her name made her jump. It took her awhile to collect her thoughts and finally realize it was Sam.

"What?" she said.

"Let me in," he cajoled, turning the knob. "Unlock the door, Darlene."

"I'm bathing. I'm in the tub," she said, hoping to get rid of him.

But his soft chuckle came through the door and she could tell he was leaning against it, practically hear him breathing though the wood.

"Open the door or I'll take it off by the hinges," he whispered.

Having no other choice, she folded the article up and stuffed it inside her shoe. She quickly put the papers back in the bookcase.

She stepped out of her dress and pushed the rubber stopper in the drain. While the water splashed inside the tub, she opened the door. Sam's big body filled the doorway, in his arm were several bath towels, a sponge, and another bar of soap.

His eyes flicked over her, and then at the tub. Stepping inside, Sam locked the door and went over to the tub where he put his bath supplies down on the floor. He stuck his hand in the water and jerked it back out.

"Feck!" he said and shook his hand. He turned on the cold water. "Sure'n that's better, ya would have scalded yourself. What are ya doing in here? You've been gone a long time."

She wanted to accuse him, ask him what he knew about Jilleen.

Taking a step toward her, he reached into his pants pocket and pulled out a strand of pearls, dangling them in front of her face. She parted her mouth in surprise and couldn't help but stare at the small white pearls, wondering where such a pretty thing had come from.

"This is for you, Darlene. I was going to give the necklace to ya after we came off the Titanic and were on our way to our new life. But things changed, you changed, being sick and all. I think now is a good time." His amber eyes searched her face and she smiled at him, trying to put aside the article about Jilleen, but couldn't.

He put the pearls around her neck and hooked the clasp.

"There, these are right grand on me woman, aye," he said while turning her to face him, studying her as if to find something new about her.

Derry felt the sleek round orbs. This was the first time in her life she'd been given a present so fine. She watched Sam lower his suspenders, and then remove his white shirt where he tossed it to land on top of the bookcase. Apparently seeing the stack of newspapers for the first time, he appeared to be puzzled, and then as though dismissing them, he turned to her and winked.

The sight of him shirtless, his chest nothing but muscles covered with dark hair would normally cause her to desire him, but since they'd arrived in New York, the sight of him naked held nothing but indifference for her. She hadn't stopped loving him, it's just that a wall had appeared. Where once she saw things clearly, she could no longer think about anything that took much thought. Sam took a lot of thought. Living took a whole lot more.

"I want to see ya wearing nothin' but them pearls," he said, and flicked his dark brow. He pushed her drawers down over her hips and helped her step out of them. Reaching behind her head, he pulled her hairpins out and placed the pins on the bookcase.

Naked with nothing but the necklace that she'd trade in a heartbeat for her rosary, she never felt more vulnerable.

"Nothin' like me woman wearin' only jewelry and the skin she was born in." His eyes wore smoldering appreciation as they raked her entire length. And then as though she was as delicate as the necklace she wore, he picked her up and placed her in the tub.

To her, the water wasn't hot and relaxing. She felt the water softly lapping around her body and steeled herself not to bolt out of the tub.

He took the sponge, and after lathering it up with floral smelling soap, ran it over her back, and down each arm.

"Relax," he urged.

His hand went to the back of her neck as he helped her to lean back against the white porcelain tub. He suds her breasts, then slowly between her legs. The sponge floated to the surface while his hand remained underwater working her cleft, stroking her.

Tears joined the water on her face. She hated being touched, didn't want to be touched.

"Don't," she whispered and grasped his hand.

To her relief he stopped his unwanted caresses. She opened her eyes to find his face red with anger. He soaped her hair, his fingers hurting her scalp. He lowered her until the water closed over her face. He held her under a long time. Too long. Her lungs felt like they were going to explode. She started fighting, thrashing, trying to breathe, trying to get her legs under her. Her mouth opened taking in water. He pulled her upright, hurting her. She sputtered, coughed, and gulped in air.

His face was within inches of hers, his voice damning. "Don't ever deny me anything, Darlene."

"Let me out of here," she begged, and grasped the top of the tub, holding onto it, afraid he would put her under again.

For once he didn't join her in the tub. Instead, he roughly hauled her out of the tub and grabbed up a towel.

The walls were slick with steam, the floor wet with puddles as Sam ran the towel over her body, making her breasts jiggle as he briskly dried them off. His gaze went to the pearls, remembering the last woman who had them in her mouth.

He was no fool and knew things were not right with Darlene's mind, that she'd lost hold of reality. At first, he'd thought it was the trauma of losing her kids, but when she slowly got worse, he thought it was the laudanum and stopped giving it to her. Now he knew better. And in truth, he had to admit even back in Belfast she was always a little different, remembering how his Mam tried to point it out. But he was being taken down memory lane, thinking of her as the innocent lass in the butcher shop, on the beach, someone naïve he could easily impress. Someone with the type of mind a man such as himself could control.

They both had kinks in their brains and were more than deserving of each other. Hell, she even had him listening for those damn voices she claimed to hear all the time. He was getting tired of it, his patience with her wearing out, and now this, her denying him what was his right to have. He wouldn't stand for it.

He moved away from her and bent to pick up her drawers. A piece of newspaper stuffed inside her shoe caught his eye. Curious, he reached over and plucked the paper out, instantly seeing Jilleen's face and the article that he'd long ago memorized.

Derry's intake of breath was sharp and he swung his head around to stare at her. She wrung her hands and folded them in front of her blonde pubic hair. She searched his face. He wanted to hurt her for daring to have this paper, wanted to hurt her for what he thought was betrayal. But her anxious face had him changing his mind. Instead, he widened his eyes in mock surprise and acted as good as any actor on stage.

"Well I'll be a feckin' blighter! Darlin' would ya look at that—'tis Jilleen. Ye've found her. And here we thought she'd died. 'Tis a blessing from The Almighty, aye? Why didn't ya tell me when I first walked in?"

"Sam," she stammered, "I found it…and…wanted to keep the picture of Jilleen. She's so pretty…and…I want me daughter…can I have her…" she faltered, her voice running down like an auto out of gas.

Sam ripped the writing away from the article leaving only the picture. He handed it to her. "If ya think yer well enough to take care of her, maybe. Can't exactly be a mother when yer having conversations with people who aren't there, aye? We'll wait and see how ya fare."

"Can ye find out if Jilleen's still there?" she asked with hope.

"Anything ya want, Darlene."

His mind raced along, he'd just figured out how to get Jilleen out of the Marsh's house.

Get Jilleen. Get Casey. And then…

Chapter Sixteen

Sunday evening found Donald getting ready to go to the Marsh's. He fidgeted with his black tie in front of the small mirror while Joe stood close by and scrutinized every move. Donald was thankful the bruises on his face had faded to pale yellow and the cut on his lip healed.

"How's that?" Donald said and adjusted the knot one more time.

Joe, leaning against the doorframe, shrugged. "Fine I guess. Never wore one. Hey, Donald, while you're gone I'm going to visit some friends." He moseyed back into the living room, whistling.

By *friends* Donald knew Joe meant his old gang over in the Lower East Side. They were thieves that stole people's hard earned cash. In the past, Donald's wallet had been lifted once too often. Since money was hard to come by, Donald had a tough attitude about the gang, or any gang for that matter. Yet, knowing why the boys had settled into a life of crime, he could feel sympathy for them. He also wanted to get help for them, and thought by reporting them to the authorities they would be rounded up and sent to orphanages. His way of thinking made Joe keep a tight lip about them. Donald also knew that since staying at his place, Joe didn't visit his old gang too often.

Donald took his dark blue vest from the peg, and after slipping it on, buttoned the six small buttons. He went to the dresser where he'd tossed his personal items and picking up his pocketknife, money clip, and key, put them in his pocket. The cheap pocket watch he'd bought awhile back was last to be picked up. Every time he hooked the delicate chain and stuffed the watch inside his watch pocket, he thought about holding his son close and exacting a promise. His family's laughter should be filling his home. He tried to put away feelings that threatened to take him down into a pit of hell so dark he'd never crawl out. Sometimes Donald envied the dead, it was over with for them, but for him grief stuck to him like a leach.

The stain on the bedroom wall was still there. The odor of roses lingered, but now he had new memories, the one of Olivia Marsh lying in his bed, her dark hair fanning out, and her guilt about being one of the lucky ones who survived. He could still feel the desperation coming from her, like if she didn't keep a strong grip on him, she would drown in memories of the sinking ship.

He slipped on his black suit coat, and rolled his shoulders, allowing the new coat to settle on his broad frame. The three-piece suit, purchased with the money Walter Marsh had left for him, fit Donald as if it was tailor made. He took his cap from the coat rack and put it on, the bill just off center, a jaunty angle he liked.

"Ya look nice, Donald, just like a proper Irishman. Maybe you'll impress the banker." Joe rubbed his nose and sniffed. "And ya smell as pretty as a lady."

"Be sure to lock the door when ye leave. Don't want another intruder like the last time." He was pleased to see Joe flash his key.

A soft knock sounded and Donald opened the door to Walter Marsh's chauffeur standing smart in his uniform, and with eye goggles hanging around his neck.

"Mr. McShane, I'm Hugh Huckaby, the Marsh's driver." He held his cap in hand, and with his uniform so pristine, Donald wondered how a man could manage to get around and not put a wrinkle in his pants.

"Mr. Huckaby, I'm glad to make yer acquaintance. That young fellow over there is Joe Gillespie." Donald put his hand out and the man was quick to shake it.

"Young man," the driver nodded at Joe.

Donald followed the driver who was probably a little older than he was. They came out onto the sidewalk where several men and women assembled around the limousine, admiring it.

A lady living in the same building as Donald smiled up at him, practically flirting. "Don't tell me you're getting inside that lovely car? Have you come into money or something?"

Donald could only nod, for he had no answer to give the slim woman. Nor did he intend to enlighten the curiosity of someone who usually never gave him the time of day and who sure as hell didn't know his name. He got into the car where Hugh held the door open for him.

The chauffeur cranked the car that chugged to life. He jumped into the driver's seat. Honking the horn, he slowly pulled away from the curb, waving at people to get out of his way.

Donald got a new perspective of being in an expensive automobile. People would stare in admiration and quickly draw back onto the curb if they started to cross in front of it. The horn was in constant use, something that Donald found to be loud and obnoxious. Relaxing against the tan upholstery, he admired the sleek interior. He couldn't help but see his distorted reflection on the shiny chrome of the door handle. Nor could he ignore the mounted flower vase on each side that held a pink carnation, its spicy fragrance most pleasant. Appreciating the mechanics of the car, he rolled the window down halfway to allow the air to circulate. Donald was where he'd never expected to be in life, his status elevated somewhat. He felt better times were ahead, especially working for Walter Marsh.

As the Village's brownstones receded behind the tall skyscrapers of Manhattan, the car joined a line of cars and horse drawn wagons coming and going. Men wearing summer straw hats escorted women whose evening attire rivaled the plumage of a colorful bird. Everyone had a purpose.

The chauffeur constantly worked the gears, slowing down or speeding up. Just to watch made Donald realize there was a lot to driving an automobile around. They turned onto Eleventh Avenue and headed north.

Donald noticed most of the vehicles they passed were similar to the one he rode in. He perked up at the sight of so much green. Massive trees were everywhere. They lined the streets and they poked over green hedges. They drove by stately homes surrounded by generous sweeping grounds and ornate wrought-iron fences. Donald took a deep breath of the crisp clean air, and glanced up at the broad sky.

The car stopped in front of a black wrought iron gate, and Hugh hopped out to open it. Ducking his head to peer through the front windshield, Donald could see the overpowering house set well back from the street. It was the same here as back in Ireland, the rich lived lofty with fresh air, and the poor were jammed together like sardines.

Gravel scrunched under the tires as the car slowly followed the circular driveway. After being let out of the car, Donald grabbed the large round metal knocker and banged it against the plate, preparing to enter the sealed off world of the rich. It wasn't long before he heard heels clicking against the floor and the door flung wide.

Olivia Marsh stood there, a cool vision in a pale linen dress the color of a summer meadow. The dress's skirt barely had a flare to it showing off her long slim frame. For some reason, she stared at him like he was a cross between the Devil and the Lord. He prayed it was the latter.

"Mr. McShane," she said offering her hand.

"It's good to see ya, Miss Marsh. Yer lookin' better than the last time we met, aye?" It was all so stiff and formal. Had she forgotten sharing her innermost fears with him? He sure as heck hadn't. He remembered the whole evening just fine.

"Yes, yes, that's true. I'm still having trouble with headaches though."

She searched his face with such intensity that he asked, "Is anything wrong, Miss Marsh? Is me face manky…er…dirty?" He ran his hand over his chin.

She smiled and shook her head. "No, Mr. McShane, your face is quite adequate."

"Just adequate?" He couldn't help but tease and when she actually turned a delicate shade of pink, he laughed. "I'm sorry, I've never been told me face is adequate. Guess that's good?"

Smiling, she interlaced her arm within his and escorted him toward a room just off the foyer. "Dad's waiting for you in the study. Mother is fussing with last minute dinner instructions and will join us shortly. We'll be eating a little later."

She took her time escorting him, and he had to admit it felt good to be next to her, although he found her constant chatter not in character. He thought of her as a woman in control of events around her, even one to make them happen. Her grip on his arm tightened as they entered the study where Walter Marsh sat in a comfortable brown leather chair. Beside his chair stood a tall metal ashtray cluttered with cigar butts.

Walter didn't bother to stand, instead, he motioned toward the camel-backed sofa close by. "Take a seat, McShane."

Donald sat on the tightly stuffed cushion, the material in browns and tans was made with a man in mind. Walter's study fit him. Donald couldn't help but give a quick glance at the ceiling-high book shelves, the dark mahogany trimmed walls, and the fireplace where no fire burned this warm evening. His apartment could fit inside this one room.

"Would you care for something to drink? Perhaps lemonade, or a man's drink, brandy or the like?" Walter said.

Donald eyed his host. "Ah…no, but thanks for the offer. Maybe later?" He glanced at Olivia who now sat right beside him.

"Are you sure?" Olivia asked. "Certainly, you must be thirsty. Perhaps a glass of water?"

Thinking to appease her, he nodded. She quickly stood and went to the fancy sideboard holding crystal decanters of liquors and a large pitcher. She was striking from the back, her stance erect, her glistening brown hair pulled up in an elaborate twisted knot, her injury cleverly concealed. He couldn't help but remember holding her close. The special moment and memory made him smile, but a glance over at Walter who puffed his cigar and eyeballed him speculatively, made Donald lose his smile in a hurry.

Olivia returned with the water. Donald no sooner accepted the glass and gulped it down when a woman, he figured was Olivia's mother, stood in the doorway.

"Mother, this is Mister Donald McShane, the man who saved me from Lapaglia's ruffians. Mr. McShane, I'd like to introduce my mother, Merilee Marsh."

Donald quickly sat his glass down on the end table and came to his feet.

"Welcome, Mr. McShane." A puzzled look creased her face, followed by a low, nervous laugh. "Goodness me, I almost feel like I've met you before, but that's impossible. I do want to thank you for getting Olivia away from that dreadful brawl."

Merilee Marsh smelled like heaven must, her face was like seeing Olivia's in years to come. Smiling, he offered his hand. "Mrs. Marsh, I feel the same way, like I've already made yer acquaintance." As he held her hand, stiff and unyielding, her reserve for the likes of his class was on her face, in her posture, even in the tilt of her head. He didn't care for the woman and had good reason not to. He let go of her hand and waited.

Merilee settled gracefully in a nearby chair and situated the folds of her skirt around her legs. Smiling, she accepted a drink from the serving girl. "Thank you, Lori Raye. Please see to our guest and fill his empty glass." She turned her attention back to Donald. "Tell me about yourself, Mr. McShane."

Donald was careful to relay only the parts he wanted them to know. He told bits and pieces about his past. His father was a furniture maker who always smelled of wood shavings and stain, and that he died before his time leaving his wife depending on her sons to get by. He spoke of his childhood, his schooling, growing up poor and hardworking in Ireland, and of being the middle son. Little was mentioned of Sam. And Donald omitted telling about Aidan's shooting and his brother's quick rush to get him out of the country. Instead he filled them with the sadness he felt from leaving his wife and two children and coming to a strange country where he found work and saved to send for them.

The Marsh's politely listened and asked questions when it was appropriate to do so. Donald couldn't help but feel he was being questioned for a particular reason, like they were making sure he should be working in Walter's bank, and wasn't a thief or something. They also failed to mention the main reason he was here, to meet the little Irish miss.

They'd had an excellent meal, probably the best feast Donald had ever had. The roast beef was cooked to perfection, the gravy melted in his mouth, and he'd managed not to make a pig of himself. He'd watched Olivia to make sure he was using the correct eating utensils.

Missing from the dinner table was the little lass. Normally she ate dinner with them, however Olivia explained this evening was different, and that she'd eaten in the nursery. Donald figured it had to do with wanting only grownups at the table or some silly rule pertaining to the rich.

After dinner, Donald followed Walter into his study where he had his choice of drinks. Enjoying a whiskey with a strong burn, Donald listened as Walter reiterated the job, the salary, and that he was to start tomorrow morning. They both puffed expensive Cuban cigars, and blew cones of blue-gray smoke that lifted toward the high ceiling of carved intricate scroll work.

Donald reached inside his suit pocket where he took out the calendar page from Lapaglia's and handed it to Walter. Walter's jaw clinched as he read it. Stubbing out his cigar, he went to put the incriminating piece of paper inside his desk drawer.

"I should go to the police with this, but I'm not sure it will do any good."

"Ye might be surprised," Donald said. "Yer money can open doors a poor man couldn't get through. Meanin' no offense, sir, but it's the truth."

"No offense taken. I'll try the police, but first I'm going to pull in the loans Lapaglia owes my bank. When you come to work tomorrow, I'll show you just how we run things from my end of the coin." Walter drained his cognac. "You should get some satisfaction in seeing Lapaglia squirm?"

Donald grinned. "D'ye need anything else done?"

"I might."

Olivia knocked on the door and asked to join them. "Dad, I hope you've finished with your business. Mother's gone upstairs." The look she gave her father appeared to be more of a signal than anything.

Walter nodded and stubbed out his cigar.

Donald again wondered what was going on. Then it dawned on him, at last, he was going to meet the little miss.

Walter no sooner left when Olivia turned to stare at Donald. She worried her hands together like some old sailor tying a knot and never quite getting it right.

Donald's guard came up. Something about her demeanor wasn't right. He would never peg her as being nervous about anything. "Is it time for me to meet yer little miss?" he asked. And from the wretched despair on her face, he knew that was the answer. He couldn't understand it, he was just going to talk to the child for Christ's sake, nothing more, nothing less, and it was at their request. From the slight lowering of her mouth, he knew it was going to get worse.

"Mr. McShane…oh…Lord," she blurted out, "I don't know how to say this—"

"Why not just say what's botherin' ya then? You've been acting like yer walkin' on hot coals ever since I stepped foot in yer house. Ah…maybe it's the closeness, the…er…touches, from the night ya got hurt, aye? If yer upset or embarrassed at my havin' taken off yer clothes, don't be. I kept you covered with a sheet—didn't see a thing. Yer engaged to be married—"

"Promised."

"Promised? Promised what—"

"It's one step before being engaged, I'm promised to Myron, not engaged. And my being upset has nothing to do with you undressing me. Well…that sounded strange." She tried to be witty but it wasn't like her and her attempt at humor failed fast. "The other night when you told me about your family, your wife being called *Derry*, I—"

"What has me family to do with anything?"

She approached and placed her hand on his forearm, "Mr. McShane, please, it's your wife's name. Alana Darlene. You said Derry was her nickname?"

"Aye, I did."

"You also said your daughter's name is Jilleen and you have a son named Casey."

Agitated, he thrust his hands in his pockets. This was not what he came here for, to be dragged back through painful memories. He'd be starting a high paying job which allowed him to live better. He wanted to bask in the happiness of his good fortune, but Miss Marsh was pulling him back into the icy water of the Atlantic.

"Mr. McShane, before I bring in the little girl, there is something you need to know."

"Aye?"

"The little girl living with us calls her doll Derry, and she cries out in the night for her brother Casey." She paused as if her words were sticking inside of her. "And…well…her name is Jilleen McShane."

This was the last thing he'd expected. Hope, shock, and shattered feelings coursed through him as strong as an ocean's current. His dinner rose to the back of his throat and he hastily swallowed. Thrusting his fists inside his suit coat pockets, he strode to the fireplace where he turned and whipped out his hand to point at her.

"Ah…no…don't say such, Miss Marsh. I've got an inspection card belonging to me wife that was found in a stranger's pocket. A dead woman as cold as the iceberg which destroyed the Titanic. Trying to find me children, I looked at wee little faces all tight—blue and dead. I can't go through this again, won't. Good evening." He started to leave, but was stopped by the threesome standing in the doorway.

Walter and Merilee Marsh stood directly behind a little girl clutching a doll to her chest. Walter's hands rested on the girl's shoulders.

"Perhaps you need to look at her first, Donald," Walter said, and gently nudged the child forward.

The little girl's eyes widened upon seeing Donald and she dug her heels in, refusing to take another step. She whispered, "Nay."

She appeared frightened until Walter leaned forward. "Don't be afraid, this man will not hurt you." And once again, he urged her on.

Merilee took Walter's arm and they remained like strong columns in the doorway.

Donald watched her shyly scurry over to Olivia's side and squirm upon the seat next to her. After straightening the skirt of her blue dress, she deeply sighed, staring first at him and then up at Olivia.

Unable to stop looking at the child, Donald remained standing. She was a moppet in brown curls, the same color as his. The lass had his face. She resembled his mam something fierce. "Was she wearing a red coat when ya caught her?" he said, surprised he could talk, surprised that his knees hadn't turned liquid.

Olivia, now biting her bottom lip, nodded.

He asked to see it.

Merilee summoned Stella Lippencott and they waited in mute silence. At last, the coat was produced. Donald's hands were shaking so bad he dropped the coat. He picked it up, fumbled with it some more, cursed to himself, and finally found the label. Turning the label over, he read the name Jilleen McShane that he'd wrote before sending the coat off to Derry.

"*Jaysus—Jaysus*," he moaned, no longer able to trust his legs, he groped for the sofa behind him and collapsed on it. He buried his face into the woolen cloth of the coat, allowing tears to soak into the material.

He slowly raised his head. Everyone—everything in the room became a blur but his daughter sitting across from him, staring back at him with eyes the same hazel color as his. He flashed to the day she was born, holding a slippery, squirming little thing in his hands, her lusty cry, her eyes searching yet not seeing. He'd felt arrogant, like he'd produced a miracle, and was the only man in the world to do so. He'd put her little mouth to Derry's nipple and watched with delight as she started to suck. Together, they'd introduced her to Casey. Yes, he'd been a contented man back then. Wanting to feel that way again, to hold her close, Donald held out his hand and beckoned.

He said in a soft voice fraught with emotion, "Jilleen, come here to yer da who has waited a lifetime to hold ya."

She slipped from the sofa and stood, hesitating.

"Ah…do. Do come to yer da," Donald said.

With Olivia's gentle prod against the small of her back, she moved closer to him.

He met her halfway and got down on his knees. Not wanting to frighten her, he gently pushed an errant curl from her forehead. He tilted her chin and looked into her eyes, wide with curiosity and searching his face.

"I sent ya this dolly. It was wearing a sailor suit."

She perceivably nodded, and held her doll up. "Grandmum Ina made clothes for her, a red coat like mine."

"I've waited three years for this day. Three long years, with the last few months thinking I'd lost you forever." He took a deep breath and swallowed. "Welcome home, daughter, welcome home."

His throat closed tight and he hugged her small body to his for the longest of time. Placing his head against the side of hers, he cupped the back of her head with his hand. True happiness coursed through him. To him this was a miracle, and he prayed to that God he'd long ago cast away, accepting His love, His guidance, thanking Him, Olivia, the Marshes, and all those involved in this joyous happening.

"Are ye truly me da?" she whispered in her tiny Irish lilt. She snaked her hand around his neck where it stopped to take his earlobe between two fingers and gently tug.

Jilleen's tug on his earlobe sealed it.

Tears slipped down his cheeks. "Aye, I'm yer da. I'm father to yer brother Casey, and husband to yer mam, Derry McShane. Ina McShane, yer Grandmother, is me mum. Colin and Sam are me brothers."

At the mention of his brothers, Jilleen stiffened and pulled back to stare at him. She changed, becoming fearful as she scoured his face, making him wonder what was going on.

"Don't be afraid of me."

"Ye look like Uncle Sam," she replied, her hands nervously balling the material of her pretty dress.

Yes, he did resemble Sam and silently cursed the man for having caused him to lose the past years with his daughter. “Don’t worry about yer uncle.”

He moved to the sofa and after placing her on his lap, he smoothed her dress. For the first time he noticed Walter and Merilee were gone. Miss Marsh, dabbing at her eyes, was on her way out of the door.

“Miss Marsh, please stay,” he begged, “I’m goin’ to be needin’ yer help.”

She abruptly turned, sending the skirt of her dress to whisper about her ankles. With a look of total relief, she hurried to sit close to him on the sofa.

“Jilleen, this is for certain your father. And you know what? Your father was at the ship trying to find you, but you were with me. He didn’t recognize you because he thought you were my daughter. You have also grown and changed since he has last seen you.”

Jilleen nodded and timidly smiled. “Casey said ye would be there and…” She stopped talking and a frown overtook her face. “Casey—”

“It’s all right, Jilleen,” he interrupted, not wanting to talk about his dead son, not now, not during this happy time. It could wait. He ran his hand up her precious face, still not believing he held her.

“I don’t know where to start, Miss Marsh. I have so many questions. I’d like to take her home with me tonight. Would that be fair?” he asked hopefully.

“How can a father ask if it’s fair to take his child home? Of course, it’s just I wasn’t—”

“Nay!” Jilleen squirmed out of Donald’s tender hold and scurried upon Olivia’s lap. “Nay, ’Livia, ya got to come too! I don’t want to leave ya,” Jilleen’s voice was charged with desperation, confusion, and she gripped Olivia’s hand as tightly as her small hand would allow. She started to cry. “I dinna like this at all,” she managed to say between sobs.

Olivia took Jilleen, now almost inconsolable, against her bosom and patted Jilleen on the back.

Donald met Olivia's intense stare over Jilleen's shoulder.

"Please understand it's going to take time for Jilleen. She's gone through so much. We both have. And I've grown to love her dearly." She pulled out a lace handkerchief from her cuff, dabbed at Jilleen's tears, and wiped her nose. She kept reassuring Jilleen that her father loved her and only wanted good things for her. Olivia paused for a moment, and Donald could tell she was fighting for control.

"Can I still be in her life?" she asked.

Her plea wrenched compassion from him. He took their hands within his and squeezed. Why not? Why not have Olivia help guide Jilleen. There was no reason not to. He owed so much to this woman who had saved his child, nurtured her, brought her back into his arms.

"Would ye come home with me tonight? Help me to settle her in?" he asked, still clasping her hand. She laced her fingers through his, a natural movement for two people who already shared so much.

"Yes," she said, and absentmindedly pulled one of Jilleen's curls straight then let it coil back. "I will ride with you when Hugh takes you home. At least see her tucked in. But Jilleen has nightmares and I'm afraid she might…"

Donald could see Olivia's inner turmoil and knew she truly loved Jilleen. He tried making it easier. "It sounds like I will need your help considerably." Without thought, he ran his hand down the side of Olivia's face and paused to thumb her lips in a most intimate way. He liked the feel of her, to touch her, but then a heavy reminder fell like a curtain. Not only was Olivia the boss's daughter, there was a social chasm from here to Ireland separating them. He best get over his attraction.

Olivia's brows drew into a worried frown as she voiced her concern, "Mr. McShane, don't you have to start work at the bank tomorrow? Who's going to take care of her?"

Jilleen sniffled, yawned, and leaned her head against Olivia's chest, her hand gripped Olivia's like they were still back on the lifeboat.

"I've been too excited to think any further than havin' me wee lass back. I see the wisdom in what ye say. Maybe she should stay here until I can find someone to watch after her while I'm working. It's just now I have her—"

"No one will take your child from you again. Leave her here until she gets used to the idea you're her father."

"I've waited this long, a while longer won't make a difference, aye?" he reasoned.

"No difference at all," she agreed, her features brightened with a smile.

"Casey…" Jilleen mumbled, "Da…Casey's—"

"Shh..." he said, and seeing she was fighting sleep, he stood to take Jilleen in his arms. He nodded at Olivia. "Tomorrow, you and I will talk, Miss Marsh."

Jilleen's head rested against his shoulder as he followed Olivia upstairs. They went down a long hallway where she stepped inside an open door.

Donald carried Jilleen inside a room filled with little girl things. Dolls lined against the pillows of a frilly-canopied bed, and a brown, stuffed teddy bear was sitting in a rocking chair. A tall wardrobe was ajar with clothes. He couldn't give Jilleen any of this. He vowed with his new job and wages, he'd make sure she had more than what was waiting for her back in his apartment. A lone drawer with a change of clothes, and a small cot pushed into the corner of the living room, and he'd have to put Joe on the couch for her to even sleep there.

He sat Jilleen on the bed.

She yawned and staring at him, said, "Yer me da."

"Aye, I am. And never forget I love you, have always loved ya." He hugged her tight. Finally, he released her and stood aside so Olivia could ready Jilleen for bed.

Olivia unlaced her white shoes and removed them. Next she took off Jilleen's clothes and dressed her in a soft cotton nightgown, the sleeves trimmed with lace.

"In you go." She pulled back the crisp sheets allowing Jilleen to snuggle inside. She smiled at Donald. "I believe your daughter's ready for a good night kiss. I'll wait for you in the hallway. Oh…leave the night light burning…her nightmares, remember." Before relinquishing her spot to Donald, she kissed Jilleen on the cheek.

"Aye," he said.

"Da," Jilleen said, nervously plucking at the sheet. "Casey came to see me."

Jilleen's announcement stopped Olivia with her hand on the doorknob.

Donald gently ran his finger around Jilleen's chin. "In your nightmares? Olivia told me ya have bad dreams and wake up screamin' for Casey."

Jilleen's little chest rose and fell with a deep breath, her words tumbled out, "I was pickin' flowers for 'Livia when me brudder poked his head inside the hedge. He was funny lookin'. I was happy to see him. I thought he'd drownded, but he didn't. He was with a boy named Jimmy. I didn't see Jimmy. Casey didn't have a hat so I gave him mine." She clutched the sheet and stared up at them.

So easily said, Jilleen's words stilled both Donald and Olivia who simply froze in place.

At last, he found his voice. "When was this?" Donald's insides were vibrating like an auto's engine.

"The day 'Livia asked if I was Jelee McShane." She squirmed against the pillow, her face wary.

Olivia, standing next to Donald leaned down. "That was after I'd been hurt. Why haven't you told me this sooner, Jilleen?"

"'Cause, I promised Casey not to tell." She fixed a stare at Donald.

A stare so much like his own, he winked and smiled at her, and then without hesitation and delirious with happiness, Donald scooped her out of bed. He put his free hand around Olivia's waist and spun her around. He laughed—he yelped—Jesus, Mary and Joseph, his son was alive!

Jilleen giggled and clasped Donald's neck tighter.

Olivia laughed, her brown eyes searching his.

Donald stopped his silly dancing, and said in all sincerity, "Olivia Marsh, ye have brought my children to me."

Not waiting for her to say anything, his mouth slanted against hers and he heartily kissed her. For a moment she melted against him. Then as if realizing what they were doing, they broke apart and both looked at Jilleen whose bright eyes were mere inches from theirs.

Olivia ran her fingers across her mouth as if marveling at what just happened. And with a smile radiating across her face, she said to Donald, "I'll wait for you outside."

Remembering his manners, Donald tucked Jilleen back into bed and smoothed the sheet over her. "I promise ya this, Jilleen, I'll find yer brother and we'll be a family again."

"Really, Da, ya promise?"

"Oh…aye, I do. We'll be a family again."

Olivia stood at the end of the hallway. A clock on the nearby hall table loudly ticked off the minutes as hope filled her with fantasies. She parted the curtains to look out at a day now gone. Only her reflection stared back, that is until Donald's fine form filled the space behind hers. He stood extremely close to her. His eyes met hers in the glass. She could practically feel his nervousness that matched her own.

"Thank ya for me daughter, Miss Marsh. You could have kept silent about Jilleen and I would have never known."

"Yes, somehow you would have. Deceit and lies always catch up with a person. Even when used with good intentions and told by honest people," she spoke to his reflection. It was easier. "I must confess. At first I thought about not telling you. In the short time I've had Jilleen, she's become like a daughter to me. When Albert Flynn tossed her into my arms, I convinced myself there were loved ones waiting for her. She was afraid—I was terrified."

She clutched the velvet curtain a little tighter. "And now your son is alive, alone somewhere in the city. We must find him…" her voice trailed off as she watched his hands go to her shoulders and cup them with a grip both firm and comforting.

His fingers slid up her neck to touch her ear, then her pearl earring that he sent into a gentle sway. His mere touch sent excitement throughout her. No longer caring about decorum, Myron, or anyone else, she started to turn in his arms.

"McShane," Walter's voice boomed down the hallway. "Now that you have your daughter back, I'm thinking you will need to postpone starting at the bank tomorrow. And that sets fine with me." He strode up to them, pulling out his pocket watch as he did so, comparing it to the clock on the table.

"There's another reason he can't start tomorrow," Olivia said, wondering about her father's impeccable timing. "Jilleen just informed Mr. McShane that his son is alive."

Walter couldn't have looked more stunned. He took a few minutes to compose himself before snapping his watch shut. "My-God! I am overjoyed for you, McShane, overjoyed. What tremendous news. It appears our little miss is full of information she's kept to herself."

"Promises," Olivia said.

"Promises?" Walter's eyebrows flicked upward.

Donald smiled, and said, "A child's promise is as strong as steel. Don't ask me why, but it is. I'm just happy Jilleen broke this one to her brother."

Walter shook his head. "Aren't we all? It makes me wonder what else she's keeping to herself. Perhaps she'll tell us when she's ready.

I've left an envelope for you on the foyer table." He pointed a finger at Donald. "After you open it, I don't want to hear any arguments from you. Hugh has the car out front. Good night, Olivia, McShane." And not waiting for a response from anyone, he went inside his bedroom and shut the door.

"I take it he's left money for me, aye?"

"If it is, please take it in good faith."

Indeed, the envelope held money, and Donald couldn't refuse it. He needed money to eat and pay rent. Since Walter's enclosed note stated it was an advance on his salary, it made it all right, not like charity.

"It appears I still need yer help," he admitted to Olivia. "Tell me about Albert Flynn who threw Jilleen off the Titanic."

"Let me walk you to the door," she said, and wrapped his arm within hers.

It was a subtle movement on her part, one done with good manners. Yet, as they walked together, Donald felt that something precious and good had started between them.

Olivia began to tell him what little she knew about Albert Flynn. How he denied throwing Jilleen overboard. "…He has a wife named Lillian. And…I must say Albert Flynn looks enough like you to be your brother."

"Does he now?" Donald thought about Lillian Denbury and Derry's inspection card. And that wasn't all he was thinking about, but those thoughts he kept to himself, as if to voice them would make them true. Besides, he had a son to find.

Joe lounged on an old beat up sofa next to Frankie. The springs coming through the soiled Victorian discard threatened to give his body permanent indentations, so he shifted his behind to find a more comfortable spot. He'd been disappointed to arrive at the gang's hideaway to find only Frankie there.

Frankie had filled Joe in about the gang's latest happenings. He also mentioned a new kid had joined them. Right now, the kid was out with Jimmy and Benny trying to steal a buck or two. If Joe waited long enough, he could meet the little guy who according to Frankie was quite handy with his fists, fearless.

Joe had peeled and cooked up some potatoes and added them to the canned tomato soup he'd brought with him. He had to admit it didn't taste too bad. He'd managed to filch a few cans of soup from Donald's larder, reasoning he would be able to replace them before Donald noticed they were gone. Even though his life had turned for the better since meeting Donald, he wasn't about to forget his friends who had to constantly worry about their next meal.

"Wow, looks like you're doin' okay," Joe said and pointed to the long pants Frankie was wearing. The new pants were already grubby and dirty.

Frankie leaned forward to spit on the trash-covered floor. "Yeah, we were for a day or two. Jimmy made a haul, like robbin' the bank ya might say, but money only last us a little while. Expect we'll be movin' from here soon. Someone's hanging around, askin' questions about us. I've spotted him, tall, well dressed, think maybe he's the law."

Joe frowned at this news. "Well ya best be tellin' me where you're goin' to be movin'." A cockroach scurrying across the floor caught his eye and he watched until it disappeared under a crack in the floor.

Frankie started coughing and couldn't stop. He pulled a grubby handkerchief from his pocket and coughed so hard his face turned red with exertion. Bloody phlegm spotted the hanky. Finally he stopped and leaned back to recover.

Neither one said anything for a while.

Joe couldn't help but notice his friend was skinnier, his face skeletal, and his arms like sticks. Poor Frankie, only sixteen, yet looked like an old man.

"Make us a cigarette, Joe."

"Sure, Frankie."

Going over to the shelf on the wall, Joe stretched to reach the tin box with the cigarette supplies. After he shoved junk aside and cleared a spot on the table, he took out a cigarette roller, tobacco tin and soiled cigarette making papers. He fit the paper in the roller, tapped out the right amount of tobacco, and then rolled the first one. When he'd made a dozen or more, he twisted the ends of each cigarette to prevent the tobacco from spilling out. After stowing the cigarettes and supplies back inside the tin, he placed it back on the shelf.

Not in the mood to have a smoke himself, Joe used a wooden match to light his friend's. He sat down, careful to avoid the protruding springs.

"Yer bad sick ain't ya, Frankie?"

Frankie blew out a stream of blue gray smoke and shrugged. "Guess so. Think I have what my mom died from."

Hearing that piece of dire news, Joe gulped out, "I'll bring ya some cough drops."

Frankie nodded, his long blond hair stringing across his forehead. "Yeah, I like those licorice ones, Smith Brothers." He studied the glowing end of his cigarette with fascination until he finally took one last drag from it and stubbed it out. He leaned his head back against the cushion and shut his eyes.

Seeing how tired Frankie was, Joe figured it was time to leave. "Guess, I'll be going." He reluctantly stood. "Ya take care, Frankie. I'll bring your drops tomorrow."

Joe hurried along. He had stayed later than intended, was a fraidy-cat of nighttime, and dark sinister things that came out to roam. He could vaguely remember his pretty mother holding him close, and telling him that nothing but the blessed Lord was in the dark, and to never be afraid. Somehow those words of wisdom didn't help him right now. He also remembered standing next to her grave in Potters Field as the men lowered her coffin into a deep dark hole, and the sound of the thudding dirt as the gravediggers covered the pine box. Stern-faced women took him from her burial straight to the orphanage where he lived for a year until he ran away. He'd gone back to search for his mother's grave, but like everything in his short life it had disappeared.

Nothing but the blessed Lord, he muttered out loud.

The decaying buildings closed in around him. A ship's horn blasted from the East River, making him jump. His booted feet echoed as they slammed down on the cobbled pavement. He thought he heard someone else walking.

He stopped.

He listened.

All was silent. He let out a long shaky breath. *Nothing but the blessed Lord.* He started walking again. So did someone else, and it wasn't the blessed Lord. Joe started to sweat, his skin prickled.

He picked up his pace. He turned to walk backwards. He swirled back around, constantly scouring the black gaping holes where doors once stood, unable to see anything.

From the middle of the street, a match flared off to Joe's left. The yellow flame highlighted the mouth and nose of a man lighting a cigar. As he puffed, the smell, sharp and pleasant, carried over to Joe.

"Hello, boyo," the man said with lazy insolence, taking another puff.

"Wow, mister, you scared me." Joe relaxed. A mugger wouldn't bother to say hello. Besides, he had nothing a mugger would want, not in this derelict part of the City. He kept walking. So did the man.

"Didn't mean to frighten ya, lad. I'm searchin' for me son who's left home. His mother cries for him. I think he's joined up with a gang around here. Can ya take me to where the gang lives so I can have a look?"

"Which gang, mister? There are lots of gangs around here." Before Joe knew it, the man was next to him matching his stride. Joe picked up his pace. The man's face a blur of white in the dark, until they walked past a flickering street lamp. Even in shadow, Joe swore he was looking at Donald. But it wasn't Donald. Fear crept up his backbone like a spider after its prey.

"What's your boy's name," he croaked.

"Casey."

The words were no sooner out of the man's mouth when Joe knew he was in trouble. This was no coincidence. The thought slammed into his mind. This same man attacked him in Donald's apartment. Fear had him taking off, but the man was fast, his strong arms captured Joe around the chest. Joe, like a defenseless animal, was forced to the ground.

"Not so fast, lad. Since you were in Donald's apartment, I'd say ya know who Casey is."

"No—no! I don't know who you're talkin' about. Let me go," he gritted out. He grabbed at the man's suit coat, kicked at his legs, and flailed his arms about. He bit down on the man's wrist, tasting blood.

"Ya feckin' bag of shite."

Joe felt the terrific blow explode against the side of his head.

Shaking his bloody wrist, Sam allowed the unconscious kid to slump against the ground. He felt for the kid's pulse. Still alive. Good. Amazed that someone so skinny and young could put up such a fight, Sam took a piece of strong cord from his pocket and bound the gangly youth. Slinging the kid over his shoulder, he headed deeper into the dilapidated part of what was once a thriving section of the waterfront.

Chapter Seventeen

Myron stood like a sentinel on the mezzanine balcony outside of his office. Below him were rows and rows of tall noisy machines with whirling thread spools. Most of the machines had children working them. Some of the children stood on boxes to reach the thread spools they worked. Myron knew without a doubt if Olivia were to pay a surprise visit to his factory, she'd be appalled to learn he hired children.

He was fortunate his factory was over here in Brooklyn, but he felt the tide of the Suffragette movement heading across the bridge. Not that they'd never been here before, they had, but he only had a few children working for him then. His father had staved off a protest rally by promising the women he'd get rid of the children. Of which he did, and when the women came back to inspect, they'd left with glowing smiles. But in order to compete in the industry, Myron and his father had to hire cheap labor. And children worked the cheapest.

A boy working the machines glanced up at Myron with a hateful stare. When Myron pointed and mouthed to get back to work, the boy dipped his head, losing it under his tattered brown fedora.

Myron liked busy workers, but most of all he liked money. Huge profits were the bottom line, and those huge profits brought him immeasurable success. He'd built a mansion and had recently moved into it. The house was on a grand scale and he'd built it for Olivia. He hoped she'd like it. Olivia could be mystifying at times. She was a woman who had wealth, yet didn't want it. A woman whom he had fallen deeply in love with, but here recently he didn't think she returned his love. If that was the situation, then he planned to marry her and make her fall in love with him.

He had to admit she'd changed after the *Titanic*. The little girl who turned out to be McShane's daughter had caused the change. When Myron heard that Jelee was McShane's daughter, he'd been elated, and thought for sure the man would take Jelee out of the Marsh's home. But like everything of late, Myron's elation soon soured after Olivia told him McShane's son was also alive and she would be helping him find the boy. Another unwanted distraction to keep Olivia from his side, but this one was more lethal than a picket sign. He didn't like her being around the Irishman, not at all, and wanted the man out of her life.

Myron leaned against the balcony railing and watched in surprise as Bruno Lapaglia made his way through the maze of large machines. He stopped to look around at the operation, and talk to the floor manager who pointed upward toward the office. Lapaglia glanced toward the office. Myron signaled him to come up.

He waited as Lapaglia trudged up the squeaky stairs, his shoes scraping against the wood, his thinning dark head bent as he carefully watched where he was going. Upon reaching the landing, Lapaglia took out his handkerchief and wiped the sweat from his face and neck.

"Hello, Prewitt," he said while pushing the handkerchief back into his suit pocket.

Myron nodded toward his office. In silence, they walked down the long landing until Myron stopped in front of a large window facing the factory floor. He opened the door next to it. Lapaglia brushed past him.

Even though the smell of machine oil penetrated inside Myron's office, it was meticulously clean, and stark. A telephone was on the desk along with a stack of papers held in place by a glass paperweight. On the far wall was a bookcase loaded with books and ledgers. A clothes tree by the door held his summer linen jacket and hat.

Myron closed the door, silencing the noisy machines. He gestured for Lapaglia to take a seat in the wooden chair facing his desk. Myron pulled down the window shade cutting them off from the factory. He sat behind his desk and crossed his arms.

Watching Lapaglia wipe the sweat from his forehead, Myron knew full well that this visit meant nothing good. "Why are you here? You could have telephoned an order in, or sent it by mail. What's happened?"

"Plenty." Lapaglia's burly body was tense, his dark eyes fixed on Myron.

"What do you mean?" Myron offered him a rolled cigarette from a gold case. Both men lit up and filled the small room with thick coils of smoke.

"You know the man who used to be my accountant? That damn Irishman who helped the Marsh dame out the day of the rally…ah…riot?"

"Her name is Olivia Marsh, she's the woman I love, so show more respect."

Lapaglia threw back his head and laughed, ending it with a sneer. "Respect? You amaze me, Prewitt, simply amaze me." And then he got down to business. "During the riot, I gave McShane a choice, stay out of the fight or get fired. Surprised the hell out of me when he picked the woman over his job. But that's not all, he still had a key to the factory and he got into my office. It's taken me awhile to realize something was missing." He paused, his face revealing nothing, yet everything as he purposely withheld information. He finally said, "Want to know what it is?"

"What could be missing? What did you have there for him to see, for anyone to see?" Myron came to his feet and stood beside his desk.

Lapaglia took a deep drag on his cigarette and then blew a stream of smoke directly at Myron. "I had my wall calendar marked with the date of the deed circled and the rally noted. And in my zeal to back the…ah…your woman off, I wrote on the week beneath it, eliminate the bitch."

"You did what?" Myron grabbed Lapaglia by his suit lapels and hauled him out of the chair.

"Hey, just words, nothing more." Lapaglia held up his hands in defense.

"And you think McShane took it?"

"I'm fairly certain. Everything points toward him."

In disgust, Myron shoved Lapaglia away from him. "Well, I know why you haven't gone after him, it smacks of being a chicken. Is that all you had in your office to incriminate those involved in this?"

Lapaglia hesitated, probably too long for the truth. "Sure…sure, just the calendar."

Myron knew Lapaglia was lying. He also knew he wouldn't get an honest answer out of the man. "Get out of here," he ordered.

Lapaglia slowly stood and pointed a thick finger at Myron. "You're in no position to order me around. I think you have as much to lose here as I do. See if you can fix it. Make it right." Hatred blazed from his eyes. "Next time keep your hands off me. I'll let it go this time but never again." He slammed the door behind him.

Lapaglia had made a mess of it, and Myron knew once Walter Marsh was roused and upset he'd use his banking empire to ruin those who had upset him. But maybe not. Myron still held a trump card, or so he thought.

He reclaimed his chair and leaned his elbows on his desk. He reached for his telephone, but drew his hand back. Once again that old insecurity about losing Olivia, or never having her to lose, crept in. Keeping a woman in line and making her love you was not much different than running a factory. Keep the machine well oiled, ran by the best operator there is, and you'll get profitable results.

Again he reached for the telephone, and again, he changed his mind.

If only Olivia hadn't gone to London, he lamented. Or better yet, why did she return on that damn ship. The Titanic had sunk more hearts than one could count. He thought for sure his was going to be claimed by it as well.

It was late afternoon, and exactly two days since Donald had his daughter back. Bursting from happiness and pride, Donald couldn't wait to show Jilleen off to Eldon and Archibald.

A bright sign saying *Closed Please Call Back* dangled in the door of Johnston's drugstore and the white shade on the glass door was pulled. Donald opened the door, sending the overhead bell into a loud jangle, and held it for Olivia and Jilleen to pass.

Donald approached Eldon just as he straightened from tidying up a perfume display. He nudged one last bottle into alignment. The deep blue bottles with their fancy lettering now lined up like toy soldiers on parade. Eldon smiled while tucking in his white shirt that ballooned out below his vest.

"Here she is, Eldon. My daughter, Jilleen," he said in a voice threatening to crack with happiness. "Jilleen, this is my good friend, Eldon Johnston."

Eldon leaned over and said, "I'm pleased to meet you at last, little Miss Jilleen. Your daddy's told me all about you for a long time. Now you're with him." Eldon glanced up at Donald, emotion raw on his face. He'd been with Donald every step of the way through the darkness of hell, and right here was a ray of bright light. "This is a miracle, isn't it?"

Looking unsure about all of this, Jilleen glanced up at Donald who nodded back at her. She dipped into a short little curtsy. "Pleased to meet ya, Mr. Jonsun."

Eldon grinned. "How about a treat, little lady, would you like an ice cream soda?"

This time Jilleen sought out Olivia who smiled at her, and said, "I think Jilleen would like one very much." Olivia held out her white-gloved hand to Eldon who eagerly accepted it. "I'm Olivia Marsh, a friend of Mr. McShane's. He's had nothing but kind words to say about you."

They all watched as Archibald approached. "Hello, I'm Eldon's father, Archibald Johnston." He took Olivia's hand that Eldon had just relinquished.

"How do you do, Mr. Johnston," she said brightly.

"Fine, fine," he answered. Spotting Jilleen, he shook his head. "My—my—my, she certainly takes after you, Donald. And you, Miss Marsh, weren't you the one who put her picture in the newspaper trying to find her parents?"

"Yes, I did. When we were on the lifeboat together, I helped Jilleen. You read the article?"

Archie nodded. "Yes. Donald was in Halifax when it came out. I thought the little girl in the picture resembled Donald so I sent Joe home with the paper. According to Donald he never received it. But none of that matters now, because it's all turned out for the best." And not waiting to be introduced, Archie acknowledged Jilleen with a genuine smile. "Hello, Miss Jilleen McShane. Welcome to my store. If you see anything you'd like, just tell me and I'll make sure you have it."

"Ah, Eldon—Archie, I have more good news. I've found out from Jilleen that Casey didn't die on the Titanic. Been to see her, he has. He's here somewhere in the City."

Eldon appeared shocked and blew out a breath. "Donald—I don't know what to say. How? When?" Both he and Archie listened as Donald told what little information he had about his son.

Jilleen tugged on Donald's jacket and asked, "Can I have a soda now?"

The grownups laughed. Only a child would remind grownups of a promised treat. They followed Eldon past shelves stocked with medicines, shaving gear, and hot water bottles, finally reaching the soda fountain where the sweet smell of strawberry and chocolate syrups enticed. Donald put Jilleen on a wooden swivel stool, while Olivia took a seat next to her. He sat next to Jilleen.

Eldon cleared his throat and stood grinning like a delighted idiot. "What flavor of soda would you like, Jilleen?"

"Chocolate, please."

Her order made Eldon laugh. "You're certainly your father's daughter. It's his favorite. Instead of a single, how about I make you a double-double chocolate soda? Sound good?"

Jilleen's eyes widened in anticipation as she said, "Aye, please."

"How about you, Miss Marsh? What will make your tastes buds happy today?" Donald raised a brow at her.

Olivia pursed her lips and considered but a moment before saying, "I'm rather partial to strawberry. Make mine a single, please."

"Ya heard the ladies, Eldon," Donald said.

Eldon clanked glasses together and tried to work around his father. "I think you'll be needing help finding your boy. The City's a big place," Eldon said.

"Jilleen said he was grimy and with someone called Jimmy," Donald offered.

Eldon pursed his lips in thought. "Maybe he's down in the wharf area of the East River. Remember there are a lot of gangs in that area. Orphans running amuck, forming gangs. Might be the best place to start."

Donald glanced up at the large round wall clock, seeing they had plenty of time before meeting Paddy at his apartment. "Archie, has Joe been around lately? I haven't seen him for several days."

"No, come to think of it. But I'm sure he'll show up, you know how Joe is. Maybe he's staying at Ryerson's. Miss Marsh, would you excuse us please, I need to talk with Donald."

At Olivia's nod, Archie gestured for Donald to follow him.

They went into the pharmacy that had shelves with rows of medicines in large jars. A mortar and pestle was on the counter.

"I have something to tell you. Perhaps the information is valuable, perhaps not. While you were in Halifax a man came into the store and had me fill a prescription for his wife. I know you're wondering what this has to do with you. It's just that the man resembled you an awful lot. But, they do say we all have a twin walking around somewhere, right? And, I haven't seen him since."

Donald didn't know what to think of this news. "Do you remember the wife's name?"

"I have it written down in my records. Let me look for it."

Archie opened the drawer under the counter and begin rifling through his records, sorted by the month. "Let me see—April—no May."

While Archie searched, Donald leaned against the counter patiently waiting.

"Dammit," Archie swore, "I have it here somewhere—ah, here it is." He waved it in triumph and then handed over the small slip of paper.

Donald read it out loud. "Lillian Flynn. Do you remember the husband's name?"

Archie shook his head. Donald didn't press. He already knew the man's name. Olivia had told it to him last night.

Albert Flynn.

They went back to join the others by the soda fountain where Olivia pointed to the wall clock.

"I believe it's time we leave so we're not late meeting Mr. Riley at your apartment," Olivia suggested.

Donald agreed, and after telling Archie and Eldon goodbye, he ushered Olivia and Jilleen toward Olivia's car.

Donald opened the door to his apartment, allowing Olivia and Jilleen to enter. He quickly glanced around for Joe, hoping he'd returned, disappointed to see he wasn't here. He'd check with Mabel Ryerson tomorrow. It wasn't like the lad to stay away for more than a day, at least not since he'd started living with him. He wanted to introduce his daughter to Joe, and ask Joe to help him find Casey. If anyone knew his way around the city, it was Joe.

Olivia removed her hat and placed it on the sideboard. "I take it your young friend Joe isn't here for me to meet?"

"No, he isn't, and I'm mighty put out that he isn't here."

"Perhaps another day." She picked up the picture of Donald and his family, and said, "Be sure and show this to Mr. Riley. Is this is a good likeness of Casey?"

"Paddy's already seen it." Seeing her puzzled glance, he explained. "The night you were hurt, he noticed it. We talked and he promised to help out, but with Jilleen and all that's happened I've been too busy to get with him."

Jilleen was quick to Olivia's side. Taking the picture from Olivia, she greedily stared at it, her stubby finger pointing. "That's me mum and Casey. Da, is this me on yer lap?"

"Aye, you were nine months old at the time. This was taken a couple of months before I left Ireland. Does Casey look about the same?"

She shrugged. "Aye. He was mighty skinny and dirty. Grandmum Ina would clatter him a good one upside the head for gettin' so dirty." Appearing to lose interest in the picture, Jilleen went to stand by the window where she parted the curtains and peeked out.

Donald couldn't help but worry about his mam. He'd written to tell her what had happened with his family, his inability to find them after the disaster. He asked her to come to America. She wrote a long letter back to him of her grief over losing the golden spots in her life and was unable to accept they had perished. With no grandchildren to take care of, she wasn't sure she wanted to leave Ireland, thought she was too old, and might as well stay put. And in truth, after the sinking, she didn't know if she wanted to step foot on a liner. She had one son left in Belfast since Sam had gone to live in England. Donald was surprised Sam had left the shipyards where work was steady. He thought he knew the whereabouts of all his family, but that wasn't the case. With his good news about Jilleen and Casey to write her, he hoped to change her mind about coming here.

"Tell me more about your family." Olivia regarded him quizzically. "About your life in Ireland."

"Sure'n and I've told you some of it the other night at yer parents." And then he opened up to her. "My older brother Sam is the reason I'm here in America." Donald told of Sam's moodiness, his temper that would flash in an instant, and what had happened the night Aidan was shot. "It turned out Aidan wasn't dead. Sam had felt his pulse, not me. He was always in trouble with the law, stealin' from stores, things like that. But after he stole the collection box and money for the poor from St. Doulagh's church, that's when the true evil in him came out. My father couldn't stand the shame of it and he died clutching his heart in pain. I blame Sam for his death.

"Everywhere Sam goes, death follows. He's the oldest of us brothers, he's thirty-two, and I just turned twenty-six. Colin, my younger brother by three years is a good lad and I think Mam's favorite. Colin's so mellow he should have been a priest. I'll not be surprised if he gets the callin' someday. Right now, he works in the shipyard as a riveter. After Da died about nine years ago, we brothers, especially Colin, took on the obligation of helping our mam out.

"When I married Derry, we moved to Dublin. We were poor, but I managed to get jobs as an accountant. Like so many men in Ireland, I had dreams and visions of Ireland ruling herself. I joined the Sinn Féin to help the cause, but all I got was a bunch of trouble. I abandoned my sweet wife and family when I ran like a coward afraid of the gallows. Derry moved in with my mam. Mam wrote about Sam helping her with his wages from the shipyard. I thought he'd changed, trying to make amends, but I don't think someone of Sam's caliber can ever change. They go about foolin' people. Sam's the best at foolin'."

He didn't tell her about Sam and Derry's history. Some secrets were best left on the soil where they started.

"Is this me new home?" Jilleen asked from where she stood next to the window. She sucked in her breath. "Where's the lawn, the garden, and Sparks, where will Sparks play? I want to live with 'Livia. I don't like it here."

Jilleen's word stung, she sounded uppity and spoiled, and Donald tried being patient. "Ah…Lass. This would have been good enough fer yer mam and brother, and it will be good enough fer ya as well." He couldn't help but snap at Olivia, "See, I can't give her what ya can, so she compares."

"Do you think I've made her that way?" she snapped back, reminding him she was a suffragette who didn't need to lift a finger to help those less fortunate, but did. "I love Jilleen as if she's my own, and I've tried to keep the values she was raised with instilled in her."

"How could you possibly know Irish values—poor Irish values, aye?"

Olivia couldn't help but see Jilleen was upset. She went to her knees in front of the child and gently drew her into her arms. "Never mind us silly adults. We are both thinking of you." She rubbed Jilleen's small back, feeling her bony shoulder blades. "You must appreciate what your father has worked so hard to make here, a warm, clean home for his family. His home here is just as nice as mine, only smaller, that's all. Tell your father you like it and you want to live here with him."

"But I don't, 'Livia. I want to be with ya, please…" she whispered, all the while fingering Olivia's earring.

Oh…dear, Olivia never thought this would happen. She glanced up at Donald who was standing with his hands in his pockets, rocking on his heels. She could tell his Irish temper was brewing, and wanted to stop it before it erupted. She quickly rose and looking around for something to entertain Jilleen with, grabbed up a deck of cards and placed them on the table.

"Do you remember the game of Solitaire I showed you?" When Jilleen nodded, Olivia said, "Please play it now while I talk with your father."

And with no other place to have a private conversation with Donald, she ushered the man into his own bedroom, and softly closed the door behind them.

"Well, bloody hell," he scorched out. "Now me own daughter is too uppity for the likes of me home."

"Don't you dare say that," she hissed right back. "Jilleen is a wonderful child, and she will get used to living here. Children are so…so…resilient, they ebb and flow like a tide. Give her time. She doesn't know you. She knows me, and the life she had back in Ireland. She remembers how it was to live with her mother, her brother, and her grandmother. My family is…is just a surrogate family, something she's gotten used to for the past few months. Why wouldn't she prefer me to you? You're a stranger to her, but it doesn't mean she won't come to know you, to love you. You can't expect her to adjust overnight."

"Settle down, Miss Marsh. I'm hearin' what ya say, but it doesn't make it any easier to swallow. I thought my children dead, both of them. And now I find them alive and you not being a parent will never know the joy of that. I'm fair to burstin' with happiness, and if ya don't think I'm afraid to have my daughter here, yer wrong. What do I know about raising children? Probably as much as you, and that I imagine might fill a thimble—"

"Then you don't know a darn thing about me, Mr. McShane!" she bristled out.

"I know that I enjoy being with you. And I will never forget you made the sun shine in my life again. Miss Marsh, there is a lot about you I like—more than like," he said, surprising her with the unexpected statement, and he did it as slick and easy as turning a light on.

"Oh…you…" Olivia was at a loss for words. "I mean…well…I…" she sputtered. She drew in a ragged breath and sagged against the door. "Oh…my."

"It's been a long time since I've had the comfort of a woman in my arms and I like being near you." His hands cupped her shoulders and questions filled his eyes. "Olivia."

She could only whisper, "I'm not sure what's happening here. But right now, I think it's wonderful, and I can't get past the here and now, Mr. McShane."

"Please, call me Donald," he said in a low voice and brought her hand to his lips.

"Donald." She relished in the intimate warmth of his mouth, and when he finished with the back of her hand, all she could do was stare at the silly lock of hair tumbling onto his forehead, and at his hazel eyes now bright. And just as he started to dip his head to hers, a soft knock sounded behind her.

"'Livia? Da? Are ye through talkin'?"

Startled, they pulled apart, acting like parents caught in the throes of passion by their child.

"Yes, Jilleen we're done talking. We'll be out in a minute, darling," she said.

"Bloody hell," Donald groaned. "I'm sorry, Olivia. But when I'm around you, I forget myself, forget my manners. I'm comforted by yer presence but I turn into a lad who can't control his…em…wanger."

With her hand on the doorknob, she tilted her head back and laughed. She'd just received the nicest and most outrageous compliment ever. "Comforted? Wanger? Well, Mr. McShane, since I know what you mean by comforted, someday you'll have to explain what the other word means. But, I think I already know." Chuckling, she raised one eyebrow at him.

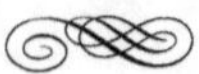

He winked at her bold comment, and reaching around her opened the door. His daughter was standing in the middle of the living room with her hands on her hips and her head tipped to the left. She wore a pout, and he wondered just who was going to be raising who, him raising Jilleen, or Jilleen raising him. He grabbed her by the hands and began twirling her around, making her giggle. "Ah…do," he urged, "laugh me wee lass." And he proceeded to dance with her, shooting a smile at Olivia. "And you and I are not done either."

There was a knock on the door and Jilleen broke away to run and open it. "Da, Mister Riley's here to see ya."

"Hello, again, my wee lass," Paddy said and tweaked Jilleen's nose, sending her into another fit of giggles. "The last time I met you, we didn't know who you belonged too. Remember when I took your picture for the paper?"

"Aye, me do."

Donald accepted Paddy's grip, strong and vise like. Donald liked the man's direct gaze and confident smile.

"Good to see ya again. It appears yer life changes every time I see ya. Not a quiet life, aye?" Paddy said.

"I'll go make us tea." Olivia excused herself and went to put the kettle on. Jilleen followed her.

"Miss Marsh called me at the paper this mornin' to tell me about yer children. That ya recently found out yer son's alive, likely livin' on the streets, and ya want me to help find him?"

"Aye, according to Jilleen, Casey, my boy was at the Marsh place to see her. She said he was with a boy called Jimmy. I wish to hell that Casey had walked up to the Marsh's front door, hammered on it and begged for help. Why would he run away instead of shouting out Jilleen's his sister? I hope this Jimmy lad isn't forcing Casey into trouble."

"Kids will always be hard to figure out. Just when ya think ya have them figured out, ya haven't. We'll search every block of this melting pot, we'll find him."

Donald picked up the picture of his family and handed it to Paddy. "Ya held this the other night, but I want to point out me son there. Jilleen's says he looks about the same. He would be three years older, taller, and probably thinner."

The shrill whistle of the tea kettle went off and was promptly silenced by Olivia removing it off the burner. Donald heard Olivia searching for cups and saucers in the cabinet and next thing he knew, she was walking into the living room holding a brass tray filled with tea supplies. She set it down on the sideboard and had Jilleen help her to serve the tea.

Paddy accepted a cup from Olivia, and then said, "Sure'n if ya add a tad of Irish whiskey to this cup of cha, I'll be forever grateful, lass."

Olivia glanced at Donald who nodded. "In me cupboard, you'll find a bottle that'll grant Paddy's wish. Both of our wishes to be certain." He pointed to his cup.

"Well, as long as you don't get tipsy, I might be convinced to do your bidding," she said, and with a chuckle went to get the requested bottle.

While Olivia was out of earshot, Paddy got serious. "I'll start first thing in the mornin'. I have some ideas where to search. The City's a big place to be lookin' for one wee lad. But with the description you've given me of the lads, their unkempt appearances, I'll concentrate on the run down section where they are demolishing and rebuilding. When the Manhattan Bridge was built, they demolished blocks of tenements to build the bridge's supports. Parts have been rebuilt, some not. Gangs of boys are known to hang out there. Regular little pickpockets they are. Having this picture will help. I can show it around. How about I print this in the Times? My paper can do a lot of leg work for me."

Olivia returned with the bottle of whiskey and poured more than a dollop in each cup.

Donald watched the sway of her blue skirt as she went to replace the bottle. "Ah—don't. I have a reason for not wantin' it in the paper. Nor do I want a story about my family and Casey. Not yet anyway."

For some strange reason he couldn't put his finger on, Donald thought keeping this hushed would be better for his son. There was a reason Casey didn't go straight to the police for help. And something definitely kept him from asking the Marsh family for help when he came to see Jilleen. Donald needed to figure out why.

Joe sat blindfolded and trussed up like a turkey in a butcher's window. He'd pissed himself the minute he was slammed to the ground. The forlorn sound of an occasional ship's horn made him realize he was still close to the waterfront. He thought he'd been here several days, but being blindfolded and unable to tell day from night, he'd lost track of time.

But the truth of his situation made his hopes sink. He was in a pickle, big trouble, and he didn't think Donald would be looking for him. Donald figured he'd gone to visit his old gang and was no doubt staying with them. Joe knew Donald had a strong aversion to stealing, always saying it isn't right, and if ya don't earn it, ya don't deserve to have it. That had made some sense to Joe. He'd promised not to steal, and hadn't.

The sound of someone walking made him perk up, yet filled him with dread. Not knowing what was in store for him scared the hell out of him. He heard a door being opened with a lot of resistance, the wood moaning and creaking. And then a rustling sound of material as if someone walked up and paused next to him.

Next he knew, the gag was jerked out of his mouth.

"You make a sound and I'll break yer scrawny neck." The man's breath tickled Joe's ear.

"Who are ya? What do ya want? I told ya I don't know your son. I have nothing to tell ya about him. I don't have any money. Please let me go. I'll tell no one—be on my way," his words tumbled out.

The man chuckled, a sound so sinister it made Joe's flesh crawl.

"Oh me, lad, ye have riches beyond compare. Why yer a walking wealth of information and I intend to get it from ya, one way or another, if ya get me meanin'."

Joe could hear the slap of a leather strap, or something equally as bad. "Mister, I don't know what ya think I'm goin' to be able to tell ya, but I've got to pee. How about untying me so I can take to a corner?"

"Sorry, lad. From the smell of ya, I'd say ya already pissed yer pants. A few more times ain't goin' to hurt ya." And then he asked, "The boy, Casey, I know he's with that gang. Can ya lure him away from there?"

Joe blurted without thinking, "Yer the one in Donald's apartment. Ya hit me on the head. Why? Who are you?"

"That's none of yer business, now is it? Answer me question, boyo. Can you lure Casey out, get him for me?"

"Go to hell!" Joe screamed and spit.

"Ya got good aim, kid. Now you'll pay."

The man's fist slammed against the side of Joe's head, rattling his teeth, almost knocking him out.

"Oh, ye'll be giving the kid up all right. A few more days without food and water ye'll be kissing my boots." The man pressed the gag back in Joe's mouth. "Yer life or his, think on it."

"Mmmmp," Joe tried to talk. He listened to the fading chuckle of the man as he walked away. The sounds of scurrying started, the soft squeaks of mice, rats, and Joe didn't want to know what else was starting to come alive in the rotting, smelly building.

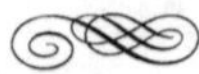

Leaving Ryerson's store, Donald took his cap out of his pocket, and giving it a good snap pulled it low over his brow. Joe hadn't been in Ryerson's since Saturday, his last day to work. Worried, it seemed Donald now had two little boys to find.

Donald wished he knew more about the gang Joe used to run with. Without a doubt, he could kick himself for not paying more attention. He took the elevated train as far as he could, and then traveled by subway, finally coming out in the teeming tenements. The spring evening was balmy and a quick glance around showed the day in the tenements ending.

He went past the old place he used to live in. In the two years since he'd moved out, the building appeared to sag into the ground more. Children played on the trash-filled stairs leading up to the front door. They played on the sidewalk, bouncing a ball. He walked down one busy block after another. With more immigrants coming off the boats daily, it was like a tidal surge of people washed up and landing in the Lower East Side. Donald hated the filth.

A vendor, a small, dark looking individual was closing down his food cart for the day. Donald's stomach growled and he almost kept going, but seeing the cart had several sandwiches left, he stopped. He pointed at a sandwich and asked what kind it was.

The man quickly nodded. "Those are both salami and cheese. And, they're still fresh. My wife makes the sandwiches and brings them to me several times a day. Want one?"

Donald plunked the required amount of change in the vendor's wide palm. He jovially wrapped the sandwich in brown butcher paper and handed it to Donald.

"Ya wouldn't know of a gang of boys hanging around the waterfront?" Donald asked.

"Gang? With so many orphans around, they have formed gangs for protection, for money, for food. There are gangs fallin' out of the trees in Central Park, and gangs ridin' the subway. There are gangs around the wharf. There's the Tenement Terrors, the little bastards make those of us livin' in the tenement's miserable. They'd sooner put a knife in yer gut then earn an honest dime. Man, ya got to know that gangs are everywhere. Who ya looking for?"

"I'm trying to find my son, and another boy called Joe."

The man shook his head and pushed his foot against the wooden brake keeping his cart in place. "Last I knew, some boys were livin' in abandoned buildings close to the East River that used to be warehouses and stores. This city is growing so fast you can walk by a building one day and the next day it's gone and already replaced by another. Bigger and taller, isn't that the phrase? Go over to Smith's saloon around midnight, they can point ya in the right direction."

Donald thanked the man and left. He ate his sandwich while walking and still hungry, wished he'd bought both. He started for a part of the city long forgotten. He walked down obscure alleys filled with overflowing garbage and children who rested against soiled brick walls. Clothes lines crammed with frayed laundry, skirts, aprons, and shirts, crisscrossed so thick overhead they blotted out the sky.

A man on a balcony looked out over his domain, and a shadowy woman who was standing in a doorway eased back inside and shut it. Not far away, a woman holding a baby sat on an overturned barrel. She was wearing a dingy white apron and a frayed brown blouse. Her age, he couldn't tell, she could be young, or she could be old, maybe somewhere in-between. A skinny lad peed against a building. The walkway smelled like an overflowing outhouse. There were no animals around, they were too smart to live here. Donald pushed on, going deeper into the misery of the tenements.

He stopped to talk to those that would give him the time of day. Most wouldn't. He asked about the gangs, about Joe, and tried to describe Casey. People scoffed, just how many blonde-headed boys did he think lived in the tenements? Hundreds. They told him he was on a fool's mission, like rounding up all the cockroaches in the city. He stopped in a police station called the Tombs, but no one had heard of a boy named Joe Gillespie, or of one called Casey McShane.

With recollections of Halifax still fresh, he forced himself to go into a dark and gloomy morgue. Inquiring about both boys, he was relieved that no youngsters had died recently, certainly none fitting their descriptions. He went into a clinic, anyplace that might give him information.

He wound up on the waterfront staring out at the East River. Behind him a fish market was closing for the night. The smells coming from it blew his way. Men joked and laughed amongst themselves as they left, their cares and worries put on hold for a brief moment.

The ships tied to the wharf bobbed in the water, their rigging slapping loud against their masts. Discouraged, Donald gave up and went back the way he'd come.

Chapter Eighteen

Olivia was begrudgingly getting ready for an impromptu dinner party planned by her mother this Tuesday evening. Even though it was a small party, Olivia knew to dress the part. Standing in front of her cheval mirror, she did a slow turn, inspecting her red satin sheath dress with its modest scooped out neckline and short sleeves.

Olivia didn't feel completely well yet. A dull pain still nudged against her temples, and just today the doctor had removed the stitches. She leaned forward to check her hairdo, happy to see that no sign of her injury lingered, and that her bruises had faded.

Myron and his parents would be here. Donald, along with his friends the Johnston's, were also invited. Merilee hadn't been happy to indulge Olivia in this, but she did. Olivia knew her mother's motives were simply to solicit Myron's mother, Grace, in helping to rush Myron and Olivia down the aisle. Olivia thought of it as *The Great Marriage Cause*.

She wondered how Donald would fare against all the wealth and snobbery she knew would be floating around in the guise of good manners. At least Paddy Riley and the Johnston's would be here to bolster Donald. Olivia liked the Johnston's. The fact that both were pharmacists and owned their own business had impressed and mollified her mother somewhat.

"Hello, darling," her mother said while breezing into the room. Beautiful in a black satin sheath dress with embroidered gold beads, she was a dynamo of boundless energy tonight, and was completely in her element of giving such parties. She paused next to Olivia in front of the mirror, pushing and tweaking her own hairdo artfully done in a chignon and anchored with glistening jeweled combs. At last, she turned her attention on Olivia.

Taking Olivia's hands, Merilee spread her arms wide and gave her the once over, the twice over, and then her opinion. "You're radiant, elegantly divine, but that necklace is all wrong."

Olivia's hand went to the pearl pendant as if protecting it. "It may well be, but Dad gave it to me for my eighteenth birthday. I want to wear it."

"Nonsense, with that red dress you need diamonds, glitter, you must sparkle like a chandelier. But most of all, you want Myron unable to take his eyes off of you."

"I'd blind him if I'm to rival a chandelier. Really, Mother, don't you know me by now? I like to blend in, silent sophistication, I call it."

Merilee's eyes were alight with a smile. "Silent sophistication, indeed. Darling, daughter, there is nothing silent about you, nor is there likely to ever be."

Feeling exasperated, Olivia dropped her mother's hands and took a seat on the brocaded dressing bench. She picked up a bottle of perfume, pulled out the chiseled stopper, and dabbed the perfume between her cleavage, and neck. The smell of gardenia now blended with the heady jasmine her mother wore.

Her mother stood directly behind Olivia, acting flighty, and fussing with Olivia's hair, adjusted the ornate comb holding it all together. "Olivia," she paused, now wearing a serious frown that etched a vertical line above her nose. "Is there anything more than a proper friendship developing between you and Mr. McShane?" Her hands cupped Olivia's shoulders.

The question surprised Olivia and made her pause to think. She felt more than a strong attraction for Donald. She found his rough edges captivating, and couldn't deny that whenever they were together he made her pulse race. Trying not to show her feelings, she put on a brilliant performance by smiling and patting her mother's hand.

"Of course not, Mother. Why would you ever think such a thing? Mr. McShane visited here one time, the night we gave his daughter to him. Have I given any indication of liking Mr. McShane…well other than Jilleen's involvement?"

"There are some things that don't need words or actions. Much can be read in a glance. And I've seen the way you look at him. I believe you may be taken with Mr. McShane." She fussed some more with Olivia's hair, until annoyed, Olivia took her mother's hand and stopped her nervous tweaking.

"Mother, I seem to remember being told you fell in love with father over lobster bisque. And I remember you saying it was the first time you laid eyes on him at a dinner party."

"Don't compare, Olivia. Your father was rich. Mr. Shane is practically penniless. And don't try turning the tables here."

"Whatever are you saying?"

"This is not about me and your father. It's about you and Mr. McShane. You appear to enjoy his company more than you should. Olivia, you do intend to marry Myron don't you?"

Olivia sighed with frustration. "Mother, please don't think me rude, but my relationship with Myron is my concern only. I have a number of reasons why Myron may not be the right man for me to marry. Please tell me this party tonight isn't designed as an opportunity for you to further encroach in mine and Myron's affairs?

As for Mr. McShane, I'm delighted and relieved that Jilleen has such a special man for a father."

"I asked if you still intend to marry Myron," Merilee said tersely.

"I don't know if I ever intended to marry Myron. That's why we're not engaged, only promised."

Merilee nudged Olivia over and sat down next to her. "Let me tell you, with Myron it's more than a promise. He has every intention of making it permanent."

Her words alarmed Olivia. "Is he planning something tonight? Mother, this was supposed to be a simple dinner party. This was not supposed to end with me being bushwhacked by Myron asking me to marry him in front of everyone. Tell me that will not happen."

Merilee skirted Olivia's concerns with stealth, merely saying, "At least I bowed to your wishes and invited Mr. McShane's friends, the Johnston's and Mr. Riley."

Olivia met her mother's disapproving stare in the mirror. "Yes, you did, at father's insistence. And I thank you for doing so. Certainly, Mr. McShane will be at ease if the Johnston's accompany him tonight. Isn't that the proper thing for you to do, Mother? Make one's guests feel comfortable in your home?" Olivia's chin came up in defiance.

"Why, you're worried senseless," Merilee extolled with glee. "You're worried how this…this…Irishman will cut it beside Myron. I've got this right, haven't I?"

"Fiddle-faddle, that's plain nonsense. You planned this little black-tie-affair to flaunt it in my face you don't think Donald is good enough for me." The second she used his first name, she regretted it.

"Donald—is it?" Merilee glared. "You're on a first name basis? You've known him how long? A little over two months? And that's counting your encounter with him on the pier after the Carpathia docked. You don't know your own mind. You're caught up in the romance of it all, this…this…mystery surrounding him and his lost family. I'm telling you, Olivia, you're not going to throw your life in the gutter for this."

"'Livia?" Jilleen hesitated in the open doorway.

Olivia quickly stood, and fighting for composure, forced a smile at a worried Jilleen. "My, aren't you pretty, Miss Jilleen McShane. With your new dress and its pretty bow, you will be the center of attention tonight." She watched Jilleen gaze down at her pale blue taffeta dress, and run her hands across the smooth material.

"'Livia, Da and the Jonsun's are here. Mr. Riley too. They be waitin' fer ya in the study."

Merilee crossed the room and paused by the door. "The Prewitt's should be arriving anytime now. I'm going to see if your father needs help with his tie. Remember what I said, Olivia."

"And what was that, Mother? You said a lot of things in a short amount of time just now." Olivia held out her hand for Jilleen. "Come on, Jilleen. Let's go see your father."

Olivia entered the study where she found Donald, Paddy, and the Johnston's standing across the room talking in animated conversation. Jilleen immediately ran over next to Donald where she tugged his hand and pointed to where Olivia stood. Donald stopped talking and turned to give Olivia a visual sweep, flicking a dark eyebrow upward in what she gathered as appreciation. He became the only person in the room she was aware of. He was dashing in his recently purchased suit and a short haircut that tamed his curls into brown waves. Looking as if he belonged here, he slowly walked up to her, appraising her, letting out a low whistle that thrilled her.

He leaned close and whispered in his deep tone, "Sure'n yer beautiful tonight, Miss Marsh."

"You're quite dapper yourself, Mr. McShane." She wanted to tell him she found him both handsome and debonair, but refrained from doing so. Instead she addressed the others. "I'm so pleased all of you could attend."

"We're happy to be invited," Archie said. "Wonderful home you have here."

"I agree with Dad," Eldon tossed in.

"Miss Marsh," Paddy said, "May I have a word with ya in private? It'll only take a moment." And without further ado, the black-suited reporter steered Olivia over to stand next to her father's desk. "I was just talkin' to McShane about the woman they claim was murdered on the Titanic."

"Yes, I read about it in the Times. Something about her aunt identifying the woman as Lillian Denbury," Olivia said. "What's this got to do with Mr. McShane?"

Paddy lowered his voice, "Did you know when McShane went to the morgue in Halifax to identify his wife's body the woman he looked at wasn't his wife at all? According to McShane the woman had his wife's inspection card in her coat pocket. That's what caused the identity mess. And now that very woman was Lillian Denbury."

"Donald hasn't mentioned this to me. How can they be sure she was murdered? I mean so many people drowned and were hit by falling objects from the Titanic, maybe that's how she died."

"I recently talked to Doctor Tory the coroner, and Inspector Mulhall who is investigating it in Halifax, albeit with little enthusiasm I might add. Mulhall thinks most of the crucial evidence went down with the Titanic and I'm inclined to agree. The coroner told me she was dead before she went into the water. Her lungs were dry, ya see. She also had bruises around her neck, bruises in the shape of fingers, squeezing tight."

Olivia reflectively touched her neck, thinking of death. "Paddy, were you able to find any information concerning Albert Flynn?"

"I'm trying to dig up information, but I don't have much. According to the Titanic's manifest for immigration, he had sponsorship of a job up in Boston. I checked with the company by telegraph, they never heard of him. Heard tell his wife was taken off the Carpathia on a stretcher. I'm up to my ears in investigations, and I hope to end up with one helluva scoop. Excuse my cussing."

"Well, let me inform you of something else. Donald McShane looks enough like Albert Flynn to be his brother."

"Ya don't say?"

Olivia felt smug. "And I most certainly mentioned this to Mr. McShane. He told me he has two brothers. One is in Ireland with his mother, and the one Donald really resembles, Sam, is working in England."

"You've given me a load of information here, makes me want to kick up my heels and think exclusive." He laughed and tugged at his tight white collar.

Donald walked up to them and nodded at Paddy.

"Mr. McShane, Paddy just told me about the woman in Halifax, Lillian Denbury. Why didn't you tell me about her?" She put her hand on his arm and watched as he covered her hand with his.

"I didn't have the time. With you being injured, me getting Jilleen back, and Casey being alive, when could I? I've talked with Vivian Denbury, Lillian Denbury's—"

"Good evening, Olivia." Myron nonchalantly leaned against the door jam with his arms crossed. His eyes swept her face questioningly, making her feel guilty. And she wondered how long he'd been there. Too long, or not long enough?

Myron immediately came to stand directly in front of Olivia and Donald. With finesse, he reached for Olivia's hand. His face was a blend of wariness and anger until he had Olivia away from Donald's side and next to his. Wearing a black suit, white waistcoat, and a rigid smile just for her, the lights danced off the sheen of his black hair as he bent his head and kissed her hand.

"I don't need to tell you how beautiful you are, but I will. You're stunning, and I'm proud to be here *with you* tonight, Olivia," he stressed.

"Thank you, Myron. I'd like to introduce you to Donald McShane, Jilleen's father."

"Hello, McShane. At last we meet in person."

Donald's hand went out to Myron's. Both equally tall, their eyes met as they came face-to-face for the first time, sizing the other up. And being gentlemen, they shook hands.

"I believe I owe you thanks for getting Olivia away from the riot." Myron possessively caressed Olivia's arm.

Donald grinned and stared at Olivia. "Aye, but she repaid me by givin' me my daughter back. It's like divine intervention. Had I not stopped to listen to her speech, and then helped her, I would never know she had me daughter."

"Yes, Olivia's good to the core. She's helped many a wet, smelly, stray dog. That's one of the numerous reasons why I love her." Myron drilled Donald with an intense stare, his words, and his barb more than meaningful.

Donald gave Myron a brief nod and smirked. "Ya know, legend in Ireland has it that good old St. Patrick pounded a drum and banished all the snakes from Ireland. Ireland has no snakes. And yet, America is filled with venomous vipers, isn't it, Mr. Prewitt?"

Olivia drew in a sharp breath, and detecting impending fisticuffs, quickly intervened. "I think we should join the others. Are your parents in the drawing room, Myron?"

"Yes," he said.

"Did you just arrive? I didn't hear you." She watched him closely.

He studied her, his mouth breaking into a stiff smile. "No, you didn't. You were engrossed with McShane—your guests. I hear his son is also alive, how fortuitous for him."

"Yes, he recently found out his beloved son is indeed alive. However, lost somewhere in this city," she offered.

Jilleen, forgotten by the adults, scooted off the couch and came over to tug on Olivia's skirt. "'Livia, I'm hungry. Are we gonna eat soon?" she whined.

Bless the innocence of a child, Olivia thought and smiled down at her. "Yes we are, and I'm hungry too, sweetheart."

Olivia took Myron's arm and started toward the drawing room where the other guests waited. She glanced over her shoulder at Donald, questioning, but he only winked at her.

Taking Jilleen's hand, Donald escorted his daughter.

"Olivia, daughter, glad you're joining us," Walter said. His bushy eyebrows pulled downward in his way of silently scolding as his eyes took on unasked questions.

Merilee, the perfect hostess, quickly introduced everyone.

"My, Olivia, you look just like your mother, doesn't she, Emil?" Grace Prewitt nudged her husband's arm. Emil grunted.

Grace Prewitt was a graying blonde with a figure that was all sharp angles and bones. Her mouth was too wide, her eyes protruded too much and looked as though she never missed a thing. Emil, his dark hair streaked with gray, was the opposite of his wife, and apart from a florid complexion, appeared to be in robust health. He took out his gold pocket watch and giving it a quick glance stuffed it back into his rose-colored satin vest. Olivia couldn't see Myron in either of his parents.

"I saw your picture in the paper, that frightening display at the rally." Grace Prewitt let it known how she felt. "I must say it looked like a lot of energy being wasted. Couldn't you apply it to one of your mother's charities, or the orphanages? Do you ever fight for their cause?"

Olivia didn't have a chance to answer Grace Prewitt's icy and unwarranted comments. Her own mother sucked in her breath and sided with the enemy. "My sentiments exactly, Grace. That picture of Olivia in the newspaper was humiliating. Disgraceful. I only hope everyone realized she was out cold and didn't know it was being taken."

Paddy smiled at Merilee. "Ya should be proud of Olivia and the work she's doing. My photographer took the picture. No disgrace was meant, Mrs. Marsh, merely the harsh realities of these times we all live in. People need to see the truth of their community. That's what the newspaper is all about, isn't it?"

Olivia couldn't help but grin at Paddy's intervention, but knew his efforts were useless. Her mother's mind was set in stone and she blamed Paddy for intentionally printing a less than flattering picture. And as for Grace Prewitt, Olivia decided to ignore her scathing remarks.

The men were standing close by and having a rather boisterous conversation. Olivia watched Paddy work the room, listening, commenting occasionally. He paused next to Donald and the Johnston's, saying something to Donald.

Emil Prewitt turned to Walter and said, "With elections this fall, who are you putting your mark for?"

"Theodore Roosevelt, without a doubt." Walter beamed.

Olivia, seeing her chance to escape her mother and Grace's cold stare, moved next to her father. She offered up her opinion. "Rumor has it former President Roosevelt is planning to create a split in the Republican Party during the convention. I hear Mr. Roosevelt wants the office for himself again. If women had the right to vote across this nation, we'd give those connivers a run for their money—"

"Olivia," her father, a staunch Republican, interrupted.

But Olivia wasn't done yet. "Whatever is the matter, Father? I thought you liked a good debate about politics," she said while snagging a crystal flute of champagne from the tray carried by the maid, Lori Raye. The bubbles tickled her mouth and nose as she took a delicate sip.

"Tell me, Miss Marsh, who would you vote for?"

The deep lilting voice came from behind her, and her skin prickled with excitement as she turned to see Donald holding a glass of champagne, and wearing an amused grin.

Myron was quick to join her, his smile plastered on.

"Why, Mr. McShane," she said and continued, "Without a doubt I'll be voting for Woodrow Wilson, the next Democratic President of our United States. And I will not rest until every child's pulled from the lines of labor mills and treated as they are, children."

"Well put, Miss Marsh," Donald said.

But not all agreed.

Emil Prewitt spoke up, "Now see here, my mill employs the young and I pay them good wages. If it weren't for my factory, a lot of families would starve."

Myron blanched and started to speak, to run interference, but Olivia was too quick for him. "I take it by the young, Mr. Prewitt, you are referring to young men of eighteen, nineteen, perhaps older? Because Myron has assured me you do not employ children in your mills. Textile mills like yours are the most dangerous of places for children to work. Too frequently they get their feet, fingers, and hands either cut off or damaged beyond use—impacting their entire futures."

"Olivia," Myron broke in sounding on edge. "We do not employ young children in the mill. Do we—Father." He glared his father down.

Merilee fluttered out a laugh. "Well, now, there she goes again. Give Olivia a soapbox and she'll talk you to death, politics, or whatever. Calm down, daughter, there is no need to question Mr. Prewitt's business practices. Why don't we talk with Mr. McShane about his new job, his children?"

Mrs. Lippencott came up beside Merilee and nodded in a stiff gesture. "Mrs. Marsh, would you like to seat your guests for dinner, or wait awhile longer?"

"We can eat now. Thank you, Mrs. Lippencott."

Merilee and Walter led everyone out of the study and into the dining room where a long, dark mahogany table was set with china blue plates and silverware. A tall bouquet of pink roses dissected the center of the table.

The room itself was Merilee's project and had her flair for decorating. It was a blend of solid Victorian furnishings and the lighter airy look of current fashion made up of French imported satin, fleur-de-lis wallpaper in creams and blues. A large sideboard held ornate silver pots of steaming coffee and tea, and covered silver dishes to surprise the guests.

Walter escorted Merilee to her chair at the end of the table, and then went to his own place at the head of the table. Merilee had conveniently placed Myron on her left and Donald on her right. Myron held Olivia's chair and seated her next to him. Olivia noticed Donald was across from her, and was helping Jilleen onto her chair. The Prewitt's, next to Jilleen, were looking at Olivia with a silly-sweet smile pasted on their faces. Paddy, slipped into the chair on Olivia's left, while the Johnston's took their places next to Walter.

Unable to keep her gaze off Donald, Olivia smiled and tried to pretend her smile was for Jilleen, but her gaze kept drifting toward him. Despite his fancy suit, he was still the knuckle-busting Irishman she was becoming more than fond of. She was drawn to him in a way beyond her control.

She felt bad for Myron, but she also felt numb toward him. Myron was a gentleman, handsome, and wealthy. He held position in New York's society. However, she didn't feel nervous and bubbly inside while around Myron. Not like she did around Donald. His grin at Jilleen flashed white while fussing and tucking her napkin to protect her dress. He was tough and gentle at the same time. Seeing him acting so, filled Olivia with so much pride she wanted to burst. The warm feeling spreading over her was like being enveloped in a comforting embrace.

Myron's hand crept to find hers under the table and give it a squeeze. She felt guilty, could feel him staring at her, but she couldn't meet his gaze. Yet, despite her discomfort she was relieved to have finally sorted out her feelings. She was going to tell him that there would be no marriage between them.

Donald leaned over to speak to Jilleen. Whatever he said made her giggle, and Olivia wished she were close enough to share in their laughter.

They ate the served courses of seafood bisque, followed by poached salmon, roasted beef, and steamed asparagus topped with hollandaise sauce. The sound of silverware scraping against china was loud. They sipped wine as conversations flittered around the table.

"Olivia, lass, I have something to tell ya." Paddy lowered his voice so Mrs. Prewitt, directly across from him and hanging on their every word, couldn't hear. "Earlier, I overheard a conversation between your father and Emil Prewitt."

"What did you hear?" she said, trying to be circumspect.

"I got in on the tail end of it, but Emil was urging yer father to take Lapaglia back as a bank customer. Sounds as though the Prewitt's do business with Lapaglia, and Lapaglia needs to order cloth from their factory. Apparently the rally and yer father pulling in his loan from Lapaglia has hurt his business."

Olivia took a sip of wine. This was news to her, surprising news. "Myron and Lapaglia?"

It was time for Jilleen to leave and go to bed. With Mrs. Lippencott holding her hand, Jilleen came around and wedged herself between Olivia and Myron. Jilleen yawned.

"Time for bed?" Olivia asked and turned her cheek to Jilleen for the expected kiss.

"G'night, 'Livia."

"Goodnight, sweetheart. And thank you, Mrs. Lippencott," she said and watched the housekeeper smile and leave with Jilleen.

Myron placed his napkin on the table and stood. He softly hit his fork against the side of his water glass for attention. “I guess there’s no time like the present, especially being amongst family and friends, to say what I have to say.” He put the fork down and reached inside his pocket to take out a small blue velvet box.

He took Olivia by the hand and brought her to her feet.

With a phony smile pasted on her face, and having found out about Myron and Lapaglia, Olivia was seething. She steadied herself, knowing now was not the time to accuse Myron of his deception.

“Olivia,” Myron said and continued, “Would you do me the honor of becoming my wife? My parents find you delightful and will welcome you into our family.” His face was all smiles.

How arrogant, she thought. His parents welcome me—indeed. She wanted to slap the smug grin right off his face. Lapaglia’s name was squeezing her mind like a vice. She glanced at her father who acted as surprised as she was. Everyone but her mother appeared dumbfounded. Merilee, wearing a wide smile of victory, nodded down the table at Walter. Again, Olivia checked her anger, unable to voice it. She had too much respect for her friends and guests.

Myron, apparently thought Olivia tongue-tied from happiness, misconstrued her silence. Before she could react, he slipped the large diamond on her finger and kissed her cheek.

The sound of glass breaking caused everyone to turn their attention away from the couple and to Donald who was holding a white linen napkin against his bleeding palm. A wine glass, shattered at the stem, lay in two pieces on the table where burgundy wine soaked into the tablecloth.

“Oh…oh my! You’re hurt,” Olivia blurted, and was away from Myron’s embrace and around the table before anyone was sure of what happened. “Here, Mr. McShane, let me take you upstairs and put something on it.”

“Olivia!” Merilee raised her voice. “Let Lori Raye help Mr. McShane. We need to toast your engagement.”

"Olivia…" was all Myron managed to say.

She stared at her mother's startled face. "No! I'll help Jilleen's father. He's my guest," she said.

Myron's eyes narrowed. He started to protest, but Olivia quickly led Donald out of the dining room and up the stairs.

They went into the bathroom where Olivia rummaged through the medicine cabinet until she found a bottle of iodine and gauze.

"Here, let me see that." She lifted the napkin off the cut. "Donald, I think this needs a stitch or two."

"I don't think so, Miss Marsh." His questionable gaze roamed her face.

A small shard of glass had embedded in his palm, so she turned back to the medicine cabinet searching for a pair of tweezers. "Don't call me, Miss Marsh."

"I see. Guess I'll be callin' ya Mrs. Prewitt here soon, aye?" He held out his hand while she pulled out the glass. She compressed her lips and generously dabbed on the iodine.

He sucked in his breath and swore, "Bloody hell!" He blew on his hand trying to stop the sharp sting of the iodine. It didn't work. "Sorry to swear in front of ya." Shaking his hand, he again blurted, "That almost stings as much as seeing ya in Prewitt's arms and him putting that ring on yer finger. I didn't know it was so serious you'd be marryin' the man. Sure'n I thought there was something special beginning between us."

"There is something special between us." She was wretched, close to coming undone, angry with Myron and her mother, hurt for Donald. "I didn't know he was going to propose. I don't love him—I'm not marrying him. I just didn't get a chance to say otherwise." She wrapped his hand with gauze, glancing at his eyes still watering from the iodine.

"Ya didn't?" he said. "Could have fooled me."

"No, I didn't," she affirmed, holding onto his hand. "I was speechless. Mother and Myron planned their little announcement behind my back. Things were taken out of my control and I intend to fix—"

"Dammit, lass—" His head dipped toward hers, his lips close to meeting hers.

"Olivia! Olivia, there you are." Her mother, with Myron on her heels, moved quickly from the landing to where they stood next to the bathroom door.

Muttering under her breath, Olivia let go of Donald's hand. She could see relief written all over her mother's face and wondered what she expected to find when she came dragging Myron up here.

Merilee apparently accepted the situation at face value, but scolded all the same. "You really shouldn't be in the bathroom with Mr. McShane. It isn't proper. Myron can help now that we see you've taken care of the cut. Was it bad, Mr. McShane?"

Donald stepped out of the bathroom. "Not bad at all, Mrs. Marsh. I'm afraid I broke a glass to your set, and for that I'll be apologizing. I was caught up with the announcement and all. Didn't realize me own strength."

"Not to worry, it can be replaced. The important thing is to keep your hand from getting infected."

"Well then, it's me turn to tell you not to worry. No self-repectin' germ could get past that iodine. *Bejapers,* I've never felt anything so brutal."

Olivia grinned at his words and watched as Donald started past her mother. Merilee slid her arm within Donald's and smiled at Olivia and Myron. "Please join us soon. We must continue with the toasts about your engagement and wedding. Imagine that, Mr. McShane, Olivia and Myron getting married," Merilee's voice echoed back as they started down the stairs. "I am so excited for her…"

Olivia replaced the iodine and gauze, and then shut the cabinet. She turned to Myron and held out her hand for him to take, but he had other plans.

"Come here, Olivia. Let's seal our engagement."

He surprised her by backing her up against the sink and crushing her against him. He started to kiss her but she turned her face away.

"Don't, Myron."

He broke off, his eyes a cold jade. "You're right, I forgot myself just now. I love you and wanted to show you how much. Forgive me, Olivia, I allowed my feelings to overshadow my judgment. Let's set a date for our wedding. How about August? August is a good month for a marriage. We could sail to Paris for our honeymoon. What do you say?"

"I'm not sure what to say. You took me by surprise tonight. I wish you'd talked to me in private instead of announcing it at the table. Did you expect me to act dutiful about this? You know me better, and if you don't, then you've wasted the past year we've been seeing each other. And since I didn't get to give you an answer when you asked, I'll give it now. My answer is no. I can't marry you."

His jaw clenched, and he spat his words out. "Yes, it has been a year, hasn't it. I foolishly fell for your mother's plans, thinking you'd be happy and accepting. I'm sorry about proposing at the table. The whole affair was done wrong. You have a right to be upset. Just remember one thing, Olivia, I'm not a fool. Don't play me for one." He pointed at her, his voice low, "Another thing you need to know is that I don't easily give up what's been promised to me."

She leaned against the sink, thoughtfully perusing him, seeing a whole different man, and not caring for what she saw. Yet somehow down deep inside her, intuition maybe, she knew it was always there, a deadly strength, that when provoked could be lethal. "Then don't play me for a fool. Tell me about Lapaglia."

His face remained stoic. "Tell you what? There's nothing to tell."

"I think there is. My father dropped Lapaglia as a customer and requested he pay his loan. Don't tell me you don't know anything about that."

"Lapaglia buys our material to make clothing. We were doing business long before you and I met."

"And yet, you continue to do business with a man who hurt me? A man who almost killed me? I'd think you'd never speak to him again, certainly stop doing business with him."

For a moment, he sagged against the wall like the wind was taken out of his sails, but he rallied again. "How was I to know you'd get hurt? Be fair."

Her mouth fell open in shock, his words a stunning revelation. "What do you mean, *'how were you to know I'd get hurt?'* Did you plan that day? Were you in on this with Lapaglia? Were you trying to scare me away from rallying against child labor?"

His expression changed, he paused, and that brief pause was an answer in itself, an admission of guilt. Too late, he blurted, "Don't be ridiculous, of course not—"

"You did. You planned it," she said, feeling desperate, her voice loud.

"Not for you to get hurt, Olivia!" He shoved off the wall and stood dangerously close. "It was an accident, all of it…" his voice trailed off.

When she started to go past him, he stopped her and again tried to kiss her.

Unable to believe what was happening, that he even had the gall to try again, she clamped her mouth shut and rebuffed him. She put her hand against his chest, backing him off. "I could have been killed, or injured for life." She saw Myron for the kind of man he was. There was no end to how low he'd sink to get her to quit championing for children. She hated being witness to it.

"But you weren't," he countered. "I'm not going to let you go. Nor am I giving you to that Irishman you undressed with your eyes during dinner. Did you think I didn't know—couldn't see? This is because of him isn't it?"

"He has nothing to do with us."

"Liar. If you'd never caught Jilleen we wouldn't be here like this. This is all just an excuse isn't it? You've been salivating to break off with me, but you didn't have an excuse. Now you have plenty."

She started down the stairs. He was right beside her.

"Yes, you're right, Myron. You've found me out—and I've found you out. But almost getting me killed is far worse than anything I could ever do to you." Stunned at his admission and her own, she didn't know what to say only to do what she must. She removed both rings, and taking his hand slapped them in his palm.

Looking dumbfounded, his fingers closed over the rings. A second later he was grabbing her hand trying to force her to take them back.

"Don't." She slapped his hand away.

The promise ring pinged against the wall and shot over the banister to be plucked from the air by Donald. The engagement ring bounced down the stairs and came to a glittering stop at the feet of all the guests gathered there.

By now Myron had lost all reasoning, didn't care who was circled at the bottom of the stairs watching. He roughly pulled her arm, preventing her from taking another step.

"Stop it," she hissed, hitting his shoulders with her balled fists, "you're hurting me." But he was too tall, too muscular for her as his body wedged hers against the curving banister. She teetered dangerously, praying the rail wouldn't break.

"Damn you!" Her father's arms circled Myron's chest, securing him, pulling him away from Olivia. "Myron, I suggest you pull yourself together long enough to leave my home with some sense of decorum. Either that, or I'll kill you."

Chapter Nineteen

The City's hastened pace had already started. The harsh odor of humanity having settled for the night was stirred up with the rattling sound of delivery trucks, and horns bleating like pastoral sheep.

Eldon, holding a bag of hot scones in one hand, was hurrying back to the drugstore with breakfast. Tired from being up late at the Marsh's, he yawned. *'Man that was some dinner party. Yes—sir. Good to know the rich could have their affairs go into the sewer as easily as the poor.'*

He and his dad, along with Donald, had talked about it all the way home. Donald had started toward the stairs to help Olivia but Eldon restrained him and whispered to stay out of it, that Walter Marsh was doing fine on his own. Mrs. Marsh had picked up the discarded diamond ring, trying to sooth the Prewitt's. Myron kept babbling something about Olivia's brain was still healing and she couldn't possibly know what she was doing. Walter, strong-armed Myron out the door, telling him after he came to his senses, they'd talk. Mrs. Marsh had stood on the front porch chattering like an aggrieved woman, telling Grace and Emil Prewitt they weren't disgraced, a small mishap only, and that everything would work itself out. Certainly, Olivia wasn't herself.

Yep, what a night.

Unable to ignore the aroma of hot pastries any longer, Eldon took out a scone and bit into it. Rich tasting with a pinch of lemon filled his mouth putting him in heaven. He tried not to think of the roll of flab around his waist, instead he focused on the flaky hot scone in his hand. Somehow the scone won out. He took another bite, then another, until his breakfast was gone.

"Paper—get yer paper!"

A new boy, a new corner, had Eldon digging in his pocket for a nickel.

The kid scratched his behind and continued to shout, "Paper—get yer paper! Read about Roosevelt's new Progressive Party!" He held up a copy of the Times, and with a pitiful look on his face pleaded for people to buy the latest news.

Eldon stopped and bought a paper. "Hey, kid," he said grinning down at the lad. "You're new here, huh?"

"Yeah—so?"

"I'm looking for a friend of mine, a young boy, Joe Gillespie's his name. Don't suppose you know of him?" Eldon was doubtful as he perused the kid.

The kid's blue eyes narrowed at Eldon who expected a big fat *no*, but the kid surprised him.

"What about, Joe?" he asked. Handing a paper to another customer, he caught the flipped nickel.

Eldon's flesh prickled, this wasn't what he expected. He tried to curtail his excitement. "I'm concerned about him. He's been missing over a week and I'd like to find him."

The boy's mouth pulled down. "Yeah, I know Joe. He mostly stays at Ryerson's groceries, or with some Irishman, don't know his name."

"Yes, I know he does. But he's not at either place. I'm a friend of that Irishman you just mentioned, and Joe hasn't stayed there since last Sunday. That Irishman's name is Donald McShane. Not only is he trying to find Joe, he's also seeking his son, Casey. You wouldn't know a Creighton or Casey McShane by any chance?"

The kid's eyes widened in surprise and he quickly bent to scratch a scab on his grubby knee. Finally, he straightened, but his homely face had closed-off. No more surprises for Eldon.

A customer jostled up to the kid, rudely pushing Eldon out of the way, he demanded, "Give me a paper." The kid quickly obliged and put out his hand for the money.

"Your problem kid, ya took too long." The shyster shrugged and walked off.

"Hey, ya fart head!" the kid yelled, and started after him.

Eldon reached out and grabbed his boney arm. He took out a nickel and gave it to the boy. "Here's your money, never mind about him. Do you know Casey or not?"

The kid shrugged and said, "Mister, be here this time tomorrow. Bring that McShane man with ya."

Wanting to shout, throw his hat in the air, Eldon did neither and settled a grin upon the kid. He held out his hand. "I'm Eldon Johnston. My drugstore is several blocks over. Come see me for a free ice cream soda. What's your name?"

"Benny Hart." The kid quickly wiped his dirty hand on his knee pants. He shook Eldon's offered hand.

"Well, Benny Hart, I'll see you tomorrow." He reached into his bag, took out a scone and gave it to the kid.

Derry stood in the middle of the busy sidewalk, confused, looking left to right. She was lost. The voices constantly whispered, telling her she was worthless and to kill herself. She looked helplessly about. People scurried by, bumping into her, shoving her out of the way, and cursing at her clumsiness.

She reached into her purse and taking out the paper with Jilleen's address, accosted a stranger. "Sir, help me—this address?"

The man brushed by her.

The voices started up in a medley of soft whispers, *"Sam's a liar. Stay away from Jilleen—stay away from Sam. You're lost…lost…!"* the voices screamed.

"I'm not lost!" she whined in bewilderment and backed into a lamppost. Derry's mouth quivered, the people around her became a blur. She no longer knew what was real and what wasn't. Jesus, Mary—not again, please—not now.

"Sam's going to kill you…kill you…kill yourself…kill yourself…"

Trying to force the voices out, she put her hands against the sides of her head, madly shaking it from side to side. "Go away—damn ya—go away!" she blurted, her mouth pulled down in a grimace, her eyes squeezed shut.

"Darlene?"

"Go away!"

Someone lowered her hands from her face.

"Darlene, what are ya doing out here?"

She tried to focus on who was capturing her hands in such a tight grip. Her vision was steeped with tears.

"It's me, Sam. I've been searchin' all over for ya. It worried me findin' ya gone." He looked haggard, as though he hadn't slept in days. His face was thick with dark stubble.

She nervously wet her lips and swallowed. "Oh…Sam," her words whispered out in relief. He had a way of always turning up. Right now she didn't know to be afraid or happy to see him. She decided happy, and breaking his hold on her, groped at his suit lapels.

Anger etched his face. Once again he pried her hands loose and secured them within his. "Why did ya leave the apartment?"

"Leave?" She tried to think, but he took up the space and air around her.

"Aye, yer standing here in the middle of the sidewalk acting like a loony, yelling to someone who isn't here." He cursed under his breath, his eyes feral glints of danger. "People are gaping at ya,

Darlene. They're dartin' by and hoping to hell ya don't grab hold of them."

She flinched and stared down at the grimy sidewalk. Not making the connection he was telling her something was wrong with her mind, she only knew one thing, and it had become like a mountain for her to climb. She brought her head up to meet his hard stare.

"Sam...please, I want Jilleen." She thrust the small piece of tattered newspaper at him.

"Ya want Jilleen? Well so do I, darlin', so do I. If ya can pull yourself together we'll go get her—now." A slow smile creased his mouth.

"Now? You'll take me now?" she said in disbelief and pushed at her hair that had loosened from its combs and straggled around her face. "Is it far?"

Sam's glance was sharp. "Aye, clear across the city from here. But what do you care? Ya want yer daughter, let's get her." He shoved her, making her stumble.

Derry cried out, "Stop it!"

He steadied her. Becoming somewhat gentle, he put his hand against the small of her back and guided her through the crowd toward the trolley line.

Her determination to see Jilleen overshadowed her fear, and she fought against the abyss of unseen voices threatening to pull her down.

"Go back...Sam will kill you."

Fighting to see through her tears, Derry shouted, "Get away from me!"

Her outburst appeared to surprise Sam. He stopped walking. "Do you want me to leave ya alone, Darlene? I don't know how to help ya, or what ya want. Let's go home." He took her by the arm and started to turn back.

She dug her heels in. "No! I have to get Jilleen. Please, Sam, help me to get there..." Desperation washed over her like storm water crashing over a pier, tears streamed down her cheeks as determination lifted her chin. She reached up to touch his raspy cheek, examining him as if truly seeing his dark troubled face. "I'm hanging on with every thread of my being. Don't be cruel to me, Sam. Please help me."

His face relaxed in hopefulness as his stare softened. "Are ya back with me darlin'? Are ya your old self, like back in Ireland?"

She nodded, trying to convince them both. She tried to shut out the voices, tried to smile at Sam, tried to reassure, when all the while another thread of her sanity stretched and tore loose.

Traveling by hot and stifling trolleys and trains, they reached the end of the line. Sam took her hand and helped her step down. She used her white handkerchief to dab at the small beads of perspiration on her upper lip.

"We don't have too far to go, several blocks over, then uphill a ways," he cautioned.

"I don't mind walking." And she latched onto a distant memory of long walks she used to take with Donald. How they'd wrap up food, put it in a basket and climb the nearby hills. Casey would turn somersaults, yelling at them to watch as he rolled like a ball down the sloping meadow. Donald was quick to catch up with Casey and swing him high into the air, the both of them laughing, darting wide grins back at her. Oh…to be there again, living in happier times. Derry fought back tears, and tried not to break down in front of Sam.

"If ya want yer daughter, just do as I say." Sam walked with long urgent strides, instructing her with what he wanted done. "Can ya do this for us?"

She nodded. Yes, she could do this. She glanced from one side of the street to the other, trying to take in the large houses. At last he stopped in front of an imposing mansion set back from the road and guarded by a black wrought iron fence and a deep thick hedge.

"This is where Jilleen's at," he said pointing beyond the gate at the dowager structure. "Are you sure yer up to this?" He took off his hat and slowly ran the brim through his fingers.

Derry wondered how she was going to see Jilleen. This was not what she expected. The place looked like a fortress. She didn't answer him, instead stared at the house with a frown on her face.

He pinched her chin. "Look at me when I'm talkin'. Do ya need me to escort ya to the feckin' door?"

She swallowed hard, terrified to go beyond the gate, terrified not to. "Can ya not get her for me?"

"She's your daughter. Ya want her—get her." He started walking off.

"No! No! Don't leave me. I'll go." She ran after him and took hold of his arm, desperate, gripping it as though it was a lifeline. "Please?"

"That's a good lass," he said, pulling her to him, showing kindness, encouraging her, kissing her forehead.

"What if I'm stopped?"

"I'm telling ya, Darlene, do exactly what I told ya and you'll be able to steal your daughter right from under their nose." He opened the gate set within the scrolls of the wrought iron. "Take yer time." His hand went to the small of her back guiding her through.

The gate clanged shut behind her, startled, she jumped

"Remember to go around to the back door, not the front. Follow the driveway around back," he reminded.

"Aye." Standing just inside the gate she hesitated.

As if feeling her dilemma, he encouraged her. "I'll be right here. I won't leave ya." The black scroll work shadowed designs across his face.

Merilee, alone in her bedroom, thought of herself abandoned by Walter and Olivia who had both gone off to the City. Walter went to work at his bank, and Olivia fled to the suffragette's office. They'd left Merilee to stew about the fiasco of a wedding proposal gone terribly wrong. *Wrong* was an understatement, and she was brokenhearted for Myron. In the time it took the diamond ring to bounce and roll down the stairs, their planning had rolled into oblivion.

Stupid man—stupid man. What on earth possessed Myron to admit his involvement with Lapaglia? Olivia wasn't permanently hurt. If she had been, it would have been a different matter. And Walter, how was she supposed to know his bank had loaned Lapaglia money?

She rubbed at her forehead and the headache that settled there with intense ferocity. And now this, she scowled at the vicious note in her hand, delivered first thing this morning. The message was a threat written in bold stabbing letters, the ink splattering with hurried blots. In a precarious position of her own making, Merilee didn't know how to handle something like this. Certainly she couldn't show it to Walter. Not after last night. Thinking to deal with it later, she opened her dresser drawer and put the note inside.

Going to the front window, she pulled the curtain aside to peer out. A man and woman stood there at the front gate. The pair had Merilee grabbing up her opera glasses, spying on them. At first she mistook the man for Mr. McShane. But he wasn't. She could tell from the bowler hat and his silhouette that he was the same man she'd encountered at the gate weeks ago. The woman came on alone and disappeared around the corner of the house.

A warm breeze rustled through the giant trees, making the green leaves quake and dance, cooling Derry somewhat. The voices started, joining the whispering leaves. *"Go away. Kill yourself…"*

"Ah…no," Derry groaned. "You go away."

Her tongue stuck to the roof of her mouth, the cobblestone driveway now a haze. She put one foot in front of the other. At last, she stood a safe distance from the monstrous house and the backdoor. She pushed the voices down, battling with them, suppressing them inside her fragile mind. What was inside the house was more important than anything the voices said. Yet, her resolve started to crumble.

The door opened and a tall slender woman with gray hair stepped out onto the porch. Beside her a small black and white dog barked.

"May I help you?" the woman asked.

Fear shut off Derry's air. Words failed her. Everything wavered, fading in and out. The dog padded toward her. Derry staggered forward, stretching her arm out, reaching, and then she was falling. She heard the woman yell, 'Hugh.'

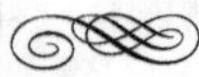

Curious, Merilee left her bedroom, crossed the hall to Nathan's old room, and went to the shuttered window. There, she pulled the wooden slats open, again training her opera glasses for a better view.

Shocked, Merilee watched her housekeeper and chauffer help the woman towards the house. It was apparent the woman had fainted. Her head lulled against Hugh's shoulder, and her feet were limp and dragging.

Something like this happening in her own home was not going to get past Merilee. This whole situation was mystifying. She quickly went down the stairs and headed to the back of the house. At first she wanted to confront her servants and the stranger, but changed her mind. Instead, she slipped into Lori Raye's bedroom right next to Mrs. Lippencott's where she could hide and listen. Besides, Merilee figured she was in enough hot water to just observe for a change.

Chapter Twenty

Something wet dabbed at Derry's face making her think Sam was washing her. She didn't like it and batted at him to stop. "Don't…Sam…don't!" she cried out. Her eyes fluttered open to see an elderly woman's blue eyes peering at her with concern.

"There—now, no need to hit at me." The woman, a slender reed of a person, wore a smile that broke her sharp features. She dipped the washcloth into the basin next to the bed, wrung it out, and gently dabbed at Derry's face again.

"Wh…happened?" Derry asked while groggily glancing around.

"You fainted dead away. Hugh helped carry you in here. I'm Stella Lippencott."

Derry started to sit up, but Mrs. Lippencott gently stopped her.

"I think you should remain still a while longer. Why were you outside?"

She didn't know at first what to say, and then she remembered what Sam had told her. "I've…ah…well…'tis about the housekeepin' position, aye?"

The woman clucked her tongue. "You must have the wrong house, we have no openings here. I should know as I'm the head housekeeper for the Marsh family."

Derry searched for the right thing to say, trying to pull words from her fading mind. "…I'm…sorry…I'll…leave." She started to rise, but a firm hand on her shoulder anchored her.

"Posh!" Mrs. Lippencott said. "Not until I get a cold drink of lemonade down you, and make sure you're steady on your feet." She placed the cloth across Derry's forehead. "Here, keep this in place."

Derry watched a little girl come bounding into the room with the dog behind her. The closer the child came the realization set in that she was Jilleen. Derry wanted to scream with delight. Jilleen was close enough to touch. Her daughter whom she thought was lost to her forever. She wanted to leap up and snatch up her baby. Run from the house with her. Instead, she held the wet cloth in place, keeping her face halfway hidden and trying to stop her hands from shaking. *Do as Sam says. Do as Sam says.* The dog kept sniffing at her, going up and down her arm that was close to the edge of the bed.

"Missus Lipencod, is 'Livia gonna be home soon?"

"I would imagine so, Jilleen. And please stop running in the house. Little ladies do not run, they walk."

"Aye, Miss," she said in her small voice.

"Sparks—get away from the bed," Mrs. Lippencott ordered the dog.

"Who's that lady?" Jilleen asked.

"Why…I don't know her name. She fainted outside and we brought her in here. What's your name, dear?"

"D…em…Lillian," she stammered. "…Please, somethin' to drink…"

"Yes, how silly of me. Jilleen, would you keep the lady company while I go get her a cold drink? Sparks, come."

Hearing the housekeeper's footsteps fade, Derry sat up slowly. She soaked in Jilleen's image. Her daughter was as pretty as a picture in a plaid ruffled dress, her hair a mass of brown curls framed by a large blue bow.

Jilleen gasped. Her eyes widened in recognition, forming tears.

Derry held out her arms which were shaking so much she could hardly control them. She begged the Lord, the Virgin Mary, to give her a sane moment, just a small amount of time.

"Jilleen, come to yer mam."

Without hesitation Jilleen ran to her. "Mammy!" she cried.

Derry hugged her to her bosom, feeling her little body, kissing the top of her head, and constantly murmuring endearments against her curls. "Yer so pretty. Oh me, baby—me wee, Jilly. I've missed ye so." She rained kisses all over her face.

"Mammy, Casey's been to see me."

Derry couldn't believe what she heard. "Casey's alive?" She held Jilleen at arms length, searching her face, watching as she nodded. Derry's mouth quivered. She felt like she was going to collapse again with all the excitement, her joy hard to contain. *Blessed Mary—Jesus—Jesus, bless you. Bless my children.*

...Go away...kill yourself...

"Ah...no...don't do this."

"Do what, Mam?"

The hollow, thudding sound of heels hitting the floor announced the housekeeper was returning. Derry pulled on inner strength that was quickly waning. "Listen to me, Jilly. I've got to go. I'll wait for ya by the front gate. Come to me darlin' angel. Come to me, and don't tell a soul yer doing so."

Mrs. Lippencott sailed in carrying a tray with three glasses of lemonade. "I thought we could all use something cool to drink. Why, there you are sitting up. Are you feeling better?" She lowered the tray down to both Derry and Jilleen.

"Sure'n I am," Derry said.

Mother and daughter smiled at each other.

...Kill yourself...kill your daughter...

Merilee went back upstairs. Thoughts rattled around inside her head like ships bobbing at anchor. With opera glasses in hand, she went straight for her bedroom window. The man who greatly resembled Mr. McShane still waited at the gate. The woman downstairs was Jilleen's mother, making her Mr. McShane's wife, making him still married and making him unavailable. She wanted to squeal with delight.

She watched the woman walk toward the gate, and not long afterward, Jilleen followed.

Merilee made no move to stop Jilleen. Her smile of malicious intent formed into a smirk. This couldn't be more perfect if she'd planned it herself. She and Myron had been too quick to push their plans. If only they would have waited one day, a week. With a little finesse and wrangling on her part, perhaps she could salvage all and mend broken feelings.

Derry practically raced down the long pathway and stepped through the gate.

Sam said in a worried voice, "What happened? You look upset. Bloody hell, don't tell me it went all wrong."

She clutched her handbag against her chest, trying to find the words to explain. "No Sam…me wee Jilleen…well, she…" She gave up and pointed at Jilleen who was walking up the path at a fast clip, and holding a bulging pillowcase.

The dog was making a racket in the window, barking and scratching at the glass. Jilleen glanced back over her shoulder at the dog, hesitated for a moment, and then turned to see her mam.

Derry opened the gate and Jilleen stepped through. Her innocent child's eyes peered around taking in her surroundings, and then they settled on Sam.

She screamed, "No!" She whirled around and started running toward the house.

Sam moved fast, and just like on the ship, scooped her up. Her knapsack fell to the ground, her legs a blur as she kicked. "Put me down—let me go!"

Her little fists were ineffective against his chest. He nestled his head against hers trying to calm her. "Ah…sweet, Jilleen. We've missed ya. Yer Mam's cried every day fer ya."

Derry watched in silent confusion at the scene before her. At last Jilleen stopped kicking, but she seemed frightened, as Sam continued to hold her. Derry went to Jilleen's side and took her hand.

"Mam?" she said.

"Baby...I've been sick…couldn't come sooner. Sam wanted too. Now we're together. We'll be fine…you'll see."

Sam put Jilleen down and picked up the pillowcase. "Listen to yer mam."

"Where are we goin'? I brought me things, just in case."

"What do you have in here, Jilleen?" Sam asked while groping inside the knapsack. "Nothing that would make them think you've stolen anythin' and come searchin' for us, aye?"

"Jest me dolls." She glared at Sam. "Mam, can we come back and visit 'Livia?" Jilleen pleaded.

Sam answered for Derry. "Of course. We best move on." He glanced at the house, and still holding the pillowcase started down the hill.

"Where are we goin', Mam?" Jilleen stared up at her, accepting that she knew what she was doing, accepting her without hesitation.

"We're going for a ride on a train. Would ya be likin' that?" The voices began their damnable whispering, hissing, *"Go away…go away…"* As tears of failure and bafflement pooled in Derry's eyes, she felt Jilleen tugging on her hand. She stopped, but Sam kept on walking.

"I want 'Livia."

Agitated, Derry looked down at Jilleen who was staring back at her with eyes as moist as her own. "Who is this Livia woman?"

"She caught me when Uncle Sam threw me off the big ship."

Derry's mouth fell open in protest. Sam would never do that. Why was Jilly accusing him of such a horrible thing? "Jilly, did Sam really throw ya off the ship?"

"Aye, Mam, he did. 'Livia was in the lifeboat and caught me."

"Well, there ya go. He threw ya in the boat to save ya," she affirmed, feeling better.

Jilleen shook her head. "I hate Uncle Sam."

Trying to ignore her daughter's venomous outburst, Derry pulled her by the hand and hurried to catch up with Sam who was waiting for them. If what Jilleen just said is true, then Sam had lied to her about Jilleen and Casey dying on the Titanic. Sam could have brought Jilleen to her on the *Carpathia* when she lay paralyzed with guilt, but he didn't. How could he let her wallow in such mind-rendering grief, almost destroying her? With her thoughts more muddled than ever, she teetered between belief and disbelief about Sam's actions.

…Sam's bad…Sam's bad…

At last, the train whistle sounded in the distance.

"Mammy. Let's go back. 'Livia will take us where ya want to go." Jilleen dug her heels into the ground, slowing her down.

Sam stepped in and taking Jilleen's hand forced her to run. "C'mon, lass. We don't want to miss the train. Have you ever ridden in one?"

"Nay," she said, her little legs working to keep up.

They reached the station where the train had stopped to unload people. After purchasing tickets for the three of them, Sam quickly helped Derry and Jilleen onboard and ushered them to seats.

Derry smiled down at her daughter, but not satisfied with a mere smile, Derry hugged her close. She tried to smooth the puckered little brow. "Ah…me wee lass, I never thought to see ya again." She ran her hand over the expensive material of Jilleen's frock. "Such a fine dress. Isn't she pretty, Sam?" She relaxed into a timid smile, searching his face for approval.

"Aye, she is."

Jilleen acted terrified, which only increased when she glanced out the window to see the train clacking along.

"Mam?" She grasped Derry's arm, her face pinched with fright as she motioned with her finger to lean down. "Casey said not to tell Uncle Sam about him. Ya won't tell him, aye? I promised Casey," she whispered.

"Shhh, Jilleen…please..."

The voices clanged around inside of Derry's head like a church bell. Her daughter was pulling her one way, the voices another.

Fear covered Jilleen's face, showing Derry how much she was afraid of Sam and of him knowing about Casey. Jilleen's fingers nervously plucked at the lace on the pillowcase and she collapsed against Derry's chest and sobbed. "Promise, Mammy."

Derry took her daughter's hand and held it, trying to make things right. But how could she when she'd messed things up for so long? She knew she couldn't take care of Jilleen, not with the quagmire her mind had become. She gently stroked Jilleen's back. "It's all right, me wee baby, I promise. Want to show me what ya have in your pillowcase?"

Jilleen raised her head. Her face was flushed from crying, her eyelashes spiked with tears. Sniffing, she settled back on the seat, her legs sticking straight out in front of her. Hiccupping and taking a deep quaking breath, she took up her case.

She pulled out two dolls. "These are me dollies Mr. Marsh brought me." The dolls were porcelain with Victorian faces. One was a blonde the other had black hair. Each one was dressed in fine clothing. Next was Derry doll, wearing the coat Ina McShane had made for her. "This is Derry, 'member Da sent her to me?"

Derry could only nod, barely remembering when Donald had done so. She tried to remember all the good there was about Donald. But she'd lost him, thrown him away like everything else in her life.

Sitting across from Jilleen, Sam thought back to the *Titanic,* how he'd heard Casey yell at Jilleen that he'd murdered Lillian. He wondered if Jilleen could forget her brother's words, let time work on her memory, let it fade as most childhood memories had a tendency to do. He hoped that would be the case. But whenever he looked at his niece's face, he saw Donald's face, and he didn't know if he could live with the constant reminders of what he wanted most in the world to forget.

He smiled at Jilleen, hoping to wipe her frightened stare away. But it wasn't happening. Darlene didn't look any better. Her hair was stringing around her face. Perspiration darkened her red blouse giving her the appearance of a washerwoman after a hard day's work. She looked as bedraggled as he felt.

He put his hand on her thigh and gave it a reassuring squeeze.

"I'm thinkin' it's time to leave Manhattan."

"Leave?" She stared at him uncomprehending.

Wearing a jovial grin he sure as hell didn't feel, he nodded at her. "We're headin' to California, the day after tomorrow."

Jilleen shrilled out, "Me Da's been to see me. I'm supposed to live with him, but he doesn't have room for Sparks. I'm not going to Cafornia with ya."

Sam reminded himself to remain calm. Jilleen's words surprised him. He didn't know his brother was involved with the Marsh woman. Nor did he know Donald had found Jilleen. He'd read the papers about Lillian Denbury being identified by her aunt. Knowing women's penchant for gossip, he wondered if Lillian had written her aunt about him. He'd tried to cover his tracks, but did he?

"If I say yer going to California, then yer going." He warned Jilleen.

The brat was staring at him. Her eyes narrowed in an accusing stare like she was saying, *I know what you did.*

He pasted on a thin smile and lifting a lone brow gave her an intense glare that said, *I don't give a feck you know.*

Chapter Twenty-One

Since learning about his son, Donald now spent his days searching for both Casey and Joe, and Walter Marsh's generosity made it happen. Donald felt Casey was safe with other boys. But not Joe. It was as if Joe had been swallowed up and Donald's concerns were tenfold for the gentle lad that he'd come to love as a son. He tried to go early enough that the streets weren't so clogged but his late night at the Marsh's had him sleeping late.

With last night's party on his mind, he'd just removed the bandage on his hand and thought about Olivia's closeness as she'd wrapped the cut. He also knew he was the reason for the cockup that followed between her and Myron Pruitt. Yet, he knew exactly how the man felt and if the tables were turned he would have done the same thing to keep Olivia Marsh in his life.

Taking a quick sip of his coffee and wanting to get started, he was jolted by thunderous pounding and Eldon's loud shouting coming through his door. Donald hurried to let Eldon in.

Donald's skin prickled at Eldon's agitated rush into his home.

"What's happened? Why aren't ya at the drugstore?" He closed the door.

"Because something good has happened. I came across a paperboy named Benny Hart who says he knows Joe." Excited, Eldon emphasized his words with a wave of his hands. "I'm supposed to have you there in the morning—at his corner where he sells his papers. And that's not all. I asked him about Casey McShane. I'm telling you that little guy also knows your son. I can feel it. If he didn't, why would he ask me to bring you there tomorrow morning?"

Suspicious, Donald suppressed any elation he might have. He sighed. "Aye, Eldon, we'll be there the time the kid mentioned. Sure'n I'm not getting me hopes up about Casey, ya understand?"

"I do understand, but you should get your hopes up. And that's not the only reason I came rushing over here. Damn it, I wish you lived in an apartment building with a telephone—"

"What's my having a telephone to do with anything?"

"Plenty. After Olivia called and asked me to come here and bring you to her place, I was thinking she could have called here and left you the message—oh—never mind. Olivia sounded upset, but refused to tell me why, just that I bring you and to hurry."

They'd left Donald's place in a rush. He fretted all the way to Olivia's. As they hurried up the walkway, Donald was trying to figure out what had gotten Olivia in such a dither.

"Wished you knew what Olivia has to tell us. Maybe Paddy's found something out about Casey?" Donald glanced at Eldon.

"Don't know—could be. But she sounded troubled not happy."

They were halfway up the driveway when the Marsh's front door flung open and Olivia came out. Lifting up the hem of her blue dress, she ran toward him in a flurry of knee-length, white lacy drawers and stockings. A view he immensely enjoyed but it was so unlike her to act this way that it struck him as strange. When she was close enough, she flung herself into his arms, hysterical, forcing him to step backwards.

Regaining his balance he held her close. "Olivia?"

"Donald…oh…" she cried out, breathless from her run.

And this frightened him, for Olivia wasn't a woman to give into hysterics. "What's wrong, darlin'?" The endearment came as natural as holding her did.

"Something terrible has happened."

He tried to calm her, feeling the rapid rise and fall of her ribs. At last, he put her at arm's length, but the distress on her face made him hesitate.

"'Tis Jilleen, aye?" He didn't want to know, but watched as she slowly nodded and latched onto his hand. Her gaze moved from his face to Eldon's.

Donald turned and started running for the house.

Olivia shouted after him, "Don't, Donald. She's not there—Jilleen's gone."

Not believing what he heard had him stopping. "Gone where?"

"A woman took her." Olivia told him what had transpired between the stranger and Stella Lippencott. "It wasn't too long after the woman left that Mrs. Lippencott noticed Jilleen was gone. I wasn't here. Only mother and the staff were."

"Have ya searched everywhere? Maybe Jilleen's hiding?" he asked with raw hope.

But Olivia shook her head. "Jilleen hasn't hid in a long time, and has no reason to. Mother was taking a nap and Sparks's loud barking woke her up. Guess it took some time to calm the poor little dog down. He was trying to get out so bad his claws scratched the window glass."

This enlightened Donald in waves. Jilleen wouldn't leave the Marsh's with a stranger. It had to be someone she knew, and that someone had to be family. He tried to sort it out, wondering just who else survived the *Titanic's* sinking.

He and Eldon escorted Olivia to where her parents were waiting.

Walter led them into his study. "We'll call in the police. We'll find her, Donald. I don't understand who would do this, or why. Maybe she's been kidnapped. People do that, you know. They want money. If so, I expect a ransom to come any time now, and when it does, I'll be paying it. Don't worry." Appearing to notice Eldon, Walter nodded hello.

"Thank ya, Mr. Marsh," Donald said, still trying to absorb that Jilleen was gone. "Olivia, would ye mind sendin' for Paddy? Oh…and ask him to bring the picture of my family. He might be able to help. Is Mrs. Lippencott here?"

Olivia took his hand and squeezed, her large eyes were searching his, reflecting his sorrow. "I've already called him. I'll summon Mrs. Lippencott."

Merilee put her hand on Olivia's arm. "You stay here, I'll go get her." And they all watched Merilee walk away, her rose-colored dress swaying gracefully with each subtle step.

"Eldon, thank you for bringing Donald here." Olivia's smile was wistful if nothing else.

"I don't think it's too early for brandy. But maybe you want coffe or both?"

"Brandy," Donald and Eldon chorused.

Walter immediately poured a brandy for the men, then cocking a bushy brow at Olivia, and getting the nod to do so, he poured one for her. After putting the crystal stopper back into the decanter, he handed each a glass of amber liquid. He then took up his own drink.

Olivia knocked hers down in one gulp like it was lemonade. "Dad, I'd like another." She held out the empty glass to Walter who hadn't a chance to drink his. With a surprised look and a shrug, he simply handed his over, and went to pour another.

Merilee brought their housekeeper into the room. Everyone drained their drinks. Without further preamble, Merilee went to stand by Walter, leaving Mrs. Lippencott on her own.

"Mr. McShane," Mrs. Lippencott said, "I feel so guilty about our little lovely. I'm so sorry. She was in my care and I lost her, lost our darling little girl." Her shoulders stooped, and she wrung her white lacy handkerchief with nervous hands.

"Mrs. Lippencott." Donald indicated for her to sit next to him on the sofa. "I need ya to tell me what happened from the very first time you laid eyes on the woman, aye?"

She sat next to him, her hands gripping her knees as though willing them to stay in place. She told her tale from the time she noticed the blonde stranger standing in the backyard to when the woman fainted and Hugh went to her aid.

"I wiped her face with cool water until she came to. She said she was seeking work as a domestic but it turned out she had the wrong address. By then Jilleen had come into the room. I asked the woman her name and she said it was Lillian. I went to get her some lemonade, and left Jilleen with her. I wasn't gone but five minutes, if even that. Jilleen was beside me when I saw the woman to the door. The woman left and I went to make Jilleen's lunch. Sparks started going wild, pawing at the window and door. I scolded him trying to make him quiet down. That's when I searched for Jilleen and couldn't find her. Oh…Lordy, I'm so afraid that woman may have taken our precious miss." Her mouth quivered and she drew in a deep breath.

"The woman gave her name as Lillian?" Donald asked, his mind churning with horrendous thoughts. "What did she look like?"

"Yes, she said Lillian. She was pretty, but vague acting. She had blonde hair and blue eyes, and her clothes were somewhat rumpled. Oh…and another thing, she spoke with an Irish accent as strong as our little Jilleen's."

Donald stopped breathing, she was describing Derry down to her hair and eye color. However, that she acted vague was something new, or was it? "No last name?" he asked.

Mrs. Lippencott shook her head.

"Lillian?" Olivia murmured while tapping a finger against her lip. "Lillian! That's the name of Mr. Flynn's wife. The man on the

Carpathia that I thought could pass as your brother. Certainly your brother couldn't be the same person, could he?"

What could Donald say? He'd already come to this conclusion, hateful as it was.

Eldon and Walter moved to stand closer to Donald while Merilee remained aloof and silent. They stared at Donald, appearing to take it all in.

"Oh…there's one thing the woman said while I was trying to revive her," Mrs. Lippencott said.

All eyes turned to her.

Donald forced his question. "What was that, Mrs. Lippencott?"

"Well, as she was coming out of her faint, she became combative like, fighting at me, shaking her head from side-to-side, yelling, *'Don't, Sam, don't.'*"

Positive proof slammed Donald in the gut. He sat as rigid as a statue. And like sand, it all began to shift and settle. At first tiny grains of disbelief that grew until Donald's mind overflowed with thoughts of betrayal. Why should he be shocked or deny it? Hadn't he been thinking this very thing while on his way here? For if the Flynn's were Sam and Derry, what they'd done to his children was so detestably wrong it sickened him.

But history had a way of repeating itself. Sam was first with Derry, and Donald, although it was his desire to do so, was never able to forget. All these years he'd allowed Derry to think she'd tricked him concerning Casey.

Donald placed his glass on the table. Turning to face Mrs. Lippencott, he forced the words from his mouth. "She said, *'Sam?'*"

Mrs. Lippencott's mouth turned down and she gave a brief nod.

The loud knock on the door jarred everyone out of their shocked musings, and brought the housekeeper to her feet. "May I have your leave to answer the door?"

"Yes, please do," Merilee said. She went to stand by Walter who put his arm around her drawing her close.

Olivia slipped into the spot next to Donald, her hand seeking his. "Donald, your older brother is called Sam, right?"

"Aye, Olivia." And with that admission he felt all his joy ripped away, his whole being hit bottom. His happiness at having his daughter back, and soon his son, turned upside down. Olivia's eyes filled with a terrible sadness, and he didn't want that at all. He couldn't look at the rest, didn't want to see their eyes mirroring Olivia's.

He wanted to shout, *don't pity me.*

Mrs. Lippencott escorted Paddy Riley into the room. "Here's, Mr. Riley. Do you need more from me, Mrs. Marsh?" she asked. Merilee told her they might, and indicated for her to take a seat close to the fireplace.

Sparks went over to sniff Paddy's shoes, and then left the room, his toenails clicking against the hard floor.

Olivia filled Paddy in on what happened. He instantly reached into a small sized sack he was carrying and taking out the picture of Donald's family handed it to him.

Donald in turn showed the picture to Mrs. Lippencott. "Tell me if ye find anything unusual about this picture?"

She stared at the picture. Her hand went to her throat, absentmindedly fingering loose skin. "That's Lillian. She's the woman who took our little miss."

"Yer sure?" Donald's gut twisted as he accepted the picture from her, his thumb rubbing over the glass covering Derry's smiling face. A memory flickered back to the day it was taken in Dublin, a young happy family, his.

"I'm positive, besides, I take pride in my sharp mind."

An awkward silence filled the room at the implications. Donald felt like a specimen under glass whose life was flayed open for all to see.

Walter, apparently sensing Donald's despair, cleared his throat. "Mr. Riley, if you would come with me, I'd like to talk with you. Tell me about this Mr. Flynn." He motioned to Eldon. "Mr. Johnston, join us. Merilee, why don't you send Mrs. Lippencott to check on lunch preparations?" And with that said, they cleared the room leaving only Donald and Olivia.

Donald went to stand by the cold fireplace that smelled faintly of ashes. The mantle acted as a crutch, and he needed support like never before. Olivia approached, and he was vaguely aware she did so. He wished the Marsh's weren't privileged to his shame, to see how his brother and wife had tricked him. His jaw firmed, he'd find Casey if it was the last thing he would do in this life. He'd find his daughter, and Sam and Derry could be damned. Damn them both to hell.

"Do you know the implications of what has happened in me life?" he said, and met her solid stare. "Do you?"

"Yes, I do," she said in a soft voice. "This means you are still married, not a widower. It means your brother, possibly using the alias of Albert Flynn, has your wife. And he may have had your wife for a long time. It also means your wife came here to take her daughter back. Under the law, her doing so is legal, and there's nothing you can do about it. Where she's been since the Titanic we may never know. Donald, we must find your son. I think Casey holds the key to all of this," her voice broke.

She spoke the truth and he hated hearing it. He'd never told her about Derry and Sam. Nor was he able to do so now. He'd choke on the words. Olivia was so caring, so enduring, he couldn't help but take her in his arms and rest his forehead against hers.

"There is one thing certain in me life, and that is I have mighty intense feelings for you, Olivia Marsh. Sure'n this is not the right time to say anything like that. But I'm beginning to think there's never a right time in me life for anything."

She put her fingers over his lips, sealing his words inside. "I...well...I've been longing to tell you I share those *intense feelings* you're talking about. And have since the day I was hit with the brick and you held me in your arms."

His hands framed her face, his thumb worked across her cheeks, her eyes, her lips. His joy in her admission of more than caring for him was no more. He had no right to touch Olivia at all. And the way it came about for him not to be free to do so grate at him. His brother had played him for a fool. His wife, whom he thought he'd known better than life itself, had once again created the ultimate sin. He could only wonder what had made her come and steal Jilleen away. Was her conscience bothering her?

Olivia stepped out of his embrace, immensely sad. "What are we to do?"

Donald's jaw clenched. "I can't resurrect her in my heart. She is still dead to me, Olivia. How could I feel anything for a woman who turns away from her own children? You said yourself ya put Jilleen's picture in the paper with hopes of finding her parents. Well, Derry didn't come forward then. She was on the Carpathia with the survivors and didn't try to find Jilleen. And Sam, damn his black soul to hell, told ya right to yer face he didn't know the child he threw overboard. He's a bold one, Sam is. A thief—a blaggard that only cares for himself." His anger was soaring and he fought against making a bloody show of himself when he wanted to punch a hole in the wall.

Apparently sensing his distress, Olivia tried to calm him. "Donald, please don't let this stand in the way of the happiness you've achieved. Don't let it drag you back down into the despair you were in after the Titanic. Please pull yourself above it all. Let's find Casey and get Jilleen back—"

"Olivia, that *despair* you mentioned will never leave me mind. It's my first waking thought and it's the last each night. How do you think I feel? I'm a man who's been tricked and led around like a trained animal. I'm married to a woman who doesn't want me. We're Catholic. I can't divorce her..." Donald paused. Olivia looked as though she'd been slapped. "Lass," he said, and struggled to find something less stinging to say, but he couldn't. "When I get me hands on Sam—"

"Donald." Paddy walked back into the room. "I have something to tell ya. You probably don't want to hear it, but in all my findings and searchin', I'm starting to put pieces of this puzzle together."

Donald and Olivia turned to Paddy at the same time.

"Aye?" Donald asked.

But Olivia interrupted both of them by quickly saying, "Wait a minute you two—I'll be right back!" And picking up her skirt, she allowed a glimpse of frilly lace as she dashed out of the study.

"What were you going to say?" Donald asked.

Paddy chuckled and replied, "Let's wait for Olivia to return. I think she's gone to bring us something of interest."

Eldon came back into the room and went to pour himself another brandy. "Want one?" he asked them, but they shook their heads.

Olivia returned as fast as she'd left and thrust several sheets of paper into Paddy's outstretched hand. "This is a few pages from the Titanic's manifest. It's a passenger list of the people that boarded the Titanic and where they embarked. I've brought you second-class only."

Paddy wet his finger and turned the pages. "Ah—here we are! Bold as brass, Mr. Albert *Samuel* Flynn. And below his name is Mrs. Lillian Flynn. They boarded at Southampton, England."

"I have a copy of that list. Here, let me see it." Donald took the paper from Paddy's hand.

Donald's eyes took on a dangerous shine. "I told ya I met Vivian Denbury, Lillian's aunt. We talked about Lillian's name not being on the Titanic's manifest. I read the letter Lillian had written her aunt, mentioning a man she'd met, that he'd given her gifts and taken her out to dinners. She also said the man was traveling on across the continent, going to California. I'm thinking this Lillian Denbury was with Sam on the Titanic as Lillian Flynn."

"Ya stole me thunder, laddie. That's exactly what I was goin' to tell ya," Paddy said. "And remember, Donald, Lillian Denbury was strangled. What we need to find out is why she was murdered and who did the killin'."

Donald fixed them with an enlightening stare. "Well, if I was a gamblin' man, I'd put me money on my brother. Is that what yer thinkin', that Sam did it?"

Olivia volunteered an answer. "He might have. I've noticed every time you mention your brother's name in front of Jilleen, she acted scared, downright frightened. I intended to ask her about it, but I forgot with all the excitement. And now I can't because she's no longer…"

Deep in thought, Paddy stroked his dark stubble. "I'll telegraph Inspector Mulhall our findings. Donald, I believe the man Lillian Denbury wrote about in her letter was your brother. Lillian Denbury could have been doing Sam a favor and passing for his wife, possibly for a free ticket to America. Your wife was in steerage with your children. Why would Sam go to all the trouble to have a woman do this? Why not just board the ship as a single man, Albert Flynn? What was he, or your wife trying to pull off? This is what puzzles me. They had to have some kind of plan."

"Maybe he wanted another woman, just in case Derry changed her mind?" Olivia offered.

Donald had a good idea what they had planned. He burned with hatred for a brother who could be so damn conniving that it sickened him.

"My sweet wife was going to be with him after the ship docked. Somewhere, or somehow, they were going to be together. But like all things with Sam, the ship sank and he came out on top. I wonder how he got off the Titanic when most of the men gave way to women and children. How did he manage to pull it off." His voice rang with sarcasm.

Olivia squeezed his hand, and he thought how she had caught Jilleen and taken care of her. His mind filled with all the good things about Olivia, and he brought her hand to his mouth for a kiss. Her warm skin beneath his lips made him feel somewhat better.

Eldon joined in the conversation. "Dad told Donald about a man who came into our store to have a prescription filled the same day we were coming home from Halifax. At first, Dad thought the man was Donald until he saw him up close. The prescription was for a Lillian Flynn."

Olivia's eyes narrowed with speculation. "Then Albert Flynn is living somewhere here in Manhattan. But where?"

"Mind if I wet my whistle, lass?" Paddy went to pour himself a whiskey. "We must find your lad. I'd like to know what's keeping your brother from moving on. If I had done this dastardly deed, I would put plenty of distance between me and my brother. A whole continent if I could."

"We might just be finding Donald's son tomorrow," Eldon said. "I met a paperboy earlier today who knows Joe, but doesn't know his whereabouts. When I asked the kid if he knew a Casey McShane, he said to bring Donald by his stand tomorrow."

"Donald, why didn't you tell me about this?" Olivia scolded.

"I haven't had time to mention it with all that's happened. But...I also wanted to meet the paperboy tomorrow and see if he's telling the truth, if Casey will be there." Donald put his hands in his pockets. "Olivia, could ya meet us at Eldon's store around nine? I want ya with me when I go to see what this Benny lad has to say."

She smiled at him with love and trust. "I'll be there."

Paddy emptied his glass. "We need the Carpathia's original passenger list. Something's nagging at me about it."

"Why do we need to see the rescue ship's manifest?" Olivia asked.

"It might give us a clue where Albert Flynn, or should I say, Sam McShane and Darlene McShane are staying."

Donald washed his hands and dried them on the white linen hand towel embroidered with a giant purple initial M surrounded with pink flowers. Even the Marsh's water closet was richly decorated, again reminding him of the wide divide between him and Olivia. After a quick survey in the mirror, he straightened his black tie and prepared to leave.

In a hurry to get back to Olivia, and with his mind still reeling about Derry being alive, he thought about all he'd learned today. As he walked down the hallway the polished hard wood floor rang solid beneath his shoes. He was heading for the elaborate staircase when Merilee Marsh stepped from a nearby door and beckoned.

"Mr. McShane, if you don't mind I'd like a word with you." And not waiting for his reply she left the door open for him to follow.

He walked into what must be her personal sitting room where a faint smell of floral perfume sweetened the air. Surprised that she wanted to talk with him here, he waited, on guard, and rightfully so.

With her ramrod stance, her hairdo pristine and held by combs, Merilee went over to a round table which held a bouquet of flowers and a crystal decanter with several small glasses. She poured two brandies. Not the usual stingy inch in the bottom of the glass, the amber liquid almost filled both glasses.

She handed him a glass, and the scowl on her face caused him to swallow his smile in a hurry.

"Sure'n I want to thank ya for all you've done for Jilleen. We'll get her back, and soon. You're very generous, Mrs. Marsh."

Ignoring him, she downed her drink, then immediately poured another. Donald knew in one gulp of his drink that things were not good. And Mrs. Marsh more than confirmed it as she turned thunderous dark eyes on him.

"Mr. McShane," she said, standing with her hand on her waist, her New England upbringing squelched, and pointing her drink at him. "My daughter and my husband like you. I don't. Since Olivia caught your Jilleen in the lifeboat, Olivia's life has never been the same, nor has ours. I've endured seeing my daughter put through the ringer over trying to find your son. Now she's in turmoil over Jilleen and blames herself for not being here. I've endured her losing the man she loved because of you. I've endured my husband taking you into our banking business—I've—"

"You keep sayin' I've—I've—I've. It sounds like it's all about you, not Olivia," Donald said, knowing full well where this conversation was going.

"If you hadn't come into Olivia's life, she would be marrying Myron. You've spoiled everything." She made another return trip to the crystal decanter. Fortified, she continued her attack. "I've allowed my daughter to take in your daughter, thinking that once found, you would take Jilleen to live in your home. I wonder why you haven't done so. But that's a moot point now, isn't it?"

Donald put his drink down and took a deep breath. "Jilleen stayed here at Olivia's request. I'm sorry if anyone in your household was put in danger today."

Her mouth snapped shut at his reply. She moved to steady herself against the back of her settee. "Mr. McShane, you're very clever with words, so listen to mine. I don't want you to see Olivia anymore. You can come up with any excuse you need, but I want you out of my daughter's life and I want it done now."

Still upset from his recent discoveries and the shame of it all, he cautioned himself to think before he spoke. He tried to be gentle with Olivia's mother, but she'd riled him. He found himself using the only weapon he had against her. "Enlighten me please, Mrs. Marsh, how much money did *you* pay Lapaglia to hurt Olivia?"

The blood rushed from her face and her hand flew to the lacey front of her dress, fussing, and picking at it. "Whatever are you talking about?" She eyed him, her bold demeanor now sagging.

"I went to Lapaglia's office at your husband's request. I have it in writing, Mrs. Marsh. A handwritten note by Lapaglia saying you and Myron Prewitt paid him to create a riot during the rally. Tell me, was the price worth almost getting Olivia killed? Was it so important to get her to stop workin' for children's rights?"

Merilee put her glass down on her dressing table, her posture becoming erect. "If you have it in writing then there is no sense in trying to deny it. Do you plan on using blackmail to get Olivia?"

Sad and disgusted that she thought so little of him, Donald said, "I'm not like that. Being devious appears to be how you approach life—you and Myron that is."

Taking on a new bravado, she pushed. "I still want you out of her life—ours. Once you find Jilleen can't you do that? Make it like it was before Olivia ever met you, let her go back to her life as it was?"

"Sure'n I don't want to be where I'm not wanted. I've never forced meself on anyone and I don't intend to start now." He started to leave, yet paused halfway to the door, compelled to say, "Don't worry, Mrs. Marsh, I won't be telling Walter and Olivia your part in paying Lapaglia."

Walter stepped inside the room. His face ashen and lined with devastation as he glanced from Merilee to Donald. "You won't have to, McShane. I overheard enough to know I'm sickened."

Donald wanted to bite his tongue off, retract the words he'd just uttered, and take back the hurt he'd caused his friend. He started to speak, but Walter held up his hand to silence him.

"How could you, Merilee? How could you?"

She stood still, caught in a sticky web of her own making. Her face blanched white to match her husband's. "Walter, I did it for Olivia. Myron wanted her away from the suffragette movement, child labor, all of it."

"Of course he did. He hires children. Think of it—he does exactly what our daughter fights against, child labor. If Olivia had been permanently maimed, I bet he would have high-tailed it back across the Brooklyn Bridge so fast you wouldn't know he'd disappeared. Myron's not the type to be saddled with an imperfect mate," he paused as if to let his words sink in and then continued, "Lapaglia forced his way into my bank, threatening me, telling me he had a secret and if it got out I'd be ruined. Well, how ironic to discover…darling wife…that you are Lapaglia's big secret." His laugh filled with irony.

"Walter," she whispered, the lamplight shadowed her bewildered face. "What are you going to do?"

"About Lapaglia, or you, Merilee? Lapaglia's easy. I've already told him I'm calling in his loan. I'll close his doors. You, my dear, are the hard one. How does a husband get over the hurt when he finds out the woman he loves more than life has undermined his very beliefs with deceit? Not to mention placing our daughter in dire danger."

Uncomfortable to be witnessing the Marsh's personal agony, Donald wanted to go. "I'll be getting Eldon and leaving."

"No, you're not, McShane. Merilee and I can finish this conversation later."

There was a soft knock on the door and Olivia walked in. "What are you doing up here?" She hurried to Donald's side. "Paddy's left, and Eldon's waiting for you…" her voice ran down like the fizz in a stale bottle of champagne. Puzzled, her brows knit into a frown. "What's wrong?"

Donald didn't know what to say. No, that wasn't true, he wanted to tell Merilee Marsh to go to hell. Instead, he said, "Olivia, I think it's best ya stay out of me problems now. With Paddy's help, I can find Jilleen and Casey."

"Don't be absurd. I feel guilty about Jilleen. I should have been here." She put her hand on his arm in a loving gesture. "You're upset. You don't know what you're saying."

"Listen to me, Olivia, I know exactly what I'm saying. I've pulled ya into the muck surrounding me. It's best I leave ya be." His gaze raked over her lovely face and he wanted to take her in his arms, wanted to take back his words to her mother, wanted to tell Walter

Marsh he'd heard wrong. Regretting to do so, Donald removed her hand and started for the door.

Olivia stepped in front of him, blocking his way. "Don't I have a say in this? After we find your children, I can only hope someday, you'll find it in your heart to include me in your happiness." She glanced around as if for support from her family. "Mother? Dad? What's going on here? Mother what have you said to Donald? You've ordered him to stay away from me—haven't you? My word, he's just found out some dreadful news, he's wounded, his daughter's missing, and you're acting this way? How dare you, Mother, how dare you do this to us," she cried in frustration. "Donald, don't do this, please…"

"Don't go, McShane," Walter said. "I think it's time Olivia hears the truth from her mother."

Donald shook his head and said, "Nay, Walter. Leave it be for now."

With a look of gratitude directed at Donald, Merilee hurried to her husband's side. She tried taking his hand but Walter shied away. Tears came to her eyes as she turned to Olivia.

"Go ahead, Mother, tell me what is running Donald out of here and has Dad so upset."

When Merilee hesitated, Walter nodded at her. Her tongue nervously darted across her lips, obviously not wanting to tell, but forced to do so, she began. "I was in on Myron's scheme to have Lapaglia scare you. And I was guaranteed it was all he'd do."

"Mother—you were in on this plan with Myron?" Olivia's mouth parted and she slowly shook her head in disbelief. "I'm numb. I knew you hated my work, but I always thought you loved me as a daughter, and would never hurt me physically or otherwise. The otherwise is just as hard to deal with as the injury to my head." Her emotions anguished across her face.

Merilee quickly sought Olivia's hands. "I never thought Lapaglia would have a brick thrown at you. He was supposed to do some heckling, maybe take away your signs, a shove or two. Never was he to touch or harm you like he did. I thought he'd verbally try to intimidate you, frighten you off, hopefully to rethink your involvement with the suffragette movement. Myron didn't want you hurt either. He told me it all had gone terribly wrong, that you were injured. Guilt kept me from your side that night. Dearest, I never, never, meant for you to be hurt. You have to believe me."

"Mother…how much did you pay, what was it—"

"The price isn't important, Olivia," Walter said. "What's important here is what are we going to do after hearing about this? How can we ever mend our family?"

Donald knew how both Olivia and her mother felt right now. Family betrayal wasn't easy to take. He'd been living with Sam's sadistic muck for as long as he could remember. The ache that sliced through his soul and shattered his well-being was named Sam. He couldn't stand the thought that his words were as lethal to Walter, Olivia and Mrs. Marsh, as what Sam and Derry had done to him. The comparison was too much for him. Caring for Walter and Olivia the way he did, he tried to help. "Olivia, I believe your mam did this because she loves you."

Both Olivia and Walter opened their mouths in sputtering protests, but Donald raised his hand to quiet them. "Lass, I know yer hurtin', but try to see yer mam's side of it all. She fears for ya. Sometimes mothers do awful things. Remember, no one knew Lapaglia would try and harm ya like he did. 'Tis certain, yer mam and Myron didn't know what kind of man Lapaglia is. I do. I worked next to him for three years, saw his corrupt side, and yet I did little to help anyone who suffered under him. Don't be so hard on yer mam."

"Well, I can and will be hard as hell." Walter patted his suit coat, feeling, and opened it to take out a cigar from the inner pocket. Not having a cutter with him, he bit the end of it off, and placed the discarded piece on Merilee's fancy table. He lit the cigar, and in a cloud of smoke, finally turned to Merilee.

She stared back at each of them, finally settling on Walter, waiting.

"Merilee," he said, pointing at her with his cigar. "Do you realize the implications about Myron and yourself in this…this…stupid plot? And for you to be involved with an unscrupulous man like Lapaglia is just plain suicidal. Now that I've been enlightened, I can tell Lapaglia where to put his blackmail scheme."

Merilee's mouth flew open in shock. She blurted, "Mr. Lapaglia's blackmailing me. He's sent me threatening notes, demanding money from me."

"My God—this goes much deeper than I realized. Do I dare ask what you've done about it? Don't tell me you've given him money," Walter said.

"No, I haven't. I kept putting him off. He said he was going to the newspapers, tell them all, that he'd ruin our good name."

"I must say, Merilee, when you decide to come off your society high-horse you do it in a grand manner don't you." He removed his spectacles from his nose and rubbed at the indention it left.

"I only wanted Olivia away from the organization, to be safe, happily married." She gave Olivia a pleading glance and then turned back to Walter. "I wanted our daughter to have what I have with you, a wonderful life, prestige, society—"

"How about love? I don't hear you mentioning love, that you love me," he said with a deep sigh. "And you certainly don't know your daughter at all, or me, for that matter. None of that social claptrap means anything to Olivia. Someday these damnable so-called social structures will tumble down like a house of cards and I'll be glad when they do. Can't you understand Olivia's stance in trying to help abused children? Even if Donald didn't exist, once Olivia found out about Myron's factory making money off the sweat of children, it would have been over between them. Now, this brings us back to you and me. What's going to happen to us?"

Her brows knit a line above her nose. "What do you mean?"

"Somehow I knew you'd say that." He puffed his cigar, stalling. And then the words slipped from his mouth, "I'm leaving you, Merilee."

"You can't do that—my word, Walter."

He replied as gently as possible. "Yes, I can and will. Tomorrow I'll have my things taken to the club."

Merilee's lips parted, dumbfounded, she could only stare.

Olivia moved to her father's side. "Dad, maybe you and mother…"

"Some things are irreparable." He walked toward the door.

Benny lugged his empty bag up the stairs. He'd sold all his papers and felt great. His new corner was going to be a good spot for him. Opening the door, he walked in to find Frankie sleeping. Jimmy and Casey were lolling on the sofa. Frankie coughed, even in his sleep he coughed. Benny was worried. They were all worried about Frankie. Benny dropped his bag, and rubbing his aching shoulder, went in search of something to eat.

"Have ya ate yet?" he asked while shuffling through cans stacked haphazardly on the counter. He slapped at a cockroach but it was too quick and scurried inside a crack in the wall.

"Nay, we haven't. Been waiting fer ya," Casey answered.

Benny, tossing a can of vegetable soup between his hands, went over to stand in front of Casey. "What's yer last name?"

Casey shrugged. "Why d'ye want to know?"

Jutting his chin out in defiance, Benny put his hand on his hip. "Is it McShane? Are ya Casey McShane? Ya never told us, ya know."

Casey shot to his feet and balled his fists. "Who told ya me last name?"

"A man did. He bought a paper and asked about our Joe. Said he was a friend of Joe's. I told him Joe might be staying at Ryerson's or at the Irishman's place. He said no, Joe's missing—"

Jimmy butted in. "What do ya mean Joe's missing? Frankie said he was here the other night."

Frankie rolled over and slowly sat up. "Jimmy, roll me a cigarette, will ya? What's going on? What this about Joe?"

Benny shrugged. "Just that he didn't make it home the other night."

"What's this Joe got to do with me last name?" Casey blurted with impatience.

Benny darted a scowl at Casey. "Hey, Joe's part of our gang…well, he used to be. I think he's in trouble. The man said the Irishman Joe stayed with is Donald McShane."

"He really said that?" Casey screeched, his blue eyes wide as saucers, his grin big and loopy. "D'ye tell him I'm here? Jimmy, did ye hear? Let's go! Let's go guys, let's go find me da." Casey started for the door, but Benny grabbed his arm.

"I didn't say I knew ya. The man's bringin' McShane to my corner tomorrow."

"What was the man's name who talked to ya? Did he say?" Jimmy asked Benny.

Benny wearily eyeballed Jimmy. "Said his name is Eldon Jonsun. Owns a drugstore near my paper corner."

Casey started jumping up and down with excitement. He giggled. He hooted. He grabbed Benny and danced him around the room. Casey's eyes brimmed with tears and excitement. Tomorrow he'd be back in his da's arms.

Chapter Twenty-Two

Sam watched the gray shadows disappear as the sun came on, breaking over the tall dilapidated buildings, warming the broken sidewalk and the trash filled street. He shifted, feeling the familiar hard metal of the pistol and holster poking under his arm. He'd bought the pearl-handled Colt automatic in a gun shop.

Desperate to find Casey, Sam knew the minute the kid was reunited with Donald, he'd tell about the murder. Sam could see the headlines now: MURDER ON THE TITANIC, LILLIAN DENBURY MURDERED BY EVIL SAM MCSHANE. No, he didn't want to be a hunted man with a reward on his head. But then, they never found *Jack the Ripper*. True, but they didn't know who the Ripper was. Casey sure in the hell had witnessed him popping those beads out of Lillian's sweet dead mouth.

No matter how much Sam threatened the lad he'd abducted, he wouldn't talk. The stubborn shite. Giving up, Sam no longer cared if the boyo lived or died, and hadn't bothered with him for days now. Sam kept going back to the area where he'd snatched the lad. He searched block by crumbling block, looking for signs of life, trying to find a place where a gang of boys might be living. And perseverance had paid off last night in the form of a lit window in the back of a foul looking building. The very building he now watched.

Going around the side of the building, he paused before a boarded up door. Several boards hung loose and used like a pendulum. Swinging the board to the left revealed an opening big enough for young skinny boys to ease through, but not him. Sam wrenched the board free, tossed it away, and then savagely kicked the next slat, splintering it. Tearing away all the boards, he stepped inside the dim interior. The opening helped shed some light inside, but not much. He started up the stairs that groaned beneath his weight.

He reached the second floor landing where he opened a door leading into a room with a rotted floor and busted windows. Birds took flight making him jump. He shut the door against the smell of a dying building. Using the sole of his boot to light a wooden match, he held the flame aloof and eased up another flight.

The floor gave up secrets as he saw a trail through the dust which ended at the end of the hall. Fire from the match reached his fingers forcing him to shake it out. He turned the doorknob and pushed open the door. Daylight barely crept into the room from the lone window, outlining the pitiful furniture. He took out his gun and crouched. The odor, like an outhouse, made him gag. He wanted to leave but forced himself to stay and let his eyes adjust to the dreariness of the room. The place was quiet and empty, disappointing him, until he noticed movement on one of the lumpy mattresses.

"Did ya forget somethin', Jimmy?" A weak voice sounded from the bed.

"I don't think so, boyo." Sam moved fast and pounced on the kid. He smelled like month old garbage and Sam didn't know if he wanted to touch him. Sam's nostrils flared at the stench as he whipped the covers off to bare a grimy union suit. The kid was sick with something bad. He had dried red crusts on the corners of his mouth.

"What's wrong with you? Are ya contagious?" Sam asked with caution.

The kid shook his head while staring down the barrel of the gun.

Sam slowly cocked it. "Tell me where Casey McShane is."

"I don't know." The kid wheezed then went into a fit of coughing, groping for a piece of cloth to cover his mouth. Red phlegm burst out.

Anticipating the kid would say no, Sam pinched his boney cheek hard between his thumb and fingers. "Where is he? Where's the rest of yer gang?"

The kid remained silent. Sam popped him upside the head with the gun barrel.

The kid cried. "Yer the fucker that's been snoopin' around. We ran you off back when."

"Right ya are. Where's Casey?"

The boy hawked and spit at him.

Drops of spittle hit Sam full in the face making him grimace. He wiped away bloody phlegm. Enraged, Sam hauled him off the mattress and busted him across the mouth. The kid's skinny body skidded across the floor.

Getting on all fours, he started crawling, his filthy blond hair stringing across his face, coughing, scrambling to get away.

Sam dragged him upright.

The kid wheezed and held up a hand to ward Sam off. "Don't—don't hit me again," he whined. "Casey's gone to meet his dad."

This news put Sam in a panic. "Where—when is he meeting him?"

"This morning, around nine or so. At Benny's corner where he sells papers."

Out of patience, Sam shook him hard practically snapping his neck. "What corner—what street?"

The kid spewed his guts, telling all. No longer useful, Sam dropped him to the floor, and thought to put the kid out of his misery. He pointed the gun at the kid's head, cocked it, and then thought the sound of the gun might bring the coppers around. Besides, what did he care if the kid lived or died? Putting his gun back in the holster, he pounded down the stairs and out the building.

Frankie crawled to the closest mattress and slowly pulled himself upon it. He had to get to Jimmy and Casey. He'd meant to give Benny's old corner not the new one, but his mind was fogged with pain. Shaking so bad he could hardly move, he picked up a pair of grimy pants from the floor and pulled them on. Too weak to worry with shoes, he tried to walk but his legs felt liquid and it took forever.

Holding onto the wall for support, he managed to make it out the door and to the landing. Unable to take another step, he grasped the banister and slid to the floor. His chest was on fire. His breathing became labored, forced, and the only thing he could do was rest his face against the wooden stair rail.

Casey lugged two tied bundles of newspapers while Benny carried his stuffed newspaper bag. The bundles were heavy, the twine cutting off the circulation in Casey's fingers.

"C'mon, Jimmy, don't go so fast," Casey hollered while struggling to keep up with Jimmy's long stride. "What don't ya grab a bundle, they're heavy."

But Jimmy just turned, and walking backwards in a lanky gait, yelled at both Casey and Benny, "Slow pokes. Get the lead out of yer asses and get up here."

"Yeah," said Benny, "get your ass back here and help us."

Casey knew by Jimmy's grin he was only teasing. But Casey didn't take teasing well. Jimmy he didn't mind, but when Benny did the teasing, he didn't like it. He didn't get along with Benny, and liked to thump him a good one. Benny had taken to picking his nose and wiping it on Casey, laughing at the explosion it always resulted in. Well, he better not be wiping any snot on him today, Casey wanted to look his best for his da.

Last night, Casey thought Benny was lying and being mean about Casey's dad. But Casey had never told his last name to any of the boys, not even Jimmy. When Benny blurted it out, Casey knew it must be true. And yet, they still planned to be cautious. Casey was going to remain hidden until the two men arrived and he could see if one of them was his da. Even though excited, he was taking no chances with Uncle Sam being one of those men.

To Casey's relief they finally made it to Benny's corner where he dropped the bundles on the cement. He rubbed at the red indentions the string had made in his fingers.

While Jimmy played lookout, Casey helped Benny set up his corner, stacking the papers just like Benny wanted them. The crowd thickened, people going about their business, the smell of unwashed bodies as strong as car fumes. Casey was right there with the best of them, his weekly bath just a memory. He scratched his head, and inspecting his dirty fingernails, made sure he didn't have head lice. Cleanliness was the one thing Grandmum Ina had insisted on. She'd become enraged when he'd gotten nits at school. She'd shoved his head under the pump and scrubbed his hair with bed-bug extermination liquid until his head flamed red, almost straightened his curls permanently.

A horse-drawn wagon filled with furniture rumbled by. The driver stopped and signaled for a paper. Casey ran it over to him, jumping high to put the paper in the man's hand. He no sooner took the nickel back to Benny when a car horn bugled and the driver motioned.

"Can't the bloody blaggard get out of his car and come get a paper?" Casey whined.

Benny laughed and handed him a paper to take over to the car. Casey helped Benny while Jimmy leisurely watched. Casey, always thinking selling papers was easy, learned just how hard it was. Not only did Benny have to sell all of his papers, he had to put up with moody people. Casey found out some were nice and some were pure mean.

Jimmy, shuffling trash around with his shoe, reached down and picked up a penny. He flipped it at Casey. "Here's yer luck for today."

Casey caught the coin mid-air. The penny was an Indian head, dated 1904. "Hey, sure'n this is lucky, 'tis the year I was born." He kissed the Indian and stashed it in his pocket. His stomach growled and since they had plenty of time before his da was supposed to arrive, he wanted breakfast.

"Jimmy, how about we go get something to eat at a food cart? Benny, what can we bring ya back?"

It didn't take Benny long to say, "A sausage on a stick." He pointed down the street filled with pedestrians. "Go that way three blocks and then turn right. You'll find a cart there with the best sausages on a stick ya can eat. Watch out for the owner, he's a mean Italiano who'll eyeball ya to death." He laughed.

The boys took off, leaving Benny to sell his papers. The rush of foot traffic began to thicken. Most men hurried up to him, bought a paper then left. The women were the nicest always having a smile for him as gloved fingers placed a nickel in his hand.

"Mornin', sir," Benny said to the tall stranger while handing him a paper.

The tall man winked down at him and flipped him a dime. Benny moved coins around on his palm and picking out a nickel started to give him change, but the man held up his hand.

"Ya keep the nickel, lad. Might say, it's fer doin' me a good deed being here with yer papers and all." The man clamped his lips around his cigar and puffed. Throwing his head back, he blew a cone of smoke in the air. He took the cigar from his mouth and offered it to Benny. "Here ya go, lad."

Benny couldn't believe what was happening. "Gee, thanks, Mister." And without hesitation, he accepted it. He puffed the cigar, trying to act important.

The man grinned and walked off in the same direction Casey and Jimmy went.

Benny watched him go, wondering what he meant by good deed. With all the customers now circled around him, he stubbed out his smoke and putting it in his pocket, quickly forgot the man and his words.

Casey and Jimmy loitered around the food cart stuffing their mouths with Benny's recommendation. One bite into the spicy meat sent warm juices squirting down Casey's chin. He wiped his mouth on his shirtsleeve. Jimmy did the same.

"Boy, Benny's right. These are good," Jimmy remarked, his brows going up a notch.

Casey, with his cheeks bulging, could only nod and keep chewing.

The owner, short and round, with greasy black hair and a thick, droopy black mustache, kept darting scowls at them. He gestured for them to go away.

Jimmy finally shrugged and said, "Hey, Mister, I'm buying a couple more of these for my friend. Ya got a problem with money or somethin'?"

"Why ya no say so? I've been thinking yer bad boys, a wantin' to steal." He stood by his cart where steam slithered off the cooking meat.

They ate two sausages apiece, and then bought two for Benny. Each carried a sausage as they started back.

Jimmy led the way in a hurried stride, his lanky body parting the crowds.

"Wait up, Jimmy," Casey yelled, trying to push through the jostling people. He felt someone's presence right on his shirttail. Black-clad arms snaked around Casey's middle lifting him up.

"Act happy to see me, lad," his uncle whispered against Casey's ear.

Casey dropped Benny's breakfast and for a fleeting moment he thought how mad Benny was going to be about his food.

"Help me, Jimmy!" he screamed.

When Casey opened his mouth to yell again, Sam stopped him with a stuffed handkerchief. Casey resembled a bagged bird under his uncle's arm. He kicked his legs in the air. He pummeled his uncle's hard chest with his fists. But he could have saved his energy. Uncle Sam had a death grip on him and ducked into a nearby alley. Casey thought for sure he was a goner.

Jimmy came out of nowhere and tried to free Casey by grabbing his leg and pulling.

"Get away," Sam snarled. He put his hand across Jimmy's face and shoved him a good one.

Jimmy landed on his behind.

He scrambled to his feet and blurted, "I know who ya are. Yer Casey's Uncle Sam. I'm not lettin' ya hurt him!" Jimmy launched himself onto Sam's back.

"Ya, bloody blaggard," Sam gritted.

Casey felt like he was flipping somersaults as his uncle turned and twisted, trying to dislodge Jimmy. Casey panicked when his uncle started running toward the side of the building. Like a horse trying to unseat its rider, Sam slammed his body hard against the bricks, dislodging Jimmy who hit the ground with a loud grunt.

Casey tumbled onto the broken cobblestones. He got to his knees and had a split second to see his uncle's fist fly toward his face.

Sam opened his suit coat to reveal a holstered gun to the redhead. He pointed. "If yer as smart as I think ya are, yer going to stay right there and make sure I don't see ya again today. Get me meanin' ya piece of shite?" Satisfied to see the kid's startled nod, Sam picked up

Casey's limp body. Throwing him over his shoulder, he went back out on the main sidewalk and boldly started down the street.

When an occasional passerby asked Sam what was going on. Sam would smack Casey's behind, laugh jovially, and say, "I've finally caught up with me runaway son, and by the Saints, he isn't going to run again, no-siree."

Jimmy, wise enough to keep distance between himself and Casey's uncle, kept pace with them across the street. The uncle moved rapidly. Jimmy tried staying out of sight but couldn't. Again, the uncle's coat flapped open and his gun shown. Jimmy knew the man wouldn't hesitate to use it.

Finally, he spotted Benny.

"Hey, where's my sausage?" Benny pouted, his hands on his hips.

"Benny—look!" Jimmy grabbed him and pointed across the street. "That's Casey's Uncle Sam. The one he's scared of. The one we ran off with the bricks."

"Damn, he just gave me a cigar." Always fearless, Benny started to go after Casey.

Jimmy grabbed Benny's arms and stopped him. "Stay here. If that druggist shows up with Casey's father, tell him what's happened. I don't know anything more. I've gotta go before I lose them."

Sam entered the dark, decaying building and went straight to the room where he kept the lad he'd kidnapped. He plopped Casey down hard on the debris-strewn floor, not caring if he hurt him or not. He tied him to an old pipe attached to the side of the wall. At last, he had freedom before him. Like always, things just had a way of falling into place for him.

He glanced over at the lad. No need to keep him alive now that he had Casey. It was always Casey. Jilleen hopefully would forget, and if she didn't, well who would take the little lass seriously. But these two presented a problem. He had to get rid of the both of them, together, after it was dark enough outside to do so.

Joe started grunting and Sam was quick to his side. He pulled the gag loose and said, "What do ya want, boyo?"

"I'm hungry," he cried, still blindfolded, "and I'm ready to help ya lure that kid away from the gang. Please mister, I'm so thirsty."

Sam looked at the lad. Sweat and dirt stuck his black hair to his head, and the only clean spots on his face were where his tears had dripped. He replaced the gag back into his mouth.

"Ah…no, lad, I no longer need yer help."

He pulled up a broken chair bottom and sat. Sam fixed a hard stare at Casey who glared back. Taking pleasure in having Casey right where he wanted him, he lied with malice. "I know where yer precious Da is. He thinks you, yer sister, and mam are dead. Bet ya don't know yer mam and I went to that fancy place yer sister was livin' at. We took Jilleen right from under their noses." His laugh was sinister. "If ya don't behave yourself here, I might just have to hurt yer little sis, aye?"

Casey nodded and tears crept down his cheeks to soak into the rag across his mouth.

Chapter Twenty-Three

Donald, sitting in the backroom of the drugstore, waited impatiently for Olivia. He nervously rubbed his hand across the back of his neck, trying to work out kinks. Casey was constantly on his mind and he prayed that soon they'd be together. He marveled at his son's resourcefulness, at how Casey managed to survive at the mere age of eight, especially in a large city with the odds totally against him.

He figured that Sam had more than likely kept Casey from leaving the *Carpathia* with all the other passengers. He also wished to God that Casey had gone straight to the police and told everything he knew. If so, his son could be safely tucked in his arms by now. Or would he? If Sam had killed Lillian Denbury, then he was capable of killing anyone. Knowing his brother's deceptions better than anyone, the skin prickled on the back of Donald's neck.

"Eldon, I hope this morning will not be another dead lead, or a game a paperboy is playing."

"That's crossed my mind, but I think this is different. The kid appeared to be honest. He didn't ask anything of me, just for me to bring you." Eldon rubbed his chin.

Donald rapidly tapped a pencil against the desk. "I couldn't sleep worryin' about Jilleen and Casey. And now, here I am waitin' fer Olivia to get here, and feelin' like I'm going to break apart any second."

"Give it time, Donald, it's not even nine yet."

"Aye, but Olivia's always punctual."

Eldon shook his head and reached out to stop the pencil's rapid thumping. "She'll be here soon enough."

The front bell jangled and they heard the soft murmurings of voices, Archie's being one of them. And then the loud sound of shoes hitting against squeaky floorboards as Archie led Olivia and her father into the backroom.

As both Donald and Eldon stood to welcome them, Donald couldn't help but notice Olivia acted flustered, while Walter was his usual unflappable self.

Walter rubbed his big beefy hands together in anticipation. "I'm going with you. The minute Olivia told me about the paperboy, I wanted to help."

Donald couldn't turn away the man who'd come to mean so much to him. "Wouldn't have it any other way, Walter." He glanced up at the wall clock, anxious to leave. "Guess we should be going, aye—"

"Donald," Olivia butted in. "Paddy has gone to the Cunard shipping line over on Broadway. He thinks he'll find where your brother and…er—"

"Wife, go ahead and say it, *my wife*." To even voice the words galled him, but he had no choice. Derry acting as Sam's wife tore him apart. Love? What had happened to her love for him, their children?

He looked at his friends before him, at their faces that were filled with pity. Donald clenched his jaw, and tried to stop his emotions that were worn on his sleeve more often than not.

Olivia spoke in a soft voice, "Paddy said he would call me here if he manages to locate where your brother is living. He said to go ahead and talk to the paperboy." She picked at a piece of lint on her plaid green skirt. "Mr. Johnston, I told Paddy he could call here and leave a message. Is that all right?"

"Absolutely. This is the most logical place," Archie said.

Donald captured her hand within his and held it tight. She glanced at him from underneath the brim of her straw boater and grinned.

"Shouldn't we be going?" Walter interjected. "We can take my automobile."

They stepped outside where Hugh politely stood next to the car's open door and waited for them to get in. He put on his hat, took his seat behind the wheel, and waited for instructions.

"Where's this paperboy at?" Walter asked Eldon who was sitting beside him.

"Several miles or so down the street." Eldon leaned forward to give Hugh directions.

The car was warm, the air thick, and Donald rolled down a window. When that didn't help, he took off his jacket and rolled up his shirtsleeves.

They passed a police station and traveled for several more blocks. Hugh eased the Studebaker into the diagonal slot and quickly jumped out to open the doors.

As they drew near the corner, Donald swept the area filled with people going about their purpose. He could hardly spot the small boy holding up a paper, calling out to customers. Donald stretched his neck, trying to see past the scurrying people, but he didn't see any sign of Casey. He prepared himself to be the butt of a cruel joke.

They approached the grubby youngster who held up a paper almost as tall as he was.

Eldon hurried up to him and knelt down on one knee. "Remember me from yesterday? I've brought Casey McShane's father. Benny, can you help us? Do you know his son?"

Donald eyeballed the lad who appeared wise beyond his years, yet wary. Like Eldon, Donald also went to one knee. "Hello, Benny. I'm Donald McShane. I understand ya know Joe Gillespie."

Benny stepped backwards and blurted out, "Jesus, mister, ya look like the man who was here earlier."

"What do ya mean?"

"Ya look just like the man who gave me a cigar. The man who ran by with Casey."

"What are ya talkin' about? Is Casey here?" he ground out, trying to remain calm.

"He was."

Not wanting to scare the lad, Donald gently clasped the kid's arms. "Tell me what happened."

Benny's eyes welled up and he wiped his runny nose on his shirtsleeve. "Casey's been livin' with us since April. We helped him the night he came off the ship. Someone was chasing him, so we threw bricks at the man. He ran off. When this guy," he said pointing at Eldon, "came by here yesterday and asked about Casey, I went home and told Casey his dad was going to be here today."

"Hey kid. How about a paper?" A customer rudely pushed Donald aside, plopped a nickel in Benny's hand, and took a paper.

"Then Casey's not here?" Donald asked.

Benny shook his head. "He was. But him and Jimmy went to get us a sausage. Next thing I know, Jimmy's runnin' by and pointin' to a man across the street carryin' Casey. Jimmy says it's Casey's Uncle Sam and that he's gonna hurt him."

"Are you sayin' my brother has my boy?" Donald swallowed.

"I g…guess so…" Benny stammered.

Olivia drew in a sharp breath.

Both Eldon and Walter cursed.

Donald slowly got to his feet. He went to lean against the side of the building. Crossing his arms, he bent over. He'd lost his family not once, but twice. He was sure a weaker man would have gone mad by now. In agony, he inwardly railed at God, asking how he could have let someone as evil as Sam be born. He continued to rail, asking just how much God was going to give him to bear. Miserable, Donald knew without a doubt, that the Lord wasn't through with him yet.

Eldon stayed by Benny who could only stare up at the adults.

Walter and Olivia approached Donald. Olivia immediately went to his side and taking his arm forced him to face her.

"Olivia," he started to say. But she touched his lips, stopping him.

"We'll find him, Donald."

"Appears your brother is a busy man," Walter said.

Eldon came over and rested his hand on Donald's shoulder. "I'm sorry. Instead of bringing you happiness, I've brought you more misery."

"Ah…no, Eldon. Ya had no way of knowing what would happen. None of us did, especially when it comes to my brother."

"Donald," Olivia said, tapping her finger against her lips, thinking. "I believe we have our answer about Casey. I'm certain it was something that happened on the Titanic. Something so vile and evil Casey must be silenced."

"Lillian Denbury, aye?"

"Yes," she nodded. "I think Sam strangled her and Casey witnessed it. What else would drive your brother so hard? What would keep him here when he could have been long gone? He has to silence Casey. He could never live in peace knowing he was wanted for murder."

"Then we best find my son before Sam harms him." Donald's jaw tightened, his blood ran cold with the sadistic implications. He tried to think where to begin.

"Benny," Walter said, "You're coming with us. Do you have any idea where your friend Jimmy, or the man who has Casey, went?"

Benny could only shake his head. "Maybe close to the wharf, the East River where some of the buildings are abandoned. What about my papers?"

"I'll buy them all," Walter said with urgency.

After throwing the papers in the luggage holder, they piled into the car.

Jimmy scurried around the outside of the old building that looked like it was about ready to buckle. He tried to find a window, anything to see inside, but the only windows were high up, and he had no way to climb up to them.

He waited for what felt like an eternity for Casey's uncle to come back out, but he never did. Thinking about the gun, and knowing he needed help, Jimmy took off. The only place he thought to go to was home and Frankie.

Jimmy ran like the devil was nipping at his heels. He made it to where he lived in record time. His lungs burned, his chest heaved as he paused in front of their doorway. Splintered wood lay about and the door gapped open. Without a doubt, he knew who did it. He swallowed and charged up the rickety stairs.

Reaching the third floor, he found Frankie looking like a shadowy ghost, sitting on the landing and leaning against the banister.

"Frankie—Frankie, are ya all right?" Jimmy moved with haste to his side.

Frankie's thin chest rose and fell beneath his union suit. Purple bruises on his cheek and blood around his mouth contrasted against his white pallor. His eyelids fluttered open.

"...Jimmy...help..." his voice was as weak as his breathing.

"Shh...Frankie, don't try to talk. Let me get ya back to bed."

Jimmy slid his arm around Frankie's back, and helped him to his feet. With little effort, he picked his friend up and hurried to place him on the soiled mattress.

Sobbing with fear and frustration, he gently arranged a wool blanket over Frankie.

"Was it Casey's uncle?" Jimmy asked, staring at Frankie's battered face.

Frankie nodded.

Jimmy, overwhelmed and defeated, sat next to Frankie and taking his hand, told his story.

"He snatched Casey off the street, right next to me. Took him to the old abandoned Marshall Wells buildin'. I waited a long time for the guy to come back out, but he never did. Casey said if his uncle ever found him, he'd be a goner for what he saw his uncle do." Frustrated, he wiped tears, not wanting Frankie to see him cry.

"What'd…see?"

"His uncle murder a woman on the Titanic."

Frankie, gasping for air, finally said, "…should have told me…"

"I promised Casey not to."

"Don't care…we're like brothers. The watch…give Casey—" A lung-busting cough seized him and spatters of blood dotted the mattress.

Jimmy felt Frankie's forehead. It was clammy. "Gosh—Frankie, I'll go get help for you. Ya need a doctor."

Frankie just stared back. Resignation covered his face as he tightened his grip on Jimmy's hand. "…don't leave…" He pulled in a ragged breath and said, "…not Potters Field…my mother…lost forever…"

Jimmy knew what Frankie meant. His mother was buried there and with no grave marker and no record kept, her grave was gone.

They didn't talk anymore. Jimmy sat there holding his friend's hand, listening to his labored breathing and watching his chest barely lifting the musty blanket. He thought about their friendship. Boys came and went from the gang, but he and Frankie stayed true to the other. Neither one of them had a break in life, but together they had some good times.

Tears coursed down Jimmy's cheeks, his neck became slick and wet. "Remember when we picked the same pocket?"

Frankie let out a long rattling sigh. His hand went limp within Jimmy's.

"Ah…no…Frankie. Don't die, don't leave me…" Jimmy whimpered. Like a little boy, he put his head on Frankie's warm silent chest and sobbed. He was frightened. Without Frankie the gang was finished. He wondered what was going to happen to them.

Frankie was right, they were like brothers. Jimmy continued to hold Frankie's hand. Shadows crept across the dirty floorboards. He knew he was the only person who could help Casey, yet he remained next to Frankie.

Hours passed.

He thought about Benny and wondered if Casey's father ever showed up. Nothing mattered anymore. He was tired of being beat down, tired of simply existing in a world with only a dark bleak future.

At last he straightened and covered Frankie's face. He reluctantly stood. Something glinted on the floor and he reached down to pick up the watch that belonged to Casey. This watch meant the world to Casey. Without a doubt, Jimmy knew he must help the kid.

A rat scurried across the floor and crawled upon Frankie's body. Jimmy became incensed. He grabbed up a butcher knife and began stabbing at the disgusting creature. He missed. He crawled after it, stabbing, missing, stabbing, missing. The long-tailed rodent disappeared in a hole in the wall.

Frustrated, he went into a fury at the injustice of Frankie's death. He sent bowls and canned food smashing to the floor. He tipped the kitchen cabinet over in a resounding crash. Finally with his anger spent, he stood in the middle of the room with his shoulders heaving, crying. The rat came back out of its hole and scurried over to Frankie. No way was he going to leave Frankie for the rats to eat. He couldn't.

Removing the canister of kerosene from the burner, he poured it over Frankie and around the floor. He rifled around for the spilled box of matches. Picking the wooden matches up, he struck one of them against the side of the box. It flared. He threw the flame on top of Frankie.

He stood there as long as the heat and the smell of burning flesh allowed. Satisfied to see the hot flames lick towards the ceiling, becoming an inferno, he grabbed up the remaining oil lamps, and left the door open behind him. He took the glass chimneys off the lamps and tossed them to shatter against the floor. He opened the bases and poured lamp oil while going down the stairs, stopping long enough to throw lit matches in his wake. The old dry wood took fast, while flames leaped up the staircase and swirled against the ceiling, he stepped outside. He crossed the street and watched as heat blew the windows out and gray smoke curled from them. When the fire leaped to the next building igniting it, Jimmy left.

Donald, along with Olivia, Eldon, and Walter, fanned out in the fractured and decaying part of the Lower East Side. At Benny's guidance, they'd spent frustrating hours searching through garbage-strewn buildings with doors falling off the hinges, peeling paint, and dangerous staircases.

Walter, with Benny tagging behind, approached. Walter's suit was covered in a film of dust and he was now as dirty as Benny.

"Donald," Olivia said. "I think we should go find a phone and call Archie to see if Paddy's called. We can come back."

Donald hesitated. "I'd like to stay here with Benny and keep on searching."

"Good idea," Eldon said. "Olivia, why don't you and your father go call my dad. I'll remain here."

"Hey, look at that?" Benny said, pointing upward.

They all turned to where he pointed. Over the tops of buildings, and roiling like a terrible storm, the sky was filling with dark gray smoke.

"That's close to where I live." Benny started in the direction of the smoke.

Donald grabbed the skinny kid by the arms, stopping him.

Benny struggled against Donald's strong hold. "Let me go—I've got to see where the fire's at!"

"We'll all go, Benny. Get in the car," Walter ordered.

Everyone jumped in. Hugh started driving them toward the black billowing smoke. They were forced to pull over to let a bell-clanging fire engine pass. The engine's driver sat out front turning the large round steering wheel and motioning people out of his way.

"That's my buildin'," Benny screamed. "Frankie's in there," he sobbed.

The fire grew. Two buildings were completely engulfed in flames. Firemen fought to put water on them. Another fire truck joined the first. The roofs caved in. Sparks flew high.

People started massing on the broken sidewalks, pointing, and talking. Some saying good riddance to the rat infested buildings. Eyesores they called them.

"Was Frankie your brother?" Olivia asked the distraught boy.

Crying, Benny shook his head, unable to tear his gaze from the horrible scene. "He was like my brother. Frankie led our gang."

"Benny, let's go tell the fire chief about your friend," Donald said as gently as he could. He felt Benny's anguish as though it was his.

Together, they went to seek out the man in charge. His fire hat and yellow fire coat were covered in black cinders and dripping water. The word *Chief* was barely visible on the front of his hat.

Donald hurried up to the man. "This little guy here says there was a boy livin' in the building."

The man with soot on his face sadly shook his head. "These are abandoned buildings, scheduled for demolition. If anyone was living in them, they were doing so illegally. And if anyone is in there, they are dead. No one could survive that inferno." His sharp eyes stared down at Benny.

"I made a mistake," Benny said, frowning up at the man.

Donald didn't believe the lad, but wanted to get him away from the fire and his friend who apparently died there. He took him aside.

"Why did you lie just now?"

"I didn't want to go to jail for livin' illegal." Benny stared at the fire.

"Ah...lad, maybe your friend isn't in there. I'll bet he's somewhere else." Donald knew the kid didn't believe him, that indeed his friend was dead. And Donald wondered what else could happen today to take him further away from finding Casey.

They joined the others waiting in Walter's Studebaker.

Olivia leaned forward to tap the chauffeur on the shoulder. "Hugh, we need to find a store with a phone so Eldon can call his father. Maybe Paddy's left information about where Albert Flynn is staying."

The sky turned a burnished red as smoke still churned high.

Cinders fell about them as Hugh drove away.

Benny looked out the rear window and couldn't understand what had happened. Where was Jimmy? And then a thought made him happy. Maybe Jimmy got Frankie out of the building after all.

Paddy Riley stood across the street watching a certain tenement building for quite sometime and didn't see anything out of the ordinary. It seemed to Paddy that everything surrounding the tenement was dark and gloomy. On the ground next to him was a satchel filled with cooking gadgets he planned to use as a deception.

The day was almost gone and with the tall buildings blocking the sun, dusk came early in the City. Paddy could smell the faint, acrid smell of smoke that still lingered around the East Village where a large fire had burned earlier in the Lower East Side.

He'd spent hours at the Cunard business office trying to obtain information they weren't keen on giving him. Even flashing his newspaper credentials didn't help. He was forced to go through layers of bureaucracy before finding someone willing to help him.

And that was obtained only after he made threats to expose their lack of cooperation. Looking up the *Carpathia's* passenger list, and the *Titanic's* survivors list, he'd managed to find whom the Flynn's shared a stateroom with. A couple named Ambrose and Bertha Williams. Further investigation had him getting their address.

He'd left a message with Archie Johnston, telling him to give Donald and Olivia the address and for them to hurry over there.

He could smell exclusive, eye-catching headlines blaring across the *Times*, paperboys yelling his name. *'Read all about it—reporter Paddy Riley cracks murder case'*. He was a man who took dares, and putting his investigating reporting into play, he decided to go on without Donald and Olivia. Certainly, they'd be here soon enough. Squaring his shoulders he approached the tall brick building and climbed the stairs.

He searched the tenants' names and found good old *A. Flynn* was in 102. Excited, he opened the door and stepped into the hallway next to a staircase. 102 was the first door on the left. He knocked and waited.

The door was slowly cracked open by a woman he recognized as Derry McShane. Elated that he'd hit his mark, he started with a wide grin and a hello. The hall light fell across her face. Her hair straggled about her shoulders, and her blue eyes appeared unfocused. The pretty woman in Donald's picture was buried in the ravages of deceit, and something else he couldn't put his finger on.

"Aye?" she said in a thick suspicious voice, her fingers curling around the door, holding it tight.

"Ah…Lass, from the old country, are ya?" He took off his brown bowler and nodded at her. "Now isn't that grand? I'm Paddy Riley, and right glad to be makin' yer acquaintance." When she didn't respond, he kept up his lively chatter. "I'm selling kitchen gadgets. Wonderful things invented that no woman cookin' should be without." He held up his satchel and jiggled it, making the contents loudly clang together. “Being a fellow Irishman, perhaps I could show ya a few things?”

“Nay,” she said and started to shut the door.

Paddy grabbed the door with his hand. “Are ya sure now?”

“We’re, leavin’. Please…” She stepped aside so he could see several suitcases were sitting in the middle of the dimly lit room.

To Paddy’s dismay, she also put into view, Jilleen, who was sitting on the sofa looking forlorn.

Spotting him, she instantly perked up and let out a squeal. “Paddy! Mammy, it’s Paddy from the newspaper. He took the picture of me. He’s ’Livia’s friend.” Her eyes shone as she ran toward him.

Disbelief masked Derry’s face. She started to shut the door, but Paddy blocked it with his foot. “Please, Mrs. Flynn or McShane, whatever ye call yerself. Jilleen’s in danger. She must be taken away from Sam McShane who wants to harm her.”

At those words, Jilleen’s arms clasped her mother’s hips, holding tight. “Mammy, take me back to ’Livia’s. Please, Mammy. Ye could stay there too.”

Derry’s hands went to her temples as if fighting with an inner devil. She rasped out, “I don’t like this man—Irish or not. He’s a pretender. Evil.”

Paddy could tell the woman was not in her right mind. He didn’t know how effective his words would be with someone like her. “I see,” he said. “It’s all right for you to pull off the biggest pretense of all, Mrs. Flynn, Mrs. Lillian Flynn. What would ye say if I told ya the real Lillian was murdered on the Titanic? And Albert Flynn no doubt murdered her, or should I say Sam McShane. Yer son Casey may have witnessed it. I just found out Sam McShane has grabbed yer son before Donald could get to him today. My—God, lass, think about it.”

Jilleen cried out, “Mam, Casey tolded me Uncle Sam killed that woman on the big ship. He saw him do it. Please don’t let Uncle Sam hurt me.” Her little face furrowed with fear.

Paddy knew Derry was fighting to disbelieve what he and Jilleen were saying. She looked so distraught and frightened he felt sorry for her. He figured she'd been seduced and duped by Sam McShane for quite sometime. But how much did she know?

"Do you know your son is still alive?" he asked.

"Aye, Jilleen told me." Her eyes were brimming with tears as she rubbed her hands together. "I can't believe Sam would kill anyone."

He scoffed at her comment. "Where is Sam now? Let me take you and your daughter away to safety. Mrs. McShane, he will hurt her. Jilleen knows about the murder."

Her indecision cost him dearly as she stood confused. And then as though a veil lifted from her mind and clarity pushed through, she urged, "Please help us. Oh…" Her gaze darted beyond him and widened with fear.

There was a quick blur of movement behind him. Instinct had Paddy trying to get out of the way. A hand clamped over his mouth and he was paralyzed by the sharp pain of a knife being pushed up under his ribcage, piercing his vitals.

He choked on the blood filling his mouth.

The satchel fell from his hand in a loud clatter as he clawed at the fingers locking his mouth shut.

The knife was withdrawn and plunged again. As he drowned in his own blood, Paddy briefly saw the look of horror on both Derry's and Jilleen's faces. The pain lacing through him was so incredible he welcomed the darkness.

Chapter Twenty-Four

Sam stood over Paddy Riley's body as blood spread in a wide stain.

"Mother Mary—Mother Mary," Derry blurted, crippling fear masking her face. "Tell me ya wouldn't hurt me babies." She moaned and began backing away from him.

He couldn't believe she actually believed that snooping piece of shite over him. "Shuddup! He's not dead, Darlene. Quit yer screamin'. Take Jilleen inside and I'll help him." She didn't move fast enough for him so he put his hands on both sides of her face and lifted her, propelling her back inside.

"Don't hurt, Mammy," Jilleen screamed.

Breathing heavily, he shook Darlene. "Stay here. Can ya obey this simple order, or is yer feckin' mind so bloody adrift ya can't understand a damn thing?" He pushed her down on the sofa. Roughly grabbing up Jilleen, he deposited her beside Darlene.

Towering over them both, he pointed. "Don't ya dare move yer ass off there, either of ya." He whirled around and slammed the door.

Putting his hands under the dead man's armpits, Sam drug him across the hall, leaving a trail of bright blood in his wake. Opening the door to the Williams' apartment, he pulled Paddy inside and let his body thud against the floor.

Darlene would have left with the reporter to save Jilleen. Well, he wasn't so great at being the snoop, now was he? The feckin' bastard deserved to die, spouting his mouth off, telling Darlene he'd killed Lillian—that he meant to hurt Jilleen. After all this time, her bloody children still came first. Donald was probably still first too. Sam's mouth curled in distrust. How could she think he was a monster after all he'd done for her? Darlene's betrayal just now sealed his mind with hate.

Anger fused his mind. The white haze started, no longer controllable, as he stormed out the front door.

Getting rid of Casey was now a vendetta.

Derry still quaking from the wild look in Sam's eyes peeked out the front window and watched him. Her mind clouded with disbelief. Where was he going? To Casey? Frightened sick to do so, she had to follow.

"Jilleen, go upstairs to Mr. Meeks. Door 202. He'll help you. I've got to follow Sam."

"Nay, Mammy, I'm scarit, don't leave me." She cried, her hands grasping Derry's.

"Jilleen, I must help yer brother." Derry took Jilleen's hand, led her out, and placed her on the stairs. Trying not to sob, she caressed Jilleen's cheek, fighting the voices, fighting panic. "I love ya, me wee, Jilleen. Be brave for me."

Before Jilleen could protest further Derry turned and followed Sam's bloody boot prints out the front door. She lifted her straight brown skirt to her knees and ran, her heels hit hard against the cobblestones as she tried to keep him in view. With the voices trailing along like a whispering snake, she could barely make Sam out, moving fast, already blocks ahead on the darkening street. *Kill yourself…kill yourself…*

"Please hurry, Hugh. Can't you make this thing go any faster?" Olivia prodded from the backseat. "I could get out and run faster."

Leaning forward, Donald tried to peer past Olivia on one side and Walter on the other. Here the neighborhood was thick with tall old buildings. East Village was a step above the Lower East Side, but not by much.

Donald felt the same as Olivia, antsy, that he could get out and run faster than the car. Daylight was going fast. Paddy Riley had called and said it was urgent that Donald meet him at this address. Donald prayed that Sam had brought Casey here to the tenement.

Benny, sitting in the seat next to Hugh, pointed down the side street. "I see someone down there running. Ah, just a lady," he said.

Donald looked where Benny was pointing. Even at a distant, he recognized that figure and hair. "Stop the car! That's Derry," he exclaimed.

Hugh slammed on the brakes.

Donald turned to Olivia. "Go on to the apartment. I don't see Jilleen with Derry. See if she's there. After that, come to the wharf area."

"But, Donald, how will I find you?"

"You'll find me." He quickly vacated the car.

"How far to the Flynn's apartment?" Olivia asked, still staring in the direction Donald had taken.

"There it is." Walter pointed. "That's the address Mr. Riley gave you. Hugh—there on the corner."

Hugh pulled the car to a stop right in front of the tall brick building. Several men stood on the front steps. They stopped talking and stared as Walter and the rest of them poured out of the car.

"Benny, stay here with Hugh," Walter ordered.

"Ah…jeez."

Olivia paused on the steps. "We're looking for an Albert Flynn. Is he here?"

"I'm Tom Meeks in charge here. Albert Flynn isn't here."

Walter started past him, but Tom Meeks put out a hand and stopped him. "Maybe you shouldn't go in there. A man's been murdered. We've called the authorities."

Olivia feared for Donald's children. "Is there a little girl and boy in there with Mrs. Flynn?"

"Mrs. Flynn left. Her daughter Jilleen's upstairs in my room. There's no boy here."

"Do you know any abandoned buildings close to the wharf?"

Tom Meeks thought for a moment. "The only one I can think of would be the old Marshall Wells warehouse down by the waterfront."

"I know where that is," Olivia said. Grateful for Meeks's answer, she pushed past him and stepped inside the dimly lit hallway. Walter and Eldon followed.

The blood on the floor made them pause.

Both Olivia and Walter could only stare. Eldon covered his mouth and bolted back outside.

Olivia, frightened for Jilleen, shouted, "Jilleen—Jilleen, I'm here."

She no sooner started up the stairs when a terrified Jilleen came pounding down the stairs toward her.

"'Livia," she cried, and launched herself into Olivia's arms. Like in the lifeboat, Olivia caught the little girl and held her quivering body tight. She cupped Jilleen's head and tried to sooth her.

Jilleen's arms latched around her neck, and she sobbed. "'Livia, Mammy had me. She's alive—she didn't drownded on the big ship. Mr. Riley came by to talk to her. Uncle Sam hurt him bad—he was bleedin'."

Walter followed the blood smear and disappeared inside the room across the hall.

Olivia continued to hold Jilleen. "Do you know where your mother went? And your Uncle Sam, where is he?"

Her head shook against Olivia's bosom. "Uncle Sam was so mad, he almost hurted Mam too. He told us to stay here. Mammy made me get Mr. Meeks. She followed Uncle Sam."

"Did ya see which way they went, Jilleen?"

"That way. She ran down the street." Jilleen pointed in the direction they'd just come.

Walter came out of the room Paddy's body was in. Visibly shaken, he shook his head no at Olivia, signaling Paddy was dead.

"Jilleen, is this where your mother lives?" Olivia pointed at the door on the left. When Jilleen nodded, she carried her inside and put her on the sofa.

Walter sat beside Jilleen. He patted Jilleen, trying to be of comfort. "You've been a good girl, Jilleen. Don't worry, everything's going to be fine."

Olivia paused in front of her father. "Dad, I must find Donald. Would you mind taking care of Jilleen?"

Walter started to protest then apparently thought the better of it. "Daughter, you're not going alone. Ask Mr. Johnston to go with you. Hurry. I'll handle the situation here." He smiled at Jilleen. "And you, little miss, would you mind keeping me company until Olivia and your father return?"

Jilleen nodded and moved into Walter's outstretched arms.

"Olivia, leave Benny outside, or do you need him to show you where the building is?"

Olivia shook her head and started for the door.

Dusk was settling into a darkening sky as Sam cautiously moved toward the abandoned building. Upon hearing voices from within, he pulled his gun and approached with caution. Creeping inside where the lads were kept, he was startled to see the redheaded kid he fought with earlier had untied Casey.

Both boys were working to untie Joe. A lamp hanging on the wall cast their hurried movements in shadows.

"Casey's uncle was at our place. Joe, Frankie died, and I set fire to the building. Didn't want the rats to get him. We need to get ya out of here and quick," the redhead said, and cussed at the tight knots.

"Yer not goin' anywhere," Sam snarled.

Casey gasped and stopped untying Joe. Both boys scrambled to their feet.

Joe tried to stand but couldn't. "Oh…no…it's him." He started to cry.

"Put the rag back in Joe's mouth." Sam eyed the tall gawky redhead wearing his bowler. "And stuff that one back in Casey's."

"Uncle Sam—don't. Mam wouldn't want ya to do this. I won't tell what ya did on the ship." Casey fought, trying to keep the gag out of his mouth. "No, Jimmy—don't. He's gonna kill us all."

Click. The gun cocked again.

"Hold still, Casey, I ain't got no choice," Jimmy whispered and replaced the restraint.

Sam watched with satisfaction as the kid did as told. He pondered what to do with the older boy, and decided to tie him up for the moment. Later he'd come back and deal with the scum.

He approached the smart-ass redhead and forced him to his knees. Looking at the lad's defiant face, he grabbed the hat from the kid's head and punched his fist through it. He put it back on the kid's head shoving the brim down around his neck.

"How d'ya like that fit now, boyo?" He leveled the gun at him. "Yer lucky I don't stick this barrel up the eye of yer arse and blow ya a bigger hole."

The redhead glared at him. "Ya killed Frankie."

"Frankie? Frankie who? Ah…ya mean the kid coughin' his guts up? He was already a goner. Ever hear of consumption?" Sam ripped the kid's shirt off and tore it into strips. He balled up part of the sleeve and started to stuff it into the kid's mouth.

"Wait, mister," the kid said.

"What?" Sam was in no mood to linger.

"Casey," he said, "This is from Frankie, your dad's watch." The kid nodded toward his pants pocket.

Curious, Sam reached into the kid's pocket and pulled out some coins and a pocket watch. He pocketed the money and turned the watch around, squinting to read the engraving in the dim light. *To my son, Donald, 1902.* "Well don't that feck all. The watch Da gave to hoity-toity Donald when he was sixteen." How proud Da had always been of Donald, while he, Sam was a carbuncle on the butt of life.

The only thing Sam ever got from his da was disowned after being caught stealing from St. Doulagh's and jailed. Sam reasoned he was a poor person, and the money box was for the *poor.* He liked stealing, especially what belonged to Donald. At least he had the last trick with Darlene, having her first and last, now didn't he? Didn't he? Rage burned, he wanted to smash the watch. Instead, he ordered Jimmy on his stomach, and putting the gun down, he tied and gagged him.

Turning his attention to Casey, Sam wrapped the watch chain around his neck. "Wear that to yer grave," he whispered.

Casey kept shaking his head, mumbling through the gag, his legs working, trying to scoot backwards.

Growling, Sam grabbed him up, and throwing him over his shoulder, pointed to each of them. "I'll be back to take care of you two."

Sam no sooner left when Jimmy rolled toward Joe. He stopped, and with his mouth close to Joe's tied hands, he mumbled through the material, urging Joe to take it out.

Joe fumbled with the rag, finally able to pull it from Jimmy's mouth. Jimmy did the same for Joe.

"Hurry, Joe, he's going to kill Casey." Jimmy turned his back to Joe and slid closer. He laid there enduring Joe's feeble attempts.

"I'm doin' the best I can. These knots are tight," Joe said with frustration.

After Jimmy's hands were freed, he untied Joe and helped his weakened friend to his feet.

A soft rain fell on Sam making his way toward the docks. He whistled, *'No Irish Need Apply.'* The closer he got to the water the more Casey struggled. He jovially slapped Casey on the rump. "How ya doin'?"

He approached the wooden pier that ran behind the fish market and stopped. A lone light, with rain dripping off its metal cover, burned from the side of the building. A line of shadowy fishing vessels with tall masts and spider web rigging bobbed in the dark waters. The whole place reeked of rotting fish.

A pulley used to haul barrels of fish inside the market was loose and slapping against the side of the building. Sam started at the sound, and then chuckled when he realized what it was. He walked around making sure he was alone. Satisfied, he went close to the dark water and looked down to see the white underbellies of dead fish bobbing next to the pier.

"Appears yer going to have a few dead fish to keep ya company," he said, and started to drop Casey in the water.

Darlene's voice came out of nowhere. "Please, don't kill *our* son."

He pulled his gun and whirled around to see her standing there. She was crying and wringing her hands, betraying any bravado she had taken on by following him.

Sam couldn't believe she'd had the nerve to follow him. What did she mean *'our'* son? He paused, unsure of himself, unsure of Darlene.

"Ah—no…" She shook her head as if warding off some inner demon, she whined, "Go away…not now…not…now. Leave me alone!"

Whatever or whoever she fought within her mind must have gone away for she slowly came towards him.

"Let's picnic." She gently took his arm, and it was as though Sam wasn't holding Casey and threatening to kill him. Her eyes were vague, shadowy and she had a smile only for him. "Let's take our wee one up the hill, I've packed a lunch." The last thread in her fragile mind had snapped. She ran her hands over Casey's curls, showing her love. "Casey, me angel—would ya like to go on a picnic? Yer Da here says to pack the basket. We're going up the hill."

"Darlene, what did you mean by sayin' Casey's our son?" Sam scanned her face, trying to find the love she always had for him. But recognition wasn't there. He'd lost her completely.

Donald, breathing heavy from the chase, stepped out of the shadows. Having heard all, he couldn't believe what was happening. It was Ireland come full circle. Derry, Sam, and him. A trio he'd thought he'd long put behind him. His Derry who he'd grieved over, twisted his gut into kinks thinking she'd died, now stood next to his brother, and not him.

He began walking toward them and wiped the drizzling rain from his face.

"Derry," he said, stopping within yards of her, unable to believe he was seeing her in the flesh. He wanted to turn away from her, but couldn't. The one fear she always lived with had reached out of her mother's grave and claimed her. Derry's mind had snapped. To see her like this made it somewhat easier to accept what she'd done.

Sam's mind was just as sick as Derry's. His mouth slacked open, his eyes glazed and filled with cold hate as he stared at Donald. Casey was perilously perched over Sam's shoulder.

"She speaks the truth, Sam." Donald admitted to something he never wanted to voice. But trying to keep Casey alive, he kept talking. "Put Casey down." He could see the hesitation in Sam's eyes that looked at Derry for confirmation.

But Derry just stood there slightly swaying.

A car came chugging down the pier. Both Donald and Sam whipped around in the direction of the sound. Donald shielded his eyes against the headlamps glare.

Olivia, followed by Eldon, got out of the car. Stopping next to Hugh, she leaned over to say something. As they slowly approached Donald, the car whined in reverse, leaving them once again in the dim softness of the lone light on the building.

"I've sent Hugh for the police," Olivia told Donald.

"Olivia, Eldon, stay back. Sam has a gun," Donald ordered.

Derry tugged at Sam's shirtsleeve. "Donald, do you think I'm pretty?" She canted a flirty look up at Sam.

Donald moved closer. "Sam, put Casey down. He's blood, and no Irishman kills his own blood," he spoke in a soft voice, trying not to upset his brother. "Take Derry and just go. I'll not be lookin' fer ya—no one will."

Sam hesitated and appeared to be giving it some thought. But it was only a hopeful illusion. "Sure'n and ye'll be wantin' me to take her now that she doesn't know who I am." The pistol hung loose in his hand pointing toward the ground.

Casey kicked against his restraints, he mumbled. Sam's hold tightened.

Donald held his breath, waiting, staring at the gun. With Sam it was always a gun. A gun that set Donald's course in life and a gun that might be ending it. "She'll be herself in no time. She loves ya."

"She's feckin' mad—a looney! Besides, Casey saw me kill Lillian Denbury. And those pearls around Darlene's neck is the cause of it all," he said savagely. Using the barrel of his gun, he ripped the necklace from her neck.

The strand broke, sending the precious pearls to scatter and bounce on the wooden pier.

"Oh, look at the pretty beads," Derry said.

They all watched the expensive, tiny white orbs as they rolled and disappeared amongst the cracks in the rough planks.

"Donald, take me home." Derry grabbed Sam's arm.

"I'm Sam—Sam," he yelled, swatting at her with his pistol, trying to get her off him.

The firearm discharged in a loud roar.

Derry gasped. The red stain on her left breast spread as she struggled to regain her balance.

Sam grabbed at her, but missed.

She fell over the edge.

"Darlene," Sam yelled.

Donald hurried toward his brother, trying to get to Casey.

Sam said with a snarl, "Yer not going to find happiness this night, little brother, it's gonna drown along with everythin' else." Holding Casey, he jumped into the water.

"Nooo..." Donald yelled, and plunged into the filthy water after him.

Kicking downward into the black water, Donald blindly groped around, searching until his lungs and head felt like they were going to burst, he started to surface. His leg brushed against something hard. Jackknifing downwards, he felt someone's head. Grabbing a handful of hair, he swam upwards, pulling the body with him. He surfaced, gasping for air. Holding the person close to his chest, he frantically ran his hand over short wet hair and a small face. He had Casey.

"Help!" He swallowed nasty tasting water, grabbing wood, anything to keep his and Casey's head above water.

"Donald—here," Eldon shouted from where he leaned over the pier, stretching out his hand. Olivia, ready to help, stood beside Eldon.

Donald put his hands around Casey's waist and propelled his son upward into Eldon's strong hands. He tread water as Eldon pulled Casey up, and then thrust him into Olivia's arms. Exhausted, Donald grabbed the wood of the dock, and started to pull himself out but he slipped back into the water. Eldon's hand loomed in front of Donald and he grabbed it. A stranger, a red-headed kid, appeared next to

Eldon and both of them strained and helped Donald scramble to safety.

Donald lay on the pier trying to catch his breath. He finally rolled over, and got to his knees. Sam and Derry were nowhere around.

Olivia was busy working over Casey.

Donald rushed over to them. Seeing Casey's still body, his heart plummeted.

"Is he alive? Tell me he's alive. Please…," his voice faltered.

"I don't know yet," Olivia said. Casey lay on his stomach and Olivia pushed her hands against his back. "Breathe, Casey, breathe," she ordered. At last he gagged and coughed as water spurt from his mouth and nose. Olivia rolled him over onto his back.

"Casey!" Donald said.

Sam yelled from the water. "Somebody take her."

Donald turned toward his brother's cries and quickly ran over. Reaching down, he took Derry by the arms and hauled her out of the water. Water sheeted off her straight brown skirt, the bright blood on her white linen blouse had widened into a large pink swath. Derry's head lulled against Donald's shoulder, her body still, lifeless as he went down on his knees. Holding his wife in his arms, Donald prayed, *God, don't let her be dead.* But the stain over her heart told him otherwise. He started to feel for a pulse when Sam came up and knocked him away.

Donald watched his brother take Derry in his arms.

Sam lovingly pushed the wet hair off her face. He tried shaking her awake. "Darlene…" he sobbed, feeling for a pulse that wasn't there. His hand covered the bullet hole in her chest. "Ah…no…" His lips pulled into a grimace as he held her and rocked.

The sight of Sam's face buried against Derry's body tortured Donald. He couldn't take his wife back into his arms, hold her in death as his mind had done these past months. Instead, he watched his brother acting like her husband. Sam's grief should be Donald's.

And like always, Sam loomed large between Donald and those he loved.

Sam's eyes glittered at him over Derry's body. "Damn ya, Donald, ye've killed her," he growled.

"*You* killed her, Sam. Yer actions, yer betrayal, yer feckin' gun killed her," Donald spat, and turned to go to Casey.

Olivia screamed, "Donald, look out!"

Donald turned just as Sam plowed into his midriff, knocking the air out of him, sending him crashing to the planks. Sam straddled him, and locking his fists together began hitting Donald as though he wielded a cudgel. Donald tried to ward off the blows, but failed. Sam's hard knuckles ground into his face. He managed to buck Sam off and get to his feet.

Eldon circled behind Sam, but Donald shook his head.

"Get away, Eldon."

The world narrowed to him and Sam.

"Damn ya to hell, Sam," he cried out in a hoarse voice. He threw a punch backed with all his weight, his knuckles smashed against Sam's jaw.

Sam's head jolted backwards with the blow. He recovered, his smile a satanic twist of hate. "I'll meet ya there, little brother." His fist exploded against Donald's cheek, splitting the skin.

The force of the blow caused Donald to stagger backwards, pain ripped through his face. He felt his cheek, the blood. Donald became enraged, manic. He wanted to tear his brother apart.

"This is for trying to harm me children." One after another, he smashed deadly punches against Sam backing him up toward the water. Hate filled each blow.

Sam flung his hands up trying to protect himself as droplets of blood flew from his face.

Donald yelled, "Ya conniving bastard! This is for stealin' me wife!"

He hit Sam hard enough to launch him off the pier.

Cold water splashed up over Donald, startling him, he shook his head dispelling the anger. With something akin to horror, he looked down at the inky blackness expecting Sam to surface. Wondering what he would do if he did. Would he pull him out, or push his head under? He was grateful not to have to make that kind of decision, for Sam didn't surface. Only the underbellies of bloated dead fish floated in the dark ripples.

Drawing in deep breaths, Donald used his shirttail to wipe at the blood on his face.

"Da," Casey called and ran toward him.

"Casey—Casey." Was all Donald could say as he dropped to his knees and caught his son's rush. Donald rocked him, holding him tight, their tears mingling. At long last, he put Casey at arm's length and checked him over. He was as wet as a landed fish, his golden curls matted to his head.

"Is Uncle Sam gone?" Casey asked with fear. More than one question masked his young face.

Unable to accept that he'd beaten his brother into a watery grave, Donald could only nod.

Casey blurted, his voice shrill, "Am I Uncle Sam's son? Mam said I was, and ya agreed. Am I not yer son? I don't want to be Uncle Sam's. I want to be yer's, Da." His mouth parted as both disbelief and despair covered his face. He started to sob.

Donald's throat constricted at Casey's words. And putting Casey at arm's length, yet holding him with a strong grip, Donald chose his words carefully. "Listen to me. You are my son, Casey. Yer Mam and I said that to try and stop Sam. We lied. We would have said anything to keep you from gettin' hurt. I want ya to forget we ever spoke such."

He pulled Casey tight and stroked his blonde curls. How could it be otherwise? How could such a sweet gentle little soul come from someone so evil? He couldn't. And Donald would forever defend the words he'd just told Casey.

A lie for a life.

Casey's lips quivered as he pointed to where Derry lay. "Mam's dead, aye?"

And when Donald nodded, Casey broke down, violently sobbing, throwing his small body against Donald's chest. Again, Donald held his son, trying to sooth him, simply loving him.

"I want ya to remember yer mam like she was, lovin' ya something fierce, callin' you her golden boy. Remember her that way, Casey, not the mam who became so sick in her mind."

"She tried to save me from Uncle Sam," Casey said and shuddered.

"I know she did, and love her for it." Donald thumbed the tears from Casey's face. Taking Casey's hand within his, he walked him over to where Derry lay. He nudged him forward.

Casey went to sit next to his mam and gingerly touched her cheek. "Mam, Da and I will take care of Jilly. Don't ya worry. We're together now."

Donald sat next to Derry and took her other hand. Together they sat, deep in grief, a son, and a husband.

At long last, Donald got to his feet and rested his hand on Casey's shoulder. He glanced around to see Eldon talking to Joe who was sitting down and leaning against the building. The lad who'd helped him out of the water was standing next to them both, his hands waving in the air as he talked to Eldon.

Casey pointed. "Da, that's Jimmy Kelly over there. He's my friend."

Donald watched with pride as Olivia slowly approached and stood next to Casey, filled with concern. "Hello, Casey. I'm Olivia Marsh. I've heard so much about you from Jilleen and your father. I'm truly sorry about your mother."

He sniffed and nodded. "Uncle Sam said he had Jilleen. That Mam took her from ya, aye?"

Olivia put her hand on his sleeve. "Yes, she did, but Jilleen's safe with my father right now. I can't express how glad I am that we found you in time."

Donald put his arm around Olivia. He pulled both her and Casey close. The three of them stood together.

The sound of a police siren coming on echoed off the buildings.

Epilogue

Five months later….

October was almost gone and winter nudged into the city. From the window, Donald looked down at the pavement to see a strong wind swirling and banking brown leaves and debris against the apartment steps. This past week had turned frigid and small beaded snowflakes now flitted around like shards of glass.

More often than not, his thoughts were about Derry and Sam. He'd come to accept that Derry had inherited her mother's illness. Thinking back on small happenings while still in Ireland, he realized it was just a matter of time before Derry ended up like her mam, and he would end up like her father, Hoyt O'Dea. Everything about her, the shy, smiling lass he'd married, the mother she became, the deceit, all of it, forever etched in his mind.

Derry was buried in one of the City's better cemeteries, close to a massive oak tree. He'd taken Casey and Jilleen to visit her grave and they'd lovingly put flowers at the base of her headstone.

Sam was the cold spot in his life. Even though the police had searched for Sam's body, it was never found, and that had sent

Donald into another depression. He should be elated Sam was gone, never again to torture his family. But being the person who'd put his brother in a watery grave made it hard to accept.

One day, not too long ago, Olivia had asked him if he would have saved Sam if he'd surfaced. Without hesitation, Donald said yes. He would have offered his hand to his brother, helped him out.

He'd written his mam telling her what had happened. Emotion came back in raw waves across the ocean. Her reply was full of heartache about her oldest son's death. She accepted Donald's offer to come live in America. Both his mother and Colin would be sailing in the spring.

Lillian Denbury remained buried in Halifax's Fairview cemetery in a simple pine coffin. A headstone provided by her aunt marked her grave that rested alongside so many others from the *Titanic,* known and unknown.

He'd taken Casey with him to visit Vivian Denbury. Casey told her what had happened on the *Titanic*. At Donald's urging, Casey made Lillian into a righteous person whose threats to tell the authorities about Sam's stealing had caused her death.

Murder and Love, Pearls of Death, were the bold headlines. The papers glorified reporter Paddy Riley. His courage in acting like a gadget salesman confronting the enemy would put newspaper reporting in a new light. The articles told how Sam had killed three people. Donald missed the flamboyant reporter who'd become a good friend, and by becoming embroiled in Donald's life, had lost his.

Inspector Mulhall from Halifax was glad to mark the case closed, but was sorry Donald's brother turned out to be the man who'd done everyone wrong.

Donald turned away from the window. Even though he'd moved into a bigger apartment closer to his job, his home was bulging with kids. By taking in Joe, Benny, and Jimmy, he'd prevented an aggressive social worker from putting the younger boys in an orphanage. He now lived on the third floor and the building had a wall mounted telephone on each floor.

All the kids had nightmares and silent moments. Donald tried to soothe them in the best way possible. When first reunited, Casey had spent a lot of hours dogging Donald's steps. Although Casey never asked again about his mother's revealing words the night at the wharf, Donald knew the question was there, would always be there, wanting to surface, and if it ever did, Donald would again say it was a lie.

A lie for a life.

Donald had asked Casey why he didn't go for help after coming off the ship, and Casey more than confirmed his suspicions. He was afraid too. Uncle Sam was everywhere. Casey was in a strange country and didn't know anything about America. He liked the gang, but they'd put the fear in him about the hoosegow. Besides, with Jimmy's help, he thought he could find Donald on his own.

Telling Jilleen that her mam was dead was the hardest thing Donald had to do. She'd cried a lot, but she'd accepted the news with curiosity about Heaven. When she'd asked about Uncle Sam, Donald was quick to tell her he was gone, forever.

Just seeing Casey and Jilleen together, their interaction with one another, made Donald the happiest he'd been in years.

Jilleen had sullenly fit into the apartment with the impatience of being the only girl in a cramped home full of ornery boys. But even her whining about it had become less lately, and Donald knew it was because of Joe.

At first, Joe, traumatized the most, would sit for hours on the sofa, staring at nothing, and even though Donald tried to bring him out of his nightmares, nothing worked. But then, Jilleen, using her childish wiles, started coaxing him into playing games, especially tea parties. It wasn't long before Joe's brown eyes would shine whenever Jilleen came around.

Casey, Joe, and Benny were enrolled in school. Benny's teacher had already paid Donald a visit, expressing the child was a disruptive hooligan and needed a firm hand. She even threatened detention hall if he didn't change. While all this bedlam had taken hold of Donald's life, Jimmy, who Donald thought was too old to change, had a new occupation. He'd become a soda jerk at Johnston's drugstore. Archie and Eldon had taken a shine to the red-haired reformer who made it irresistible not to like him. They also tutored him on his days off.

While Donald worked and the kids were in school, Jilleen was watched by a good-natured neighbor woman who also had children in school and a nursing baby to take care of.

The bank and Walter Marsh's good nature had become Donald's salvation especially when Walter made him head of the accounting department. Walter, still living at the club, didn't appear in any hurry to return home to Merilee. Donald wished it were otherwise.

Olivia and her mother had come close to healing their relationship. And even though Olivia tried helping her parents put their fractured marriage back together, some of the fissures were up to Walter and Merilee to close.

Donald and Olivia had settled into seeing each other when they could. She was busy trying to get laws passed for child labor regulation, women's labor, and better factory working conditions. She and her suffragettes had camped out on the capitol steps until they had promises from congressmen that they would draw up bills for reformation and see them through the Assembly.

He missed Olivia who would show up between trips, help him with the children, and then be gone again. He yearned for something more permanent, but didn't know if he should ask her. Sometimes she was too headstrong for her own good, and not wanting to be denied what he desired most in life right now, he thought it best not to ask her to marry him.

All the kids were bathed and wearing brand new clothing. They were an array of brown knee-pants, white shirts, and tweed jackets.

Jilleen had a new frock of bright red. Jimmy proudly wore long pants just like Donald's.

The plans were to take them to Eldon's for a soda. Donald pulled out his watch and snapped open the case to look at the sweeping second hand. Almost one o'clock, time to leave. His new watch made him think of the one he'd left with Casey for safe keeping, the treasure his own father had given him, the watch Sam had wrapped around Casey's neck. That watch was now at the bottom of the East River, and probably just as well, for Donald didn't think he could look at it and not think of the horrendous happenings tied to it.

Donald put his watch back into his vest pocket and went into the bedroom to get his coat, when bedlam broke out.

"Da, Benny's wiping nose-snot on me new coat. Stop it, Benny, ya bloody blaggard."

"Shit head," Benny sneered.

"Fart face." Casey lobbed back.

They hit the floor in a loud thud, rolling, exchanging blows with their small fists.

Donald hurried to break up the fight.

He pushed the squabbling boys apart. "Benny, stop it, or I'll box yer ears for ya. Better yet, ya won't be gettin' a soda at Eldon's. And you, Casey, I might have to give a good clattering to if ye don't watch yer mouth. Now that should make ya behave, aye."

"But, Da... He's wiping buggers on me coat. Look." He glowered and pointed to the fresh green smear on his new tweed coat.

Donald could only shake his head, trying not to laugh.

Benny's blue eyes twinkled. He parked his bottom on the sofa and folded his hands on his lap. He tried to act angelical, the only thing missing was the cracked halo.

Donald wasn't fooled. He glanced at the rest of the kids. Jilleen was being the perfect little lass patiently playing with her dolls. Jimmy shuffled a deck of cards and then dealt them between Joe and himself. Joe picked the cards up and fanning them apart, concentrated on his hand.

A knock sounded on the door and Casey ran to open it. Like always, Donald started to shout out a warning not to open it before he got there. He was jittery, thinking of Paddy's death in a doorway, and not wanting the kids to open the door to just anyone.

To Donald's joy, Olivia entered in a burst of energy, the black feathers on her large hat bobbed and pointed like the mast on a ship. Her cheeks were rosy from the cold, and her grin wide. She carried a picket sign by its wooden handle of which she went to lean against the wall. He couldn't read the sign as the writing was turned away, which was a good thing, he didn't need reminders of the reason they were apart so much.

She bent to give Casey a loud kiss on the cheek. Casey wore a goofy grin as he beamed a glance at Donald.

"'Livia," Jilleen squealed with delight and ran into her arms.

Olivia knelt and rained kisses on her cheeks. "I've missed you, sweetheart. You're so pretty. Did your daddy do your hair?" She patted the long brown sausage curls topped off with a large bow at Jilleen's crown.

Jilleen nodded and cuddled closer. "Aye, Da did me hair. But it hurts when he brushes it. I liked it best when ya fix it."

Olivia finally released Jilleen, and approached Donald with a smile. "Are you going somewhere?"

"Aye, taking the kids to Eldon's for sodas."

"Jimmy, would you mind driving the children over to the Johnston's?" Olivia asked.

"Ya trust me drivin' yer car, do ya?" Jimmy grinned and raised an all knowing brow.

"Since you learned to drive using my car, I think you've earned my trust. Just be careful and no showing off."

"I want ya to come with us, 'Livia," Jilleen said with a pout.

Olivia smiled and gave Jilleen her full attention. "I know you do. But I need to talk with your father alone. Please go with Jimmy. When he brings you back later we'll play with your dollies, would you like that?"

"All right," Jilleen said, and meekly smiled.

There was a flurry of putting on warm coats, striped wool scarves, hats, and colorful mittens. Jimmy herded the younger ones out. The door shut on the cacophony of laughter and teasing, as shoes pounded down the stairs.

The room became silent with only the ticking of the clock.

Olivia reached up, and removing a long hatpin, took off her glorious hat and placed it on the sideboard. She turned back to Donald while tidying her hair, and then she slipped out of her brown suit jacket and walked past him to hang it on the hat tree next to the front door. Straightening her frilly white blouse and brown wraparound skirt, Olivia was all business.

"Hello, Mr. McShane."

"Miss Marsh. Coming from another rally?" he asked, following her every move. She filled his apartment with the smell of spring, her perfume a bouquet of exotic flowers.

"Yes. I gave a speech on unions. That's what the textile industry needs, is unions. Unions can keep everything regulated, keep children from being hired. Congressmen up in Albany sing a different tune now. They are starting to pass legislation, and unionizing is another one I hope they recognize."

She went into the kitchen and put the kettle on the stove.

He caught her occasionally glancing through the open doorway at him. Donald found her darting glances disconcerting, and wondered what she'd come here to talk to him about. Certainly getting Jimmy to take the children out of the apartment didn't bode well at all.

Finally, she returned holding two cups of hot tea of which she placed on the coffee table. Another new acquisition.

"Ah…lass, do I want to know what's on yer mind? Have ya come here to tell me goodbye? That our lives are too different for us to be together?"

She tossed him a subtle smile. "Maybe yes—maybe no. I figure we have two hours of uninterrupted conversation before Jimmy brings them back."

"Uninterrupted conversation?" He swallowed hard. "Sure'n that sounds bad. Like it's gonna take that long to tell me goodbye. If that's what you've come here to tell me, just say it, and be done."

"Don't be silly." With a slight sway to her hips, she walked over and picked up her picket sign, holding it for him to see.

WILL YOU MARRY ME, MR. MCSHANE?

She raised her brows at him in expectation, and he couldn't help but chuckle with relief.

"Am I being picketed, Miss Marsh?"

She shook the sign at him. "Yes you are, Mr. McShane."

He watched her put the sign down, and then come over to where he stood.

"Well?" she asked.

He didn't know what to say, and said nothing.

"I take it by not answering you're saying no?"

"No, that's not me answer. I don't have an answer yet. Besides I thought *I* was supposed to do the asking about such things? Yer a strong-willed woman, Olivia."

"You knew that about me when you met me. Has it been so bad?" She searched his face for any kind of denial.

"What do ya expect me to say with ya staring at me? And yes, it's hard with ya away on trips doin' yer suffragette work." She had a way of muddling his mind. Putting his hands in his pockets, he moved away from her and went to glance out the window.

A soft snow was starting to stick.

"Donald, that's not all I'm here to say. In addition to asking you to marry me, I've got a proposition to make you," she said, her brown eyes searching his face

"I haven't answered your first question yet. What if I refuse?" he joked, almost choking on his lie.

Olivia's manner became serious. "Would you consider leaving New York and moving to Oregon State?"

He was more than surprised, startled perhaps, yet it all sounded intriguing. He didn't know what to say. Moving across the states had never come up before. His mam and brother were arriving in the spring and he didn't want them to travel even further.

"Well? Do you want to move to Oregon or not?" she asked, this time more firm.

"What about my job at the bank? Your father depends on me, and I like workin' there. Besides, I just settled in this apartment."

"I know Dad depends on you. That's what makes moving to Oregon even better. Want to hear the rest of my proposition?"

Something about her seriousness, made him serious, and he concentrated on her. "Yer being truthful, aye? You're askin' me to marry ya, and not just in jest. Walter knows about this?"

"Yes—yes—and yes." She wrapped her arms around him and kissed his cheek. "Hmmm, you smell like shaving soap, very pleasant." She deeply inhaled. "Where was I? Oh…yes, it's really Dad's idea, his proposition, the bank issue that is. The marriage proposal is all mine. Dad's going to ask you to run his bank in Portland, Oregon. My brother Nathan wants to come back to New York. It's really simple."

He absorbed her words. "Is that what ya think? Simple?"

"Well, yes." She fingered the wide scar on his cheek that was put there by Sam. "What's to keep us here? It's a chance for us to have a new life. We could get away from all the unpleasant memories. The kids could grow up happy with blue skies and green trees. We would have a big house. Think of it, Donald. Nathan says Portland is thick with tall, giant fir trees, and surrounded by rivers."

"It sounds like Dublin, the green trees, the rivers," he said somewhat wistful. "What about all the boys? Joe, Jimmy, and Benny?"

She nodded with each name he mentioned. "Why, they'd come with us of course. We could give them more love than they ever had in their short lives."

"What about yer suffragette work? Ya can't be a mother and gone all the time."

She was quick to say, "I know. I'll simply join the organization in Portland, which I'm told is much smaller than the one here. I'll never give up this endeavor, but I can give more time to the children there. And much more love."

He couldn't help but grin, still unwilling to accept her offer. He wanted to make her suffer just a wee bit, squirm, was the word.

Again she went for the sign and held it up. "Donald, will you marry me?"

"There you go again, being willful. Thought I was supposed to do the askin'."

"Well?" She stared in apprehension. "Then do it."

He was enjoying this too much, way too much, and he dragged it out even more. "I need more time to think about it all. This isn't like movin' down the street. Besides, me mam and Colin are coming in May. And speakin' of mam's. What about yours? To her, I'll always be a poor Irish immigrant, not good enough for her daughter."

"Mother's changed. Her close friends abandoned her when this all came out. She now sees that her highbrow friends weren't true friends. They've done to her exactly what she did to others. Losing father was the hardest for her. But the one thing for the good is mother realizes just how much she loves him. I pray they will soon be together again."

She shook the sign at him. "Are you going to ask me to marry you, or not?"

He took the sign from her. Taking her in his arms, he spoke in a voice gone husky. "I want ya, lass. Just not want, Olivia, I need ya. Need to have ya pressed against me. I want to come home to ya, sink into yer smile. I want to turn over in bed and take ya in me arms. I want to make love to ya, give ya our child. So, I guess I'm sayin', aye, I'd move anywhere just to be with you. Marry me, Olivia, be me wife."

She melted against his chest. "Oh…good, Mr. McShane, I'm so glad you asked. I certainly didn't want to organize my suffragette's against you. And the answer is yes—yes—yes, I will marry you!"

He gently pulled her onto his lap. With their gazes locked together, he began kissing her, softly at first, then with more urgency as his mouth worked against hers. He unbuttoned the top buttons on her blouse and pressed his lips against the spot where her pulse jumped. She moaned and he lost himself in the feel of her.

Casey was the first one through the door. Jilleen was close behind him. The kids shed their coats, hats and mittens and put them on the hat rack.

"How was yer soda, Son? Eldon makes the best, aye?"

"Jimmy made them. Mr. Marsh was there and he bought seconds for us."

Olivia ran her hand through Casey's blond curls. "So, Dad joined you?" It wasn't any secret how much Walter Marsh enjoyed Archibald and Eldon's company. He'd offered them sound business advice, and they were expanding, putting in another drugstore in lower Manhattan close to Wall Street.

"Aye," Casey answered. "He said to tell you hello. He was talkin' with Mr. Jonsun about their new store when we left."

Donald signaled for Casey to come over. "I have something to tell you and yer sister. Are ya listening? Jilleen? Pay attention here."

Jilleen obeyed and went to stand next to her brother. She grasped his hand and rocked on one foot while staring up at them.

Casey smiled at his da and Olivia.

Donald sat down and lifted Jilleen onto his lap. He then reached out to Casey, drawing him close. He grabbed Olivia's hand bringing her near.

"Olivia and I are getting married."

Jilleen sucked in her breath. "Casey, 'Livia's going to be our mam!" she exclaimed with awed excitement.

Donald saw tears glistening in Casey's eyes. "Are ya all right, son? Don't ya want Olivia to be yer mam?"

Casey hung his blond head.

Olivia knelt in front of him and took his small hand within hers. "Casey, darling boy, listen to me. I would never think to take your mother's place. I know how much you love her and treasure her memory. Allow me to take care of you. Let me do what your mother never had a chance to do. Let me raise you to be the fine young man she would have wanted."

Slowly Casey's arms went around Olivia's neck in acceptance.

"I love you, Casey. You're the bravest little boy I've ever met," she said.

"Truly?" he asked.

"May God strike me dead right now if I'm lying."

And when Olivia kept smiling and wasn't struck dead, Casey grinned at her.

Joe, Benny, and Jimmy stood watching with apprehension on their faces. And seeing this, Donald was quick to say, "Lads, after we're married we'd like to adopt ya. We'd raise you as our own. You will always have a home with us."

Realizing they weren't being put out again, the three boys broke into wide grins. Everyone relaxed.

Casey glared at Benny. "This means ya have to behave, Benny. No more wipin' snot on me clothes."

Laughing, Donald motioned at Olivia. "I think this calls for us all to toast our good fortunes."

"I certainly agree, Mr. McShane. Children included." She went toward the kitchen.

Casey's job was to light the lamps, which he did every night, and with great importance. His da had electricity, a lone bulb on the ceiling of each room. But Casey knew he preferred the soft glow of the oil lamps. Casey now went around and lit them, turning the wicks up and putting the ornate pink globes back in place.

It was dark as Casey parted the curtain. People walked by directly below the window, their voices carrying up to him. Unable to see anything but his own reflection, he cupped his hands around his eyes and peered out. Across the street, a match flared in the darkness. The match highlighted a man's dark mustache and beard as he lit a smoke. The match winked out as it dropped to the ground. All Casey could see was the glowing end of a cigar or cigarette being smoked. Casey felt like the stranger's eyes were boring into him. A chill ran up his back forcing his skin to goose flesh.

He quickly stepped away from the window.

Uncle Sam was dead wasn't he?

He turned toward his da, thinking to call him over, but when he braved another peek, the person started walking off, passing near a dim street lamp. The light reflected off his black bowler, and faint whistling echoed up to Casey. Within seconds the man was gone from sight as though he never existed.

Casey let out a sigh of relief. Dropping the curtain back in place, he hurried to stand next to Da and Olivia who had just returned with a tray of drinks.

Jilleen moved next to him, and both he and his sister accepted a glass of the blackberry brandy. Jilleen crinkled her nose as she sniffed at the inch of amber liquid in her glass.

Casey listened as his da talked.

"Since us Irish are a superstitious lot and for centuries we believed in charms and spells, I'd like to offer one for our safety. When going on a journey, ya pluck ten blades of yarrow, keep nine, and cast the tenth away for tithe to the spirits. Put the other nine in yer stocking right under yer right heel and the *evil one* will have no power over you, and your journey will be safe."

Olivia smiled at Donald and clinked her glass against his and each one of the kids. Following her lead, they all did the same.

Donald, brimming with pride, winked at Olivia and said, "I don't think I could find a yarrow plant here in Manhattan, but my toast is for all our life journeys to be safe from evil."

The End

ABOUT THE AUTHOR

Perhaps reincarnation might explain this author's fascination with all things historical. Or maybe it's about loving the "Good old Days," or a slower pace of life. Mercer likes to think it's the latter. Raised in the beautiful Pacific Northwest, Mercer, along with her husband still calls it home. An award winning author of many contests, Even Nectar is Poison, is Mercer's first published book.

Contact: www.merceraddison.com

www.ingramcontent.com/pod-product-compliance
Lightning Source LLC
La Vergne TN
LVHW010634110826
845149LV00014B/2843

* 9 7 8 0 9 8 9 1 9 4 7 1 6 *